# ASHES OF ALDYR

## THE OBSCURED THRONE TRILOGY - BOOK ONE

RUSSELL ARCHEY

5 PRINCE PUBLISHING

# CONTENTS

Published by 5 PRINCE PUBLISHING

PO Box 865, Arvada, CO 80001

www.5PrinceBooks.com

ISBN digital: 978-1-63112-400-6

ISBN print: 978-1-63112-274-3

Cover Credit: Marianne Nowicki

*For Symphony and Carter*

# ACKNOWLEDGMENTS

Thank you, Jennifer, for always pushing me to be my best.

Thank you, Cate, for being an editor with the eternal patience of a sleeping eldritch entity.

Thank you, Bernadette, for these amazing opportunities.

Thank you, readers, for sharing these worlds with me.

## ALSO BY RUSSELL ARCHEY

The Seven Spires

Ashes of Aldyr

# LETTER FROM THE AUTHOR

## From a Mind of Madness
### (a.k.a. A Note from the Author)

Some of the best horror fiction I've read has been in the format of the short story. Many of these were also parts of a larger mythos. Most fantasy I've read has been in full novel formats. So, the question I posed to myself is: how could I write a work of dark fantasy that fits what I enjoy and am familiar with: short story horror, fantasy novels, and a larger mythos? This book is the answer to that question.

Each of the stories you read here are separate entities. They have a beginning, middle, and end. But, so too does this book as a whole. There is a journey you're going to be taken on throughout the world of Alda and its people. You'll experience the events through multiple sets of eyes (how's that for a multi-layered horror reference?) across long spans of time.

Every story is a picture, but they all form a larger mosaic. All the self-contained narratives are separate threads weaving a tapestry of cosmic horror in a fantasy setting. All of them building a mythos that grows with each story and, hopefully, leading you back to former pages where, like a horrifying realization that something *was* watching you from the shadows, you'll find more things to be afraid of as the world of Alda grows darker and darker.

This is the first of a trilogy. These are the first of many stories to come for this forsaken world adrift in a cosmos that isn't just unfeeling, but possibly unimaginably sinister.

Thank you for reading and I hope you enjoy the ride.

# ASHES OF ALDYR

# PROLOGUE: THE RUPTURE

THE SKIES OUTSIDE WERE CLEAR AND BLUE FROM ONE HORIZON TO the other. It almost seemed poor timing to ruin such a beautiful view from high on the hillside where his home nestled hidden in the trees. But this was an event centuries upon centuries in the making. It was his work, the studies of Jermiah Colwerth, that took his Order's work from mere study, hypothesis, and conjecture and brought it to a grand scale.

He ran his old, knobbly fingers over the cover of a large tome. The barbed diamond shape engraved on the front, particularly its small dot in the center, stared back at him. This book had been his life for the past few decades. He had already grown old when he had first found it. His intellectual pursuits were many, but none had prepared him for this journey in his life. He was a man who once believed in the gods of his people, too. But he found others. *The* Others. Those that waited beyond. The traditional gods may still exist, but they were nothing compared to what he had found.

Jermiah placed the book in a satchel and left it on his writing desk. Others may come and find the book; it may be some of his Order or random passersby, but that was irrelevant. They would partake of the knowledge within, or it would partake of them. This was an original copy. Possibly the first. It practically reeked of the darkest magics, so much that it may have gained a mind of its own. It was a pleasing, but unproven, thought.

Standing shakily to his feet, he looked at the body lying on the floor. His apprentice. She had been a good lass. The fact that she couldn't understand his work—their work—left him feeling deep pangs of regret. He should have told her sooner instead of waiting until the last minute. He knew it would be a shock one way or the other. He thought that, perhaps, if she'd seen the fruit of their labors first, she would have better understood. She was talented and would have done well in their new world. Such a pity that it had come to this. Her death caused him great heartache. It was not even a valuable sacrifice, simply a loss of her talent.

He sighed and untied the loose knot holding his black robes in place. His hands trembled; he carefully pulled the robes off one shoulder, wincing as the cloth ran over the cuts on his body. The other half of the robe sloughed off his body like dead skin, revealing bleeding runes carved into his aged, withered frame.

He walked out the front door of his small, utilitarian home. From the hillside, it overlooked the town below. A little place on the outskirts of the capitol of the city-state of Carnelia, it was an unimportant town full of unimportant people.

Those he once called friends were still down there, though. Jermiah tried to explain everything to them. He wanted them to know. After he first found the profound knowledge held within the tome on his desk, he, too, had been afraid. More than afraid —he was terrified. It took much study and contemplation to finally realize what, ironically, reality truly was. Everyone from the lowliest stableboy to the archmagi and high priests, to the gods themselves, were wrong. In fact, Jermiah had never seen any proof of the existence of the gods of man, dwarf, elf-kind, or any other. But he had seen The Others. Those that waited. He no longer feared them, at least not as he used to. It was now a different fear—a reverent fear. None of his former friends or colleagues would conform to his ideas, however, and they would be lost like all the others.

Jermiah's strength continued to ebb. The blood flowed from the numerous symbols and invocations etched upon his flesh, the blood-blessed writings calling to Them. He stood on the edge of the natural stone landing in front of his home, wherein his apprentice lay with her blood pooling pointlessly. He smiled, knowing his sacrifice would open the first window. His blood would let the world of Alda see that it could hide no longer. That a new throne, the oldest throne, was returning.

Spreading his arms, he felt the wind course around his body. It tickled his skin where the blood rapidly cooled against him. His gray beard and long hair fluttered like a pennon. Others had completed their sacred tasks before him, some long ago and some even by accident, but his would be the last needed for now.

He fell backward, waiting only briefly for his body to crash into the stone of the landing. After the briefest moment of pain, Jermiah Colwerth's body, carved with the language of the forbidden, the cosmic, the profane, and the indescribable, exploded into a red mist. Not a single solid piece of viscera remained. He disintegrated into the basest elements, all deep crimson. The drops and splatters rolled into rivulets and formed a symbol matching the one on the cover of his precious tome: a diamond, with curling barbs at each corner, and a rough-edged dot in the center.

The red image stained the stones immediately, to become a place of dreadful power and unspeakable magic. The dot, which had seemed to stare back at Jermiah like a vacant eye and unsettled him despite his fevered convictions and loosening grasp on reality, deepened in color. It turned from deep red to crimson then black as the void of night where light dare never tread.

In those moments, many around the world would say they felt a small tremor but none knew that it came from that sanguine mark on an unnamed hillside. The small dot, no bigger than a fist, groaned with the cries of a world dying. To look upon it, one would think they were sinking into the world itself. The dot became a hole, a door, a passage that fell further and further into the core of the world and beyond. Alda cried out, and every creature from every continent heard.

A vicious cacophony rang out from the sky. The bright blue of the day turned to an angry red, like an agitated wound. In the blink of an eye, a veil of ghostly, hair-like strands stretched and writhed across the sky. Like a pale aurora, the strange sight ran over all of Carnelia, off to the horizons, and was visible across the world of Alda.

Scholars swore they saw patterns of stars never recorded. Others say the dark there was deeper than pitch. Then there were those who were shouting and swearing that they saw other things watching them from beyond the ghostly strands.

Very few of these people knew the name of Jermiah Colwerth, or the Order which he served. But Jermiah left his mark on the world—rather, a mark wholly belonging to another. A presence longing for the shores and fields and creatures of Alda for eons. The thrones of men, dwarves, and elf-kind were but stone and steel; the most ancient forebears of these peoples; young when compared to the rightful Lord of this world. As Jermiah asked his ill-fated apprentice: what are stone and steel against the vast majesty of the sentient nothing?

# FORGET ME NOT

THE WAVES CRASHED AGAINST THE JAGGED ROCKS FAR BELOW AT the base of the cliff. The paper in his hand felt dry, its edges sharp. The ink might have well been the dark brown of old blood, given the cost paid for it. He refused to meet with the same end as the rest of the cityfolk did. Those creatures would not take him. The memories of his family were slipping quickly. Their names already gone. The emotional connection he'd had with them, that familial essence, leaked from his memory like water through fingers.

His name was Edwin Buchanan Syriell. He was a professor's son and a student of art, philosophy, and science. He was a son and brother and lover. And he would not be forgotten. There were others he knew would remember him, if they survived. The cobbler whom Edwin was friends with. He'd gotten away before everything went completely to hell. The cobbler would remember him. And the young lass from his painting classes. The one with the large blue eyes that always stared at him and smiled during instruction. She'd escaped, too. 'Escaped' was perhaps the wrong word; he saw her leaving town with her grandmother not two days ago, and she would remember him, if only vaguely. And there were others.

Edwin hadn't yet taken that last fatal step; the final act that would take him over the cliff's edge to plunge into the cold water below. He wouldn't be dragged into a black hole of nothingness, a soulless rip in the air where the literal essence of nothing exists. He would not go screaming and flailing like the others. He would leave this world on his own terms. The cold ocean would wash his blood from the stones, and his bones would lie among them—a rugged tomb, but at least it would be some sort of resting place. His body would remain here in this reality and not lost somewhere unknown; somewhere in the black.

He looked to his left at the aldyr tree that grew precariously near the edge of that mighty drop. It should have remained blooming throughout the fall and winter despite cold, darkness, and snow. Now, it was dead—a lifeless reminder of what was happening to his world. Lush and full of timeless vigor, the aldyrs are sacred to the world. Now, they all lay dry and lifeless; broken like the world that once was.

The sounds of the world breaking, the skies rending open, and the shudder that resounded through the souls of every living thing; he regretted these would be the last things he experienced. He saw a star fall through the sky once. It was brief and beautiful and reminded him what the great philosophers and astronomers told him: there was much more to existence than their little world. It was awe-inspiring and humbling. When the sky opened, a sickly hue rolled across the sky, and an oily shimmer followed behind it. Certainly, now everyone knew there was more to existence than just their simple reality. There was nothing beautiful about it, but they were still awed... and terrified. The rupture that would, in time, destroy everyone and everything was upon them.

When the world fell, creatures crawled from the bowels of

the world that none had ever seen or heard of. If they existed there before, they hid well. Other things—he hesitated to call them creatures for they defied all description of anything that could or should be living—stepped out of the ether, materialized from the air, or stepped out of rips in the fabric of reality itself. Some small, and others the size of castles. Some were vaguely humanoid, and others resembled other nameless things. Even his educated faculties could not describe those horrors that consisted of material or essence that could only be perceived by the mind's eye, made of noisy colors and rotten sounds.

Edwin's father knew. Not the specific events, but of the horrors that would come. His father was voracious in his studies—ambitious and dedicated. His books and teachings earned a nice profit for his family and kept them comfortable. The name of Professor Corwin Syriell was spoken with respect and admiration in Carnelia. But something about such tenacity unsettled Edwin. He loved his father, but later in life Edwin noticed Corwin developed a disconcerting look in his eye. He became more and more haggard as he disregarded his personal health and hygiene to stay up all hours reading and recording tome after dusty tome.

His father's notes and scrolls began to fill up their lofty home. The words turned to gibberish, though even Edwin could still discern a pattern in them. It was as though his father began writing in some different language—but not elf-kind, dwarven, or any other remotely familiar sort. It was curled and gnarled as though roots had stamped themselves on the paper. The calligraphy was accented with sharp, wispy barbs and small round blotches of ink. Once, Edwin was curiously digging around his father's workspace and found an old book bound in cracked, dried leather. It was buried under a pile of papers that had been recently inscribed with the odd writing. This book was different from the others. It bore a strange symbol embossed in the style of the odd script and felt heavier than it looked to be. His father came in to see a young Edwin leafing through the book and its unreadable writing punctuated with profane and sinister illustrations.

When his childhood self went to greet his father, however, Edwin saw a side of him that he hadn't before: indescribable outrage. Corwin tore the book from Edwin's hands and flung it across the room. Corwin grabbed him by the shoulders and forbade him from ever looking at the book or even entering the study again.

What most disturbed Edwin about the encounter was not that his father seemed angry at him. He was angry, but not for the reasons Edwin previously thought. Edwin also felt a rush of fear coming from his father. Later that evening, Edwin peeked in to see his father at his desk with the book open, searching furiously for something. This is the most common memory Edwin has of his father in those waning years, with his head buried in one crumbling volume or another. One volume in particular dominated the professor's studies—the one that had precipitated his outburst at Edwin.

Corwin would spend hours at the libraries, both in their home town and abroad. He was obsessed with knowledge beyond that which he or his cohorts had acquired. He always pushed himself to find out more. In his youth, Edwin admired his father like no other. He wanted to be a well-respected intellectual, himself. When he saw what the studies did to his father, he opted instead for art, to his father's chagrin. But Edwin would not be drawn into the desperation and obsession that claimed his father.

Professor Corwin Syriell had become deranged, aloof, distant, and lost all his academic credentials. By this time, their mother had long since left, finding solace away from her crazed husband and closed-off eldest son. Edwin fell into himself, using art as an escape. In all honesty, he wasn't even that good. But it took his mind off the pain of his deteriorating father and collapsing family. His mother took his younger brother and moved to the far side of the city. He hadn't spoken with either of them in over a year but assumed them to be acclimating fine to their new home and new life. Edwin was only slightly bitter. It had been a long time coming. Edwin was, admittedly, more aligned with his father's personality and he chose to remain with him and try to help him out of his destructive course.

Still, the last days with his father wore upon him. He, too, was ready to abandon the disheveled old man, who grew more reclusive every day. Just when Edwin had gathered the resolve to pack his things and leave one day, and not long before Corwin passed, Corwin called Edwin into his study and confided in him. The study smelled of unwashed clothing, old leather binding, and ancient paper.

Edwin recalled looking around in pity. His father had lost his mind.

"Sit, boy. Sit," Corwin motioned him to sit in a chair currently occupied by books and scrolls.

After removing them and setting them in an unceremonious pile on the floor, Edwin patiently awaited the reason for his father's summoning. He noticed the book with the strange glyphs was opened to the last few pages.

"I know—" his father began hesitantly, sounding years older than he was, "I know that I've been unlike myself lately. But, I may have found something! A tiny morsel of knowledge so profound it may set me among the greatest of my peers."

Edwin remembered the irritation he felt as he looked around at the absolute mess that had been made, and the copious books and uncountable pages that filled the room.

"A morsel?" Edwin had spat in irritation. "Mother left us!

She took Ekkard with her! And all you have is a 'morsel' of information?"

His father was unfazed by the accusation; he only grew more fervent, "The tiniest nourishment is like a feast to a starving man, son. This book, it speaks of things that—that even I can't fully put an explanation to."

His father ran a hand—wrinkled as paper with deep blue veins bulging—below the surface over the book cover. The sight of the ghastly appendage on a black leather binding made Edwin shiver inside. The cover displayed a symbol that looked like a diamond with curved barbs at each corner and a simple dot in the center. It was physically uncomfortable to gaze upon. This was the book his father spent so much time with. After returning from a trip several years ago, it took his vigorous interest and turned into an obsession.

Edwin simply shook his head and left the room. He closed the door gently on his way out. Despite his anger, he knew something was wrong with his father. This was too much, even for him. Edwin didn't speak with him the next day. He left his meals by the door and would return later for the empty plate. Two mornings later, the food was untouched. Irritated, Edwin took the plate after several hours and replaced it with lunch. An hour later, that too was left uneaten.

The next day, Edwin tried again. Breakfast remained untouched once more. Returning with lunch, he knocked loudly after placing his father's dinner plate in front of the door and left to go for a walk.

Edwin looked to the sky where the stars were shining. It seemed a bit early for them to be shining so brightly. Far too early, actually, as it was around noon, but the sky bore the purple twilight of evening and seemed quite strange. The air had an odd quality about it. It smelled different, even had a texture to it. He could remember feeling it on his skin and wanted to go see someone—or something—but he couldn't remember who. He'd had a vague image of someone in his mind, but it slipped away as he tried to recall what he was doing.

Edwin remembered marking this incident up to simple absent-mindedness. Now, standing on the edge of a more preferable oblivion next to the dead aldyr, he knew better. Whoever it was, if they were a friend, he would never remember them now.

The first one of *them* he'd seen was through a window. Edwin couldn't remember if he genuinely knew the people who lived there or if knowledge of them was also stolen. It didn't matter now. When the gangly midnight-hued humanoids pulled the house's patron screaming into the blackness, Edwin had frozen on the spot. The things must not have seen him. He turned and ran for home.

The memory of the door slamming open and hitting the wall as he barreled into his home stood out to him for some reason. Perhaps it was due to what happened next that it was traumatically frozen in his mind. A sound like a mountain cracking open tore through all creation. The walls of their stonework house shook and cracks split the foundation. An odor unlike anything he'd experienced filled the air. It wasn't foul, necessarily, but it stung the nostrils and set him in a panic. Edwin still remembers the screams from outside.

He'd run to his father, accidentally trampling the food still sitting on a cold plate in front of the door. His father still refused to answer, so he'd tried the door and was thankful it was unlocked. Edwin had called out to his father as soon as the door swung on its hinges, but the name caught in his throat. Professor Syriell lay slumped across his desk, a red pool forming on the floor. Edwin recalled the lightless stare in his father's eyes, the gash across his throat—made by Corwin's own hand, and the letter left on the table that Edwin now still clutched in his fist. After reading it, Edwin left his father there and ran outside.

As he ran through the streets, he saw people being taken. Oval-shaped rips, hovering in midair like black gemstones, were facing him and he could see the empty voids rimmed by a strange glow on the other side. Some must have been at odd angles, as he saw people disappear seemingly into thin air, or a clawed foot stepping out of nothing. The worst were the elongated hands pulling people into the nothingness before them. The city was under some kind of assault.

Edwin could still pinpoint the moment he knew the captured were forgotten. He couldn't remember who it was, but an ache in his chest still lingered when he tried to recall someone who was pulled howling into the blackness. Even as he looked on their face, arms reaching out to him and making eye contact with this now-forgotten person, their memory began to slip away. Within moments of the blasphemous tear closing, he no longer knew who they were. Only a pain that someone he must have cared for was gone.

He ran again, faster and harder until he felt his sides would explode. He saw the cobbler and his family loaded onto a wagon with horses, charging from the town. He saw the blacksmith leave his wife as she was pulled away. He saw children crying in the streets.

He kept running.

When he stopped, he was near a farmhouse. He knocked and no one answered. Numb from exhaustion both physical and emotional, he'd just walked in. No one was there. A fire was burning and a pot of stew cooking, but no one waited to eat it. He looked out into the wheat fields and saw a scarecrow standing there. He thought it turned and looked at him, but he wasn't sure. He didn't tarry there for long. He wandered for days, passing caravans of people fleeing one horror or the other. He traded information with them. No one knew what happened; some said the gods had forsaken them at last. Others said that errant magic was responsible; that magi were being hunted like witches. Edwin didn't speak much, only told them of Carnelia and to avoid it.

After some time, Edwin wasn't sure exactly how long, he made his way to where he now stood. It would be easier, even in the slightest, if he knew that these were the only creatures that accompanied that awful sound that shook his house and the strange smell that drifted out of the sky. The letter in his hand, the stories from the migrants; they spoke otherwise. There were others. Many others. Worse ones, more powerful ones. They were all over the world. He saw the aldyrs withering before his eyes as he traveled the road that led to the cliff. The unique trees grew in thickets and this one hugged the side of a steep cliff. Elf-kind worshipped them; said they were tied to the soul of the world. Now they were dying. Both the trees and the elves.

Edwin stepped forward a bit. It was time. He would die, but he would be remembered. And he would leave this dying world behind. He felt pangs of grief for his father, but something tugged inside him that said there should be others he should mourn, but he couldn't recall anyone else that mattered.

At least his death would be quick and maybe the fall would be slightly euphoric. At least he wouldn't suffer whatever ungodly fate belonged to those taken by those night-skinned monsters. He would be taken by the sea and his memory would live on, somewhere. He stepped over the edge.

The wind rushed past his face. He smiled for the first time in days. He could hear the waves and smell the salt sea air. He waited for that brief, crushing moment—

He jerked to a stop, nearly lost his breath as his heart slammed against the inside of his chest. He was hanging in midair looking down at the waves crashing against the rocks, their white, foaming crests so very close. He could feel the ocean's spray just slightly on his face.

He looked over his shoulder, and his mouth fell agape in a silent scream. A face, a dark-as-midnight face with soulless, shark-black eyes and no mouth stared back at him. The smooth skin had a wet gleam; the limbs were too long for the shoulders they were attached to. The fingers ended in sharp, vicious claws and Edwin began to feel their sting as they flexed against his skin. The creature gripped effortlessly onto his ankle. Another one of them appeared from the roiling edge of the tear in reality and grabbed him with its hooked, elongated fingers. Edwin howled in pain and terror as they dragged him up into the inky blackness with the strange, out-of-sight glow.

The only sound that remained other than the peaceful crashing of waves on gray stone was the gentle flutter of a letter that caught on a stray cliff-side branch on its way down. It was filled with the hurried writing of a man gone insane, but still aware enough to make an apology to his eldest son. It rambled on here and there, but eventually, its point was made. Words such as 'accident' and 'regret' were tossed around frequently. It was the final few lines that sent Edwin fleeing from the town altogether: "We let them in. The Black Gnarl lied and we let them in."

SOMEWHERE, a young woman with large blue eyes was huddled in a corner and surrounded by strangers. All of them were cold and terrified. It was dark and smelled of shit and decay and misery. Too many people with too few supplies were crammed into a logging camp outside the doomed city of Carnelia. Sometimes, she would comfort herself by thinking of the young man from her painting classes in her hometown. She fantasized that he would come to rescue her. He was smart and kind. His family had respect and money. They had shared a few moments together in their art gatherings that she certainly remembered, surely he remembered her?

That night, as she tried to fall asleep by entertaining herself with thoughts of a smart and kind man and her hopeful rescue, a tear rolled down her cheek. Try as she might, she just couldn't recall his name. Even his face had faded. When she woke, all that remained was a deep heartache and sorrow.

# A GARDEN SWEET AND SANGUINE

THE SOUND OF A QUILL SCRATCHING SOFTLY ON PAPER IS THE MOST comforting sound in the world to me. So many words built from so few letters. Each stroke, each serif and spur, every line that made up the languages we use to communicate has something soft and magical in it. Writing is no different from a symphony to me. There are three things in the world of unique and unparalleled beauty: writing, music, and Nayomi.

She was so lovely, the way she drifted into any room she entered. She had a haunting charisma that charmed any person, regardless of social standing or innate willpower, into acquiescing to her desires. There was no magic or seduction or other base tricks involved in the way she manipulated others. She simply had a way about her that made one want to be in her favor and her thoughts.

"Henrick, how are you?" she beamed. Her eyes glittered as though she hadn't just spoken to me earlier that day.

"I'm well, Nayomi," I sputtered quietly. I was mildly awkward on my best days. This was not one of my best.

Nayomi leaned over to see what current scrollwork I was copying for my employers today. It was late morning and the salty odor of the ocean may have been refreshing to some, but I found it nauseating. I did enjoy the soft, rolling sound of the nearby waves, though. It soothed my anxious mind, which was only aggravated by the presence of Nayomi. I had a very particular way of doing things, and I was very good at my craft, which was unceremoniously described as sedentary, clerical work. I feel, however, that the skill of proper calligraphy and scrollwork, especially after the tenth or fifteenth repetitious copy, requires a certain dutiful mind. My focus, my purpose, and my composure, all come crashing apart like waves upon the nearby shore when she's present.

"You're well? Is that all you have to say?" she asked in mock annoyance. "Well, I can be just as pithy. I have something for you."

That was the first time since she entered the room that I stopped writing. In fact, I was so surprised that I dragged a serif too far and would have to begin my current page from scratch, though my surprise also left me feeling too anxious to be frustrated.

"You have something for me?"

"Yes. I should say, it's for both of us. I know you would enjoy the scholarly aspect, and I would desperately like to know more about it myself. You would be able to do more research more quickly."

I'd a dawning suspicion of the nature of her intentions which tempered my excitement over her need of my assistance; but she still thought of me when she needed help. "This wouldn't have anything to do with my ability to access certain restricted areas of the Pearlstone Library, by chance?"

She actually blushed. My heart fluttered as much as I assumed hers did. She covered her embarrassment with an impish grin that informed me she may have wanted me to come to such a conclusion.

"Perhaps."

I couldn't fault her. It wasn't everyone in the city who had access to the great, old library's best archives. It was a favorite place of mine in the rare times I left my home and place of business. Of course, she would know this. And, I had to admit, my curiosity was overwhelming me.

I frequented the facility and had grown to know the various, elderly archivists who dwelt there, including the Head Chronicler, Germanius. It was he who eventually granted me passage to the library's restricted section. This had always been my favorite area. It was isolated, quiet, and smelled of books old and rarely touched. I had to admit there was a slight thrill at the mystery of what may lie undiscovered in the rows of tomes, ledgers, and scrolls that lined the walls.

I PLACED my quill to the side, near the inkwell, and turned to face her. I always had to steel myself for this. Her dark skin and captivating eyes always turned my well-meaning words into nonsense. I suppose this made me look quite aloof or even cross, but it was far better than to reveal the clumsy, foolish truth. The question of what she wanted from the restricted section immediately began teasing my higher reasoning skills.

Admittedly, much of the restricted section was limited to the mundane. Many books of recorded history and bureaucratic archives that had yet to be copied for posterity and preservation comprised the bulk of the selection. Scrolls of personal information regarding merchant sales and noble lineages filled in the gaps. However, there were a few volumes of ill repute that gave the restricted section its air of forbidding allure. I'd seen books detailing the Fourth Sect: the magic of death, necromantic practices, and disreputable alchemical applications. Their bindings were sealed with small locks that only Chronicler Germanius himself could access.

I loved knowledge, including the sharing of it. Why I never chose to pursue more scholarly aspects other than mere scribing I can't entirely say. Perhaps because I was very good at transcription, and the comfort that was afforded by sitting and writing was both very appealing and amicable to my fragile health. Perhaps it was because of my knack for learning languages. I knew nearly a dozen. Three of which were archaic tongues long dead to the world.

This was also why I so loved Nayomi: she knew what brought me pleasure in life and her gift for me today was that of knowledge. Truly, the only kind of adventure that I would long for.

"There's a book I'd like you to find in the restricted archives. I know it's there—don't look at me that way! I can do my own sort of research, Henrick; however, for this, I need your help. I'd like you to ask the Head Chronicler if you can bring it here for a day or two. I'd like to look through it. Just you and I."

She smiled sweetly and squinted her eyes playfully to emphasize those last words. As reserved and indifferent as I appeared on the outside, internally I was in turmoil. I felt my face flush, all the power to resist hemorrhaging from me. I smiled back, hopefully without much awkwardness.

"I suppose. I have to finish my work here, but then I'll make my way there before they close the doors for the evening."

Her face lit up. Even when leaping across a room, she did so in a graceful manner. She threw her arms around me and thanked me over and over again. My shoulders stiffened and I froze. The smell of citrus perfume overwhelmed my senses. The sudden contact was awkward but so welcome at the same time. When she finally released me, I smiled back.

"Absolutely," being the only weak response I could muster.

She floated away, leaving me with a wave of her delicate hand and a sing-song "'til this evening." I breathed a dichotomous sigh of longing to see her again and relief at the chance to return to my comforting work. Returning to scribing contract ledgers, I saw the mistake that I made upon her arrival that required correction. I was annoyed. And grateful for the distraction.

That evening, I walked quickly to the Pearlstone Library. At least, as quickly as I could. I'd borne a slight limp since I was a child, caused by a fractured shin which itself was caused by weak bone structure. My day's work had been slowed by Nayomi's visit and my thoughts distracted by this mysterious tome she wished to peruse. I sincerely hoped I wasn't too late to find it for her.

My pace always allowed for time to take in the city, although I was barely ever inclined to do so. The districts that stretched into the mainland that were called Ligothi. The part of the city that stretched along the coast, was old, which is why it was often creatively referred to as Old Ligothi. It was a small but potent city-state, though; holding its own against others like Felkirk in the south and Carnelia in the north.

Old Ligothi was a city of stone. Stone buildings lining stone streets with triangular spouts of ivy pouring from windows and the occasional wild growths. Vibrant green growth crept amid the brown and grey mortar work of civilization. It may have been beautiful if not for the closely packed people, shouts and droning buzz of conversation, and the smell of market stalls and other, more unpleasant, things. The salt air was slightly nauseating, but it was heavenly perfume compared to the streets.

Yes, these walks occupied my mind, but also reminded me why I wanted to reach the library as quickly as possible.

By some fortuitous twist, I made it to the library with time to spare. Germanius had left for the evening, but the acolyte in his stead recognized me by my scholarly attire and, as he rudely put it, my "weak gait." After such a comment he mentioned that Germanius had clarified that if I showed, I was to be allowed entrance into the restricted sections. I huffed inwardly at his snide remark, but was grateful for Germanius' foresight. In typical fashion, he had left instructions for me to be allowed to conduct any research necessary to my profession. Though, this evening's business was for an admittedly different purpose.

Perusing the forbidden registers slowly, I took in the ancient smell of parchment and leather bindings. I cherished this place. It was my haven against the bustle and drama of people. All people except, of course, for Nayomi: my reason for being here this evening. True to my word, I searched every cover until I found the book about which she inquired. It was no surprise I hadn't come across it before. It was tucked away in a small pile of non-descript books atop a disregarded shelf in the darkest, mustiest corner of the archives. The symbol on the front was exactly as she had described: a rough, broken diamond shape with curled, uneven barbs where each side met in a corner. In the center was a plain, unassuming, and rough-edged dot or circle.

It was unusual and, despite being a geometric shape, it appeared organic in its layout. The longer I looked, the harder it became to look at. I felt dizzy, and suddenly had the sensation I was falling. Specifically, falling into that uneven dot in center of that strange, barbed diamond. Had it turned into a hole? In the book itself?

I thought perhaps my hurry to get here and the agitation at the rude librarian was taking a toll on me, but after a few moments, I realized I was looking at that circle during the entirety of the light-headed episode. I blinked a few times, which strangely stung my eyes and set them to watering, and shook my head to clear it. Feeling a little better, I asked myself what Nayomi had brought me into. The book wasn't locked, so I assumed it wasn't among those taboo volumes of the Fourth; though it must have been arcane in some fashion to have such an effect. Needless to say, I hesitated to touch it.

My hand trembled as it hovered over the shriveled leather cover. This was, indeed, a strange kind of leather. When I finally touched it, my assumptions proved correct. The cover was dry and cracked in places. It was incredibly old, but still in surprisingly good shape. I didn't open it yet, as Nayomi wanted to share that together. I placed it carefully in my satchel, making sure to check that the librarian was nowhere near. I departed the library without incident or even recognition by the sole remaining caretaker.

My walk home was a mess of conflicting emotions. I thrilled at this little adventure Nayomi had started me on: the search for an archaic tome even I knew nothing of, the mystery of what awaited within its pages, and the prospect of searching through them with her. It was, admittedly, exhilarating. On the other hand, I had abused the trust the old Head Chronicler held in me. I stole, even if temporarily, a book from the library I hold so dear. I took it from the restricted sections that I had been generously provided access to due to my scholarly interest, professional necessities, and harmless intents. By the time I reached my home, away from my place of work and the nauseating sea air, I wasn't sure how to feel.

That confusion quickly dissipated after opening the door. Nayomi sat in my domicile, waiting for me. She let herself in, knowing she was always welcome at my home. She had sconces lit and a fire going; plenty of light was prepared for our clandestine studies. The shadows flickering off the walls made the room seem almost romantic—if I were inclined to such whimsy. Nayomi smiled from ear to ear when I came carrying a satchel bearing the large tome. It was far heavier than it looked and I dropped it with a weighty thud on a table.

Nayomi clamored to see it, having gasped when I first removed it from my satchel..

"Henrick, this is so exciting!" she chirped.

Looking at the barbed diamond shape, I felt the same subtle vertigo begin to take me. A sense of nausea curdled in my stomach as well. The weight of the book and my hurried pace home might have had something to do with my ill state, but I doubted it would have done so to this extent.

"Henrick, are you alright?" Nayomi asked with genuine concern. She took my chin in her smooth hand and turned my head to look at her. She looked in my eyes with worry, causing me to become flushed.

"I'm alright," I said, turning away awkwardly. "Let's see what's so important about this book you had me steal."

The concern on her face melted away and she opened her mouth in mock offense.

"I did no such thing! And you stole nothing. This book will be returned in short order, I promise. I would have been more than happy to go to the library and look through it myself, but I'm not as fortunate as you to have access to it."

"As I said. I stole it."

She waved her hand and scoffed. "Come, now. Let's just look at what we have here."

She ran her hands tenderly over the book. Her forefinger traced the emblem on the cover; she didn't appear to be as affected by the symbol as I suspected I may have been. Quite the opposite, in fact. She had an even bigger smile on her face than when I brought the book in.

"So old," she whispered.

I nodded in agreement. "It may be one of the oldest I've ever seen. It doesn't have a title, do you know what it is?"

Nayomi had only described the book's appearance to me. I realized I'd forgotten to ask for a given title. I tended to make mistakes in that manner around her. I also never opened it, as she made me promise. She wanted the two of us, together, to be the first to have read it in "centuries," she'd said.

She took a breath, seeming to freeze for a moment. I'd never seen her with such a stern manner before. She opened the book slowly, her fingers gripping the cover as though it might bite her. Inside, the book was filled top-to-bottom, margin-to-margin with the most professional and artistic inscription. It was beautifully crafted; the serifs were curved with what must have been the slightest flick of the wrist. The ligatures were perfectly formed, and the lead letters of each page were artistic works in and of themselves with majestic swashes that brought the whole of a page together. My mouth gaped open and I reached out to touch the page but feared damaging such incredible work. Reverence stayed my hand. How had such old pages survived in such fine shape? This work was the very definition of not judging a book by its cover. I hesitated, my hand hovering over the open book until reason gave over to emotion.

As I ran my hands gently over the page, Nayomi sighed. It was not one of delight, as I would have hoped and expected, but, rather, one of exasperation.

"Can you understand any of it?" She said, frustrated.

"Of course I can. It's an older version of the Ligothi language, but it's still quite legible."

Nayomi looked at me, squinting in irritation. "Do you think I'm stupid, Henrick? I speak the Ligothi tongue quite well. This is gibberish!"

She made an angry gesture at the book. "The letters are practically faded away and the pages are... brown? Yellow? Some of both?" She scoffed and grunted in frustration and disgust. "I think some of them are even mildewed."

My eyes, still bulging in surprise, looked at a completely different set of pages before me. They were nothing like she described, and I told her as much.

"Nayomi, I mean no offense, but these pages are immaculate. The writing even more so. Yes, the cover is ugly and worn, foul even, but the contents are wholly different."

She looked at me in disbelief. Pinching a corner of the current page with equal parts care and disgust, she turned the page. She flipped through a few more pages, shaking her head at each one. I, however, saw no change in the exquisite quality. After a few pages, she stopped and seemed prepared to throw the book from the table. Then, her eyes opened wide and her face softened, to a small extent. She put her hand on top of mine, which still rested on the open page. She looked to me, some new understanding dawning in her eyes.

"You can read what the pages say?"

"Yes," I responded hesitantly.

She looked to the book and back at me, "Well?"

I cleared my throat nervously, withering under her expectant gaze. I stepped closer, seeing the words in their eloquent legibility. How could she not see this? The ink, though faded, was still quite vibrant. The pages were slightly dry from age, but not nearly as fragile as I would have thought. Although the language was Ligothian, a variation on the many human languages spoken in Alda, it was an archaic dialect not used in hundreds of years—making the quality of the pages even more cryptic.

I picked a random verse from the page and read aloud:

*"...THE names that are spoken in quiet places. In the peat and the mold and the rot. Rain and blood are their nourishment, and perpetuate the fruit of their flesh. All is life and death and stagnation and growth through Them: Mariamyn in her Molded Gown, Hitala'vi and Namt-*

*inugga the Twin Sickness, Suhpona's putrid domain, and Carti-carneah The Root and Blood. Many are their names, and all are beautiful to their father, Ygiddra, in whom they dwell."*

I STOPPED, feeling my heart beating faster upon speaking those fetid words. I looked to Nayomi, my face feeling pale and cold. Her eyes were wide, and a hint of a smile curled her lips.

"Gods, Nayomi, what did you have me bring to you?" I gasped. The words were not so much spoken as they were vomited from some fearsome pit of my better reason.

She put her hand on my shoulder, but didn't take her eyes from the page. "Keep going. This is fascinating."

I swallowed, feeling the scratch of my dry throat. I wet my mouth and continued.

*"BUT THERE ARE none more loved and dreaded than the Timeless Garden, Ygiddra. He is the sower of the sanguine groves and the reaper of their soul-filled harvests. He lives to make us his, to enrich us in the sweet soil of viscera and consciousness. His greatest pain is that we are not his children, and he seeks to make us so. We are nothing like his precious daughters or the children of their twisted wombs. But, He will adopt us. Make us His. Plant us in the claret-mulch and make us His. We pursue this dream. We long for this embrace."*

I STOPPED READING, feeling I could no longer continue with the pages' contents. They grew more descriptive and exponentially more disturbing. I began flipping pages, to see what else this book contained. Perhaps I was morbidly curious, or it was seeing the intense interest and frustration on Nayomi's face that forced me to continue reading. In either case, the book continued on about this putrefaction god. If that's truly what he, or it, was.

Some other indecipherable language, apart from the antiquated Ligothian, adorned the margins of the book. I thought at first they may be dwarven, but decided otherwise. This script was older than even the dwarven languages I've seen—and far more sinister, as well. Drawings of flowers, roots, and strange fruit were accompanied by short descriptions, with similar descriptors as those in the paragraphs I read aloud. None of the images were of things I'd seen in any of the hundreds of encyclopedias and almanacs I read or transcribed. Some of the descriptions were written in that same strange language.

I reached a pair of pages that caused me to stop and stare. Nayomi covered her mouth. If she wasn't seeing the same contents as I was, I could only imagine what she was seeing now. Covering both pages was a drawing, sketched in charcoal or some similar medium and colored in with simple paints. It depicted what I could only assume to be Ygiddra himself. A circle of people, so small they could scarcely be illustrated, surrounded what appeared to be a set of ruins. Encircling the ruins were curling vines that grasped the remains of the unknown structure like the tentacles of some abyss-dwelling beast. Blossoms, fruit, and human-like appendages adorned the vines. Mold-covered skeletons could be seen rotting in between the leaves and tendrils. The drawing made the creature seem both flesh and vegetation. The crude coloring of the illustration only worsened the effect. On closer inspection, some of the tiny human shapes were involved in sacrificing entire groups of individuals, soaking the ground and the outlying, curling vines in blood.

All the horror displayed by these strange and offensive writings constituted a mere pinch of the pages in the massive tome. I slammed it shut, and suddenly had a strange taste in my mouth.

I recognized the acidic bite of bile, rising to protest the things I had just witnessed, the words I had just spoken, perhaps even the names I had just invoked.

I looked to Nayomi, and she stared at the pages in disgusted silence; however, there remained a curious glimmer in her eye. She grabbed the book and shoved it back into the bag I'd brought it home in. She picked it up and began to walk toward the door. At first, I didn't believe she was trying to leave with this foul work that I immensely regretted 'borrowing' from the library.

"I need to take this to him. Please, Henrick! I'll return it to you tomorrow, I promise. This is so much more than I thought. I need to delve a little further."

I felt a stab of anger rise up in me momentarily. I never shy away from confessing how she can allure me into so many things I would otherwise retreat from, but this was a line. I steeled myself for the response.

"Nayomi, no." Once the first words escaped the others came more freely. "I'm sorry, but, if you're to take that awful thing anywhere, I'm going with you."

"Henrick, I can assure you I'll be safe."

I sighed deeply, "It's not for you. It's for that manuscript. It's evil. It's wrong in ways I can't describe to you. If you can't tell already, then I'm not of the ability to explain it right now. I borrowed it, I'm staying with it."

She looked at me for the first time with hurt in her eyes. There wasn't even any anger there. Either real or feigned, she shrank away from me emotionally.

"You don't trust me?"

I hung my head. Partially in shame, but also to think without having to see in her eyes the sting that my words inflicted upon her.

"It's not that. I don't like that thing. I don't know how it escaped Germanius' notice or why it isn't sealed like the other illicit works, but I will not allow myself to be responsible for its distribution outside the walls of my home and the library, which is already one place too much. If it leaves here, I go with it."

I placed no small amount of gravity on my last words. Nayomi pursed her lips. Her eyes darted to the book in her arms, then she sighed in resignation.

"Alright, that's fair, Henrick," she said with a nod of her head. "All I ask is that you not judge me based on who I am taking you to see. My contact was one of the most intelligent men I've ever met," she said with raised brows to emphasize her point, "Unorthodox, but intelligent. I hope you'll be as riveted by him as I am."

I'm not one opposed to an enlightened conversation, but the fact that these people were so interested in a book so vile did not endear me to their intent or purpose. The fact that Nayomi seemed to be so willing to take advantage of my good nature did not incline me to assist her any further, either. But, given her resolve to get this book to these people, the mystery surrounding its unnoticed residence in the library's restricted section, and the strange way in which it affected our physically viewable interpretations of it, I found myself admittedly intrigued even further by the situation as a whole.

"Who—who are these people? That you're taking us to? Why is there so much secrecy surrounding this? You cannot deny, Nayomi, that this sounds incredibly suspect."

She sat the book down on the table and pursed her lips. She looked to me with a tilt of her head and seemed to be searching for an explanation as her eyes drifted to the floor. After a few moments, and a few hesitant false starts, she seemed to find her resolve.

"They're called the Black Gnarl. At least, that's what they told me."

A weight must have been lifted from her chest. The old Nayomi returned, and her charming smile spread across her face again, along with the gleam in her eyes. She leaned forward, looking at me in that way that set my heart to flutter.

"Apparently, they're a small group; dedicated to finding and cataloging a very specific set of tombs and relics like this one," she grabbed the pack containing the book and looked back at it briefly, "That symbol on the front? That seems to be the mark of their order or a variation of it. Their order is so old there's no record of their origins; how they began, their founders... It's so irresistibly cryptic, Henrick!"

Cryptic, yes. A name such as the Black Gnarl invokes other, more concerning, descriptors as well. I'd read of many old orders and organizations, not all of which were benevolent or even benign. I'd never heard anything along the lines of this one and that made me suspicious. I had little to do in my life other than reading and learning. If I had heard little to nothing regarding this order, it was my first reason to, at the least, doubt it and, at the worst, fear it.

"Are you meeting them tonight? Or were you taking the book until a later date?" I asked.

"Tonight, yes. Remember, I promised to meet you tomorrow to return it?" She put her hand over her chest, "You didn't believe me, did you?"

I raised my hand, beginning to protest, when she continued anyway.

"And it's him. Not them. I'm only meeting one representative. He's the only one I've ever met from their order. They're very secretive. He won't just be waiting at a park for us; we'll have to find him."

I grimaced. Meeting one individual did seem safer. If we traveled together then we could at least offer the illusion of numbers, though my ability to protect anyone was limited, to say the least. I also didn't like the idea of some kind of scavenger hunt to find this person. The idea of this adventure began to curdle in my stomach.

I simultaneously questioned what insanity was driving me to follow through with this and was also somewhat excited at the prospect of discovering more about this mysterious old tome. Perhaps that answered my question. This was a first for me; to do something spontaneous and almost adventurous. And who would I be to deny an intellectual 'first time' for something?

"How far is the meeting place? I'll need some time to get there," I said, hesitating on my final words.

"The Graywater District," Nayomi answered, grimacing. "They wanted to be inconspicuous."

"They will be," I replied with a marked lack of enthusiasm.

There were a few hours yet before we needed to leave. I asked Nayomi to enlighten me on how she met this 'interesting' man. Her answers were cryptic and smacked of reluctance to divulge any information at all. The most I managed to piece together was that her introduction was a result of an overlap in her various social and intellectual circles driven by her interest in life's mysteries and willingness to pay coin to pursue such interests.

The sun grew low in the sky, casting an orange radiance on the bleak stone structures of the city. This signaled our time to depart. The evening crowds would start to thin and we could make our way to the impoverished section of town known as the Graywater District.

The walk was fairly slow going, given my body's propensity to weakness, but Nayomi was as patient as ever. She practically danced around me in circles with enthusiasm at the prospect of meeting her contact with the book in hand. I couldn't help but be inclined to think that she believed I wasn't going to go through with the uncouth snatching of the tome from the library. I was happy to have proven her wrong, even if just for the radiance she sent my way.

The air began to feel thicker as we worked our way inland. We found the small river that broke off from the shoreline and led into the heart of Ligothi. On the border of the old and the new, the stonework began to wear thin like old skin. Boards and planks filled the gaps in decrepit buildings like rotten teeth. Tattered shawls of cloth draped over windows and toppled masonry like filthy bandages. Here, the stonework of Ligothi's streets turned into what had become colloquially known among the other castes of the city as "the Bruise." I found this quite distasteful, but I could see the analogy.

The paved streets had worn thin and muddy soil pock-marked with filthy puddles took their place. There were more trees in this district, but they were sad caricatures of vegetation. They appeared more like old, dry bones clawing their way from the ground. People toiled away at their daily tasks, casting distrustful stares our way. Mendicants called for alms as we passed. When I saw a girl that looked no older than twelve, I couldn't help but offer a few coins from my pocket. Nayomi's expression said she understood, but was anxious to find where we needed to go.

With a stern look to me, Nayomi pointed to an old, dilapidated building at the end of an equally dilapidated street. This structure was still fully constructed of stone, although it leaned in ways that said it would soon crumble like many others. It appeared to be holding together by sheer force of will and the desperation to endure.

The rotting front door creaked as we entered. Inside, there were no candles or torches lit. The setting sun had turned from vibrant orange to dull purple. We had just enough light to see the sad state of the single room that comprised the building's interior. Everything was in disarray. Books lay tattered on the ground. Sparse furniture was tipped over or broken. The musky smell of mold pervaded the sheets and curtains that lay in clumps here and there on the floor.

"What could we possibly be looking for?" I whispered in disbelief.

Craning her neck to look among the rafters, Nayomi answered, "He said when we have the book, we'll know what we're looking for."

The images inside that tome crept back into my mind, causing me to shudder.

Nayomi stopped, her head swiveling over to me and her eyes wide. "Henrick, get out the book," she said, pointing at the shoulder satchel holding the dreadful book.

"Why?" I questioned, when I realized exactly what she was proposing.

We flipped one of the overturned tables back into a usable position. Nayomi found a candle resting in a corner. She picked it up and swiftly exited the room to the street outside. When she returned, the candle was lit and she moved more carefully, as the delicate flame flickered with every step. I pulled the book from the satchel and set it on the table. Nayomi set the candle beside it.

The dark cover looked like a pool of congealed blood in the low light. There, in the center of the cover, was the object of our search.

"That," Nayomi said, pointing to the barbed diamond shape on the cover, "That's what we're looking for. I guarantee that symbol is somewhere in this room and will tell us more."


I KICKED ASIDE PAPERS, piles of clothes, and all manner of foul refuse. The sound of chairs dragging across the floor resonated from Nayomi's side of the dwelling. I gave a deep sigh, looking to the one window opposite the entry door. It was fogged over with dirt, mud, and gods knew what else. I realized I missed the seaside view of my home. With nothing to see out the grimy window, I lowered my head in dejection. Casting my eyes to the floor, I saw a carving in one of the floorboards.

"Nayomi, over here," I said, almost in disbelief.

She came to my side and followed my gaze to the carved symbol on the floor, near filled in with dirt. "That's it!" she cried. Her hands slapped over her mouth as the sound echoed around us like thunder.

I smirked at her excitement, barely able to contain my own. We went to work feeling for where the boards may be loose enough to remove, assuming that this was a sign of some hidden door.

We assumed correctly. A number of the boards were attached to one another, pulling up together to reveal a circular hole cutting into the ground below. A ladder ran along the rough-hewn stone that formed the vertical passage. With a furtive look to one another, we began our descent.

Nayomi had the foresight to bring the candle, which provided necessary light to safely descend down the ladder. A few dozen feet down, we reached the bottom. Torches lined a musty hallway that may have once been lined completely with stonework, but now had fallen or crumbled away, exposing the damp earth beneath. Where the stones held, a few sconces held burning torches that fought a losing battle against the darkness.

The tunnel wasn't very extensive. A mere few dozen feet later, a large stone landing waited for us, leading me to believe this entire setup was once one large basement or perhaps shared cellar between several of the old houses above us. The landing was better maintained than the rest. The stone flooring and walls were still mostly intact, with obvious replacements for pieces that had crumbled away. Several candles sat on a solid oak table. Surrounding them were as many torches on this single landing as lined the entirety of the hallway. Two empty chairs sat on either side of the table, reminding me that Nayomi was expected to be alone.

Behind the chair opposite the both of us hung a thick curtain draped over what I could only assume to be a passageway. The bottom of it fluttered from a draft. As the thick cloth trembled, I saw the rough edges of a hastily dug tunnel peeking from behind it. This must be a new addition to the decrepit basement.

We waited in the dank-smelling quiet and darkness. I offered the chair to Nayomi, which she thankfully accepted. She asked that I draw the book from its satchel and place it on the desk. I thought for a moment that she intended to try and read it again. I felt a hollow pit expand in my stomach. Not because I was repulsed at the idea of seeing those writings again but intrigued by it. Perhaps this endeavor—the thrill of the hidden passage and the anxiety of awaiting this mysterious figure—had set upon me some sort of drunken euphoria of forbidden adventure and knowledge. Regardless, it was wholly new to me and I was apparently quite receptive.

The moment never came, however. She didn't try to open that heavy, scab-like cover. The book merely sat there on the table, waiting for its current visitor.

A slight shuffling came from behind the curtain. We both waited, holding our breath, when a hand pulled aside the curtain. Out from the darkness within the tunnel stepped a figure clothed in what appeared to be that self-same darkness. Their black robes and cowl made the paleness of their hands and lower face stand out all the more, like a shimmering ghoul reflecting the moonlight.

The hooded head looked to Nayomi, then to me, then darted

back to Nayomi. A scowl formed on the thin face and my heart grew instantly cold.

"You were to come alone," he growled. I suddenly had the feeling I was alone in a deep ocean, facing a circling shark.

"Gideon, I—" Nayomi began, but then choked on her words. The hooded man stepped forward in a sudden but subtle gesture that instantly made Nayomi aware of some mistake. I had to surmise that she was not to use names.

"I—I owed him. He's the one who recovered the book. Without him, we would still be trying to retrieve it from the Pearlstone."

The hooded head, darkened by the cowl so that only the lower half of the face was visible, slowly looked to me. I felt a piercing gaze hidden under its shadows. He stared at me for several moments before lifting his pallid hands and pulling the cowl back, revealing a middle-aged man with a shaven head. Deep lines creased the sides of his mouth, giving him a severe appearance and one of utmost gravitas.

"I suppose we owe you our thanks," he grumbled. He nodded at the book on the table. "This is it? This is genuine?"

I remembered the feel of the cover, leather of the most foul origins, and shuddered. "Absolutely."

He sat down, casually, and opened the ponderous tome. It creaked and echoed in the still chamber. He flipped pages— slowly, purposefully—one at a time. We watched with rapt patience. Neither Nayomi nor myself dared to interrupt. When he'd reached the last page, he closed the book with a heavy *thump*.

"There is nothing new here," he said, shaking his head. "You may have it back."

Nayomi let out a deep sigh.

"Nothing new?" I asked, confused. The book was quite large

and I didn't dare guess how long we'd waited as he perused the entirety of its contents.

He looked at me with barely contained impatience. "Yes. We have another copy of the Dread Praises. From a collection belonging to a noble in Felkirk. This is a second copy of the same book. I cannot find any more here than I already know."

"What about me?" Nayomi asked. "Does this secure my induction?"

The man, Gideon, grimaced. "You did as you were asked. You will be contacted soon."

A smile spread across Nayomi's face, larger than any I'd seen before. My brows furrowed and I mentally noted to ask her about what she meant after we'd gone. I felt Gideon's gaze on me, still, and I withered inside as I turned to look at him. He was staring at me from the corner of his eyes, one hand still resting on the book.

"Are you not curious?" he asked in low, gravelly tones.

"About what?" I whispered, too frightened to make much noise. "Nayomi's question?"

"No," he said flatly, his eyes never leaving mine. "Not that."

His thumbs caressed the side of the book, along the pages that sat between its covers. I couldn't help but feel he thumbed along those very pages I had read earlier that evening. Those that spoke of the sanguine garden.

He pushed the book towards me. His eyes darted to Nayomi for a moment, then returned to me. He reached into his robes and when his hand was once more revealed, it held a hideous-looking dagger. He held onto the blade, carefully, and offered the grip to me. His eyes continued to linger on me, looking into me, through me. I felt like he was reading my inner thoughts, my very soul, like a book.

"The Obscured Throne seeks those who are worthy. Ygiddra is not the old one whose information I seek, but if you are interested in finding out more the book will oblige. Like His garden, it will provide… if it is fed."

Gideon stood and cast a glance at both Nayomi and me before pulling his cowl back over his head. He looked once more at Nayomi and uttered the phrase, "*Via Infinitum Mortis.* Remember these words." He turned and exited through the curtained tunnel entrance. I yet gripped that dagger he had offered; it felt like it squirmed within my grip.

Nayomi's smile had faded, but her eyes were still alight from the hooded man's comment. She would be contacted soon. Another question for when we were in a more appropriate place to talk openly.

Returning the book to its satchel and adding the strange dagger, we returned to the ladder and surfaced into the world above. The difference between the underground chamber and the upper streets felt like wholly different planes of existence. In spite of the crushing poverty and decaying buildings, the air felt lighter. A weight had lifted from my shoulders. Though, this still did not make the walk home any easier.

I asked Nayomi to carry the satchel by the time we reached the edge of the Graywater. She didn't mind, though she also appeared distracted. Her eyes lingered on distant buildings. Her answers to my inconsequential questions to pass the time were brief and disinterested in tone. I stopped talking, stopped trying to fill the quiet spaces in our walk, and listened instead to the sounds of the bustling city.

We reached my apartment after sundown. Building caretakers had lit the torches to light our way, but the inside of my dwelling was quite dark. Light from both moon and torches allowed us to just move around safely within my small home. Once the fireplace was lit and the warmth spread, finally, into my bones I was able to think more clearly.

I took a seat at my table and placed the book, The Dread

Praises, upon its surface. Gideon mentioned it was a copy. As a professional in this area, I admired the dedication of its scribe. I wondered if that same scribe was the one who included the artwork, as that was not a service I offered, myself. Though, even as a copy, it was incredibly old. I traced the symbol on the front of the book with my finger. The strange sensation that once assailed me upon looking at it no longer seeming to have an effect. The image drew my mind to the conversation with Gideon and his words to Nayomi.

"You want to be a part of the Black Gnarl," I asked, my low voice resounding in the silence.

Nayomi hesitated before responding. "Yes, I want to join their order."

"So you used me to prove your worth." I didn't mean the words to sound as harsh as they did, but perhaps such hard truths were necessary.

Nayomi's mouth dropped open. Her expression spoke to hurt feelings, but her eyes flashed in anger.

"I did no such thing, Henrick!"

"You sent me to get the Dread Praises—to *steal* it. And then you asked the hooded man, Gideon, about your induction. You used me, Nayomi."

Her arms crossed her chest. Her lips pursed and she looked as though she were about to rebuke me, but then her eyes fell onto the table and, though her arms remained crossed, her shoulders dropped.

"Henrick, what are you doing?"

It shames me to admit that my emotions began to get the better of me. I didn't notice that I'd been gripping the dagger tightly, my knuckles white.

I eased my grip and looked at the dagger, turning it over in front of me. The blade was polished to a sheen and very sharp, though it had a strange color to it. The grip was also finely polished. Upon closer inspection, I found the handle and the blade to be carved from one singular piece of something. Whether the material was bone or wood I couldn't say. I tapped the tip of the dagger against the table. It stuck firmly each time. It was quite inflexible, but didn't break when I experimented further.

"A strange and ugly thing," I remarked, looking at its design.

I remembered the words spoken to me; if I yearned to know more, I only had to feed the book. How does one feed an unliving stack of paper and binding? Then, a shudder coursed through me from head to foot as I took in the possibility that, perhaps, this book was not quite as unliving as one would think. I recalled the pages wherein the images of Ygiddra and his supplicants were drawn in stark images of debauchery and sacrifice. I felt the slightest twinge of that old, unsettling feeling that came from gazing on the barbed diamond; the symbol of the Black Gnarl imprinted on that hideous cover.

"Henrick!" Nayomi shouted from somewhere in a deep fog. Had she left the room?

I heard my name repeated again, and Nayomi followed with, "Be careful, stop!"

I blinked, my eyes having gone dry, and felt a burning sensation in my hand. When reason returned to me, I saw I held the dagger firmly in one hand while my other gripped the blade itself. Crimson fluid ran down the blade and dripped onto the cover of the Dread Praises. I relaxed my wounded hand and the sudden release of pressure caused the blood to flow more freely. It pooled onto the cover of the book and I watched in rapt horror as the diamond shape turned as black as night. It could be perceived that the lines of the symbol had not just changed color, but fell into the book leaving more of a deep carving than an imprint. The hole in the center of the diamond seemed to grow ever so slightly. It pulled into itself like a collapsing building, leaving an empty hole that must have run through the entirety of the book. All the air in the room seemed to snuff out as I struggled to breathe. Nayomi placed a hand on her chest and I assumed she, too, was struggling to breathe.

It only lasted a moment, but it was a moment too long. Where once I thought I would pass out, I now found myself quickly recovering. Nayomi was staring at the cover, dumbfounded.

She took the knife from me and looked first to me, then to the blade in her hand. She put her hand on the cover of the Dread Praises, though her hand came away dry. The blood was no longer there. She swallowed—a thick, slow motion—and ran the blade across her hand.

Nayomi made a fist and squeezed, holding her hand over the book. We both expected to see rivulets of blood pouring onto the binding as it was no weak cut that she made. She opened her fist and her palm was unharmed.

Leaving her hand open, her fingers splayed and palm exposed, Nayomi ran the blade across her hand, grunting in expected pain. The force with which she applied the knife to her hand should have cut to the bone, but no such thing happened.

She tossed the knife down harshly, shouting in frustration. She covered her eyes with her hands, rubbing them harshly. I imagine she must have been seeing stars when she pulled her hands away.

"Henrick, I'm very tired. I think I need to rest."

I nodded. "Yes, I think we both need rest. We're obviously exhausted and possibly hallucinating." I chuckled, trying to alleviate the mood. Nayomi was not entertained.

She nodded and avoided eye contact. Turning sharply, she left the room without so much as a goodbye. The door shut softly behind her and then all was quiet. The fireplace spat lazily. Insects sang outside.

I sat staring at the book for what may have been hours or merely minutes. It would be impossible to tell. One thing was for certain: for the first time since I could remember, I wasn't tired at all.

I WOKE to the sounds of Nayomi calling my name. She must have burst into my apartment as I woke, startled, to the sound of some distant banging noise in the foggy space between sleep and consciousness. I also noted that I fell asleep at the table, my head resting in my folded arms on the table's surface.

"Henrick, you have to see this!" Nayomi shouted. I was still shaking off the weight of a disturbed sleep when she came over and put a hand on my shoulder, shaking me gently. "Come, hurry!"

Following her outside, I noticed the sun rose to near midday. I had vastly overslept. My attention quickly shifted to the sight of several people lining the streets and leaning out their windows. A buzz of low voices hung in the air as all heads turned to the north.

A strange light curved on the horizon, sickly strings of colors twining together like a nest of snakes. The phenomena seemed to be focused over Carnelia, but stretched into the horizon to further parts unknown.

"So strange," I mumbled.

"But beautiful, in a way," Nayomi added.

I had an odd sensation wash over me. It was neither pleasant nor unpleasant, more like a strange sense of foreboding that something was coming. It was like a strong wind at the end of winter, foretelling a sudden and harsh change in the weather was inbound.

"Let's go, Nayomi," I said quietly and gently took her hand.

"Oh, Henrick," she said, pulling her hand from mine. I thought perhaps she was upset with me, but then she gently took my right hand in hers and opened my fingers slowly. "Your hand... we never tended to it."

In the rush of strange events from the previous night, I'd completely forgotten. I pulled my hand back and looked at it. A small scar was already present, the wound having closed overnight.

"Strange," I muttered, noticing the odd tinge of color on the scar. It was an earthy, muted green rather than the stark white of typical scar tissue.

"Is it infected?" Nayomi asked, concerned.

My brow furrowed, confusion marring my face. "No. It doesn't even hurt."

I looked back up at the strange display arcing across the northern sky. The scar tingled.

"Let's go, Nayomi," I said quietly.

We returned to my apartment, the strangeness of the last twenty-four hours lingering in the room and drifting through the open windows. We were both quiet for a time, I sitting at my workstation and Nayomi on the chaise overlooking the shoreline. Time became lost between us. Eventually, I heard Nayomi ask, "Henrick, how long has that been there?"

I looked up from my workstation where I was absently staring at an unfinished manuscript. Her face, scrunched in a quizzical expression, was looking toward my table where the Dread Praises still lay. I turned and saw nothing. Standing from my desk, I stepped next to her to see what she was looking at.

There, I saw on the stone mantel above my fireplace the focus of her concern. A black and green patch of growth was spreading over the wall. I approached it cautiously, like it as some living thing that would jump out and assault me. It was a strange substance and I feared to touch it. I looked as closely at it as I dared. It didn't appear to be mold, or a fungus, or some kind of lichen. Rather, it appeared to be some form all three and yet something completely different.

"That is wholly new. I don't have a mold problem. I'll have to have someone come look at it."

I don't know why I lied. I needed no expert. I was learned enough in the subject. Perhaps it was over concern for Nayomi and what she may think of some unknown species of plant growth in my home. But, I also felt something else. Something tied to the odd heaviness in the air that I felt upon seeing the strange phenomena on the horizon, that I felt upon seeing the scar on my hand, that I now felt seeing the strange growth on the wall.

If I wanted more knowledge, I need only feed the book. Ygiddra would seek a worthy sacrifice. The knife refused Nayomi, but it cut my hand—took my blood, my offering.

"I want to return to the safehouse," I said suddenly, confidently.

Nayomi, seemingly forgetting my tainted mantel altogether, looked to me with wide eyes.

"In the Graywater? You want to see Gideon again?"

"Yes. Is that possible?"

"I don't know," she said, stumbling over her answer to my bold request. "It took money and connections to even get my meeting. Maybe when I'm contacted by the Black Gnarl again, I can arrange it."

I shook my head, my mind a flurry of half-formed thoughts. "No, I need to see him sooner. Or someone, anyone from the cult."

"Organization," Nayomi corrected, her voice tinged with a hint of offense.

"I'll go back this evening. It's worth a try."

Nayomi stood from the chaise, a look of concern on her face.

"Henrick, do you think you can handle that? Your health, I mean. Let me come with you."

I felt elated at her offer, compounded by her nearness and the lingering scent of citrus and flowers that hung around her.

"Of course. Why don't we eat before we go? I'm famished."

She looked at me, incredulous, but agreed. It's true I've never been one to be overly hungry. She was right to be concerned. But, I reassured her that I was quite alright.

We left to eat, finding a nice place in the market district. I ate more in this one meal than I had in a week. It was a strange sensation, to be so hungry and then eat my fill and not feel nauseated to an extent afterward. If anything, I already looked forward to my next meal. Nayomi thought it was odd, but humorous.

After our meal, we departed once again for the Graywater. We made good time as I didn't need to stop and rest, or slow down due to exertion. Even Nayomi asked if I needed a break, to which I surprised even myself when I told her I had no need to slow down.

We quickly found the same derelict dwelling and entered; similar eyes from similar shadows followed us. The poor and the sick looked at us no differently than they did the day prior; perhaps with more curiosity as this was our second visit in as many days.

The interior of the dwelling was untouched. If anyone else had entered since our first visit, then we couldn't tell. We immediately approached the corner where the marked panel rested on the floor. It was here that we were shocked to a standstill.

The symbol was no longer there. Prying at the sides of the boards, we found the panel remained. Pulling it up, a distinctly different flow of air came from the darkness below. The ladder was still in place and we descended into the foreboding nothingness. We only made it partway down when I noticed something different. No torches burned along crumbling walls, making the area pitch black. I asked Nayomi to retrieve the candle from our last visit. She quickly returned, handing me the small, pitiful source of light.

At the bottom of the ladder, the candle allowed just enough light for me to not trip over my own feet. Nayomi huddled close to me for the same reason. The walls of the chamber were barely visible, but what could be seen struck me as different from our last time here. Walking over to one of the walls, I saw that it was indeed an entirely different material. These were wooden walls and not crumbling stone barely clinging to musty earth.

"Nayomi, we need to find light," I said, desperation on the edge of my tone.

After what seemed like minutes of fumbling in the weak light, Nayomi found a fallen plank and some cloth to fashion a makeshift torch for the time being. After lighting it, we both stood in rapt, confused silence. The light of the burning cloth illuminated not a crumbling chamber and stone landing, but a typical, albeit rundown, basement. The room was utterly empty save for cobwebs, a few more broken wood planks, and scattered, moth-eaten fabrics.

"Are we in the same house?" I asked, spinning slow circles in a vain effort to make sense of my surroundings.

"Yes, guaranteed," Nayomi replied, breathless.

"The Black Gnarl. I assume they use magic?" I asked.

"Most definitely. Though I'd rather not say the sect or the source."

A rumble shook the basement. Then, a cacophonous blast sounded above. We were shaken so violently we fell off our feet. Pieces of the basement ceiling fell around us, including whole planks that cracked and tumbled mere inches from our heads.

"Gods, what was that?" Nayomi cried.

The residual tremor lasted for what felt like an eternity. I insisted we leave, fear crawling into my stomach and turning my newly-acquired confidence to pudding. We ascended the ladder, returned the panel to its place, and put out the quickly dimming torch and candle. I opened the door and half-stumbled onto the street, longing to be out of that strange place.

Around us, the street was abuzz with frightened and confused people. The quake had knocked some of the barely standing buildings down. People were pointing in the direction the blast must have come from.

Nayomi and I fled the Graywater, returning home as fast as we could. I couldn't remember the last time I had the strength to run for more than a few paces, but I kept pace for the duration of our panicked flight.

It took a few moments, but I noticed, as we ran, that there was something floating in the air around us. It was too early and far too warm for snow. Regardless, small motes of some material floated lazily here and there. They were very few in number, but they were there, hovering just on the periphery of my vision.

When we made it back to the busier districts, we saw the horrified looks on everyone's faces. They stared skyward, their mouths open, fingers pointing, some clutching onto their loved ones. I feared to turn and look.. When I did, I turned slowly and held my breath. It was fortunate that I did, otherwise I may have cried out myself.

A great, luminescent gash lit the sky where the strange phenomena once laced the horizon with its ghostly lights. It appeared to be a ghastly wound, red and hellish on its edges, but a deep bruise color on the inside. Then, the worst happened.

A sound unlike anything I'd ever heard in my life came from everywhere at once. It was deep, resonating within my skull and my soul, but screamed in my ears. After the ringing stopped, I realized my breaths came in quick rasps. I felt a pain in my hand

and thought at first it was my scar. Then, I realized Nayomi was
holding my hand, squeezing until it hurt.

"Henrick," she said, barely above a whisper, "let's go inside.
Can I stay with you tonight? I don't want to be alone."

Her eyes were locked onto the great, ghastly rend. She, too,
breathed in short, rasping gulps of air. She needed me, wanted
my presence. I had never before felt I could protect anyone, but
she found comfort in my presence.

This was both the most horrifying and thrilling experience
of my life.

WE SAT on the chaise together, turning it more toward the ocean
so we could look away from the horrible scar behind us in the
quickly dimming sky. It was a poor attempt to repress the
strange and terrible events of the day, but so far little more than
awful feelings had resulted from it. I chanced a look back, once,
and saw the scar had faded significantly.

The sounds of the waves lulled us once more into a sense of
calm. Nayomi's head sat gently against my shoulder, her arms
crossed in front of her chest. Her head trembled from a slight
cough. I looked out the window, staring at nothing, letting my
mind wander. I saw once more the floating, barely perceptible
motes pass by my window. Nayomi coughed again, more heavily
this time.

I offered Nayomi my bed, while I slept out on the chaise. She
insisted it was unnecessary, but I practically demanded it. I think
my sudden boldness caught her off guard. But, her cough had
worsened and she looked like she was exhausted. She relented,
taking my offer to sleep in comfort—I'd always rather enjoyed
spoiling myself with a plush bed—and I took to the chaise.
Sleep didn't come as easy as I'd thought. My mind was far too

harried by recent events. However, sleep did eventually find me. And I dreamed of gardens both beautiful and terrifying.

Morning came and I inexplicably woke before Nayomi. She was slow to rise and I helped her home that morning. For once, she required my support. I wasn't sure if I would see her that evening, but I had work to catch up and was grateful for the opportunity to do so.

Sitting at my desk, copying the manuscript that sat delayed for days, I found my mind constantly wandering. A rare occurrence, but I found it difficult to focus on my beloved work. My eyes refused to focus on the paper in front of me and kept drifting to the door, waiting for Nayomi to walk through, or to the windows. As the day wore on, I noticed the strange motes grew denser.

Sometime in the afternoon, with very little completed and a day wasted, I went to one of my windows. This time, it was not the one overlooking the shore, but rather one overlooking the street below. People walked as if the strange snow-like material wasn't falling all around them. I noticed something else, as well. I'd looked from this window many times. I was very familiar with the layout of the narrow street and the stone walls with their sparse, decorative vegetation. This greenery had expanded quite noticeably. Tufts of vines and ivy had grown, their stalks thickened and crawling over the wall like an angry spider emerging from the dwelling.

I retreated back inside, pondering this discovery when I looked at the spot above my mantel. It, too, had grown. It seemed to have grown larger since this morning. I walked over, put my face within an inch of the substance, and tried my damnedest to make sense of it. I was struck with the realization that I wasn't afraid. I was intensely curious, drawn to this strange new phenomenon that pushed the scar on the horizon back into my memory.

Right away, I noticed a beautiful, perfumed smell radiate from the green and black, furry and leafy patch. I stepped back and watched, frozen with curiosity, as one of the floating motes dropped from the growth on the mantel and floated from the room. The strange curiosities drifting among Old Ligothi were spores.

I stepped outside and went for a brief walk in the city. I noticed fewer stalls and shops were open today. I made my way to Nayomi's home, not too far away. When I knocked, no one answered the door. She lived alone, so I assumed perhaps she'd decided to take a nap. She didn't seem in a condition to wander when I took her home this morning.

I returned to my house and attempted to work once again. I made very little progress before finally giving up near dusk. I poured myself a glass of wine, an airy rose being all I could usually stomach, and watched the growth on my wall with what must have appeared to others as a disturbing interest. I had no desire to tell others of it. Except for Nayomi, who already knew. Eventually, sleep came for me again while I sat there.

The next several days came and went with no word from Nayomi. This wasn't unusual; we weren't, unfortunately, attached at the hip as the saying goes. But, given recent events, I expected to see her sooner rather than later. I missed her dearly and was quite concerned, but I did have to work at some point. I did get to enjoy more walks than usual and actually looked forward to being outside. I seemed to find myself, once again, of the opposite mind of everyone else.

The greenery of Ligothi began taking over. Strange ivys and large, curling vines grabbed at walls. Blankets of fuzzy moss and lichens began taking over the streets. The motes grew thicker and were whipped into flurries. Day after day I saw more and more of it all.

On the fourth day after the strange phenomenon in the sky, I found my own apartment missing various essentials. I discovered most stalls and shops closed. At a stall selling fruits and vegetables I asked the owner—a gray old-timer with a gruff, wise voice—what news he had of the state of the markets, hoping to garner some insight on the greater affairs of the city.

He complained of all his stores, even the most recent foodstuffs, rotting at an accelerated pace. He cursed the thickening greenery and wondered what insanity was at work. He blamed some stray magic, like most people tended to do when something was amiss. I asked if it could be due to the spores and pollen, to which he shot back, rather rudely, "What pollen?"

I looked around me. Certainly, he saw spores and pollen thick as snowfall around the city? He looked at me like I was a man crazed. He said his eyes saw nothing, but his nose smelled plenty. His other complaint was a foul stench that had settled over the whole city. Like that of rotten meat, rancid vegetables, and stale water. I admitted to him that it was my turn to admit that I hadn't experienced such an odor. He said he thought at first another stall's goods had turned, but the stench followed him home, and to his sister's house after that. He feared it might be him, but then heard complaints from customers and merchants alike of the stench.

I finished my purchase and left, returning home. I took in a deep breath, remembering his words, and could smell the scent of the many new blossoms. I entered my home and found the dark patch nearly covering the whole of my mantelpiece. Large vines had begun to curl out of the fireplace now, with fresh shoots already sprouting to claim further territory.

I poured myself a glass of wine—a fuller, more indulgent red that I would never have been able to enjoy mere days ago—and sat to ponder the growth further. None of this struck me as strange. I reasoned that it should, but instead I could only marvel at the beauty of what was occurring in Old Ligothi and wonder if it spread to the other areas of the city. My outings became daily as I felt a deep concern for the city. I couldn't help but also feel a deep kinship with Old Ligothi for the first time in my life.

As the greenery grew thicker, the daily crowd grew thinner. Scattered coughs echoed among the stone streets. Eventually, more and more individuals began to look fragile and made their outings for only the most dire necessities. The blessing of verdant abundance continued to overtake the man-made gutters of stone. Bodies, sickly and frail, began piling up along the sides of the streets. Those who attempted to flee dropped to the road-sides. One would think a plague had struck the city rather than the copious blossoming of exotic life.

The quiet, the sun-dappled snowfall of His life-altering spores, the sweet perfume of the flesh-colored pustules that became of those who gave in to the flesh's weakness. Old Ligothi was being reclaimed. The unworthy fell all around and I... I continued on.

THE BLACK PATCH, tinged with green and blue and purple hues like exposed muscle and vein, encompassed near the whole of my wall. Vines continued to curl out of the fireplace and stretch out across the floor and walls like the arms and legs of exhausted lovers. The last I looked, the furry, ever-so-tiny leaflets that comprised the lichen-like material didn't just cover the stone of my wall and mantel, it had started to consume it and become part of it.

I had lost track of time. Like a sapling in a grove, I was content to wait for the nourishment provided by the greater forces. Ygiddra feeds, Ygiddra loves, and Ygiddra provides. Almost everything, at least. I still missed her. I hadn't seen

Nayomi since she last left my home however long ago. Days? Weeks? Months, even.

Resolving myself to action, I stood from the chaise where I could watch the blossoming of different life on my wall grow like living art. I felt a strange sensation as my skin stretched, the fibers of the sanguine garden pulling from me with a sound not unlike ripping a plant from fertile soil, bringing the precious roots with it. It wasn't physically painful, but I felt like a babe pulled from its mother's arms. I would be back, but I needed to see her. I needed to know if she was ok.

My walk, slow and purposeful, took me through all the familiar places I once knew. They looked very different now. I was reminded of the depictions I'd seen in books of ancient ruins in the even more ancient elven forests, taken back by nature. This was similar, but still very different.

Bulbous growths that once languished on the ground rose with the stems that carried them as they grew up the buildings. The dark, crimson, life-giving fluid constantly seeped from their pores and crevices. Some still retained a level of sentience, an entirely new amalgam of flesh and flora, as their elastic appendages reached out, pining for something, and then recoiling. The process repeated in an endless dance. Trembling flowers, the color of brain tissue, grew in fragrant bouquets with some bluish, hair-like tufts of moss at their base.

Near Nayomi's house, I saw a shadow out of the corner of my eye. My head was very slow to turn, so I missed what it could have been. I hadn't seen any animals, even vermin, in some time. However, it did appear somewhat human. I saw it again, darting across the street in front of me. I realized this was not the same creature, but a separate being, as the side street from before didn't cross onto my current avenue. I thought it was a child, but its loping gate and pronounced spine, doubled over and giving it the stance of a gaunt quadruped, said otherwise. When the last vestiges of the setting sun caught its lidless, bloodshot eyes gaping at me, I smiled. It was, indeed, a child—one of His true children. I bowed my head slightly, an inferior creature such as myself not belonging in their presence. But it left me alone; I had the gift of safe passage.

Nayomi's house appeared much like any other. The stones quickly being hidden behind the new growth of the garden. Her door was open and I let myself in.

"Nayomi?" I called out, the sound muffled by a fresh carpet of lichen and moss.

Suddenly, the growth ended. The floorboards were blackened and crisp from a recent fire. Burned vines and roots curled, blackened and lifeless, like the gangly legs of shadowy insects onto a bare section of flooring. Much like the stone landing where we had met Gideon some time ago, an area of Nayomi's home stood apart from the rest. It was untouched by anything green or pleasant. It still maintained the coarse furnishings of what was before: wood and stone and metal fashioned by the hands of man. This area so far untouched by the garden was a small, semicircular area outside of Nayomi's bedroom.

I entered to find her in bed, a fragile imitation of what she once was. She looked to me, her skin sickly and her eyes sunken. Her burning of the sacred garden kept her from His embrace, for a time, but it only left her to suffer longer. I heard a weak choking sound uttered from her cracked lips. It may have been my name, but I couldn't be sure.

"I'll take care of you," I said, my heart aching.

I put both my arms under her, the new strength of the sanguine garden leaving her weighing as much as an emaciated doll. She muttered something else, but I couldn't make it out. I left her room, with its cloying darkness and rank smells of the inadequacies of the flesh: food, incense, and the artificial softness of blankets and cushions. I carried her out to the open air of the city with its sweet smells of resplendent growth and ancient peat.

She gagged as we passed through the front door; I imagine her sense of smell had become quite accustomed to the situation she was living in. The air would do her good. The ghostly motes, the spores of Ygiddra's new life, flurried around us. It was like the fairy tales I never thought I would find myself a part of.

She didn't utter a word as I brought her back to my apartment. Laying her on the chaise, I felt confident I could return all the kindness she once showed me when I was once so frail and in need of so much care. Now was my time to tend to her.

I took a seat at my work station. Books were of no use any more, but I wanted to sit. I wanted to be able to see when Nayomi needed me, to watch out the windows as the garden continued its work. I felt I had returned to more than just a home. I felt my grateful roots sink into nourishing soil once again. I breathed in deep, prepared to exhale in blissful relief, but it never came.

ONCE, my mind was my most precious possession. My eyes and my hands my most precious tools. I no longer have use for any of them. My eyes, though can still be utilized when I want. I no longer have need of ears, but the sounds of the city are mine when I wish. I have all but forgotten smell and taste, but can partake of them should I ever desire to relive some part of my old life.

Opening them today, I see the same thing I've seen for decades. At least, I assume it to be decades. Time is another concept of no consequence as a bearer of Ygiddra's blessings. And blessed I have been. My apartment has become indistinguishable from any other dwelling; all are a great, quivering mass longing to sing His praises.

I watch the garden grow indiscriminately, but where the sweet crimson nectar flows, it grows best. Like all great things in nature, a level of equilibrium must be attained. Blood is plentiful when it can be pulled from the very world itself.

I can see the streets through the eyes of the true children. I see what remains of my body as it treads the line between flesh and vegetation. In my mind, it is the best of both. The skeleton is the most stubborn part, as it sits in my chair with just the barest of tissue and tendon leaving a remnant of something once human. All else has become entangled in the spindling shoots and coarse undergrowth of the garden. My skin is a pungent green film that is more pleasing to Ygiddra, as opposed to pale and offensive flesh.

And I can see her. Her body is in much the same state, though much more decayed, it appears. I regret seeing the silent scream and rictus grin that adorns her face now that little more than brittle and decayed bone is all that remains. I enjoy the sight of the thin sheets of lichenous growth binding themselves together where her dress once was, creating a verdant gown mingled with thin layers of flesh required to feed the new growth. This lasting memory of her, of what she once was, reminds me that I still, regrettably, maintain a level of appreciation for some fleshly weaknesses, such as Nayomi's fierce mind and striking beauty.

But, as I promised, I took care of her. I brought her here, to be in the place where my small sacrifice fed Ygiddra's dormant and hidden pollens. That hand still grips the dagger given me by the hooded man, Gideon. That hand, which brought forth the sacred and sanguine garden, changed somewhat differently. Bark-like, fibrous growths cover that part of what remains of my physical body; merging with the bone to create something wholly different from the rest of me. Perhaps, as a sheath for the sacred blade? I don't know, but I have plenty of time to ponder.

I think on many things throughout the days, weeks, and decades. We are one in the garden. All those consumed shall live eternally, a part of this sacred place. All is shared as our bodies, minds, and souls become as countless blades of grass in a single field. I have been given more providence for my part in seeding the Timeless Garden's new field. I can see the memories of those that now fertilize its grounds, I can swim through this collected consciousness of my own accord. As far as I've gathered in my time as His humble groundskeeper, I am the only one offered this precious gift.

The multitude of conscious beings embraced by this garden that transcends physical boundaries toil and fight against the majesty of Ygiddra, but it is quite fruitless. Though they lack the freedom to peruse the sea of memories like me, their awareness is without a doubt vital to the ethereal power of the garden, as much as their bodies are vital to the mulch that expands its physical boundaries. I try to remind them of this in my wanderings, though it does no good. Whether they can't comprehend me or choose not to, I cannot tell. That leaves me only time to view the events both current and in the past, through the windows of a thousand souls.

I can see those of the Black Gnarl who remained to study Ygiddra. Their studies became my own and revealed new secrets of Ygiddra, Himself. The spores of the Timeless Garden, like any other, lay dormant when they cannot grow. And they were dormant for eons, unlike the weak creations of Alda that would fade to dust after so long. Trees and bushes and brambles held the smallest pieces of Ygiddra, though He waited, trapped in some dark place at the foot of some Obscured Throne, waiting to come back and bring His blessings where they could blossom and bear their fruit.

I see valleys on the other side of the world, thick with sanguine mulch and broad-leafed displays of Ygiddra's bounty. His true children roam those valleys, tending His garden, protecting it from fleshy, humanoid pests, and using their bodies to feed it. Some are far away, but what are miles for roots to travel compared to the infinite greatness that is He?

I saw Gideon as he boarded a ship bound for parts unknown. This was most lamentable, as sharing in the knowledge his potent mind would provide is truly a treasure lost. His body was frail and would not provide much from being transformed into one of the ever-bleeding, life-sustaining polyps; however, his soul would be most enriching for the garden to spread. Alas, he is gone. A no-doubt powerful man off to continue his research.

Research. The old librarian, Germanius, yes, I remember him now. I used to look up to him. I used to call him friend. I'd forgotten him, lately, but recalling our history together I can find so much about him in the consciousness of the garden. He had his fair share of secrets. I see dealings with the Black Gnarl. Access granted to the restricted section to the most sinister-looking of people. Of course, I can see Gideon there among them. I can also see him meeting with Nayomi. I can see through her eyes, hear through her ears. She needed the book, The Dread Praises, but it was Germanius that recommended I be the one to retrieve it. Strange, Nayomi never mentioned this.

This is the first time I've ever allowed myself to see a part of her in the garden's gathered minds. Again, my sentimentalities have led me to see that as a personal violation of someone I deeply care about. I instantly regret it and resolve myself to never call upon her memories again.

Although in many ways I miss the days past where we would spend time together as inferior creatures of flesh and sinew, I take solace in the fact that we are together here at the heart of

Ygiddra's new garden—sweet, sanguine, and eternal. She, too, either refuses or is incapable of perceiving me when I call out to her among the ephemeral sea of bound souls. Like so many others who have yet to reconcile with the beauty of their new eternity, she continues to scream decades later. I can hear it echoing throughout the city. Even among thousands of other voices, I can hear it.

# AMONG THE MIRRORED HALLS

TAMORA COULDN'T SEE ANYTHING. THERE WAS NO LIGHT; ONLY THE deepest possible darkness. She felt nothing. No sensations either physical or emotional stirred in her. She didn't know how long she'd been here. Her memory was as blank and empty as the void that surrounded her. Was she dead? Is this the great journey that awaited after one physically ceased to be?

It was disappointing.

The deafening sound of shattered glass made her flinch. Her ears rang in the aftermath. Better than the null void of the supposed afterlife, she supposed. Reality shuddered and she felt herself falling. It was abrupt and brief; she crashed onto a hard surface and felt dull pain radiate through her where she landed.

Her vision began to return. Perhaps she had just been unconscious? An accident had knocked her out; yes, that made sense. And now she was returning to the conscious world. That must have been what happened. She felt a tingling in her hands and feet as feeling returned to her extremities. She called out for one of her servants, but her voice broke. Her throat constricted and all that came out was a strained gargle. She tried again and wheezed a slightly more coherent call.

Slowly, she continued to regain her faculties. Her vision was no longer blurry and she could stand with the aid of a small table within arm's reach. She composed herself and looked around. She was in one of the halls of her tower, that much was clear. The strong stonework was familiar, as were the rich rugs on the floor. Each of these had been hand-picked by her and came from all corners of the world.

But something was wrong. In the darkness of the stone hall, the lit candles on the walls caused shadows to dance along the masonry and light to sparkle in countless shards on the floor. Why was there so much glass?

She walked as quickly as her unsteady legs would allow. Disoriented, she only recognized this hall as somewhere within her tower, but couldn't tell where exactly she was. She turned and looked behind her. The end of the hall, where she'd just staggered away from, was a dead end. She now realized this was the top floor of her beloved home. At the end of this hall a large ornate mirror should have hung on the wall; the largest and most expensive of all the luxurious mirrors she owned. Rather, she gawked at what was left of it. The mirror was broken, altogether irrecoverable. The frame was charred and cracked, as though it had been burned. The lovely glass was laying in pieces at her feet. Someone would be flogged for this.

"Fools! Who did this!" she shouted. "Who has ransacked the halls of the countess?"

She is Tamora Lisbeth'Nyall, Countess of Thayn, and Lady of the Tower. What low-born pigs dared vandalize her home?

"Guards? Guards?" she shouted.

The lack of replies only made her anger grow. In her fury, it had taken time for her to notice that the windows of her tower were boarded up. She banged on the closest window, one without glass and usually open to blue skies, to little avail. The boards were firmly in place and made of thick oak. They were not giving in. She noticed something else quite strange: the boards were attached on the outside.

She inhaled audibly. Whoever was responsible would spend the rest of their few remaining days in dark, foul misery in the tower's underground cells. She ran her fingers through her silky hair—an old habit to calm herself. Her long, brown locks were washed daily and combed until they were as soft as a spring wind. Having fallen on the floor, however, she was somewhat disheveled. She pulled some stray curls behind her ears with her dainty fingers and stopped short. Her cheeks flushed and her heart sank.

She ran her hands over her ears again. They should have been long, soft, and distinctly elven. Instead, they were short, round, and scarred along the top ridge. Did they cut her ears? She caressed them, felt for the rest of them with longing fingers. Her delicate touch traced harsh, hideous scar tissue. Her hands began to shake.

*They'd cut off her ears.*

Fiends! villains! They would suffer for this, and they would suffer slowly. Her torturer was renowned and he would be put to his best work. First, she needed to see it. Tamora had to see what they did to her.

Her largest and favorite mirror was broken, but there were several others. She walked quickly down the hall and saw yet another, this one silver with entwining serpents forming the frame, shattered into pieces; however, the frame was still intact, unlike the former. She growled and went to the door to the next floor down. The tower was old, ancient even, and constant renovation was required to keep it in acceptable shape. The top floor was a room at one point, but gradually became little more than a hall as more and more was required to reinforce it for safety and stability.

The second floor down was more properly arranged for

living, though the only room was Tamora's personal chamber. It was large and airy; the room itself took up the whole of the floor save for the stairway. She felt instinctively relaxed when she entered her private room. It did not last long. It was too dark. The windows that normally surrounded the room were boarded up much as the top floor windows were. The candelabras provided enough light to see, but the room was still thick with darkness.

Instead of the usual incense, perfumes, and dried flowers flavoring the air, there was a cloying stench that tainted her nostrils. She went to her bed and found it in disarray. Her armoire was covered in a thick layer of dust. The source of the stench came from a bowl of long-rotted fruit and a plate of what had been cheese at some point. Now it was a brown, disgusting clot that even the mold would hesitate to grow on. She peered into the water pitcher sitting nearby and realized how parched she was. Thankfully, there was some still there. She took a drink and spat it out. A thick film of dust had settled onto the top. How long had she been unconscious?

Tamora opened a decanter she always kept by her bed. The scent of sour, stale wine wafted out. It wasn't empty, but might as well have been; this was undrinkable. She tossed it aside in frustration. The expensive crystal shattered and spread across the floor like so many of her mirrors.

Finding nothing of use here, she took the stairway down to the next floor. When the door swung open on its creaky hinges, a horrible odor poured through the stone frame. Tamora put the sleeve of her dress up to her nose as she gagged. This floor was like all the others; stone walls, stone ceiling, and stone floors covered with thick rugs. Glass shards flickered in the candlelight, and half-way down to the next door a dark figure was slumped against the wall.

She ran up to the shadowed lump on the floor leaning

against the wall. Another of her mirrors hung on the wall above
the stranger. On her way, she stepped on a pile of broken glass
and cut her foot. She cursed herself for not thinking to grab
shoes in her chambers. The prospect of finding someone else
drove her on past the pain, as did thoughts of what was to be
done to those responsible for her situation.

As she drew closer, however, she realized the stench came
from the body upon the floor. They had been long dead. It was
well-decayed and beyond recognition. She put her hands to her
mouth to stifle a cry and feebly attempt to hide the overpowering smell. It was a woman, that much she knew. Her dress was
in tatters, and in one shriveled hand she held a large shard of
glass. Though her body was decayed, Tamora could make out
the grievously large gashes on the dead woman's wrists. She
could no longer stare at the ugly corpse. A haunting familiarity
settled over her, and it left her trembling. A sick pain stabbed
her in the gut, and Tamora felt as though she were going to
vomit. Why would she kill herself? What had happened here?

Raiders, perhaps? Had some vagabond army assaulted the
town and her servants holed up in the tower? How had they
boarded up the windows from outside? Too many questions.
She investigated the rooms on this floor and found them much
the same as her own chambers. Darkness, rotten food, and dust.

Then there were her mirrors. All of them that she had found
were destroyed, most irreplaceable. It was no secret that
Countess Lisbeth'Nyall was a beautiful woman. She could have
had any nobleman she desired should she decide to accept a
marriage proposal, but she preferred her tower as her husband
and her mirrors as her children. She was not as vain as her
subjects liked to think. The mirrors also made the tower feel
more open. As much as she loved the smooth-worn stones, it
had been constructed during a time when grandiose design was
favored over defensive purposes.

She abandoned this disfavored floor and went below again. There was only one other floor left after this one. The air felt thicker here. A foul, familiar odor hung in the halls. Here were the dining room and guest chambers; surely there was food to be found. Her hunger was already gnawing at her stomach and overpowered her fear of the smells of death lingering around her.

She entered the great dining hall slowly. "Hello?" she called out. "Is anyone here?"

Her voice echoed through empty halls and off lonely stones. Torch sconces were blazing and, strangely, all the candles on the table were lit. They should have been doused unless the countess was entertaining guests. She didn't dwell on it for long. It provided additional light, and for that she was grateful. Unfortunately, they illuminated nothing of import. The table was bare. Not even place settings were there. Only the many-pronged candelabras sat on the dust-coated wood.

She checked the kitchens. Candles and torches were lit, of course, but nothing else. She walked to the pantry and fell back in fright. Another shriveled body, another woman, lay on the floor. Visible through the long tangles of hair that draped in ragged strips across her face, her teeth were chipped and broken. To her horror, Tamora saw that she held a strip of leather in her hands. This poor woman had starved to death.

She ran from the dining hall in a panic. Fear had finally taken an unshakable hold on her. She barreled through the guest rooms, one by one, and found only further terrors there. In one room, another woman's body was curled up in the soft sheets as though she had simply laid down to die. Another room was covered in blood with nothing else to show for it. Common to all of them, the broken mirrors. Why she continued to be distressed over them Tamora couldn't say. She only knew that something was wrong, more so than just the numerous bodies.

Their shattered faces represented something evil, and worst of all she could not reconcile this fear with a specific reason.

She decided it was time to flee. She would leave this tower behind, find who was responsible, and, after their long suffering had ended, she would reclaim her home. The next floor was the last. A tall, looming antechamber that received her visitors and where she dispensed her regional authority. It was possibly the most luxurious portion of the tower. Countess Lisbeth'Nyall always made a good impression. It would be here that the bodies of the guilty would hang on display.

She smiled at the thought of retribution, at the dream of escape, and when the door refused to open she let out a scream quite unbefitting a noblewoman. The door steadfastly refused to move. It was more than just locked. There was magic holding this door. Magic, and the putrid stench that crept from underneath it. She banged on the unmoving planks. She grabbed the wrought-iron handle and pulled it furiously.

Then, she recoiled in dread. Much like the mirrors, she had a sudden presentiment of what lay beyond that door. It was a thought on the edge of consciousness. A hint of the awful and an inkling of the unthinkable. She began to cry in futile rage. The last hour spent in fear was not something she typically tolerated, but this went deeper than she imagined.

Tamora must have laid there in tears for hours. When she came to her senses, she stood and leaned against the door. It was silent on the other side, but that came as little surprise given its sturdy design. Having pitied herself enough, Tamora marched over to one of the candelabra stands against the wall. She removed the candles, still burning, and tossed them aside. She returned with the ornate stand and swung it like a halberd against the door. It reverberated painfully up her arm and into her shoulder and chest. The vibration also served to shake loose her fury and she unleashed it upon the door. She hacked and stabbed, attempted to wedge it beneath the door and to its sides. A few barely noticeable nicks in the wood were all her ferocious assault managed to do.

She backed away and tossed the stand aside, feeling spent. She dropped to her knees, suddenly dizzy, and a sob escaped her. Tamora's eyes began to cloud and her vision turned black. Tamora felt her body falling, but could only reach out a weak, lazy arm to stop herself. A jarring pain coursed through her for the briefest moment, and then all was nothing once more.

WHEN CONSCIOUSNESS RETURNED, there was still no indication of what time it was or how long she had been comatose. The candles still burned, but the wax remained untouched. The sealed door, the eternal candles, the dead, starved guests; the lowborn scum had revolted! They found among themselves one proficient in magic and laid a trap for her. They would all pay for this in kind. She knew many skilled magi herself; a few among them with little scruples where coin was involved.

A throbbing pain quelled her anger. One wrist was swollen and sore. The hazy memory of landing on it when she fell returned with force. It hurt awfully, but wasn't broken; just one more thing to add to their list of wrongs that they would account for.

Her stomach screamed with hunger. Her lips cracked from thirst. If she didn't find food and water quickly, she would not have a chance to dole out her justice. She checked all the rooms once more, carefully avoiding the corpses that still struck her with a creeping and familiar fear. She found nothing that appeared fit to eat. Of the rancid food that was available, the smell alone was enough to make her retch.

The situation with water and wine was just as grave. After

another few hours, or so it felt, she was checking for leaks and hints of rain against the boarded windows. She was so thirsty, anything would suffice right now. With great reluctance, she returned to her chambers. The pitcher of tainted water remained. She grabbed it with two shaking hands and put the musty container to her lips. She took a sip and found it revolting, but her body craved it regardless. She began gulping the water as fast as her body would allow. It began to pour around her mouth and onto the floor. Tamora forced herself to slow down. It would have to last until she found a way out.

With part of her craving sated, she suddenly felt tired. Despite the amount of time she had spent unconscious, she was still so very tired. Her bed called to her. It was much softer than the stones she had woken on twice now. She removed her tattered clothing. She could already see the effects of the imprisonment on her body. To have access to one of the mirrors was a bittersweet prospect. Tamora crawled under the soft sheets and felt a modicum of comfort for the first time in an eternity. She felt the tears begin to come again and forced them away. She would rest; then, she would renew her efforts again.

THE PASSAGE of time became a maddening unknown. The candles refused to burn down, and no light at all filtered through the boarded windows. Their denial to her of any knowledge of the outside was complete.

She only knew time still existed because of the hunger. If time was standing still, she would not continue to grow so famished that the rotten food became a genuine temptation. The pain in her stomach marked the slow passage of the days, which she still did not know how many were to be counted.

Despite further efforts, the locked door would not be broken.

She tried striking multiple objects and many surfaces: walls where mortar appeared to be crumbling, the boards covering the windows, and others. Her strength continued to grow weaker; she was reaching a point beyond hope of recovery.

Starvation continued to drive her mad. She began trying to sew the tears in her bedsheets, albeit poorly, out of boredom. She sang to herself to combat the silence. Eventually, she found herself clawing at the walls until her fingers were raw and bloody.

She found a large shard, larger than the one held by the still-decaying body in the hallway. Holding the sharp piece of mirror to her face, Tamora looked at her eyes. They were sunken, dark-ringed, and did not look like her own – at least not how she remembered them. The once-brilliant green of her eyes appeared to turn to a drab olive. The life was literally seeping from her. She didn't wish to see any more. She could feel her body dying. Looking into that piece of glass, she felt a twinge of that unexplainable fear. The shard fell from her hand. It broke into several more pieces and was gone forever.

The door to the countess' chambers creaked open slowly. Tamora emerged, still unclothed, and walked in a daze down the hallway. The glass cut her feet as she carelessly walked over it. She no longer cared. This was going to be the last effort she would be able to make. This would lead to her demise or her retribution.

The door sat in sinister accusation. Its stalwart curse defied her, stared back, and dared her to face its terrors. Tamora had looked through the keyhole many times. Only darkness lay beyond. Her choices were twofold: darkness in death or darkness beyond the door. At least one offered hope. She still was not used to the smell, but she would rather take it to chance than die.

Tamora pulled a tiny hairpin from her mangled and dirty

locks. She knelt by the lock on the door and, with trembling fingers, began to twist the pin inside the mechanism. Her fingers were hard, even painful to control. Her weakened body strained to control them.

She knew nothing of how to pick locks. The idea only came to her in a fit of desperation. This was her last effort. Either a despairing bit of blind luck would free her or death would claim her where she now knelt on the cold stones.

"Work. Please, work," she whispered. "Please."

The lock mechanisms clicked softly as she blindly fumbled with the needle-like pin.

"Please," she repeated.

Her body growing cold, Tamora felt the last of her strength seeping from her. Tears began to build in her eyes.

"I'm sorry," she said, just above a whisper. "So sorry. Please, let me out."

The lock clicked. Did she actually pick the lock? She didn't know. She didn't care. The door creaked open, a sliver of darkness running along the frame. It was enough to allow an unspeakable stench to crawl from the other side. She became sick, and dry-heaved painfully. There was nothing for her stomach to give.

She began to laugh. Whatever was on the other side, she would deal with and she would do so gladly. The door had opened. She pushed on it gently and found it swung on its hinges quite easily. The smell was unbearable. It was also familiar. Her elation was quickly stifled by the scent and the irreconcilable terror that accompanied it. The great alcove was lit by the same torches that refused to burn out, and the same candles whose wax did not melt. This was a grand room, however—the darkest of them all. The light simply could not reach much of it. She knew it well, though. It was still her home.

The windows on this ground floor had large shutters to seal

them against the weather and other elements. They were, of course, closed with no hint of light peeking through them. They were likely boarded along with every other window in the tower. A touch of fresh air would make her feel like the richest woman in the world right now. As it stood, she could hardly breathe for the stifling air and the horrid smell. There was something else here. A shadow that pressed down on her; an evil so profound that it carried with it a tangible weight.

She had nothing left to give it, however. There were no tears left in her eyes or any contents left in her stomach. Nothing but raw fear and anticipation was left of the woman that was once the Countess of Thayn. Her drive was to press forward and reach the door to the outside world.

The stone stairway was cold against her bare, bloodied feet. It was so dark she couldn't see but one step at a time. She watched her feet closely. The handrail provided some support, but she was weak and couldn't rely on her own strength to much extent. She cursed the ill light. She was so close to freedom and could only take the steps one by one and so very slowly.

The countess quickened her pace. She was ready to be free of here. Her fingers could already feel the gilded handle of that last, wonderful door. She would be out of this forsaken tower and likely would never come back. She would kill every one of the peasant wretches, order her guards to burn them in their houses, and flee from this place.

Cursed light! If only one of the torches were within reach. She looked up at them. They required stepstools to ignite. She would never be able to reach one on her own. Maybe she could jump and knock one down.

Her feet suddenly fell out from under her. She fell into the darkness and waited for the floor to meet her and shatter her bones like the numerous mirrors. Instead, she landed on something soft and slick. She was grateful at first. She was alive, but the fall felt much shorter than she would have imagined. Her memories of the grand entry recalled that there were many more stairs left; she should have fallen from much higher. The stairs must have broken and fallen away. Then what broke her fall?

Tamora put her hands down to push herself up and they slipped from beneath her. Her face landed in a pile of something that she hoped to never see. She held her hands up and could just make out a dark, wet substance on her hands. She knew it to be blood. The light was weak, but she knew this to be the truth.

In the paltry glow that managed to reach her, the countess took in her surroundings. She was surrounded by a mass of dead bodies. They were all in varying states of decay. Was it hundreds? Was it thousands? She couldn't tell. Arms and limbs and bodies were piled upon each other so that one could not tell where they ended and began.

Panic began to set in. What new horror had she found? Had there been a massacre in her home? Did the village rebel against her honored guests? Or, gods, was this the village? Perhaps it was an invasion and the army killed everyone and flung them into her tower. Such a thought was unthinkable and such an act almost too brutal and barbaric. But it was possible.

Tamora didn't scream. She refused. She had to find the way out. But how? There were so many. Tamora tried to stand but only fell time and again in the blood and decay. The rush of terror was wearing off, and she found herself exhausted. She dared not lay down. A moment of respite and she would continue trying to find the wall. It was a giant circle. If she made her way around she would eventually come to the door.

Her feet actually sank into the macabre, tangled mass of bodies. Crawling seemed to be preferable. She could slowly get across the bodies if she didn't try to walk across them. Sliding on her stomach, she finally reached out and touched stone. Glorious, solid stone. Her hand was covered in blood and viscera, but she felt a solid wall. There was also more light here, closer to the torches.

The stairway caught her eye first. Where she had fallen, the stones had crumbled away. The rest of the stairs could be seen jutting up from a mass of limbs. Thankfully she didn't land on those broken stones or she would have certainly died. The light revealed something else; something far worse than a broken stairway. Worse, even, than a mangled carpet of corpses.

Such was the grandiosity of her greeting chamber that two rows of windows were built to provide ample light; this singular, oversized floor was twenty feet tall. There was one row of windows for each floor. The second row was clearly visible. These were the ones she saw when walking down the steps. The second row was only partially visible; it was at least half-buried in decaying bodies.

The door was buried under the dead. It wasn't a carpet of dead villagers, but a sea of them. Despair set in once again at the thought of her macabre, impossible fate.

"No," she whispered harshly, then shouted, "No!"

She beat her fists against the wall. It renewed the pain in her poorly healed wrist. It created a new pain in her hands. She pounded against the stones and willed them to collapse and free her. Her starving frame beat against the wall with impotence. Her shattering mind lost all focus. She lowered her head and leaned on the stones. There she beheld something wholly unbelievable.

The light flickered against one of the less deformed faces. It was more than just familiar. The mouth, frozen in a scream, once had a lovely shape. The cloudy eyes were once a marvelous green. The matted hair was no longer soft. It was a horrid rendition of herself, having been dead for quite some time. She fell back in shocked silence. Grabbing at her face, she needed to know it was just a trick. It was hunger, or exhaustion, or the lighting. It was not her.

She crawled back over the grotesque mass. The face that lay within the flickering, sickly yellow light waited there near the wall. The visage stared back, its scream piercing into her. There was no trick. It was herself.

A mirror. She needed a mirror! Just one of the shards; she needed to see her face. She crawled frantically over the twisted mangle of bodies. One after another, she looked upon their faces. They were all her. Some were missing their eyes; unhealed gashes ran above and below the dark sockets. They look to have been clawed out. Others were too long deceased to be recognizable, but she knew them. Tamora recalled the bodies in the hallways above. Their familiarity now apparent. If she only knew then, she would have joined them.

When she reached the remains of the stairs, she tried to climb. Her hands were too slick and the rocks too smooth. It was no use. She couldn't get enough footing to jump. She would only slip or sink further each time.

The atmosphere of this room, of her tower, was saturated by more than fear. The evil weight she felt before was in full force here. It threatened to crush her soul; promised to shatter her sanity. She heard the screams of the countless bodies in the room. They echoed in her memory. The door to the outside, to freedom, was far out of reach.

Tamora screamed. She screamed from the depths of her being and added her voice to the others. One more time, and always once more, she cried unto the careless stones and broken glass.

～

OUTSIDE, the skies were grey and the air chill, such had it been ever since the surrounding villages were abandoned. The wood and stone buildings surrounding the tower all lay empty with not even ghosts willing to haunt them. All, save for one.

A sorcerer kept vigil over his work. The people, their hate for the cruel countess who ruled over them, had readily accepted his offer of retribution when he had arrived at their villages. One after the other, they discovered a single-minded purpose with him. They could punish the countess for her long lifetime of malice and live their lives in peace. The sorcerer had said there would be a price. They agreed they were willing to pay whatever it was. He took their gold, a pittance and unnecessary given what would come after, but had he accepted no monetary payment it would have certainly drawn suspicion. The weight of their hard lives and poverty overshadowed their logic; he had hoped for this. The citizens of other lords and ladies, no matter how down-trodden, had not been quite as single-minded and would have made the process much more difficult.

After her tower was sealed, both magically and physically, he set about his work to place the powerful necromantic curse upon the structure and its callous occupant. This would be his finest achievement: the breaking of another seal. An ironic hell served justly, eternal torment paid to the living damned. His was one of the last few remaining of the initial forty-four. Certainly, it wouldn't be long now.

The dread powers that flowed through him settled among every stone in the tower. After the first screams echoed from the tower, signaling the first of the countess' many deaths, he knew his work was a success. Less than a year passed before the first villagers left, no longer able to abide the consequences of their decision. Soon, all the nearby hamlets and hovels abandoned their homes to escape the memory.

He would never leave. This was part of the price he paid, as steward of the great curse. His body would last long in the decades to follow, a nexus for the power that fueled the dark magics enveloping the tower. After he died, the area would be so saturated in foul magics that his presence would no longer be required. His black robes would be all that remained in the tiny structure he called home. The countess, however, would long outlast him. Suffering in perpetuity. She was truly the Lady of the Tower, now.

Nearly a decade after his work was finished, when drudgery became commonplace, he had seen in the distance a great scar on the horizon. It had finally come. The sky ruptured. The earth bled. The Obscured Throne was aware of them, coming to reclaim their world.

Now, yet another decade later, his body having grown frail with age, he lies on his bed. Breaths come in weak, rasping fits. He knows his time is coming. The great darkness closes in on him, with things just out of reach to pull him into his masters' domain. He smiles, hearing for one last time the muffled screams again. They stopped, as they always did. Sometime after, in the uppermost reaches of the cursed structure and as the last bit of life left him, he heard the sound of shattering glass.

# SLIP AWAY QUIET

"Where are you headed?" the dark-haired dwarf asked. His voice was husky but soothing. He sat hunched over, with his elbows on his knees, waiting for Mykal's answer.

"That's the big question, isn't it?" Mykal replied. "We've been on the road... just over a year now? I don't think we have a place in mind, even now."

They sat around the campfire, he and the dwarf, Vincen, on one side and his wife and two children opposite them. Two other dwarves that accompanied Vincen sat just outside the light of the fire, their eyes reflecting almost menacingly. They had maintained a cold distance ever since the three of them met Mykal's family at the base of the mountains. They were quite unlike their companion that Mykal spoke to now.

Vincen was friendly. He had been the first and only one of the three to say a word to them. His dark blue eyes were gentle but sad, like a still pond that had seen too many drown in its waters. Mykal knew this because he had a gift.

In his village, he'd heard what others always said about him. He wasn't a physically intimidating man. He wasn't an intellectual or blessed with artistic talent. He was a hard worker, a loving husband, and doting father. He was plain and unassuming. These were the whispers and off-sided comments the villagers made that they thought he couldn't hear.

Mykal saw how his old community treated one another in public and when they thought there were no lingering eyes to watch them. He knew the good, honorable folk that could be trusted with his own children. He knew the subversive, dishonest ones that would smile to his face then seek to take what they could behind his back.

This talent of astute observation came as second nature to him. He was plain and unassuming – but he could watch and he could listen. He could see the intent in a man's eyes, hear the measure of truth in a woman's words, and all of this without effort. It was not a practiced art or some form of long-reviled magic, though others sometimes thought otherwise.

Mykal knew he couldn't trust the other two dwarves. He'd come to call them "Skunkstripe" and "Redbeard," for their most dominant physical traits. They'd yet to give their names and Vincen had yet to introduce them to Mykal's family. He knew right away he'd keep an eye on them both. But he could trust Vincen.

The fire crackled and the sun grew low along the western hills. Vincen grumbled something and tapped his hand on his knee. "That's a long time."

Mykal shook his head and looked at his family. They were eating a dinner of meat and potatoes, pure luxury for them after all this time, provided by the dwarves – or Vincen, rather.

Upon first meeting and realizing neither party was hostile to the other, the dwarves immediately set up a camp and fed the haggard, half-starved couple and their children. Mykal's wife and children were taking their time, as though they'd never get another meal like this again.

"They deserve better," Mykal whispered aloud.

"Aye," Vincen agreed, "They do. Especially the wee ones. This is no kind of world for them."

"You have children, Vincen?"

The dwarf was quiet for a moment. "A daughter," he finally answered.

Mykal looked at Keera, his own daughter. Not yet ten but older than her brother by two years. She had her mother's green eyes. His son, Kellen, had Mykal's narrow jaw and strong cheekbones. They both shared a bit of their mother's bloodline with slightly pointed ears.

"Does she have a home? There in your mountains?" Mykal asked.

"Aye. A decent enough home, admittedly."

Mykal looked to the ground, thinking on his next words. He hated asking, but they'd come so far. "Would we be able to find one? Work for our keep? Will you take us with you?"

Out of the corner of his eyes, Mykal saw the dwarf purse his lips. Vincen ran a thick-fingered hand over his mouth. The question made him uncomfortable.

"Where you from, Mykal?" Vincen asked, dodging the more uncomfortable question.

"That's a complicated story," Mykal sighed.

Vincen looked over at him. His fleshy lips turned upward, lifting his thick mustache. "Well, we've got some time, now, don't we?"

Mykal smiled back. If he wanted to get his family somewhere safe, he needed to be on Vincen's best possible side. So, Mykal told him of his old village; memories he thought he'd left behind.

He explained how his family was the same as any other. His father's grandfather had come to this camp with many other families. Mykal didn't know what the dwarves endured during those first months or years, but the outskirts of Dermouth became the safest place to be after the world fell. The forests were rife with stories and legends long before the unspeakable things came after the sky ripped apart. But the once-small camp, built for nothing more than logging the surrounding woods, was close enough to civilization to keep out bears, wolves, and other wildlife as well as provide that precious, rare feeling of security for the fleeing survivors.

They had all heard the stories passed down through their parents and grandparents of that cursed day that changed the world forever. Stories of blood oozing between the mortar and stones. Accounts of the unbearable cold that seeped from the black eyes of nothing that winked open seemingly at random. Witnesses who told of the frostbitten bodies that fell from the sky. All those who had memories of those final days were left with an emptiness in their eyes that was a reflection of their souls. They were left bitter and desperate.

It was their grandparents who were the last generation of survivors that had memories from that day. A few clouded thoughts of horror still lingered among the handful of elderly townsfolk, but that's all they were— spectral motes of fear and things they still spoke of in reluctant stories. Stories that faded on dead lips before Mykal was born. These days, that was all they had— stories. The disparity rooted in lost hope and unforgettable atrocity grew over the years and spread its canopy over the new settlement— still simply called Dermouth— and smothered them all in a shadow of cynicism.

"It sounds like you had a good place. Not perfect, but a home," Vincen commented. Mykal couldn't disagree, thinking on it more as he explained it. "What made you want to leave?"

Mykal thought for a moment. He smirked, remembering what had started their year-long trek. It made him second-guess their pilgrimage altogether, but who could have known? He continued explaining what drove all the people from their village.

It wasn't the dark things they had heard about from their parents and grandparents that drove them out. Although travelers brought word of terrors of every kind, both human and otherwise, no one in Dermouth had personally experienced anything more frightful than the calls of wolves or death from a sudden fever during the cold months. Dermouth had been safe, but quite imperfect. The land was sick. Crops were struggling alongside the people. Each year they grew back smaller and feebler than before. The land itself was giving up.

Those who wanted to leave met little resistance. Some wanted to return to the city, to the broken ruins of their ancestors. None who left returned and some believed that, perhaps, the city could be reclaimed. If it could, it would mean a new start for everyone.

The dwarf grumbled. He looked up at the stars and spoke softly. "My parents were city folk. A rare couple of dwarves who forsook the mountain stone, and the hills, and took up trade in another city not far from here."

He looked at Mykal and smiled weakly – at the memory of his parents, no doubt – but his eyes glistened a little. "We learned a hard lesson, too. We fled back to our ancestral home, then. Found out most dwarves did. We sealed the gates behind us."

His voice caught a bit. He cleared his throat and patted his knee again. Mykal could tell he was uncomfortable, so he continued on.

He described how a small party of souls braver than he opted to see the city for themselves and vowed to return with good news or not at all. Two of them returned, one with his arm heavily bandaged. They refused to answer questions and retreated to their homes. They spoke of no good news. One was found hanging from their rafters the next day. The other, the young man with the bandaged arm, disappeared and was never seen again. Whispers and rumors began immediately.

Mykal noticed a few things that didn't seem to make the rounds among the town gossipers. There was something different in the men's eyes when they returned. They no longer had a look of despair or surrender. They had a new look. One of true, unmistakable fear. They had seen the things from which their ancestors fled. It was then Mykal truly understood that there would be no going back to Dermouth. Also, and perhaps more unnerving, was that the injured man who disappeared left with his doors locked and all his belongings stored away.

The community became divided. They began to feel afraid. Not the familiar fear of the cold winters or poor harvests. Not the fear of brigands raiding their settlement. It was a new fear, but old as the first men: the fear of the unknown, the indescribable. The itch at the back of the mind that tells you something is wrong. The things that haunted their ancestors were coming for them, or so many thought.

Mykal knew that itch. He felt it when he spoke to the dishonest blacksmith and when wolves lingered just inside the shadows of the trees at night. It resonated within him. That was his gift. He felt that itch as the bickering grew among the others. Some arguments came to blows. Villagers began packing up their things and leaving. Some alone, others in small groups. His had been one of the largest. His instincts told him this was the best way and so he followed it.

"I'd like to think I made the right choice," Mykal said to Vincen.

The dwarf looked at Mykal's family. There was a softness in that look. Vincen turned his head toward Skunkstripe and Redbeard. His look hardened and it appeared to Mykal that he almost sneered.

"You did, boy. You did," he replied.

Mykal looked at his wife again, sitting across the fire. He remembered the concern in her voice when she'd asked, "How long do you think we'll have to be on the road?"

"I don't know, Ira," was all he could answer. He remembered smiling, putting his hands on her shoulders, and looking deep into her green eyes – as green as the aldyrs her people cherished. "You'll just have to trust me."

Their hurried caravan had departed from the village quietly. The creaking wheels of a few wagons and the snorts of a small number of beasts of burden were all the goodbyes to be said. The settlement had been a place of coexistence and survival. Now it was abandoned, left to whatever specters desired to haunt its splintering walls.

The road ahead would be long. It would be difficult. He second-guessed every moment at first, wondering if he did right by his family. His instincts had never led him astray, but there was a first time for all things. He could only remember the words of his grandfather as he looked back on the village growing smaller as they headed south: "Stay away from the city."

"Good advice," Vincen cut in. "So you hit the open road. For a year." The dwarf shook his head.

Mykal sighed in agreement. He smelled the smoke and ash of the campfire. He breathed in the lingering odor of cooked meat as though it would be the last time he'd smell it. Though, he hoped he could come to an arrangement with Vincen. A funny thought occurred to him.

"I miss the smell of the aldyrs. I can smell the pine nearby in the mountains. It reminds me of them."

Vincen nodded. "I remember them, too. Completely different smells, though. You did not find much greenery on your way here? Things must be worse than we thought."

"No, plenty of greenery," Mykal answered. His voice ran hollow and Vincen took notice.

"You alright there, son?"

Mykal blinked and came back to his senses. "Sure, just thinking about the aldyrfruit. You remember them? Big, wine-colored monsters."

"The size of yer fist, aye. Sweet as pie and twice as addicting," Vincen finished with a chuckle. "Gods, what I wouldn't give for a basket of them, now! I'd toss these two to a pack of wolves," he gestured to his two companions, then grumbled, "They'd probably just toss 'em back."

Mykal laughed for the first time in what seemed like years. He thought about the strangely beautiful and uniquely wonderful white-blossomed trees. The only memory of them now were the dead glens of aldyrs that dotted the forests like open sores. They grew everywhere, even in the mountain realms of the dwarves.

"Her people sure loved 'em," Vincen said, nodding to Ira. "Thought they were the soul of the world or some such, right?"

"Close enough," Mykal answered. "We used to walk in the woods near the village. Try to find some that were still alive. There was only one glen we could find without having to stray too far for comfort. It was dead. Just like all the others we've heard about."

"Strange thing, that." Vincen commented. "The old folk practically worshipped them. Trees like that? Growing on mountainsides? It must have been quite a sight."

Mykal nodded in agreement. Their wine-colored fruits grew in abundance and were slow to rot. It was no wonder the elves, his wife's people, considered them extensions of the world's soul. They were a strangely beautiful and uniquely wonderful thing that grew like blossoms amid the common greenery of a typical forest. The world was still green in the places Mykal's caravan had observed in the weeks since they'd left—except for the dead glens of aldyrs. He missed seeing them during a tranquil walk in the woods with his wife and children. He missed many things from the stability of their little settlement.

Vincen huffed. "We can see what's left of 'em now. Sprouting like old fingerbones from the rocks, hands up like a dying man begging for his life before he became a shriveled corpse." He shook his head, then turned back to Mykal. "Speaking of corpses, if you're all the way out here, you must not have found any towns left. Human or otherwise."

"Well," Mykal said, hesitating, "none that—that were worth staying in."

Mykal had gradually become aware that there was no tranquility to be found as town after town revealed itself to be dead or dying. Those were the better ones. Others looked to have far worse curses laid upon them.

They had ventured near one city, one whose name had been forgotten, and they were greeted only by a handful of gaunt, hollow faces from dark windows. The streets into the city had been blocked, haphazardly, with overturned carts and barrels. Rotting roofs and putrefying streets were all that awaited the weary travelers. Mykal's group didn't press their luck.

Small villages were the best chance one had at a normal existence. Or even smaller settlements, like the logging camp. A new hamlet established by their convoy would be ideal, but they couldn't find an appropriate place that everyone could agree on.

The travel and wear on his family began taking its toll. All Mykal wanted was to see his children smile and play. To see his wife with a sparkle in her eyes again. He knew things were getting worse. They were on the road with their last belongings tied to a small cart he could haul with a rope around his chest. He would busy his mind with all the tales of monsters in the deep parts of the woods, or in the hollow parts of the moun-

tains where the dwarves dwell. These things that were so horrifying – where had they gone? Once, his grandfather had shown
him a book with illustrations and near-death accounts from the
first settlers in their settlement. Yet, the worst they had faced
during Mykal's time was hunger, cold, and fear of the
unknown.

After months on the road, Mykal and his group found that
few of the smaller villages remained, as well. Many were
nothing but charred ruins, raided not by monsters, but men.
Blackened, cracked bones of wooden frames stood from the
earth or leaned against air choked by ash and death. Not even
specters remained to haunt these forsaken places. At first, they'd
held out hope that a garden or two remained, growing wild and
untended. Those hopes were trampled again and again. Their
stomachs were left as empty as the blackened soil rife with only
wilted husks of lost harvests.

"And now you're here. Next to our mountains with none of
your caravan following you. What happened to the others, son?"
Vincen didn't sound suspicious. The look in his eyes and tone of
his voice told Mykal that the dwarf pitied their situation and
knew what sort of story was coming.

Mykal swallowed. His eyes grew warm and wet as he looked
into the night sky. The embers drifted from the fire, disappearing as they mingled with the stars. He wished the memories
of those he traveled with would do the same. Instead, they
continued to burn in the back of his mind like the smoldering
wood between the rocks in front of him.

"So many things," Mykal began, but had trouble finding the
words. "I don't quite remember which happened first. We lost a
few to wild animals, some dragged off in the night by cougars
and bears. Our hunter, Henri, pointed out the tracks and found
blood stains and remains when he searched for them. Some
simply went their own way after a time. The house... I'll never

forget the house." Mykal's voice grew soft and broken at this last statement.

"The house?" Vincen asked.

"It was some sort of farmhouse or maybe a rundown estate. We couldn't tell. All we knew at first was it looked like much-needed respite after a particularly long stretch of wandering. A man lived there. I didn't like anything about him. From the moment I saw him I knew something was wrong, but Jerol and Mora insisted we see if we could stay for a few days."

"Friends of yours?" Vincen asked, referring to the new names in Mykal's tale of misery.

"Not really. Acquaintances, more like," Mykal clarified. "They became the leaders of our group by power of will. They were very confident. Strong personalities. Jerol was also one of our more skilled fighters. Everyone trusted them to keep us safe."

Vincen cocked his head. "But, you didn't."

"No," Mykal said, faltering, "but this time I knew they were wrong. I begged them not to trust him. After a day or two, I began to doubt my own initial feelings. He'd fed us well. He lived alone. He told us his only family was long dead. He still had cattle and a garden."

Vincen winced like he knew what was coming.

"It took a few days, but one family in our group went missing. A husband and wife. The man said they must have left on their own."

"The man? You never got his name?"

"I didn't care about his name. I was keeping an eye on my wife and children every waking moment. I barely slept. I didn't like the man or the feel of his home. It even smelled strange. No one believed him about the couple disappearing— Lillen and Derrik, I think their names were— but everyone else was too comfortable and enjoying not having to worry about food to question too deeply. I finally convinced Jerol to investigate with me. We—"

Mykal took a breath. The memory, the smells, and sights of that day, came back in a swell. He tasted bile in his mouth.

"We found the bodies outside, where the man slaughtered his cattle. We overpowered him. Hung him. We couldn't bring ourselves to take any food or other supplies from the sickening house. We didn't dare think about where the food came from and left it."

"Gods," Vincen muttered. "That's unthinkable."

"They trusted my instincts from then on," Mykal said. He glanced over to Redbeard and Skunkstripe, who were glaring back at him. He looked to Vincen again, whose eyes creased in disgust at his story.

"You truly have been to hell and back."

"There was worse," Mykal replied flatly.

Vincen's eyes widened. Mykal didn't give him time for questions. The words trickled from his lips in exhausted, rote fashion. However, this was the first time he recounted their ill-fated meeting with another group outside Old Ligothi.

There had been several heated arguments on their way to the city's outskirts. Few of them carried weapons. Most had rusted or broken on their journey and the blacksmith opted not to travel with them when they left the village. Only Henri with his bow and Jerol with his sword had decent means to protect them. The rest had a few hand-made spears carved from stout branches and some farming tools in the carts. One side argued that this was not enough to protect themselves if they remained on the roads for the rest of their lives. Another portion argued that was the point exactly—what would they do to defend themselves if Old Ligothi was occupied by people not exactly friendly to outsiders? Or some other evil?

The decision was made when both Henri and Jerol took

sides with the city-seekers (as those who wanted to continue into Old Ligothi came to be called). No one wanted to part from them. So, they spent another three days making their way to Old Ligothi by the sea. As they grew closer, they came upon a small crowd of people with two wagons pulled by two under-nourished horses.

One of the wagons had carried the old and young and was uncovered, giving Mykal's group a clear view of the fearful looks shared among those gathered in that wagon. The other cart was covered. It looked more like a rundown carriage with side windows that could be slid open. They were all shuttered and the carriage was given a wide berth.

There were, perhaps, a dozen total miserable souls in this new group. Twelve weary beings much like Mykal's own caravan. This new group's eyes were also sunken and tired. Their muscles strained and their nerves even more so. There was also a peculiar odor that one could smell when the breeze blew. Mykal had assumed it was from the group. He'd thought perhaps they had been on the road for a long time without a chance to clean themselves, or that some were sick. The smell was vaguely familiar, but Mykal couldn't quite place it. He eventually let it alone as greater concerns presented themselves.

Upon seeing other people, a slight spark lit in the eyes of the forward vanguard of that party: a young, dark-skinned woman and two men that appeared to be faring better than the rest of their company. The spark was not to last.

Mykal stood with Ira and listened to Jerol and Mora speak with them. The woman, whose name was Minerva from what Mykal could overhear, had brought her group from the east with her uncle and brother—the two men with her. They were a gaggle of survivors from a small collection of towns and hamlets and they had decided to travel north to Old Ligothi. They had their own stories of tribulations on their journey, but nothing compared to what they found in the city.

"What did you find?" Mora pleaded, desperately seeking to know if their journey was for naught. Minerva had turned her head toward the direction of the city and looked on in silence. It took her a moment to answer, the breeze full of hollow promises.

"The city is gone," Minerva said flatly.

She spoke so quietly, Mykal barely heard her. He thought, at first, that he'd imagined it. The news didn't surprise him. He'd almost expected it. Jerol and Mora went pale. Mykal heard Henri nearby cuss and spit into the dirt. They had laid all their hopes on the safety of that city and, instead, were left sitting in the broken outskirts of a lost city with nothing but spoiled hope and strangers.

"No," Jerol had whispered sharply, "No. I don't believe it. I refuse. The whole city?"

Mora leaned over and whispered something to him. Jerol put his hands on his hips and lowered his head. Mykal saw his shoulders rise and fall in one long, slow breath. The breeze was the only movement or sound for several seconds. Minerva's face was a blank mask.

"Don't you smell it?" she asked.

Mora looked around. "Smell what?"

"The blood. The rot." Minerva answered, her voice breaking.

Mykal's inside's grew cold. Was that truly the source of the smell? That was indeed the familiar smell, like a bloody nose. Clotted, metallic, but also old and stale. The sharp tinge of something similar to peat or garden soil was there, too.

"I don't believe you," Jerol grumbled.

"Jerol," Mora began, but a raised hand from the old guard stopped her.

Jerol turned and walked back towards his cart among the caravan to retrieve his belongings.

"I'm going to the city. Henri can scout it out safely from a distance. You're coming with me, right, Henri?" Jerol said self-assuredly. He looked to Henri in a manner that assumed the hunter had already made up his mind to go with Jerol.

Henri grimaced and asked Minerva, "How far did you get into the city? If I could find a good vantage point, I may be able to see more. Find a safe place within the city walls, perhaps."

"I can tell you plenty," Minerva said monotonously.

"I'd rather see for myself!" Jerol shouted as he wheeled around on her. "If any of you wish to come with me, you're welcome. I'm done living on the road."

A number of Mykal's group exchanged looks. Some were fearful and others resolute. In the end, less than half had picked up their things and gathered near Jerol.

Mykal recalled the grim look on Henri's face as he ran a hand over his graying beard. He shook his head, crestfallen, and walked toward his friend.

"Wait," Mykal barked.

The old hunter walked toward Jerol and straight past him.

"You'll get yourself killed," Mykal had whispered harshly.

"I have a good feeling about this," Henri replied with an unconvincing smile.

The two armed men—the only ones skilled with weapons among them—left with a number of their own people, including Mora. All that remained were Minerva's band with their carriage and wagon and Mykal's group. All of them down-trodden and full of empty stares.

Mykal watched as Minerva and her uncle exchanged glances.

"It's a day's walk to Old Ligothi. We'll wait three before leaving," Minerva called out, her face an impassive mask. Mykal had seen this look before. She had endured something beyond what the rest of them had. Most people had become numb to 'mundane' daily suffering, but this young woman had seen something beyond that which marred the rest of their souls. It was a look shared by her uncle and every rider in the open wagon. Even the children.

MYKAL DIDN'T REALIZE he'd gone silent for some time. He didn't notice until Vincen gruffly asked, "Are you ok, son?"

Wiping his nose with his hand for no reason other than to make himself move and shake the memories, Mykal quietly replied, "Yes."

"They never returned, did they? The hunter, the guard, any of them." Vincen stated more than asked.

Mykal shook his head. "After the first day, people began getting nervous. After two, they started leaving. Even Minerva's brother took off with a few others. Her uncle argued with him, but Minerva just let him go. By the third, there was just Minerva, her uncle, a young man from their group named Lenik, and my family. Desperation and fear set in, unlike anything I'd ever seen before. It was this shroud, Vincen. Some dread weight that pressed on your chest until you couldn't breathe. Then I noticed something. Something horrible."

"You notice a lot of things, Mykal. Doesn't take knowing you a long time to realize that," Vincen interjected.

Mykal clasped his hands together. They were shaking and he didn't want the other two dwarves, the ones he didn't trust, to notice. He had to take another moment, stare into the fire until it burned his fear away before he could tell Vincen about the carriage.

. . .

IT TOOK Mykal three days to notice the strange behavior of Minerva's group regarding the carriage. Nothing felt wrong about any of the people, but there was something slightly off about their behavior.

Mykal was on the opposite side of the last of Minerva's group, with the wagon and carriage between them. Two more people took their leave and gave the carriage a wide berth, almost flinching as they walked by. It finally occurred to Mykal that anyone who passed by the carriage reacted the same way. Minerva's uncle had been casting side-long glances at the faded, worn thing and Mykal always assumed it was because the man was making sure no one was trying to steal anything.

Lenik had never left the carriage's side. Not since that first day, and he was the only one who remained near it. Mykal had wanted to investigate further, but that night would be the last before they would all leave the next morning, realizing Jerol, Mora, Henri, and those that'd left with them were not coming back.

Mykal had even asked Minerva if those who left might have found a safe place in Old Ligothi, after all. She assured him they hadn't. She then cast a subtle glance at the carriage. The motion was quick, almost instinctive, but fear shadowed her brown eyes, and lips pursed just slightly. It was then Mykal knew he had to have answers about the carriage.

They all decided to travel together. Just the six of them now. They headed in the only direction they had left: further south to the Gauloth Mountains, where they hoped for one last desperate bid to seek shelter with the dwarves; or any that may still be alive.

. . .

"AND YOU FOUND US," Vincen chuckled. He looked over to Redbeard and Skunkstripe who remained silent and sour. "And there's still quite a few of us left, for now."

The last sentence was uttered with a heavy dose of melancholy, Mykal noticed. His son yawned, followed by his daughter then his wife. They chuckled softly. Mykal's heart grew warm for a moment.

"You still haven't told me what happened to the rest of your people, lad."

Mykal's heart chilled instantly. He cleared his throat and tried to find the words to explain something that he remembered as though it just happened moments ago, but his mind was constantly wanting to push it away.

MYKAL EXPLAINED how they traveled for a few more days. Minerva and her uncle had been silent the entire time, barely even speaking to each other. Lenik remained near the carriage and would mumble quietly to himself here and there. Mykal began to regret insisting they travel together, but felt they would be safer in numbers. And he needed to know why Minerva's band feared and, at the same time, obsessed over the carriage.

The Gauloth Mountains were in sight and the air smelled of salt from the sea that rolled near them via an inlet that cut sharply inland. The sound and smell were calming, so they stopped for the night. Mykal agreed to the first watch. As the waves of the sea lulled the others to sleep and the moon cast silver light on the water's surface, Mykal moved quietly toward the black silhouette of the carriage.

A small campfire had been built to keep away predators. As Mykal drew near the back of the carriage, the fire cast dancing orange shadows that glinted on the handle of a small door. Mykal had held his breath. The crickets chirped, the fire crackled, and the ocean whispered. He reached his hand out and gripped the small, tarnished handle. It was unsettlingly warm. He turned the handle and was disappointed to find it locked. He turned a little harder, a little sharper, just in case it was stuck and not locked. No luck.

"Damn," Mykal had cursed under his breath. He started to turn away in frustration, giving the handle one final jolt in defiance. He felt the handle give, and with a soft crunch the grip pulled down and the small door opened with barely a creak. Small pieces of splintered wood came off the carriage frame and the lock tumbled to the ground. It must have become dry-rotted. The carriage had certainly seen better days.

Mykal gently swung the door open. The smell that assaulted him from inside the dank carriage made him gag. He recalled the reflexive dry heaving that he tried desperately to repress before someone had woke up to find him looking into the forbidden carriage. A carriage that would better be described as a tomb. A tomb overflowing with the smell of stale blood and wet, putrescent soil and rotting flesh.

Bodies were lining the floor of the carriage. Three of them. At first, Mykal thought they were covered in some sort of thick shroud and surrounded by belongings or other random items. To his eternal horror, the light of the campfire flared and revealed the bodies were covered in a carpet of moss, lichen, and other plant-like growths. Slender vines curled out from wounds in their flesh and climbed up the interior walls, some curling up onto the ceiling and sticking there like glistening snakes. Red blossoms unfurled like wet wounds along the thicker portions of the vines, and Mykal swore they dripped with blood.

The state of the bodies was beyond words. Some portions were still well-preserved and whole. One face belonged to some poor man and Mykal could still see the final scream frozen there, while one of the blood-flowers obscured the rest of the horrible visage. Mykal told himself he didn't see one of the milky eyes twitch as the firelight flashed over it. Other portions of the bodies were so putrid that little was left but a black goo over brittle bones.

The fire also highlighted small motes that hovered like specks of dust in the air. They moved heavily, lazily, and even the breeze of the open door didn't cause them to float outside into the crisp seaside air. Mykal realized these were likely spores from the demonic vegetation. One wouldn't be remiss for thinking the listless particles were remaining inside on purpose.

"What are you doing?" a voice had said. It was low but surprised. Mykal recognized it from the constant mumbling he'd heard since Lenik had joined them.

"Why did you open that door? *How* did you open that door?" Lenik asked, his voice a sharp, harsh whisper.

Mykal had wanted to explain the situation with the lock, that he was only curious and had no interest in taking anything from them, but Lenik grabbed Mykal by the shoulder and pulled him away from the carriage. Lenik placed himself between Mykal and the unspeakable things that now lay behind the black mouth of the carriage door. The once quiet, mumbling guardian of the carriage was staring at Mykal with barely contained anger and dread.

"Who are they?" Mykal had asked, his eyes wide and his throat sore.

"Stay away from them," Lenik threatened.

"I— I think one of them—" Mykal began, but he dared not finish the thought aloud.

"Stay away," Lenik repeated. He stepped toward Mykal, his eyes filled with a growing madness.

"Okay, calm down," Mykal said, raising his hands. He stepped back, away from Lenik, and felt his heel strike against a log sticking out of the campfire. He nearly tripped, but caught his balance.

Lenik's eyes began looking around, haphazardly. "I'm sorry," he said, then, again, "I'm sorry."

"It's okay, we'll figure—" Mykal stopped when he realized Lenik wasn't talking to him.

"I'm sorry," Lenik kept repeating. He began speaking faster and faster, his voice lowering until it became a frantic mumble. As the crazed man began to turn, Mykal saw his foot land on the lock that had fallen from the rotted doorframe.

Mykal didn't have time to call out. Lenik's ankle rolled on the metal mechanism and he fell backward into the foul interior of the carriage. Lenik screamed, the sound muffled by the carriage.

"What in the hells—" another voice shouted. It was Minerva's uncle. "What have you done?" he'd shouted at Mykal.

"He tripped!" Mykal replied, but the large man pulled Mykal back, practically over the fire.

"Lenik!" the large man shrieked. "Oh gods, Lenik…"

Everyone had been wakened at that point. Ira held her and Mykal's children close, covering their eyes and ears as best she could. Minerva and her brother ran over to see the scene that played out before them.

Mykal froze. Lenik had managed to find his footing against the back of the carriage and his hands gripped the sides of the doorframe. The fire only provided a faint light, especially against the dark mouth of that sinister tomb. But, it had been enough to see Lenik begin to pull himself up and out of the door. His head and chest were covered in something green and black, with traces of red trickling down his arms.

Mykal looked over to see Minerva staring blankly at the unfortunate man. Then, her eyes widened. Mykal followed her gaze and saw Minerva's uncle rushing to Lenik. He must have been trying to help Lenik. A sane mind would've liked to think that Lenik tried to reach out to the larger man, but as the firelight flared once more Mykal saw something else that would remain buried in the deepest recesses of his thoughts; locked away for his own sake. Something else was holding Lenik back, and something else was reaching out for Minerva's uncle when he tried to grab Lenik.

As tears built in Mykal's eyes and a scream swelled in his throat, a flash of light crossed Mykal's vision. One of the logs that were partially ablaze, like the one he'd almost tripped over, flew into the carriage's interior. Another quickly followed. The inside of the carriage began to burn and soon the entire interior was engulfed in flame.

Both men fell into the carriage interior—because Mykal still refused to say they were pulled—and the screams became unbearable. Minerva approached the carriage that now had gouts of flame bursting from the small windows on each side. With conviction, she slammed the carriage door shut and led Mykal and his family away.

Ira, Keera, and Kellen had cried themselves back to sleep. Mykal and Minerva never took their eyes from the carriage. When the screams stopped and the blaze was roaring, hopefully reducing every evil root of what had lain within to ashes, Minerva found a large, flat stone to sit on. It was overlooking the waves that rolled onto the nearby beach; a peaceful, stark contrast to everything that was winding down behind them.

When he was sure that his family was asleep, Mykal went to Minerva. She was staring at the waves, cresting and reflecting the light of the full moon. Her face appeared softer, but still morose.

"We're lost," she said softly. The first words she'd spoken since their groups met over a week ago.

Mykal had just shrugged. "Well, we're still headed to the mountains."

"I mean us. As a people. Humans, elves, dwarves, more powerful and more evil things have laid claim to our world. Our homes."

She looked back at the wagon, still bright and burning. "Most of us are going to die horribly. It's just a matter of time. The best most of us can hope for is to die on our own terms. Of our own accord."

Mykal sighed. He looked back, also, but not at the carriage. He looked to his family. "I have others to look out for. I have to hope for something better."

"So did I," she replied flatly. "One is over there in that fire. The other left and might be dead already, too. To think any differently just makes you a fool."

"I guess we'll see," was all Mykal had offered.

VINCEN'S eyes were fixed on Mykal with a hard stare. The dwarf's face was a mask of stone as unreadable as the mountains he called home.

"I went to my family," Mykal said as he looked at them now, having fallen asleep in their bedrolls near the fire, "and stayed awake as long as I could. I fell asleep just I saw a sliver of light on the horizon. Minerva never moved. When I woke up, she was gone. I found footprints leading into the sea."

The dwarf was silent. He made no noise, not even a huff or groan. His two companions had leaned in to listen more closely when Mykal described what he found in the carriage. Their grotesque curiosity was evident. Vincen remained quiet for some time.

"You don't believe me," Mykal said.

"I believe you whole-heartedly," Vincen replied, "and I think that woman was wrong."

The dwarf ran a hand through his long, curly hair and then placed a heavy, gentle hand on Mykal's shoulder.

"I don't know what in all the hells was in that carriage. We," Vincen gestured to Redbeard and Skunkstripe, "have our own horrors to deal with. Things that would turn your bowels to jelly. I know plenty of people that have died screaming. I know others that have died quiet, in their sleep. And *that's* the best we can hope for."

Vincen nodded towards Mykal's family. "That's the best we can hope for them. Quiet, with a full belly, and in their sleep. You're no fool, Mykal. You made it here, through all that you've shared with me. You made it here."

Mykal nodded, biting his tongue to keep from crying. His children and his wife were sleeping quietly, feeling safe for the first time in years; and out in the wild at the foot of a mountain range, at that. He wouldn't let the other two dwarves near them, but he trusted Vincen. This was someone who meant well.

The dwarf slapped his knees. "You must be exhausted, lad."

Vincen stood from the tree stump he'd been using as a seat. Mykal remained seated, and the dwarf still barely stood taller than Mykal's head. He was almost able to look Vincen right in the eye. The dwarf smiled at him. "Get some rest. You're going to be fine." Vincen glanced over at Mykal's sleeping family. "All of you."

Vincen went over to a cart hauled by two mules that the dwarves used to bring down the food and supplies for their rendezvous. He turned the spout on a wooden cask that held some ale that had been shared that night and filled a brass cup before handing it to Mykal. "One more drink before bed?"

Mykal stood and patted the dwarf on the shoulder, grateful for all that had been done for his family. He and the dwarf downed one more drink together. Mykal eyed Vincen's companions one more time as he went to his bedroll next to Ira. Vincen noticed and looked over at the other two dwarves.

"Don't worry about them," he scoffed, "they're not going anywhere." Mykal could hear the threat in Vincen's voice that was aimed at Redbeard and Skunkstripe.

Mykal curled up into his bedroll and felt more comfortable than he had in a long time. His eyes grew heavy, and his mind grew thick and cloudy. All thoughts of sandy footsteps, grotesque carriages, and glaring dwarves had slipped away into velvety darkness.

"FOR SOMEONE SO OBSERVANT, he failed to notice you nursing one drink all night. And not taking more than a sip or two, at that," Mullin said, his red mustache curling into a sneer.

Vincen eyed the red-haired dwarf. "Shut it, Mullin."

"And gods-almighty, did you have to know his life story?" the dark-haired dwarf whined. Vincen sneered as he looked at his other beady-eyed companion with the white stripe in his hair he always found oddly funny. "Same goes for you, Thorik."

"If he's a talker, he won't last a week in iron pits," Mullin commented.

Thorik smiled. "Wife's pretty, though. Always liked the elven ones. Kids are fuckin' useless, though. Don't even know why we take 'em. All they do is use up food and space for years before they're good for—"

Thorik reeled back as Vincen backhanded him with a massive fist. His bodyguards were taller than Vincen, and younger, as the more recent dwarven generations had resulted from interbreeding with captured slaves. Vincen was shorter, but his muscles were thicker and his hands larger. Thorik just felt the equivalent of a leather-covered mace strike him in the face.

Vincen had been stretching the truth when he said there were plenty of them left. To prevent inbreeding, desperate and despicable measures had been taken by many dwarven nobles. It had been occurring for over a century.

Vincen was done with it. This rendezvous point was observable from a forward observation post in the nearby mountain pass. When Mykal's family was spotted, a 'greeting party' was formed, and Vincen was once again tasked with sweet-talking another group of people into joining the 'safe haven' of the dwarves.

Vincen would have refused the orders a dozen times over by now, but his own family would be at risk for his insubordination. This time, Vincen had plans.

"You'll fuckin' pay for that, ol' man," Mullin seethed as Thorik nursed his bleeding and swollen lip. "You're lucky they're nice and passed out. They wake up and get away and it'll be your arse."

Vincen glanced at the barrel of ale. It had been brewed from a species of mushroom that grew in the more moist parts of the mountain interior. His people called them 'dreamcaps' and fermented this drink for times when someone needed to be unconscious.

He casually sat down on his seat by the fire and pulled a thin, reedy pipe from inside his leather vest. He added a pinch of tobacco and lit it. The bitter smoke swirled in his mouth and he exhaled long, curling tendrils out of his nose.

"I won't be paying for anything, friend," Vincen said in a husky voice as he looked at the family laying peacefully by the fire, "and neither will they."

"What's this now?" Mullin said, putting a hand on the grip of the sword at his side. "You think you can let them go?"

"No. I know I can't. But I don't have to let you fucking pigs take them." He practically spat the words.

Vincen was stockier than his companions, it was true. But they were leaner and quicker. By the time Vincen had dropped his pipe and stood for the fight he knew was coming, Thorik had already circled around him as Mullin drew a short, wide dwarven blade. A searing pain shot through Vincen's side as Thorik withdrew a dagger now coated in blood.

Vincen shouted in pain and rage. In a single, swift motion, he grabbed the axe that was leaning against his stump and brought it around in a large, arcing swing. Thorik's head with its dark hair and ridiculous white stripe thumped to the ground as his body fell to one side.

Mullin was on him now, and Vincen had just enough time to bring his axe up with both hands on the grip to block a blow that would've carved him from his shoulder down to his belly. Pain shot through his body as he felt warm blood gush down his leg. He was feeling weaker by the moment. As froth from Mullin's screaming mouth sprayed his face, Vincen let go of the grip with one hand and drew the dagger from his belt. He shoved it up into Mullin's throat and listened as the despicable excuse for a dwarf choked on his own blood. Letting go of the handle allowed Mullin's sword to drop lower, however, and it cut deep into Vincen's shoulder.

With both dwarven bodyguards dead and his vision quickly fading, Vincen slumped against the wagon. He heard a slight splatter and, for a moment, thought it was his own blood. He looked over and saw the spout from the ale barrel dripping rhythmically onto the dirt. He smiled. He'd added something extra to this batch. Just a sip or two, that's what Mullin had pointed out. It may have slowed Vincen down for the fight, if he was being honest. But that didn't matter. Vincen didn't plan on coming back from this.

The outside world was dangerous. Three dwarves not coming back from an outpost wouldn't be unheard of. His family would have to deal with his loss and, for that, he was truly sorry.

"Forgive me," he whispered as his strength continued to fade. He hoped his wife and children would know how sorry he was.

As his vision continued to dim, he looked at the family laying by the fire. Mykal and his elven wife, Ira, and their children, Keera and Kellen. Asleep, peaceful, almost smiling. He meant every word he said to Mykal. The man was no fool. He met Vincen on a good night, with a plan that succeeded perfectly. The woman, Minerva, was right about one thing. This was the best they could hope for. Departing this hellish world peacefully, without fear or pain. Their bellies full of warm food and their bodies warm by a nice fire. He hoped their last thoughts were hopeful ones. He smiled, and slipped away quietly himself.

# THE RED LINE

THE AIR SMELLED STALE AND HUMID. THE LEAVES LAY IN LIMP PILES upon the ground, neither fully dead nor alive. Portions of their dried edges crunched weakly as his steps carried him across the drab gray-green spaces between the trees. Here and there, strands of black-painted rope were tied around their trunks, marking them as impure.

Thin white fingers of mist still hovered about the air. There was a slight chill in the early morning, but not so much as to be truly cold. Everything here was always something "in between." Leaves and plants were never fully in bloom or wilting. The air was never hot or cold; it was always still and tepid. No true winds blew, only whispers of air. No real snow fell, just a smattering of flakes here and there. No actual rain relieved them, rather a light drizzle would grace their crops time and again. The day was never as bright as it should be, as though a haze or the lightest of fog was ever-present.

But the night... the night was true to its name. The night was as deep and as dark as any he'd ever experienced. Fires burned weaker and warmth fought feebly against the chill. The light never reached far from its source.

This was their home.

He began his patrols earlier than usual this morning. A ceaseless scratching in the night, coupled with sounds of digging, had left him wondering if something was trying to get into the village. His rounds started with the shoulder-high drystone walls that surrounded the whole of their settlement. It was built quickly when they arrived here, and decades later its hasty construction continued to show.

The beasts in this wretched stretch of woodland were quite unlike the terrors that drove them from their original holdings. These were simple creatures; they were afraid of fire and steel. Fire was plentiful enough, so long as they took care to guard against the blackvein. Steel, however, was preciously scarce. His hand tightened around the worn and faded grip of his blade. It remained sheathed in its wood and hide scabbard at his side. It made him what he was. It gave him purpose, it kept him fed, and it made the others hate him.

He had long learned to shrug off their spiteful words and hateful gazes. In the long silence of the morning patrols, however, sometimes he was tempted to use the blade to end his own suffering, but those thoughts were quickly shrugged off. He was alone with his thoughts and boredom, and it made his mind wander.

The silence was deafening, and whatever he had heard in the night left no signs of their presence. He found no footprints or droppings. No ground was disturbed and no brush was broken.

It was a relief of sorts. His biggest concern would have been the wolgs. He had seen plenty of wolves as a boy. He could barely remember their small numbers that roamed the thickets back in their other town; that one that had been forgotten by the elders and never spoken of to the newest generation. The wolves that stalked their cattle and wounded the occasional hunter were fierce, but not something to be terrified of.

The wolgs, however, were a different beast. Here, in this hellish purgatory, the wolgs sought after every bit of flesh and blood that wandered too far from safety. They looked similar to wolves but were bigger, more vicious, and more cunning. Their teeth were white as bleached bone and their hackles were thick and coarse as dead reeds. Strangest among their physical traits were the chitinous growths along their shoulders and flanks and the extra pair of eyes set in their foreheads. This made them a strange and horrific sight. Only he had seen one close enough to discern these traits. None of the other villagers had seen one within a hundred feet. At least, not a villager that had not been dragged away by them.

Their worst quality, beyond their grotesque deformities, was their baleful howl. He only heard it for the first time when he last killed a wolg several months ago. He had tracked it back to its den. It was the last of its pack and seemed to be aware of it. The beast had taken a fisher who wandered too far from safe grounds, and the man's screams alerted him. He followed the scattered and blood-soaked leaves to a small, dark mouth amid a landslide along the southern mountains. For a moment, he thought the wolg had a second victim still alive in the den. It chilled him to the core when he recognized the subtle difference between the wolg's hideous call and the final cries of the dying. Oft times the sound resonated in his nightmares and woke him at night.

The memory sent shivers along his skin; he shook it off to continue his patrol. By the looks of the undisturbed forest floor, such a vicious thing was not the cause of the scratching. Few other animals existed here, and, even with the thinning of the wolg numbers, no new animals had been seen among the glens and boughs. Townsfolk often spotted a few scattered birds overhead, but none rested among the branches of their forest. Nothing resembling a deer or elk had been seen in years. A pathetic manner of boar could be found here and there, but they bred sparingly and their young rarely survived to adulthood. The last few he found he let alone in the hope they would produce more. That was two years past.

That left the duskrats; the only damnable creatures too foolish to find a better place or too successful in these woods to attempt such. They seemed to be built for the Black Arbors. Fat, greasy creatures that always appeared wet and well-fed, they could be found under hedges, in thick gatherings of fallen leaves, and along the banks of the Stillwater. They were normally whisper-quiet, however, and it made little sense that he would be able to hear them scratching and digging about around the wall.

He kicked up several leaf piles that had accumulated around various recesses in the wall. He did, indeed, turn up several rats but nothing so large as to make any discernable noise. He curled his nose at the little shits and continued his patrol.

The sun, that sickly-yellow orb that cast barely amicable light through the persistent ever-gray of the sky, had risen fully. He had made his way to the banks of the Stillwater. He saw a fisher already at work casting a net out into a deep portion of the lake. A length of rope and a heavy iron weight gave the net ballast and allowed the fisher to cast it in areas further away from shore. It often did little good. The fishers were a lot who had little other talent and were sent to find food in a lake that bore no catches since they arrived here. The Keeper of Lines only insisted on the effort because splashes would be heard coming from the lake throughout the day and night.

He watched quietly as two, three, then four retrievals came back empty. Nothing but a handful of moss and black lakeweed was left to show for his troubles. Finally, the fisher noticed who was there.

"WHAT'RE YOU LOOKING AT, FANG?" he sneered.

Fang squeezed the hilt of his blade. "Still no fish."

"Still no fish." The fisher repeated with bile. His name was Mott; he was a particularly dimwitted little sod and wholly unlikable. "Have you caught anything?"

"I found a few duskrats. I can find them again if you like."

"Bugger that. I'd rather eat boiled leather." He gave another heave of the net and it hit the surface of the water with a thick, sloshing splash.

Fang turned and left him to his chore. No doubt he was in for a long and fruitless day. He followed the edge of the lake and looked out over to the mountains that rose along its far opposite side. He remembered when mountain caps used to be covered in snow. It gave them a wistful beauty, but those were mere boyhood memories. The dull brown peaks of rock and dirt that gripped the banks of the Stillwater were just as plain and unparticular as everything else.

After he finished walking the length of the wall again, he decided to move inward and peruse the dirt streets of their village. The gates were little more than a wooden door fit to an iron post that was forced into the ground. Scrap-built and useless, really, but it helped keep what animals there were out of their crops.

No sooner had he entered the village, he heard the cursing of Thomys, an elderly farmer. "Little shits got into the crop again," he was complaining.

"Is there a problem, Thomys?" he asked. His tone suggested he couldn't have cared less, but he was under dutiful obligation.

Thomys spit on the ground and ran a wrinkled, spotted hand

over his mouth. "Duskrats," he said, and spit again. "They chewed the corn down to the nubs and dug out the damn pota-toes. Must've gotten through the wall." Fang looked with disdain at the pitiful gate.

The old farmer glared at Fang. "You're supposed to keep those things in check, Sword-bearer. Go see to the ditch, why don't you? And if you see any of those things, kill 'em! Take 'em to Maggy."

Fang let his eyes linger on the old man a few seconds longer. He was upset at the loss of some crops, and that Fang could understand. They needed all they could spare. His disrespect, however, Fang would not abide.

"Well?" Thomys said impatiently.

"I'm not your sheepdog, farmer."

Thomys' mouth curled at the retort. His face became a mass of wrinkles. "Would you kindly see to the drainage ditch, m'lord?" he mocked, his words dripping with venom.

Fang walked away, still eyeing the old farmer as he did so. Miserable prick.

Thomys' fields were less a farm and more of a large garden. There were far too few people to work a decent amount of farm-land, and the soil here would barely support even meager crops. Fang walked the entirety of the small fields in little time. He reached the point where a small ditch ran through a hole in the base of the wall. This was fed by the Stillwater and brought water to the garden. A small grate was forged by the smith and haphazardly stuck into the soil and wedged into the stone to prevent duskrats from getting inside. It appeared that, over time, the vermin had managed to slowly work it open. A few seconds later he had the grate wedged back into place; a simple and thankless task for the 'Sword-bearer'.

Fang looked at the sad rows of vegetables that had been raided by the rodents. The consistently insipid weather allowed them to grow crops nearly year-round. However, the meager and withered results required many harvests just to keep food on the table. He kicked at some of the dirt. It was gray, crumbling clay that left a disconcerting film on his boots.

Nothing else of note occurred within the tight confines of the nameless village. Fang spent the rest of his time walking the forest and checking his snares. Once, he would find a small variety of animals waiting for him. Now, only the oily duskrats would be squirming in the makeshift traps. By the time he returned to the village he had almost a dozen of the vermin.

He took them to Maggy, the village butcher and cook. She was plucking a large bird when Fang entered. He was genuinely shocked to see that a goose had been caught and was being prepared for barter.

"Ghil brought her down just now," she said, hearing someone enter. "All the other huntsmen are congratulating him still. Saying he's to be getting some sort of trinket from Della out o' the feathers."

When she noticed it was Fang, her mood quickly soured. "Suppose'n you'll be getting the lord's share o' the meat, no doubt."

Fang grimaced and set the duskrats on one of the wooden tables by the door. "I prefer these."

She scoffed at his lie. No one preferred duskrat.

There were none in the village who could be called fat; it was a luxury to eat anything that would make one desire more for the taste alone. Being the cook, though, she no doubt tasted and tasted again the food she prepared to ensure it was at least edible. She prided herself on the miracles she could work with the leavings this world gave them for food. As a sign of pride in her own work, she certainly had a healthier level of weight to her than most others in the village. She wiped her hands on her apron and mocked the catch Fang brought her, then examined it and set the rats one by one in a pot of boiling water.

"Take the better part of the day to cook the musk and oil off 'em. They'll serve, though."

With that, Fang took his leave. It was time he got some sleep before the evening watch. As always, sleep came with difficulty and in broken stretches. As soon as he slipped into its embrace he heard the howling in his dreams. That dreadful wailing that woke him with cold sweats. He saw the mangled remains of the fisher, those which he told his widow he dared not bring home to her. He felt the sting of her hand upon his cheek again. The images were vivid and the sensations tangible. He woke many times a night, trying to shake the images from his head and howls from his ears. He would never fully rid himself of the fear; it was the only kind of fear he still felt so strongly. In the daily purgatory of existence for this little mote of humanity, fear was something left buried under the weight of tedium. Every day was another slog through the mire for survival. They only remembered fear when the threat of starvation or a deadly fever was immediately upon them; when death was rapping impatiently at their door. Otherwise, their dread was left in the opened caverns and black, hollow cavities that remained of their old home.

Fang was beyond even this apprehension. Any spark of fright that the world drew from him was long snuffed out by the perpetual gray of this lakeside misery. Only the distant howls that echoed in the hollow of his soul could strike a modicum of terror in him still.

The evening watch was uneventful, as most watches were. The smith mockingly offered a slag-ridden iron pitchfork for Fang's steel. The water shop owner filled his waterskin with freshly-boiled water to make sure the cooled portions were free for the other villagers. Maggy provided him with a bowl of duskrat soup and burnt bread. Everything was as it had always been for Fang. More duskrats were jostled from their warrens next to the walls, but he didn't bother with trapping any. The snares would be full tomorrow. He checked the small shack that served as their armory and took inventory: two bows made of unsoiled blackwood, a dozen arrows with pitiful bone heads, a few makeshift blades made from the femurs of the last wolg, and a suit of patchwork leather that smelled too horrible to wear. Fang shook his head. It seemed they had forgotten what they escaped. That, or they saw little use in fighting it again if it ever came for them. The latter was the more likely conclusion.

The end of the evening watch came at dusk, and Fang retired for a few more hours' rest. A handful of hours were all he could manage at a time. The night watch was coming, and it would be most difficult of all. He dreamed of the scratching again that night and heard growls and other guttural noises. It was so loud and sudden that he found himself bolting out of his bed and grabbing his sword.

He was awash in a chill sweat again, and it made the outside air feel bitter cold against his skin. His small dwelling was located directly next to the wall, and he ran to the enclosure as fast as he could. By the time he reached it, whatever had been there was gone. He heard nothing, but the air smelled wrong. It was ripe with a wet musk, but not quite as pungent as the duskrats.

He laid a hand on the tepid stone and listened carefully. No chirping insects or croaking toads broke the silence of that deep night. The silence was something he had become accustomed to, and was now made wholly new again. He ran his hand along the rough surface of the wall just to hear the shuffling sound of skin on stone. It sounded like a roaring wave in his wanting ears.

When no threat or, truly, nothing of any living nature had appeared he retired back to his daub and wattle home and closed the rough wooden door as quietly as he could manage. He crossed the single room to his bed, sat on the edge, and rested his forearms on the crossguard of the blade's hilt. His heart was beating faster than normal, and he felt the cold sweat return. He took several deep breaths, now agitated at his fear, and sought to quell the feeling before it made him any more irrational.

He slept no more that night. He lay on the straw-covered sack that was his bed and listened to the silent void of night. He felt every prick of the dry contents of his cushion but welcomed the rustling it provided. He heard no more until, at last, dawn finally came.

He couldn't see that it was sunrise so much as he felt it. They lacked for seasons here in their nameless new home; they had only the perpetual cool of the gray sun and sky and the limp trees of the Blackwood. His body, however, had seasons of its own. Four watches: morning, midday, evening, and night. His mind was attuned to them, and his body would wake when it needed.

The morning watch saw him lingering heavily near the eastern edge of the Stillwater. It bordered the heaviest section of the woods. Most of the fishers were gathered near there after word of activity in the water had spread. One of them swore he'd had something tugging in his net, but he'd pulled up an empty haul. It was true that something lurked out in those calm, dead waters. The occasional splash could be heard, and the fishers became anxious with possibility. It made Fang anxious for different reasons.

Nothing had ever been caught from that unnerving mirror. He felt a cool touch on the back of his neck and looked quickly behind him. Some of the fishers noticed and looked at him expectantly.

"You see something there, watchman?" A young woman called out.

Fang didn't look back at her. The lake was eerie, but it was the woods that caused a visceral reaction in him. Something was in there, now, watching them. He couldn't see what it was, but a life of cautious vigilance left him with a sense of knowing when eyes were on him. Whether it was the sullen, pitiful eyes of the villagers or the malicious omniscience of those cursed trees, he *knew*.

He drew the blade and walked slowly into the woods. Behind him, the fishers must have been watching intently as no sounds of breaking water from their nets could be heard. Black blood oozed from the trees. He sneered at the cursed sap and kept his distance. A great many of the trees here were tied with the tell-tale ropes. The weight of the eyes on him was heavy. He was prepared to cut down every tree here to find them. It caused the hair on his neck to prickle and the cool sweats he had been experiencing at night to return. Suddenly, he felt surrounded. It was as though the whole forest were looking down on him in spite.

A bit of motion out of the corner of his eye caused him to turn violently and bring his blade down hard. A sharp squeal accompanied the splatter of blood as two halves of a duskrat flew apart.

Laughter came from the lakeshore as the fishers observed what happened. "Ratslayer!" One of them called. "You've earned your keep, sir!" Bellowed another.

Breathing heavily, Fang looked about the thick gathering of trees. The feeling had dissipated. It burned away in his rising embarrassment and confusion. His head was a fog and the braying of the fishers was like buzzing flies in his consciousness. He sheathed the sword sharply and walked back over to them. They were content to ignore him while they cast their nets back and forth in futility. Fang stayed more out of a desire to observe the woods than to keep watch over them.

A few hours later, one of the fishers began shouting abruptly. He hooted and bellowed causing Fang to grip his sword tightly. He turned, prepared to unsheathe it when the other fishers joined in and he saw they were smiling. The net was drawn through the shallows with water lashing about wildly. They'd actually caught something.

The fishers gathered around the net like it was a precious treasure. Fang grabbed the nearest by the shoulder and pulled him back.

"Clear out!" Fang shouted. Who knew what the fools could've pulled from out of the Stillwater. He needed to ensure their safety first. They were so thrilled by the haul that they moved out of the way with little resistance and not a sideways glance at him.

Fang turned a few of the fish over with the edge of his blade. They were fish, no more and no less. That disturbed him more than if they had been some sort of twisted amalgam. Silver-scaled with blue backs, they were nothing if not normal. Fang sheathed his blade.

One of the fishers elbowed him. "No fiendish duskrats, here, watchman! Just fish; whole, honest fucking fish!"

The trip back to the village was alight with joyous conversation and talks of grilled fish, spit fish, and fish stew. The fishers, for all their past uselessness, had hope for future catches. Fang had to give them that. It was the first catch since the founding of their little garbage ditch. It proved that something lived in the water that wouldn't kill them.

Upon their arrival, the fishers were greeted with smiles and cheers from the others. Fang walked past them all with no love shared or lost. Once he made his way from the rabble he heard the unmistakable sound of vomiting. He followed the sound to the back of the tanner's hut. There he found a young man doubled over on his knees and a young woman gently holding his shoulders.

"Grayce?" Fang said. He noticed the straight blonde hair of the Keeper's daughter in a long single braid. She was in the cloth pants she favored despite the urgings of her father to wear something more ladylike.

Grayce looked at him and gave a weak smile. Unlike Fang, the villagers took a liking to her. "He drank straight-water."

Fang groaned. The boy had to be at least seventeen. He knew by now you only drank water that's been boiled, never straight from the Stillwater. The only water here was from the tepid lake, and the only streams for miles originated from it. Many boiled their own water, but pots and pans were scarce and small. The water shop, however, provided purified, boiled water in larger quantities and it was freely given, which begged the question, "Where and why did you drink straight-water, you idiot?"

The young man dry-heaved for a moment, his stomach spent. "This morning... out in the fields. It was just a sip... a handful." He said miserably.

"A sip is going to cost you a painful day or more." Fang shook his head and looked to Grayce. "I'll have Heldings help you to the edge of town and bring you a cot and blanket. He'll have to dig a hole. A deep one. Your stomach and bowels are going to be busy for a while."

The boy groaned and dry-heaved again. Grayce stood and crossed her arms. She continued to look at the young man with a mix of pity and irritation. "I'll take care of him. No need to get the apothecary involved."

Fang nodded. "Make sure to get him extra water from the water shop. He'll need the fluids."

"Gods help him if he took more than a sip."

"He'll live. He won't want to, but he'll live."

Fang put a hand on her shoulder, in thanks. Grayce was the only person in the village, besides the Keeper, who seemed to appreciate his presence.

Fang left them to their business. A goose caught yesterday, fish today, and a trained farmer's apprentice drinks straight-water. Oddities abounded, so he half expected someone to have burned veined wood next.

He walked past the remaining drystone and daub houses until he came to one fortified with actual mortar. A smokeless chimney was built into the side and a door fashioned of clean wood was fastened to iron hinges, providing a front door. The Keeper of Lines didn't ask for these luxuries, but the villagers gave them to him readily. His presence was a semblance of authority, order, and normalcy. This was just as vital to keeping the people alive as clean water and food.

"Come in, Fang."

His elderly voice was still strong, but the years made it crack like a falling oak. It was enough to carry through the open windows. Fang entered to see him sitting by a lit candle writing in the massive tome that was the Book of Lines.

The village was small, and new blood was a scarce thing. The rare traveler that came through didn't often stop to barter let alone join their haggard ranks. The Keeper was not just the elder or the leader, but the sole man responsible for keeping the bloodlines as pure as possible. Marriage was not only undesirable but impractical. Men and women were paired by the Keeper so that inbreeding was avoided; for the time being, at least.

Sitting across from the Keeper, Fang saw the upside-down clusters of names and the colored dots below them that designated their lineage and skills: blue, green, yellow, black, brown —a lot of brown, teal, purple, white... only one color was missing. The keeper flipped a few pages back until he came to the page he was looking for. There, Fang saw that rare and missing hue. Under his own name, the Sword-bearer saw the multitude of red dots smattered under his name.

"Like blood on the page," Fang mumbled to himself.

The Keeper looked up to him. "You'll have to speak up. I'm old, you know."

Fang took a breath and nodded. "Nothing. Talking to myself."

"Mental illness. That could get you a few purple ones." The Keeper smiled. Fang did not.

"The most colorful thing about this place is that book of yours."

The comment seemed to catch the Keeper off guard. He was always world-weary, but now he looked sullen and sad. He stood and walked over to the meager row of books on one of his shelves and traced some of the letterings with a bony, claw-like finger. Fang didn't know what they said; that was the Keeper's work.

"I've read these so many times. Histories and thoughts from all those that came before us." He turned to Fang and smiled weakly. "It wasn't always like this, you know; suffering day in and out. True, men worked hard but there was happiness as well. The world wasn't reduced to half-rotten vegetables, tainted woods, and sick water."

"Among other things." Fang thought with a chill.

The Keeper nodded and stared out the window momentarily. "Those days are gone; hope is behind us. Magic has betrayed us."

"I've heard stories of my own, Keeper. I was told many times what happened to the old town. The things that crawled out of the earth. Those days are not gone. Those things are also behind us, and may not stay there. Magic hasn't been spoken of for decades. I still have this," Fang lifted the blade partially out of its scabbard, "which won't be enough. If you know any magic now would be a good time to tell me."

The old man shrugged. "I know nothing of magic. Our village wizard and his apprentice were killed by those damned things from below. They helped us escape, but—"

"I know the stories," Fang sighed. The old man always found a way to reminisce about lost and broken things—especially magic. "I ran into Grayce today. She was helping a farmer's apprentice earlier. You might send her to Helding's and get her started as an apothecary."

"Yes. Grayce is quite adept at keeping my ink pots full, but she's going to need a real profession soon; no matter how much she thinks otherwise."

"If not Helding's, you could always give her a net."

He waved dismissively. Fang was not known for a sense of humor, and the Keeper knew him well enough to see that he was trying to goad a response from the old man.

"She's more talented than that," the Keeper scoffed. "I threatened her with such already. She should have had a path set for her years ago. She's well beyond the age for having been appointed as an apprentice. She's a grown woman for gods' sake."

"The village likes her. Perhaps she should apprentice under you."

An old, wrinkled hand waved the idea away. "I already have Ansel. That young man is apprentice enough. She's too restless for these books anyway."

They both regarded the shelves of books and scrolls that lay throughout the otherwise empty room. The Keeper was one of the few in the village who had a home with multiple quarters within its walls. His study, being where he accomplished his work, was the largest.

The old Keeper coughed dryly into one hand. "I read

through these pages every day and into the night, especially the Book of Lines." He caressed the massive leather cover. "It's become all I know. It's everything I can do to help Ansel remember it all."

"He's sharp. He'll serve you well."

"He may. He's a good boy." The Keeper pursed his lips. His old eyes lifted to Fang and suddenly he looked wearier; if such a thing was possible.

"I hear you haven't partaken of the good fortune that's come to us lately."

"The goose and the fish?" Fang shrugged. "I don't trust it. How often have we heard noise from the Stillwater and yet caught nothing? And, suddenly, we have a large catch?"

"And the goose? That's a lot of stew and a good meal."

Fang shook his head, "I don't like the meat."

"Horseshit."

He leaned back in exasperation. "Don't concern yourself with me. You know I'll not take anything from them that I don't have to."

"You despise them."

"They despise *me*."

The Keeper closed the large tome. "They envy you. Every moment they strive through mud and shit and pain to see another day. They are feeble and weak; children are lucky to live a decade any more. But you... you are strong and healthy. You carry the only sword left in our little home. I refuse to let the smith melt it down because I will not have us entirely defenseless. I need you fed and ready to fight."

Fang walked to the window and looked out among the homes and gathering people. There were many smiling faces for once. Maggy's place was surrounded by people sharing in the goose stew and cooked fish. It was a relief for them all to have food that one could genuinely enjoy.

"They may be right." Fang pondered. "What if we escaped it all? What if we found such a forsaken place that even monsters refuse to tread here? I've run off the last of the wolgs. I've seen no sign of them for years, now."

"And if they come back? If some other horror from the bowels of the world should crawl to the surface again?"

Fang gripped his sword tightly again. "One man with one sword isn't going to do much against them. Neither is a small number of bone-tipped arrows."

It was quiet for a moment. The Keeper's voice was cold when he responded, which was enough to make the hair on Fang's arms prickle.

"The sword isn't for the monsters. It never was, Fang."

Fang turned and looked at him. His eyes were downcast. His hands were clasped firmly together.

"You can't mean—"

The old man remained silent. Fang turned back to the window.

"I'm no protector. I'm an executioner," Fang growled, his face burning in the heat of the epiphany.

"Fang—"

"I should've known. I was a damn fool for not realizing it sooner. I wonder if they've figured it out as well."

"It may not be soon, or ever, but if those things come here... if something worse comes here, I will not let our people suffer that way. My daughter; never. Do you hear me? This conversation would have to happen sooner or later. I can feel the age in my bones. I may not have much longer to do it."

"You'd just leave it to me to kill them all." Fang listened to the sounds of laughter from the crowd. They hated him for what he was. The Keeper was right about all of it. They hated him for bearing a weapon they couldn't possibly have understood the use for. Perhaps they were unaware of why the Keeper had kept the 'Sword-bearer' around. Possibly, the old man wanted them to hate him and vice versa so that his duty would be easier when the time came.

He couldn't decide if the Keeper of Lines was brilliant or a bastard. He was probably both.

"There's another reason I wanted to see you today." The Keeper finally said, breaking the silence.

"I'm listening."

"I found a solution to two problems. Grayce needs to find a purpose in life, in this village. You won't live forever, and if we're to stay here for some time, you'll need an apprentice of your own."

"I'm sure Grayce would be very happy about that."

The Keeper was rubbing his temples. "Are you being sarcastic? I find it hard to tell."

Fang looked back out the window. "No, actually, I'm not."

"Think about it, Fang."

The Keeper requested the remainder of the evening to himself. His age left him little strength for such difficult conversations. Fang found that he, too, could use some time alone.

He walked to the stable where their remaining horses rested. They only had a handful of breeding pairs left, so they were accounted for daily and used sparingly. One of them was missing. Fang glanced around, but he knew that Grayce had taken it. She often left the village on outings with a fast, black stallion she'd grown fond of. Her father being the Keeper and she being a favorite of the village, it was often ignored. It also reminded Fang of what the Keeper had said.

*Grayce keeps my ink pots quite full.*

He surveyed the bleak landscape. Everything within eyesight was not something he would call colorful, and the Book of Lines was dotted with vibrant colors. He would make a point to ask Grayce about her sources upon her return.

IT WOULD BE a ride southeast today. After helping the farmer's apprentice, her time would be cut short. Grayce had to urge the sleek black horse ever onward to reach the glens on the outskirts of the Blackwood. Their location was something she kept to herself. She felt a pang of guilt over such a thing, but nothing of any real use could be found here that would make the trip worthwhile. It would be several hours ride more to reach any clean wood without the poisonous taint of the blackvein. The lichens and berries here were inedible, as well. Mostly, she just liked having a place to go where she could be alone.

She always felt odd wanting to be alone. They, as a people, were as alone as one could get according to her father. Before she was born, when the earth opened and the fiends within took their lands and lives, they lived in richer fields neighboring towns. When they fled, they found the most remote location they could.

She rode into a clearing and found one of her best locations. Near the mountains, rocky outcroppings sprung up around a swath of flat masses of stone that cut through the trees. A dribbling creek ran in thin sheets over the rock's smooth surface. It wasn't enough to efficiently provide water of any sort, but it was fed from another, cleaner source and allowed a layer of the lichens and vines to grow.

When Grayce first discovered this location, her father sent several scouting teams to try and find the source of the clean water. None of them returned. Having lost too many horses and men, her Father called off the searches and added another apprentice to the master of the Water Shop. This kept with what she had come to call her father's unspoken motto, "Safe and Unhappy."

She sat down by a thick patch of the lichen and opened her

leather satchel. Inside was all she needed to gather and produce her father's precious inks for his book. A stone mortar and pestle from the apothecary, copper inkpots of various small sizes tied shut with string—courtesy of the smith's wife, a small sharp knife from the smith himself, and various powders and solutions to strengthen the hues and lengthen their usage.

She started with the brightest green of the lichen, mixing it with a touch of water and grinding it to a smooth paste. This color was simple enough. She continued with this until she had sufficiently filled the inkpot and tied it firmly shut. She moved on to some moss that was a dull grayish brown. This would have to suffice until she found something that would make a better, earthier brown. She moved along with each color that she needed to replenish until she came to her favorite.

The inedible berries were a striking red when mixed and ground. She opened the small pot, the tiniest among them, and washed out the blob of unused, congealed ink. She sometimes wondered why she would bother with replacing it, but she so enjoyed the color that she didn't mind refilling it as needed. When finished, she rinsed out her mortar and watched the vibrant red run in streaks over the wet stone. This was why she kept the place to herself. It was a touch of beauty in their drab world.

Once her satchel was strapped back onto the horse she took him by the reins and walked into the woods. Father only needed a few of them replenished so she had spare time before needing to return. She would relish this as her responsibility for the village, but it simply wasn't possible. It was too much of a luxury when necessities were already scarce.

Grayce walked among the trees until she found another clearing. The trees surrounding the glade were different. The oaks of the Blackwood were broader, but here the trees had a more graceful look about them. They were tall... very tall. She remembered a picture of these that her father had shown her. They were special, somehow.

If they were so special, she wondered, why were they all dead? No leaves had grown on these brittle branches for some time. Even shriveled, though, she still saw where they could once have been beautiful, like an old statue that had cracked and faded but the memory of its extravagance was made clear in the minds of onlookers.

Aldyrs. That's what they were. She remembered her father called them aldyrs. They didn't appear any different from other trees, but her father said they were sacred in generations past. She reached out to touch one but stopped short.

"Idiot." She cursed herself out loud. Just because it was a different kind of tree didn't make it any less dangerous.

She'd never ventured far into this region before, so it didn't surprise her to find something new. Calling it new, however, was a poor choice of words.

Outside the cluster of aldyrs, a cabin stood decrepit and rotting among the thick trunks of felled trees belonging to species she was more familiar with. Tall grasses grew around it, and the old thatching had collapsed and left holes in the roof. She walked by the felled trunks and saw that the wood looked clean. Her heart jumped. Could she have found a copse of clean lumber in the Blackwood? If so, there could be more.

She had reached out to touch it when she jerked her hand back. There, in between the rings of the tree were thin waves of dried black sap. When she looked closely she could see the black striations in the outer layers of the trunk. No, these trees, too, were affected by the blackvein; but oddly, not nearly as much as most others.

The blackvein was more than a nuisance. No one knew the cause, but it was present in most trees in this region and thus earned the forest around their home its dubious name. Their woodcutters earned a hard reward for their labor. Trees had to be cut to see if blackvein had infested it. If so, the tree was marked with a rope to designate it as untouchable. Even those that appeared clean could have the blackvein waiting deep within, in the heart of the tree.

Having the black sap touch one's skin was bad enough. It would cause a rash at first, and then blisters would form and they hurt something terrible. Days of treatments from the apothecary would be needed to make it disappear. Burning the wood was worse. The first to try were a few trappers who made camp instead of returning to the village. They burned veined wood and the smoke from the smoldering infestation got into their lungs. They were found several days later with blood seeping from their nose and mouths. Those that even inhaled some of the wispy remains of their fire were laid out for weeks with a racking cough and continued to wheeze with every breath thereafter.

These trees showed the vein thinner but deeper into the heartwood. They suffered from the blight long before others. The trees around the clearing were otherwise large and their trunks thick. They blocked much of the sunlight so that it was difficult to see when she neared the cabin.

Nearing the square structure of rotting timbers, she felt a weight upon her chest. It sent a chill through her and caused her to hesitate. Her footsteps ceased and she looked about the silent grove. She was accustomed to stillness and silence, but this smacked of something sinister.

"It's a cabin," she said aloud, "a fucking cabin."

Fear angered her, and she gripped onto that familiar warmth. She used it as an anchor to pull her steps forward. With its hold upon her lessened, she made her way to a dry, rotted door that nearly fell off its hinges when she opened it.

Inside it was quiet and dark. It smelled of dust and age, and the air was dry. She saw an oil lantern on a rickety table and smiled at her fortune. Only a handful of them were available in their village. She would bring this with her when she left. She tested the wick and to her delight, it held a soft yellow light. Some of the oil yet remained.

She looked about with the lantern and noted the eerie shadows cast upon the walls by the decayed and collapsed furnishings. This building must have existed before the world fell. The furniture and shelving were made from wood not sick with blackvein. It was also designed with rustic beauty and not out of simple utility. There was a rug, once colorful, now all but rotted away.

A shelf of books lay in disarray. Her father taught her to read, so she could just make out a number of the volumes. Books on the animals of Alda and the old kingdoms long destroyed were also among those her father had in their home. She found one about mythologies that were new to her. She opened it and carefully turned through the pages. They were barely legible and the pages were brittle, but she could still read them. Most of the stories were ones her father had told her before, so she continued past them. When she reached one page, however, she pulled her hand back. Someone had written large letters across the length of both pages:

*GET IT OUT.*

Grayce looked through the remainder of the books and saw the words written again at sporadic intervals. She put it away and looked through other volumes. Coming upon one title, "A Summation of Monsters and Mythical Beasts," she found her curiosity piqued again. She looked through the book and its brief descriptions of myriad creatures. Simple illustrations were drawn next to each description. She came to the entry for the banshee and was unable to read anything for the copious scratching of a single phrase across the page over and over again: '*NOT THE MOTHER.*'

She found nothing else unusual until she came to the pages for wolves. Again, they were filled with hastily scrawled writing. This time, the word '*NO*' was written in every available space on the pages. Another entry with the ominous inscriptions was the subsection on wolgs. The word '*WRONG*' was scrawled across the entire page. Several torn sections of the page indicated where the writer appeared to have stabbed the pen into the book.

After returning the book to its shelf and preparing to leave this ill place, Grayce saw something that, due to the initial darkness upon entering, she had grossly overlooked. She shouted and jumped back involuntarily, nearly crashing into the bookshelf. The skeletal remains of a person were slumped over a desk in the far corner of the room.

She approached slowly and saw the tattered remains of their clothing hanging from the pale bones. This person had been dead for a very long time. Her eyes first went to the skull. It was resting on top of something, and though she desperately wanted to know what it was she was also hesitant in moving the remains. The skull was lying on its side. From where she was standing it gave the appearance of grinning at her in mockery of her fear.

She firmly but gently gripped the base of the skull with two hands and lifted it. It seemed to not want to move at first but eventually began to give. It occurred to her that whatever was on the table was protruding into the skull. No sooner had she seen the small statue stuck in the skull that it dropped heavily onto the table. The noise made her jump and the skull fell from her hands and broke upon the floor.

She picked up the statue and held it up to the lantern to inspect. It was surprisingly heavy but had other properties that could not be seen or felt with a normal touch. It felt... wrong. Holding it gave her the feeling of being reviled, like she had trespassed upon some ancient sacred grounds. She placed it back on the table and reflexively wiped her hands on her clothes. She placed the lamp on the table next to the object so she could inspect it without touching the thing.

It was made of smooth, gray stone that reflected some of the light. A humanoid figure, what appeared to be a woman, leaned seductively against a stone obelisk with one arm held up to caress the stone above her head. The other arm was placed on the head of some creature sitting obediently at her feet. A second creature was lying down around the woman's feet with its head lifted attentively. The creatures looked frighteningly familiar. They looked like wolgs, but larger. Their chitinous growths were not only about their shoulders and flanks but their heads as well, and they had an additional pair of eyes, six total, set above the others, not unlike a spider.

The figure itself was a twisted caricature of the female form. It was slender, muscular, and nude. Its breasts were full, as a new mother's would be, except there were eight of them. They lined the front of her body like the teats of a wild beast. Its fingers were long and sharp. The hair upon its head fell in thick clumps about its shoulders. Its face was hideous to behold; the eyes were too large and devoid of any detail. The mouth, far too wide for its face, was open in a silent scream. Sharp teeth lined the gaping maw and its vaguely human visage stared forward in a shouting, glaring rage.

As Grayce stared at the horrid obelisk, she felt herself being drawn into that hideous face. The demon-wolgs seemed to smile as she saw the gaping maw grow and her mind began to list forward. She felt off-balance but unable to move. A ringing developed in her ears and she became nauseous. The leering wolgs and their vicious master encompassed her vision. The ringing melded into a prolonged, high-pitched scream.

Grayce grasped upon the last mote of her sanity and swept the table clean, hurling the statue and the table's contents to the floor. She shouted and covered her ears, which now rang in a more natural sense. She sniffed and touched her nose. When she pulled her fingers away they were tinged red with blood.

*"What are you—"* Grayce thought.

She dared not looked upon the malicious object again, but she did see several pages on the floor next to it. She reached down to pick them up when she felt a sharp pain and jerked her hand back with a shout. A thin line of red marked the tips of two of her fingers. When she moved the pages, she saw a sword laying underneath a pile of yet more books. She found its grip. It was smaller than Fang's and had small patches of rust along one edge, but otherwise appeared to be usable. She smiled and looked about for... what did Fang call it once?

*A sheath, yes.*

After a moment she saw what she was looking for. It was made of leather and wood and fit the blade perfectly. An old weapon from an old world; she put it aside as she grabbed some papers laying next to it. Grayce saw that they had been hastily written on. Most of the writing was quite illegible. Some of it could be made out:

*"The Mother calls... I cannot listen. I will not listen... yet I hear it still. The nightmares come in my waking hours now. The Mother calls to me. Night and day, but at night much worse. Howls and screams and wails and shrieks and moans... shouting at my soul... The Mother calls... silence, sweet silence... silence the screams..."*

. . .

THE WRITING BECAME LITTLE MORE than scribble and indecipherable gibberish. Grayce dropped the pages. She felt like the walls were shrinking in this dark, unnatural place. She stepped outside where even the stale air was a welcome relief from the inside of the cabin. What was this place and what was that thing? She waited for her thoughts to collect themselves and went for her horse. She tried to walk him to the cabin but the creature wouldn't enter the grove. He tugged at first and then outright refused to enter once they reached the clearing.

She left the stallion where it remained and approached the cabin door. She took a deep breath and entered again. She brought a pack with her and quickly stuffed the obelisk and papers into it. If anyone could venture to explain this, it would be her father. She took her findings, including the blade, and left the horrible place behind. When she approached her horse again the creature whickered nervously. When she tried to attach the pack, the animal reared and whinnied in fright.

Grayce decided to carry the pack and walk her horse back as far as they could go. When nightfall was approaching she stroked the animal's muzzle and calmed it as best she could in order to get the pack strapped down. The stallion could smell something in the air. It whickered nervously and was anxious to be back at the relative safety of the stable.

When she arrived back at the village there was but a sliver of light left along the sky. The lantern helped light her way, but the village was soon easily spotted. A cluster of lit torches and lanterns created a bright patch on the north edge of the wall. Something had happened.

She kicked the horse into a gallop and saw a number of heads turn when she closed in on the crowd. Their voices were harsh and quiet by this point, but the anger on their faces was easy to see. She noticed the thick robes and gray hair of her father in the middle of them. She also saw Fang standing next to the Keeper, near a head taller than the old man.

She also noticed that he was bloodied all about his chest and arms. She hopped down from the stallion and ran over to them. Her father was talking brusquely with Old Kar, the lead trapper, when he saw her approach.

"Grayce, where have you been?" He said as he grabbed her in a fierce hug.

"Gathering for your inks. What happened here?" She looked at Fang and saw the fierce reflection in his eyes. He'd been fighting. He always had that look when he'd been in a fight, but the last time he'd looked like that was when the wolgs were still menacing the village. She found herself looking down at his feet and saw a large sack soaked through with blood.

"Oh," she whispered.

"We lost a trapper," Fang said gruffly. "Marl."

"You lost a trapper!" Old Kar shouted. He pointed a finger at Fang. "What do we feed you for, Sword-bearer, if you don't keep us safe while we work?"

His accusation stung even Grayce. Fang looked at him in a manner that, coupled with his being covered in blood, sent a chill down her spine.

"Had he listened to me he would be alive. I told you this already."

"Bah!" Old Kar scoffed. "You let one of us die, Fang! Killed the wolgs? Scared them off maybe and now they're back and they're thirsting for blood!"

The shouts from the crowd were unanimous with the lead trapper. Fang shook his head.

"Wolgs can think!" Shouted a voice from the crowd.

"They *know*!" said another. "They've come for blood!"

Many others joined in and soon they were shouting amongst themselves as much as at Fang. He looked at the Keeper and said he was going to wash and that, come morning, he would be hunting. The Keeper nodded solemnly and Fang left, shouldering his way past the angry village-folk.

Before he could address them, Grayce leaned forward to speak to her father. Not wanting to pull him from the irate crowd and draw more attention, she told him she needed to talk to him later before he slept. She stressed its importance and ran to grab the pack from the horse. She grabbed the blade as well but hid it as best she could.

She ran after Fang, trying to catch up to him as he stalked away hurriedly from the crowd. When they were safely away from prying eyes, Grayce called out to him.

"Fang? Fang!"

He turned and had the look of one truly startled, though his composure returned quickly. "Grayce. Where's your horse?"

She turned back to the flickering torchlights where the villagers still gathered.

*Damn.*

The black silhouette of the stallion was still there, patiently waiting to be tended. "I'll get to him. I need to show you something."

He didn't look at her; he only slowed his pace slightly. "I'm covered in wolg's blood and spent the better part of the evening being harangued by ingrates. Can it wait?"

"For as long as it takes to wash. Otherwise, no."

He sighed and looked at her. "I'll be home in a few minutes. Meet me there."

He did, indeed, return in a short time. The blood had been washed from him and he was wearing fresh clothes, for as much as something could be called clean anymore. He brought with him a pail of water and a bit of pig's fat soap from the provisioner. He sat down on his bed and began to attempt to wash the blood out of his clothes.

"What was it you had to show me?"

Grayce looked at the water as it turned several shades darker. "What happened?"

Fang stopped washing momentarily. He seemed to be pondering whether to answer her. "Marl was a fool. I told him I saw something in the brush among the trees. He waved it off and proceeded to insult me. I told him not to go anywhere and went to inspect. I was right. I saw its hackles rising above a patch of saplings. My sword was already drawn but I hesitated."

He stopped for a moment. Grayce was about to speak when he continued. "I killed them all, Grayce. I slaughtered every wolg I could find. There should have been none left out in those woods. I heard a scream and ran back to where I'd left Marl and he wasn't there. I heard something coming through the brush and I saw Marl running with his eyes as wide as I'd ever seen. He'd ignored my warning and wandered off. I ran for him but one of them jumped from the brush and took him to ground. It dragged him away screaming. I tried to catch them but the other one made a go for me. Its head is back with your father."

"Were you hurt?"

"Just scratches. The beasts were wilder than before. Or angrier, I couldn't tell. It leaped at me carelessly; I ran it through." Fang wrung out the pink water from his clothing and tried to scrub out what he could. "What did you want to show me?"

"I found something while I was out in the forest." Grayce set her pack down and Fang instantly noticed the small sword. She glanced at him and saw a confounded look on his face.

"Sweet mercy, where did you find that?" He reached out and she let him take it. It looked small in comparison to his blade, but it still fit well in his hands. He removed it from the sheath and twisted it in the lamplight. The metal was tarnished, but Fang looked impressed.

"Father will probably just want to melt it down," she said, sighing inwardly.

Fang sheathed the sword and handed it back to her. "I doubt it."

She crinkled her brows. "What do you mean?"

"You should speak to him."

"I plan on doing just that tonight."

Fang returned to washing his blood-stained clothes. "Was there anything else?"

Grayce regarded the pack and the vile obelisk that sat within. She should show her Father first. He would know best how to handle the thing and the ill presence it carried with it. The Keeper would also like to know before revealing such a thing to Fang.

"I found something else." She decided against hiding the obscene statue from Fang. "I'm not sure if you will even know what you're looking at. I surely didn't. But it's not right, Fang. It scares me and I would have left it where I found it if not for the creatures on it."

Fang looked at her strangely. He looked over to the pack and back to her with calm but piercing eyes that glittered in the lamplight.

"I'm surprised you haven't felt anything yet. I knew something was wrong the moment I stepped into the cabin where I found it."

"What are you talking about, Grayce? A cabin? Where? Was anyone living there?"

She opened the pack, but couldn't quite bring herself to remove the horrid statue yet. Her hands refused to grab it. "Nothing was living there. A skeleton was by the statue; but now that I think about it, there was no life at all in that place. No insects, no snakes, not even a spider web."

She jumped a little when she realized he came to stand next

to her. She was too enthralled with trying to gather the strength to remove the cold stone obelisk from its confines.

"Try not to look at it for too long."

Fang truly regarded her queerly then. She swallowed her mounting fear and pulled the object from her pack and set it on the bed. In the light of the weak lamp, it looked even more horrifying. She noticed, out of the corner of her eyes, Fang take a step back. She looked at him and he was covering his eyes with one hand and covering one of his ears with another.

"Fang, are you okay?"

She recalled the maddened writing: *The mother calls. I will not listen.* Fear grabbed her and she shook him by the shoulder. "Fang!"

Fang grabbed her wrist and looked at her. Growing up in this place would accustom one to fear; make one grow numb to most of its simple effects. The fear she saw in Fang's eyes reverberated in her. It was a fear more primal than those their little village learned to ignore. This was the fear of the rabbit in the snare. The terror of the rodent tucked away in its hovel with predators prowling the night. This was true, inspiring fear that drove sane creatures to flee.

Fang was sweating and breathing heavily. He grabbed a skin of purified water and drank until it flowed down his chin. She knew Fang to be a man unshakable. He was twelve years her elder and she looked to him as one that is iron-forged; that broke the terrors that came in the night for their village. Here, he was shaken and scared. It almost chilled her more than the hideous screaming thing carved in the stone beside her.

"What is it, Fang?"

He appeared to have calmed down and walked back over to his dirty clothes. He continued to wash them, but slowly and absentmindedly. "Those things look like wolgs, but—"

"But bigger," she completed for him. "And different. The

growths on them, the eyes. Do you know what the other thing is?"

Fang shuddered as the scream reverberated through his soul, calling to him from beyond his subconscious. "No. The Keeper would be the only one I could imagine would know something about that—that thing."

They gathered the statue and sword and packed them carefully. The villagers were still riled at Fang and the two of them wanted as little trouble as possible until they reached the home of the Keeper of Lines.

When they emerged from Fang's dwelling they found the streets relatively empty. Torches along the wall and scattered houses lit the streets with weak, flickering light. It appeared the Keeper had dispersed the crowd. Someone had also taken the stallion to the pens, as it no longer waited patiently where Grayce had unintentionally abandoned it.

They reached the Keeper's home to find light peeking under the flap covering the window to his study. Fang stepped ahead and knocked gently on the door. It was only moments before the Keeper answered, "Val, I told you it will have to—oh, Fang. Grayce? What are you both doing here so late?"

The Keeper looked at Fang with concern. "Shouldn't you be walking the night's rounds?" It was then he noticed the pack that they carried. His frown deepened. "What's this?"

"We need to talk," Fang said flatly.

The old man nodded and waved them inside. "Come, come."

They gathered in his study, swamped in darkness save for the flickering of a single candle. The Book of Lines was open. On the exposed page, the entries could be seen with their associated dots; a few names were scratched out with a single, neat line. A fresh line was added for the trapper that fell.

The Keeper closed the massive tome and motioned for them both to sit down. There was only one chair, and Fang pulled it back for Grayce to sit. He stood with arms crossed and his face stoic. Grayce set the pack on the table and opened it. Its contents, even in the candlelight, were plain to see.

"Good gods, a sword. How did you slip that past the villagers?" the Keeper gasped.

"I managed," Grayce replied. "It's the other thing I want to talk about first." She pulled the statue from the pack and placed it on the table, wiping her hands on her clothes afterward.

"Don't look at it for long, Keeper," Fang warned.

"Especially the female figure," Grayce added.

"Sweet gods," The Keeper breathed the words. He grabbed the statue despite Grayce's reflexive shout to leave it alone. Fang uncrossed his arms for a moment as though he was going to intervene, but the Keeper stopped them both with a raised hand.

"It's frightening, to say the least, but I feel you're…"

The Keeper's voice trailed off. He sat back heavily in his seat. He placed the statue on the table and covered it with a piece of cloth. He wiped the sweat from his brow and placed a shaking hand on the Book of Lines.

"Father—" Grayce began. Fang put a hand on her shoulder.

"Give him a moment."

His voice was brusque but compassionate.

The Keeper licked his dry lips. He ran his hand over the cover of the tome and then stood abruptly. He hefted the book and returned it to a special place among his others. He paused for a moment, seeming to think on something, and reached into his robes. He withdrew a small key and knelt next to the chest sitting by his bookshelf. Not many lockable chests remained in the village. They had little need for such things, but the Keeper always maintained one. The lock clicked and he opened the old wooden box as dust came wafting from it. He moved a few things aside and pulled a dust-covered book from within.

He returned to Grayce and Fang and sat down in front of them. After placing the book on the table, he simply stared at its cover for a moment. Grayce craned her neck to see what it said. She read it aloud for Fang.

"On Obscurum and Myth."

The Keeper continued to sit and ponder. Fang and Grayce regarded each other with concern. Both were unable to reconcile their thoughts. The Keeper ran his hands over the book while staring at the obscene statue, still obscured by the cloth.

"I've never seen anything like this before. It has some kind of dark power or malevolent aura about it."

The Keeper opened the book. "Things were so much better, once." He spoke in a low, sad voice that carried an ominous weight. "We weren't just a cobbled mass of fear and starvation. We were a people, a community. The sun was warm, the winters were cold; water was fit for drinking, and lakes ripe for fishing. Animals could be hunted. Trees could be felled and timber could build homes without threat of illness or death."

Grayce put a loving hand over her father's. "You've told me this before, father; the time before the sky bled."

"And the earth opened and the mountains wept." Fang continued.

The Keeper shook his head. "Your parents were young. I remember seeing your father pulled into the earth by the scorpion demons. Your mother—I took a different path from the others. They gathered more people and fled west or south. I took us east. I was not much older than a child myself, barely a young man, but I did the only thing I knew. I grabbed you, Fang, from where you fell. Still swaddled, you rolled out of your mother's arms as she screamed. She was pinned to the ground by the stinger from one of those beasts."

The Keeper was shaking. Tears welled in his eyes. He repressed as many memories as he could of what came from the earth that day. The sky turned red, the world shook, and unspeakable things came unto their world. The demons that assailed their village looked like massive scorpions, but they had the faces of men. They hissed and screamed as they took one person after another down to wherever they came from in the earth.

"I rallied those fleeing, screaming, terrified people and we ran. We ran as fast as we could. Desperation... such desperation. We had no choice but to rest when we found this place. Strong men were sent in all directions to find a more hospitable location to settle. Those in the north came back with news of nothing different other than a vast ocean. Those returning from the south spoke the same. The eastern scouts never returned. No one ever returned from the east. Going back was never an option. This is the best hope we had. We were safe, if not prosperous. And now... now you bring me this. What am I to do with this new horror?"

He opened the book and turned through multiple pages. He was looking for something specific. He must have found it, as he made an audible grumble and tapped the page.

"Not exactly what we appear to be dealing with, but similar. Perhaps it will help. Grayce, would you mind reading this for Fang? I need water."

"Yes, Father."

Grayce sat in the Keeper's place. He stood and gave Fang a gentle pat on the shoulder as he left to his chambers to get a drink. Grayce took a breath, not enjoying what she saw. The creature looked similar but lacked a quality the obelisk contained in great quantity. The creature depicted in the book looked dangerous and powerful, but not unutterably malevolent. The drawing beside the description was menacing but didn't invoke the reaction that came from the statue.

"What does it say?" Fang asked.

"It's an entry on Lilitu, Queen of the Banshees. According to this, she's not quite a goddess, but much more potent than a 'typical' banshee. Her screams are enough to kill a man where he stands. This isn't right, though. She doesn't look the same as the figure on the statue. And I don't know to describe this, but this image doesn't frighten me as the statue did. I don't feel—"

"Terrified. A fear that gets into your soul, and you can't explain." Fang finished.

Grayce looked at him. He was staring into nothing as if he was reliving some horrible moment.

"Yes," Grayce said softly. "When I found the statue in the cabin, several books had been defaced by the person who lived there. One entry was on a banshee. They were looking for the same answers we are. Whatever that was, it isn't this, either."

"Did they write anything useful?"

"No. It was mostly gibberish, except for something about 'the call of the mother'."

Fang turned white. "The Mother calls," he corrected.

"Yes, that's right," Grayce replied, a pin of fear pressing into her heart. "How do you know that?"

Fang was quiet. Finally, he said, "Get some sleep, Grayce. Tomorrow, we start your training."

"My training?"

"You're my apprentice. I'll teach you to use that weapon, and one day I'll give you mine."

He left the room without another word. He closed the door softly, and her father returned from the other room. Grayce looked up at him. The Keeper was staring in the direction Fang had left.

"Did you hear?" Grayce asked.

"I did. I approve."

She scoffed. "You approve of your daughter apprenticing to

be the next Sword-bearer? I wonder what the village will say to that."

He took a sip of his water. "They will say nothing. They like you, so they will tolerate it more than they did with poor Fang."

"He doesn't deserve such treatment," she said, adding emphasis to her father's feelings. "Why do you let them get away with their behavior?"

Her father held the cup close to his mouth. He only grunted some non-committal reply. Grayce continued flipping through the book. None of it was helpful. She turned the pages without reason, giving her hands something to do while her mind wandered. Then, she came upon a leaf of paper near the back pages.

Opening the aged, crisp document, she saw it was hand-written. It was not an original part of the book. Its letters were not hastily scrawled gibberish like what she had found in the cabin. This was something written by a scholarly hand and included in this book for academic purposes. She read it quickly, but its contents were easily discernable. It renewed a tentative dread in her.

"Father, look at this."

She handed the paper to the Keeper. He frowned; he didn't like discovering that he may not have known every page in every book as well as he thought.

"This was written by Jermiah Colwerth. He was old even before we fled the village."

"Who was he?"

"The town wizard. Not many wanted to hang around our dull little berg, but Jermiah liked the quiet. He was an odd one, but his apprentice was a good lass."

"What—" Grayce paused, gauging if her question was worth it. "What happened to them?"

"They both died holding off those monsters." The Keeper

said flatly. Perhaps so much talk of it tonight had begun to numb him. Grayce stood and gave her father his seat back. He sat with numerous cracks of bone and creaking of wood. In the candle-light, he read the content of the letter aloud;

*Within these pages are the beasts and creatures that prowl our world in darkness and light, in forests and mountains. Some appear humanoid while others are quite unlike anything a common man would recognize, even in his own nightmares.*

*But even these fantastical things can be quantified and correlated to some explainable emotion or sense. I believe there are others. Or 'Others', as their disposition warrants greater recognition.*

*They are the things that defy explanation, perhaps even percep-tion. We cannot understand them, and they possibly do not deign to understand us, no more than we care to understand the life's purpose of a single pebble. Among their conscious level, we may not even register as worthwhile sentience; perhaps even as living.*

*Our fragile, mortal minds would seek to reconcile Their being with something we can understand or explain: the masculine or femi-nine form, a bestial nature, debased 'natural' urges, or mayhap some social or psychological taboo. I fear, however, that when we seek to rationalize the inexplicable, we tempt recognition of Their fathomless dread. They may be insulted by it, or they may be drawn to it in yet another way we can fail to describe. Regardless, these are the Ones who dwell outside existence. They are not of our reality, or maybe They are the real and we the conceptual, seeing as we would be so easily ruined by Their presence.*

*I have witnessed a modicum of Their work. In my arcane work-ings, I stumbled upon something I could not have expected. I witnessed something that I could not have known. I thought at first I had stumbled upon the gods themselves. I realized that if it were just that, I would be a better man for it. What I gazed upon—and I use that term in the loosest sense, as I could not truly ascertain if I was* indeed using my own eyes or those of another consciousness; I was dreaming, I hope—was beyond any religious allegory.

I lost any manner of faith I had that day. I realized if the gods allowed such a place and such inhabitants to exist, it would only be to serve as a Great Nemesis. No deity would stand by while such abomination roamed in-between time and all things. What I feared, even more, is that perhaps These were the closest things to gods we had.

It didn't matter, in the end, as I became aware of something I never should have. They were numerous and horrible to behold. The stars would not be enough for them. Many did not notice the mote of humanity that had intruded on their plane. These other-things were great and small, but infinite all of them.

When I felt the heavy weight of recognition by one of those presences, I woke screaming. My apprentice, bless her, came running to my side. I recognized the morning light between the curtains of my window, but she informed me that I had been awake and speaking incoherently for over an hour. My waking mind required time to adjust to the sane world.

My dear apprentice kept her distance that day, and I believe she feared me. It took a number of days before she would speak to me again outside of her lessons. I saw, to my shame, the fearful gazes that the other townsfolk put to me. It has not changed much in the time since. I can see that I am no longer the same. That surreal journey undertaken in slumber has marked me; My mind no longer processes clearly. I find my thoughts wandering, trying to replicate those images I saw in the spaces between reality. Whenever I try, I cannot remember. It is only the fear, unshakable, unexplainable, that remains.

I leave this addendum for this particular tome as cautionary reading. Do not seek too much in the manner of the fantastical or the unknown. Do not quest so far for knowledge that you find yourself in forbidden territory. I now believe not all things are meant to be known, or even dwelt upon, for there are those Things, those Others, *that seem to be seeking us out, but unaware of us; we should greatly desire it remains that way.*

THE KEEPER calmly folded the old document and returned it to the book. Grayce recognized the look of worry on her father's face.

"What's wrong?" She asked.

"Jermiah was very withdrawn during those last months. Others were worried. They said he wasn't behaving like himself. I thought nothing of it."

"But now we know he found something."

"Stumbled upon it, rather."

Grayce thought for a moment. The statue was certainly not Lilitu, nor anything else in the massive tome of worldly creatures. It was the closest thing they could relate it to, but it was still different, something eldritch and outside conventional knowledge. However, Jermiah may have inadvertently encountered something similar in his dreams; if that's what they truly were.

"Father—" she began to ask a question but struggled for the words.

"Yes, dear?" he replied quietly, lost in his own thoughts.

It was a few moments before she could gather enough courage to ask the question. "Do you think Jermiah brought this upon us?"

The Keeper returned only silence. He drank the last of his water, placing the cup quietly on the table. He retired for the evening, placing a gentle hand on Grayce's shoulder. He never answered.

She left for her hovel. The night felt cooler than usual, just a kiss of cold compared to the tepid monotony. She fell into her cot and tried to force the stone-carved image of spider-eyed wolves and screaming mouths from her mind.

HER TRAINING HAD BEEN ongoing for a matter of days, but Fang could already see the potential in Grayce's swordplay. She was quicker than he had ever been but sloppy. A good, solid hit from Fang, and she was sent reeling, often losing her sword.

"If your blade is lost, so are you," he said.

She walked over to where the smaller sword, now polished and honed to a finer edge by the smith, lay in the limp grass. It looked like an artifact of the gods compared to the gray-green strands of the new world.

She took a deep breath to help relieve the exasperation. "Again."

Fang was drinking from his canteen. He corked it and tossed it to the ground. "You need a break."

"No. Again."

Fang smirked at her tenacity. Had she ever seen him smile before? Had he *ever* smiled before?

He adopted a two-handed stance. She perched on the balls of her feet. Her sword was smaller, so she couldn't try to overpower him. She had to outmaneuver the larger opponent. Grayce wondered if she was hesitating. They were using sharpened weapons, not the training swords Fang told her they once used.

"Never needed one; there was no one to train with. Besides, they would never waste the clean wood," he had told her. Instead, they trained with practice armor made from boiled duskrat leather. It was uncomfortable, it stank, and became brittle quickly, but it served its purpose. They wouldn't suffer any fatal wounds so long as they didn't try to run each other through.

They were both beginning to tire. Fang's breathing grew labored, and Grayce slowed down considerably. She needed to be in better shape, and he was getting old.

"How have you been sleeping?" she asked.

Her question caught Fang off guard. She nearly landed a blow to his back, but he spun out of the way.

"Good try. Underhanded, but effective."

She grimaced. "That's not what I was trying to do. You've been looking worse for the wear these past few days. I'm concerned."

"Don't be," he grunted, bearing his sword overhead and having it parried to the side. "Once I feel you're capable of surviving a hunt, we'll be off. I will sleep when we're done."

"I haven't been sleeping much either," Grayce persisted. "I can't get the image of that statue out of my mind."

"Neither can I. Stop, I need to rest."

They sat together on a large rock and drank deeply from their canteens. They'd both been provided 'new' equipment on orders from the Keeper. Even Grayce was not spared from a few scathing glances that day.

Fang wiped the sweat from his brow. "How is your father? We haven't spoken much since your training started."

"He's as well as can be. The letter from Jermiah affected him more than I thought."

"He knew him well?"

"To hear father talk, you would think he knew little more of him than most others in the old world. But his actions speak otherwise."

Fang's brow curled. "He never spoke of him before."

"Did he share everything with you?" she replied, finishing off a pull from the canteen. The water was warm and stale, but clean. Fang thought he heard a hint of sarcasm in her question. It brought back memories of an earlier conversation with the Keeper; his eyes dropped to his sword laying in the grass.

"Not everything, perhaps."

Grayce stared into the silent woods. Her father told her of how, once, birds used to sing in the trees. Cool winds would blow and the leaves would rustle a soft lullaby. She had seen birds on only the rarest of occasions, and always far away. Except once, recently, when a goose was slain for their consumption.

She remembered how sad she was. The creature looked so graceful. It didn't seem to belong to the world anymore, and Grayce wondered if the creature knew it. They felt the stirring of an unseen evil and fled where they could because they could fly. They could find a place that only their wings could show them. All those cursed to the ground were left to run from the lurking malevolence in every shadow.

"I want to hunt, Fang," she said suddenly, breaking the quiet.

"You will, soon."

"I need to now. It's something that I have to do."

Fang looked at her with concern. "It's the battle-rage, Grayce. You'll feel it every time after a fight. There's not much fighting to be had, so you'll learn to control it."

She knew it was more than that. It wasn't physical. It wasn't something in her blood that needed time to abate. It was in her heart, her spirit. Her father's disposition of late, the fiendish statue, the return of the wolgs, the meager home and life she had was being threatened. A creeping fear had settled over her ever since she found that rotted cabin, and it followed her home. It infected those around her, Fang and her father most of all, and suddenly the wolgs returned.

The wolgs; those wicked things that scorn nature. She was so happy when Fang said he had scourged them from the forest. They were native to the Blackwood, by all evidence, and thankfully so. Their extinction was cause for celebration. Now, with the discovery of an unwholesome effigy, they returned to stalk their village. The pressure had been increased on Fang and his new apprentice to extinguish their presence again.

"I want them dead, Fang," she said quietly. "I don't just want them extinct; I want their very memory erased. I want that statue destroyed and I want to *forget*. I never thought I'd see something that would make this life preferable to something else, but I wish I could go back and never find that horrible cabin."

He understood. Unfortunately, he knew too well that nothing could ever be taken back. There was no magic that could roll back decades of pain and destruction. The priests had prayed to benevolent gods for guidance and protection, but, if there was anything out there greater than themselves then it surely cared not for their well-being, if it was capable of caring at all.

"I don't know if that's possible, Grayce," he said quietly.

"You've killed them before. You can do it again. We can wipe them out together; you're not alone this time."

Fang shook his head softly. "You don't understand. The wolgs? Those can be killed, yes, but, where they come from—"

"They come from whatever twisted the world. We've seen them bleed, so we know they can die."

"But the statue," Fang pressed.

"Is just a statue. It's horrific and perverse, but I've been thinking about this. The creator of that thing was probably that body I found in the cabin. He was ill in the head, and we've let ourselves get worked up over this."

Fang breathed deeply. He sat up straight and stretched his weary muscles. He craned his head and looked at the darkening sky. The light of the stars seemed dimmer, and that felt oddly appropriate.

"No. It's much more than that."

"Would you care to explain?" she said, frustrated.

"Has your father ever told you of the old ways? The gods of our grandfathers?"

"Yes. He spoke about them frequently when I was younger. Trying to give me hope or comfort, I suppose. It never worked."

"He told you of how they used to be worshipped? They would have their own houses built, and statues and effigies constructed solely to honor and adore them?"

"Yes. Seems wasteful, but then again I hear so often of how those were times of plenty." She spoke the words bitterly as she ate some of the dried and salted duskrat meat.

"That statue looks like what I would imagine the ones built to worship the old gods did."

He grew silent for a moment, he hunched over and rested his elbows on his knees once more. Grayce continued to chew the pitiful food as quietly as she could, but was failing.

"You think that she-thing is a goddess?"

"I don't know. From what the Keeper said, no one truly knew what our gods looked like, either. We only have the words and texts of ancestors. I can only imagine what sort of person would picture that."

Grayce shuddered. She told herself many times that she had let fear get the best of her when she remembered her reactions to the strange obelisk. She would always have to remind herself once more.

"I've been thinking, also. I haven't slept well in months, maybe years. Lately, I haven't slept at all, so I've had a lot of time to consider these things."

Fang had to take a moment to consider them further. He was afraid to speak what was going through his mind; of putting to words the insane idea that had also made a horrible amount of sense the longer he dwelt upon it.

"I don't know if the depiction of the statue is real or just some grotesque form of art. Our fathers' fathers had a different way of life than we did. Perhaps they had ways about them that we'd rather not understand. It was their time that brought about all the destruction, after all."

"Fang, what are you trying to say?" Grayce interrupted, but she did so with patience and care. She could see he was struggling.

Fang licked his dry lips. Finally, he was able to connect his thoughts into something resembling reason. "I think if our ancestor's gods were real, perhaps they were young or weak. These other things; the woman-thing on the statue, the beasts that crawled from the ground and forced us here, maybe even whatever tore open the sky and broke the mountains that we hear about, maybe they're real. They're older than our gods, perhaps they've been the only ones that have ever existed. Maybe none of them existed, our gods, these other gods. Maybe they're something else entirely. Whoever made the statue was trying to put a face on something he didn't underst—"

A gentle hand touched Fang's own. Grayce saw that he was shaking and how his eyes grew haunted. At her touch, he ceased trembling and calmed slightly. Though, the unfamiliar touch of another person brought a different kind of discomfort for Fang.

"It's ok," she said. "Let's go back to the village. We'll talk to father and go from there."

Fang took a deep breath. He was embarrassed for many reasons. He was the Sword-bearer: stoic and unshakable. The grip that this unexplainable fear had on him was stretching him thin. Perhaps, speaking with the Keeper would help.

They took their few belongings and made the short walk back to those sad, short walls. Smoke from the usual fires was dissipating into the evening sky. The walk had been quiet, but not uncomfortable. Grayce would give him a comforting smile when he would look to her and try to think of something to say. Fang thought he might be able to offer some words of encouragement in return for her kindness. Unfortunately, he found none. She simply gave her smile, thin-lipped and genuine, and they walked on. He wanted better for her. She deserved more than this place; both she and her father. On rare occasions, he would feel pangs of guilt for not feeling the same way about the villagers in general, but these feelings seemed to only manifest for Grayce and the Keeper. They were the only positive emotions he seemed to know.

The village was going about its usual business. Their path to the Keeper led them by many folk who ignored Grayce and Fang alike. Their indifference meant nothing to Fang. However, he could tell that she was hurt by it. Unfortunately, he had finally found the manner in which he could repay her kindness.

"It will get better, in time," he said in a low voice.

She kept her eyes to the ground, not sulking, but refusing to let them see her hurting at their childish reactions.

"I'd never have thought they would be so..."

"Ungrateful?" Fang offered.

"No. I haven't earned any gratitude as a new Sword-bearer yet, but just the fact that I am one has drawn their ire. I don't understand."

Fang looked around. At one point he would have answered, "Neither do I." Then he remembered his discussion with the Keeper.

The Keeper's dwelling was dark. No candle was lit within, which was unusual. The Keeper was always reading or working in his book. Fang and Grayce both thought little of it and felt hesitant to disrupt him if he happened to have gone to bed early. However, they greatly desired to speak with him. Fang rapped on his door sharply, still regretting the intrusion, but hoping the sharp noise would wake him.

When no answer came, Grayce approached one of the windows with their simple cloth covers.

"Father?" she called out. Still no response. She called out again, then moved one of the coverings aside. She looked at Fang and shrugged her shoulders.

They opened the door slowly, hearing it creak on old hinges. It was as quiet as it was dark. Once inside, they could see a faint glow coming from the bed-chamber. Grayce looked at Fang and nodded. She would wake him. Fang watched her stop at the entrance to the chamber. She stood there for several moments, unmoving. It became disconcerting, and Fang was suddenly gripped with panic.

"Grayce?" he called out. When she didn't answer, he walked quickly over to her.

His eyes were drawn to her first, and it spared him the sight that caused her frozen stature. He saw tears falling freely down her face, but otherwise, she simply stared. Her lips did not so much as quiver, and her body remained as still as the dead. It shook Fang to see her in such a manner, and then he saw what had caused it.

The Keeper's feet hung a few feet above the ground, swaying ever so gently. The rope he used was old, but it served its purpose. Fang approached him slowly and saw his skin had grown pale and cold. Veins were raised along his weary face, and his eyes were bloodshot and horrible to behold. It was a cruel mockery of the man he knew. He must have been here for several hours. There was no saving him, and Grayce knew this, as well.

He was gone.

"Grayce," Fang began, but what could he say? Even he was wracked with pain at the loss of his friend. Truly, the loss of the only father he had. He let his words end there.

The soft light resulted from a single candle lit on a small

desk next to the Keeper's bed. A few pieces of vellum, the Keeper's private reserve, were stacked on the desk. A single page was separated with a few lines scratched into it from a small inkwell. Fang picked up the page and stared at it in frustration. He wished he could read it himself before giving it to Grayce, but he knew the Keeper wouldn't say anything he wouldn't want Grayce to know. She was one of only three people in the village who could read. She was also the most likely, other than Fang, to find him.

*Damn you, old man.*

Grayce came to stand beside him. "Let me read it."

Fang handed the page to her wordlessly. He didn't even look at her.

"My dearest daughter," Grayce began to read aloud, so Fang could know the Keeper's final words, "and my dearest friend, I know you will not forgive me for this. I will never forgive myself, either. I am weak. I cannot abide any longer this world and its damnations. I led this ragged lot of people here, far from our home, to land less cursed. Though, not free from curses. When I saw that statue and heard the wailing in my soul, I knew that we would never be free from whatever has cast itself upon our world. I can no longer bear to see it come further undone. I am leaving it behind for whatever else waits on the other side of the veil."

*You left us, you coward,* Fang thought as he listened. Grayce continued. Her stoic reading of the letter changed at the next lines. Her voice broke, and new tears came, but she continued.

"Grayce, I love you. My greatest regret and fear is that I leave you behind to this world I can no longer bear, but I hope that you find something better in it. I will not deign to hope. Please, just know that I love you."

The final lines were spoken in hesitation.

"Fang, friend, remember what we discussed."

She looked up from the letter quizzically at Fang. "What does he mean?"

Fang was silent. The Keeper never told her. He left it to Fang. *Gods damn you, you cowardly old fool.*

"It's—"

"What is it, Fang?" Grayce pressed.

"Grayce, I—your father…"

"Fang!" she shouted. He'd never heard her raise her voice before.

"Your father left me with a blade so that I could provide mercy to the village should the creatures find us."

Her eyes widened. She said nothing else: no curses or condemnations. She made no action towards him. She didn't hit him, or slap him, or push him away. She only stared.

"I don't believe you," she whispered.

"He just told me a few days ago."

"I don't believe you," she whispered again. It sounded as much like she was trying to convince herself as trying to besmirch Fang as a liar.

"An awfully stupid lie to make up now. What else could he have meant?"

She drew her weapon. Fang, for the first time that he can remember, stepped back.

"Grayce, what are you doing?" He put his hand on the hilt of his own blade. Then, just as quickly, he removed it. If she wanted to cut him down, he would let her. The Keeper wasn't the only one who wanted out of this life, but Fang would not take his own or someone he cared about. She would have to take the final swing.

The short sword clanged onto the ground. Grayce threw it aside; in disgust or surrender, she didn't know. It was likely both. "I don't know what to say. You and my father, you both lied to me."

"I lied about nothing. I wasn't going to tell you until you were ready," Fang countered.

"Ready for what?" Grayce shouted. "To slaughter all of them? Or were you going to go get yourself killed and leave that to me, too?"

"You know me better."

"I thought I did!" she accused. "I thought I knew my own father, and the man I knew would never have done *this*."

"Grayce—"

"Both of you—the two people closest to me—both of you lied. Father kept you around like some sort of attack dog? I thought you protected the village."

"I did!" Fang finally yelled back. "Every day, every night I patrolled alone for those bastards, every one of them! And they would rather spit on me for it? Your father didn't tell me why he really kept me around, let me be dogged by those haggard shits day after day, until just before you found that thing that killed him. Your father was a coward! I respected that man, I loved him. He was the only father I ever had, and I found out he was a fucking coward!"

It was exhilarating; letting go of all of that. He felt a pressure come off his chest; it was like he was breathing for the first time. Then he remembered who he was speaking to. He expected to feel the sting of her hand across his face or, knowing Grayce, the ball of her fist in his gut. Neither came.

She was silent, looking up at her father and his red, blood-filled eyes. His body remained there as they argued his intentions and his legacy. When she spoke, it was just above a whisper.

"You're right."

Fang's chest was heaving. The emotional exertion was more than any physical strain he knew. When she said that, however, his breath caught.

"He was a coward. He failed both of us."

Then, he began to feel regret. The weight of his words began to replace the weight on his chest that he had so gloriously removed. It felt oddly comfortable again.

"We all want to run away, Fang," she continued, "but we stayed. He abandoned us. You, me, the village, everything. I hope whatever waits for him is worth it."

Fang had a pit in his stomach. "I doubt it."

She rolled up the vellum and tossed it aside. They would have to inform the village and hope Ansel was prepared to take his place. It required both of them to cut him down, and Fang cursed him the whole way. As they regarded the dead in silence for a time, Fang thought how having the Sword-bearers informing the village of the Keeper's passing would be interesting indeed.

The people were in a fit when Fang and Grayce called them together and gave them the news. Grayce told them he had passed in his sleep. It was the only way to prevent further harm in the community. Any other reason—poisoning from black-vein, straight water, or even the suicide itself—would have caused nothing but blame and possibly violence.

Fang remembered his words to the Keeper about Grayce becoming his apprentice. It would have fit her just as well if not better than the next Sword-bearer. The turmoil that had over-taken their recent days had been hard on her, but they were making her harder. That would only be to her benefit.

The crowd wanted to see him. They wanted to look on their Keeper a final time. Ansel came forward to help calm the scared and belligerent mob. He puts his hands in the air, begging them to remain civil. The uproar turned to a low murmur, and the new Keeper turned to them.

"I'm sorry, Grayce. You have my condolences," he said sincerely.

Grayce gave him a weak smile, but no more.

"It does not surprise me to hear that the strain of your father's position finally claimed him. I wish I had longer to train, but the village will wait for no one."

"We'll survive, Ansel," Grayce said, with a noted lack of commitment. "We may not thrive, but we'll live."

Ansel hung his head. The weight of his newfound responsibility had, perhaps, become more real. Grayce was looking toward the lake, but there was an emptiness in her eyes. Fang simply stood with arms crossed, his unreadable demeanor having returned.

The new Keeper gave word that the burial would be held in the graveyard outside the town's walls immediately. Several hands were raised to volunteer to dig the grave. The Keeper was loved by most, if not all, of the villagers. He was unique among them all in that manner.

The grounds where the dead were interred lay several hundred feet outside the village walls. Genuine concern for the safety of the living is what first caused the makeshift cemetery to be located there. In the first days of their settlement of the Blackwood, they knew not what lurked in this new forest. If any creatures were drawn to the dead, they didn't want them wandering too near the village, as well. It was not often spoken aloud, but new-found superstitions and fears were also heavy motivators for the graves' location.

The hole was dug quickly. Several ready hands were present to take over when others grew tired. A cloth was placed over the old Keeper's body, a rare honor, and he was placed within the ground with great care. No icons, tombstones, or religious effigies marked the location of their dead. It was deemed futile by most involved. The Keeper, however, had a crude headstone fashioned by the smith. It was made of slag-ridden iron, but it was the gesture that was most important.

Despite a large number of village folk in attendance, it was eerily quiet. Ansel hung his head in solemn respect. He made every attempt to play his role, but he lacked the qualities that the old man had that made him a good leader. Grayce remained quiet and removed. She stared at the freshly turned earth, and her expression was impossible to read. Fang stared placidly into the woods. A soft breeze was blowing, and the limp leaves whispered sickly in the silence.

Fang almost swore he could hear the distant sound of howling: that subtle scream that haunted his nights and caused him to wake in a fatigued sweat. He suddenly realized just how tired he was. His eyes felt like stones, and his bones filled with lead. The Keeper. He didn't even know his real name. Or, rather, he didn't remember it. He had only ever called him Keeper for so long; this man who was a father to him.

Forgetting himself for a moment, Fang heard the rumbling of the villagers' return. It started as a murmur and built into a threatening wave. They must have seen the trepidation that hung about Fang, Grayce, and Ansel, because the fear and anger rolled from the crowd like a wave.

Much of the commentary revolved, surprisingly, around their new Keeper. Words such as 'boy' and 'unfit' were among the more subdued. Other, harsher, things were said about Ansel and, eventually, Fang. Soon, even Grayce became a target of their mockery.

"They're going to kill us!" cried someone from the crowd.

Fang reflexively looked for the source of the voice. His guilt over the grim duty placed upon him by the Keeper, or former Keeper, still weighed on his mind and conscience. It took several moments for him to realize that they were not referring to him, but the return of the wolgs.

"We're going to die!" cried a separate voice.

Ansel raised his hands again, "People, please!" he pleaded to them, "We have not one but two Sword-bearers, now! The wolgs are not long for this forest—"

"Lies!" "We've heard this before!"

The tide was turning angry. The waves of fear and hurtful words born of despair began to roll against the new Keeper and his Sword-bearers. Ansel attempted to shout over them and placate them with practiced words. He was not winning them over.

Fang stalked toward the crowd. They continued to shout and ignore him until he drew the sharp steel blade from its sheath. Gasps of disbelief rolled among the first rows of the villagers, and soon those behind them went quiet, as well.

Grayce, a sudden jolt of surprise gripping her gut, put her hand on her own smaller blade. She tensed for whatever the suddenly volatile Fang was prepared to do. The people constantly pushed him to his limits, and she feared he had passed a breaking point. After learning of her father's plans for the Sword-bearer, she expected the worst.

The crowd stared in disbelief as Fang sneered at them. He looked from left to right, his red, tired eyes likely mistaken to be glowing with hate at the filthy mass. Many of them looked to him in fear, some in outright terror. Mothers held their children close. Husbands sheltered their wives. Others glared at him, daring him to do what they expected him capable of all along.

When he spoke, his words were near a growl: feral, exhausted, and spent. Those in the front heard clearly, but he spoke almost more to himself than to the crowd. His words were soon passed on to those further back: "None of you are dying today."

The sword gleamed in the hazy sun. They all stepped aside like a parting pool of muddy water. The villagers made way for Fang in a display of fear and apprehension. There was not a sign of respect in their actions, not even in mockery. They expected him to lash out and cut any number of them down right there. Few had seen him display such outward aggression.

He returned to the village and packed food and clean water for several days. He needed nothing else for his journey. The villagers were still nowhere to be seen, likely avoiding the village for fear of crossing him. He was fine with that. He made his way out of the village and headed east, toward the recent encounter with the wolg.

Fang heard the rapid progression of footsteps behind him. They were distinctly human. He turned, expecting to see an angry father, mother, wife, or husband raising their hand to him. Instead, he saw Grayce come to meet his stride.

"What are you doing?" he asked.

"You're going to kill the wolgs," she replied, "I'm coming with you."

"You're not prepared for this. I don't know what I'm going to find out there; it may be wolgs, it may be worse. But I'm not coming back unless it's with blood on my hands."

She scoffed, "You'll change your mind if you find worse. You need me."

"They need you. Ansel is a good man, but he's weak. The village will eat him alive."

Grayce opened her mouth to protest, but then Fang suddenly stopped. He looked back at the village and then off toward the eastern mountain range. His brow creased in heavy thought.

"What is it?" Grayce asked, concern marring her voice.

"I've changed my mind. You can come," he said straightforwardly.

"Well, your permission is welcome," her sarcasm was apparent.

"I want you to take me to that cabin."

It was then that Grayce stopped. Fang turned to look at her. Her face had turned to stone.

"You know what I said about that place. I wish I had never gone there to begin with."

"But you did. Nothing is going to change that, or what has happened as a result. There may be something we can still learn from there."

"I am not going back there."

"That is where I'm going. I'm not just going to hunt wolgs. I want to know if I can discover something more. I will not continue this cycle. The cabin you found is the only other place we might learn."

He turned to see her still standing there, no fear present on her face, but unmoving.

"You wanted to come with me. Then do it."

She looked at him in a manner he hadn't seen since she discovered her father's secret about the Sword-bearer. She glared at him as she walked by toward the eastern range. This, he decided, was decidedly worse than that.

They walked until night fell. Grayce explained that she was on horseback when she first discovered the cursed grove. They had at least another day's walk ahead of them. Fang and Grayce built a fire, then portioned their food. The night was strangely cold. Having lived in such tepid environs their entire lives, it was both unsettling and uncomfortable for them.

Grayce was sitting close to the fire. "This cold, I've never felt anything like it."

"Neither have I," Fang replied through clenched teeth. It made him regret not bringing blankets, but never once had he experienced such conditions.

"It's the cabin," Grayce said as she stared into the flames.

Fang remained silent.

"I don't know how or why, but it has to be," she continued.

They sat in silence. Finally, Fang said, "I believe you."

"What?" she asked, watching her breath materialize in a fine mist.

"The cold, the grove, I believe all of it. I don't understand any of it, but I believe it."

He stared at the fire. For the first time, he felt a kinship with those who came before. Fire had cleaned their water and scared away the occasional animal, but it never warmed them. Though he thought he had remembered a cool night before, he never experienced cold. The night became something altogether different. The tepid weather threatened to drive them insane, but it was bliss compared to this bone-touching chill.

Grayce came to sit beside him. They moved closer to the fire and together, tried to ward off the chill and accompanying unease. Talk was futile. They were uncomfortable and unfamiliar with their situation. Fang was accustomed to working alone. Grayce was his apprentice and, though she learned quickly, still had much to study. For her, there was also the ever-looming thought of returning to the grove.

They spent their time in silence. Neither wanted to admit to their fear. Neither wanted to complain of the cold. They sat in misery, huddled next to one another for warmth, as they waited for the insipid sun. Fang had spent many sleepless nights waiting for the gray dawn, but this was the longest night in memory.

For Grayce, time seemed to stop. The fire cracked and spat weakly. Fang's breathing became even and spoke of one asleep. She found it comforting but became anxious at the silence and darkness that refused to bring the comfort of sleep. She sat for a moment longer, listening to the fire, when she decided to rise quietly to her feet.

No insects were stirring and no wind blew. Things felt subtly off. It reminded her of when she'd had just too much to drink.

Grayce looked up to see that the stars still shone, but seemed farther away. She felt small and suddenly afraid—like a child in a dark room. She turned to wake Fang and saw he was no longer there. The fire had died out and the gray light of dawn began to show.

"Fang?" she called out.

A whisper came from behind her. Turning, she saw only empty woods and dead trees. Were the trees always dead? She walked toward the whisper, drawn to its faint location, and saw her breath exhale in chilled wisps. Her steps kicked swirls of morning fog about her feet. Strangely, this was the first time she didn't feel cold.

As she continued among the gray, wooden sentinels a clattering of voices could be heard. They were quiet, attempting to keep their debate unheard, but there were many of them. They buzzed like a ghostly swarm of hornets. Her pace quickened, and she hoped to see any human face. The voices always remained just out of sight. The fog rose to waist height, and its evanescence tickled her nose.

"Who's there?" she demanded. Where was Fang?

She began to jog, and when her frustration peaked the voices ceased. She saw a group of shadows ahead. The fog now sat thick in the air, obscuring the source of the voices. They were in a loose grouping and spread about the forest.

But this forest wasn't the Blackwood. These were all aldyr trees; the very same kind found in the glade. Where was she? Where did the shadowy figures lead her? Grayce called out to them, but received no reply. She tried again, and the silhouetted figures only moved slightly, shifting on their feet. The sound of her sword drawing against the leather of her sheath was a boon of comfort. Approaching them, she calmed her breathing and prepared for the worst. As she drew closer, her courage fell to her stomach. The bodies were corpses. The whispered conversation of a hundred creaking ropes met her as she beheld them all hanging from the boughs of the trees by their necks. They were hanged precariously low, their feet nearly brushing the ground. Her sword arm lowered, but her feet pressed on. She became surrounded by the swinging corpses. Grayce turned back, unaware of how far she'd walked into them, and her courage left her. Her hands went numb and her sword fell. The mouths of the bodies were moving, but made no sound. What they said she couldn't ascertain. Then a familiar voice could be heard. Behind her, she turned again and saw one figure facing the opposite direction. Looking at the vile gathering was a man dressed in a red robe. He hung in the same fashion as the others, but his voice could be heard. Her father spoke flatly; no emotion or emphasis was placed on his simple, repeated phrase: *She sings to us. She screams to us.*"

Grayce felt her legs give way. She fell back, awkwardly, and pain exploded in her ankle as her heel caught on an exposed root. She cried out in anguish, both physical and emotional, as her hands landed in moist, gray leaves. She looked around at the others, swaying in the trees so gently. She recognized many faces of the villagers. They were all here. Tears rolled down her face, and she wished for the indistinguishable whispers once more. The words that caressed her ears like sharp fingernails only aggravated the pain.

*"She sings screaming... cradlesongs in the dark... mother of fear..."*

She grabbed her sword and cursed Fang for not being there. She began swinging at the ropes, hoping to cut them free from their fates. At first, her swings were wild, and she shouted in anger. After the first half dozen, she began to calm. She steeled herself and regained her nerve. Her cutting became instinctive and without feeling. Once her head had cleared, Grayce realized she had not yet cut the rope that still bore her father. Damn it, where was Fang? She walked up to him, still swaying and whispering, and felt the tears come again. She looked at his dead, white eyes. He was clearly not living. Yet, his mouth continued to speak frantically. She choked on her grief, for a moment, and then cut the frayed line.

The body fell to the ground, disturbing the fog and causing it swirl about him. He made no further motion, no twitches of life remaining or fleeting. Grayce's arms suddenly felt tired. Her muscles were sore. She looked upon her father's face one last time. His body was still, but his lips continued their infernal whispering.

She turned, slowly, and feared what she might see behind her. She breathed, trying to control the chill that touched her. It was as she had thought: the villagers she had cut down lay unmoving on the ground – whispering, lifeless dolls.

"What is happening here?" she said in breathless frustration.

A guttural moan drew her attention to a stretch of woods just out of sight in the fog. A large, four-legged creature stepped into her view, though only barely. She could make out the caricature of a large wolf... absurdly large. It was perhaps the size of a small cow, with hackles like knives. It was the source of the unnatural moan. Then it made a very recognizable growl. She heard a bark in response, a second creature. It was less of a bark, and more like the pained shout of a wounded man. She feared for a second that it might be Fang, wounded or dying. The cause of her fear shifted when she saw the second shadow stalking within her peripheral vision. The dual, menacing figures snarled but came no closer. The wolgs, as that is surely what they were, moved closer to one another. Grayce found this odd, as they would normally have surrounded her for the kill. With her sword gripped tight and her muscles renewed by a vigor for survival, she was prepared to make them earn their meal.

Then, a third figure joined them. This was not a wolg, nor any animal. It was tall, lithe, and feminine. It whispered in a hiss-like fashion. The wolgs bowed their heads and skulked over to it. Grayce could not make out any defining features, but this woman was impossibly tall, her calves too long and her thighs too thin. Her arms moved like the fog in smooth, fluid strokes. She looked at Grayce. Her face was hidden, but her eyes shone like metal catching moonlight. Grayce felt something freeze inside her. A part of her mind refused to see any more, despite her eyes catching the cold emptiness of that gaze. It caused her to feel sick, and she stepped back, fighting the urge to lay down and cede to whatever this woman-thing wanted.

Grayce opened her mouth to scream. Nothing came out.

*"Nothing screams lest it be for me"*

Grayce screamed again, but it was out of her control. Her heart shuddered, and the voice that spilled forcefully from her throat was painful and raw.

*"Yes..."*

The Mother of Screams threw her head back in ecstasy. Grayce continued to scream, until she could almost feel her throat tearing. The Mother's chest heaved. The massive wolgs... her children. Grayce knew that now. These two were her children, progenitors who bore the line that now stalk the Blackwood that she claimed as her own. Something spoke that to Grayce through her internal screams. The children were now seated at her side, shuddering in anticipation. Their black tongues panting and shining saliva dripping on the forest floor. More tears fell from Grayce's eyes, but these were tears of pure pain. The screams became choked and she tasted blood. The wolgs began slavering and chomping in barely-contained excitement. The Mother began moaning, her multitudinous teeth catching the cold light.

Grayce's eyes fluttered open. Her chest pounded. She felt paralyzed and her arms and legs tingled in unbridled fear. She took several shaking breaths in and out. She was too afraid to move. She felt like a child again; small and powerless. It was that childhood feeling of waiting until the bad passed and hoping it left you alone. She sat up, feeling numb for a time, and saw Fang looking at her strangely from across the fire.

"Bad dreams?" he asked casually.

She looked into the flames, seeing something warm and comforting. "Yes."

Fang looked into the fire and nodded. "Was it her?"

Grayce didn't answer. Fang likely already knew. She rubbed her ankle, still feeling sore despite her now being awake. She coughed, her throat also feeling sore and throbbing. The thought of sleep was all but impossible. They drank some water and waited out the night.

When the faint glow of morning crested the eastern mountains, they were still too tired and sluggish to move on. It took another hour or more before it felt warm enough to move their cramped and barely-thawed muscles. Grayce was the first to rise. Her youth no doubt assisted in her effort. Fang was older, and he had never felt his age more than he did now.

They had walked in silence, and the cabin wasn't far. Grayce could think of nothing but the nightmare she'd had the previous night. It was so clear in her mind, she began to think of it as less than a nightmare. She thought of Jermiah's writings. She had read them over and over before they left. He spoke of the things that had been set free, the consciousness that had been awakened and made aware. They could do things that were difficult or impossible to explain. What the beings of Alda had called reality was too simple a concept for the things Jermiah found 'in between', as he called it. Could Grayce's nightmare had been real? Or, at least, could it have been happening without happening? The idea caused her both a headache and to fear the possibility of such a fairy tale—albeit, a dark and horrifying one.

Finally, the silence weighed too heavy and her curiosity too burdensome. "Fang," Grayce asked, "I have a thought."

"Can't wait to hear it," he said sardonically.

She ignored his cynicism. "Last night, in my dream. I was in a forest, covered in fog." She would conveniently omit the part with her father and the villagers. That would only bring about complications of its own. "I saw her, and the creatures that were with her on the carving."

Fang's pace slowed slightly, but for someone as stoic as Fang it might as well have been going from a sprint to a crawl. "And?"

"I think Jermiah was writing about creatures like them and the Mother."

"She has a name now?"

"I think you know She always has. We've been skirting around it. Myself especially, but I can't ignore what I saw."

"It was a nightmare, Grayce. Dealing with wolgs has a tendency to do that to a person. If you're going to become a Sword-bearer, you'll need to accept it and deal with it accordingly."

"I haven't known you to be afraid of much, Fang. Nothing, really. But you're afraid of them. You're afraid of Her."

He stopped and wheeled on her. His stare penetrated her, and the shadows and circles under his eyes deepened by years. "I'm terrified of Her."

An uncomfortable silence, and he turned and continued walking. She followed, and listened.

"But I can't explain what's been happening. Once I heard the wolg's howls, the nightmares came and never stopped."

He walked quietly after that. Grayce was lost in her thoughts. It must have only been a few minutes, and Fang continued.

"The only dream I've had in *years* that didn't involve me waking in cold sweats was—"

He hesitated, took a deep breath. Grayce didn't truly expect him to continue.

"I had a dream that we found some magic. Your father mentioned that there used to be a kind that could mend wounds or even treat the insane. I dreamt, once, that we found some relic or manuscript, a scroll or some such thing, I can't remember, but it was something your father could use. I could sleep and stop having the nightmares."

"The Fourth Sect. That's what father used to call it. I don't know if it even exists anymore, if it ever did. Did you think it would help you stop hearing her?"

Fang winced. "Now that we know where the nightmares were coming from, yes. Maybe; I don't know."

"Maybe," Grayce echoed, "One can hope."

"No. They can't. Not here. Not in this world." As if to reinforce his point, Fang grunted at a phantom ache that set upon him. "The closer we get... I don't know where we're going, but I know we're close. I can feel a weight in my chest; a tickle in my ear."

"You're not insane, Fang," she sighed. "If you are, then—"

Fang looked at her and saw doubt and fear. "Then maybe you are, too. Perhaps, even your father."

She slapped him. It was jarring for both of them. It took a moment for Fang's head to turn back to her. "It's not a lie. It just hurts," he explained. "You've felt it, too. Maybe your father did. He seemed to recognize something about the statue."

"My father was..." she began, but didn't finish.

She wasn't sure what to say. In a dark spot in her heart, an uncaring hand grabbed her. It was despair. It was Jermiah's writings. It drove him to do what he did.

"My father made his last mistake. It won't overshadow the good he did. Or at least, tried to do."

She forced the ache in her chest away. "Let's just find this damn place."

Grayce led the way on their last leg to the clearing where the unhallowed cabin sat steeped in dread. The forest, already cursed with the poison in its veins, seemed to scream against their arrival. A breeze cut through the hollow in the trees. It was soft and bitter cold; it touched upon their skin like soft blades, and the hair bristled on their arms and napes of their necks.

The first hesitant steps into the clearing belonged to Grayce. A cold shudder caused her shoulders to flinch, and it was not due to the weather. It was late afternoon when she was here last, and now at midday, it seemed darker than before. There was still the terrified silence of all things living and decent among those soft grasses. She could hear her feet disturb the occasional fallen leaf. That was when she realized she only heard her own footsteps.

She turned to see Fang standing at the edge of the clearing. He barely breached the threshold of the unsavory border. He was staring at something, but she couldn't determine what. He was looking at neither her nor the cabin. He simply stared.

HIS EYES WERE FIXED. He knew he had stepped into the grove, he followed Grayce in stride and ignored the gnawing trepidation that threatened to turn him around on his heel and send him back to the miserable village. His determination was reaching a zenith; feeling that somehow the apex of the last few days' tensions was upon them.

Now the tickle in his ears became a tingle, and then a throb. He felt a sensation of moving; his body felt disconnected. His mind was buzzing with the sound of a countless swarm. His skin prickled, and the swarm became a chorus of screams. His heartbeat quickened and the screaming halted. A sickening, sudden stillness overcame him as the rustle of a thousand whispering lips overpowered him, crawled over his skin like kissing lips, but the sound was not a voice that could be recognized by human ears. He knew, deep in a primordial part of him, that they could not be understood by any ears, mortal or immortal. He only understood because the source of the screaming whispers drew him, made him a part of it.

*She is the One who calls. Whispers in the Womb*

His eye twitched. A chill licked his ears and tickled his mind.

*O, Screamer in the Void; She, Mother of Nightmares. She is the Whisperer in the Womb. Embrace screams, calling the Night-Birther...*

Fang felt his eyes water. An emptiness—vast and cold—lay before him. Dead things played at Her feet. They rolled about, barking with throats red and raw. The exposed bones of their head and jaws clacking like dry sticks. She smiled at him from within the darkness that oozed.

*The Calming Screamer. Mother of Whispers.*

*Come, Fang.*

He shook his head; closed his eyes until the tears flowed and his ears bled.

*Scream, Fang.*

"*No,*" he thought defiantly.

*Quietly. Shhhhh. Scream for Her.*

"*No.*"

The pained, playful noises of the horrible things that rolled and tussled about her feet became a horrid lullaby.

*Hush little darling, don't say a word...*

The whispers, were they screaming now? He couldn't tell any longer. They came from everywhere; outside the grove, inside his head, tingling in his fingers and chest, and everywhere was the starless dark.

*Scream for Mommy, like a dying bird...*

*It's Me, Fang.*

*Whisper to Me, Fang.*

"No."

*Louder...*

"No..."

*Louder. Softer.*

"NO."

*Mother wants you Home.*

Was that laughter? He saw flashes of teeth, cradled obscenities, and blood-covered, quivering nothingness.

*Mine now...*

*Mother of Whispers, Mother of Sorrows, Mother of Madness. Mother. Mother.*

*Fang...*

"Ok."

His face stung. He saw another face, decayed and weeping. The emaciated body stood before him. It reached out to him with tapered fingers. Clawing his face and leaving it raked with red, weeping gashes. The creature stood back, crying and screaming, but the sound was soft and muted and tugged at his inner being. He felt a pull on his very soul. He reached up and touched the skin on his face, and felt it wet and sticky. He looked at his hand and saw no blood. He tried again, and there was nothing.

He closed his eyes again and put his head in his hands. He screamed. The sound he heard was not his own. It was the braying of a thousand howls. His breath felt like ice, and his mind felt open and exposed. In an instant, all was silent.

No. There was more screaming. Why? Why was there more screaming?

"Fang, it's me! Stop it, Fang!"

He looked around and saw pale light filtering through gray trees. His vision blurred. He tried to focus; he commanded his eyes to focus, but everything was spinning. He smelled the pungent familiarity of mold and mud. The air no longer reeked of sinew. He reached out and felt something rough and solid, but stable. The ground was no longer a mirror of rippling darkness.

Was he in a grove? Was he alone?

"Fang!" a voice called out. Who was with him? It wasn't Her. This voice was... normal. Human. It resonated within. It was what he remembered voices are supposed to sound like. He looked toward the voice, tried to find where it came from. He saw a fuzzy shape in front of him and his heart quickened. Was She back?

No, his vision began to clear. This was a familiar face. A beautiful face. Grayce. His friend. She was the one yelling. Why did she have a sword drawn?

"Grayce?" he mumbled. His tongue felt thick and dry. His face still stung. As his consciousness returned, he recognized that pain. It came back to him in a loose connection to the imageries of teeth, saliva, and exposed muscle that were still fresh in his memories. She had slapped him. Again.

"Why did you slap me?"

Her eyes widened, and she sneered at him as though she was privy to some knowledge he was not.

"Why were you behaving so— What were you doing?"

Fang looked around now that he could see clearly. He was still leaning on the tree, his head pounding and stomach heaving.

"What was I doing?" he asked breathlessly. He felt as though he had been running for miles. It was a genuine question. He couldn't recall what, in fact, he had been doing. His recollection of the last several minutes were quickly fading.

"You don't remember? The things—the things you said?"

Her look of disbelief no doubt matched his own. "What did I say?"

A dreadful feeling was swelling within him. Grayce had a look of genuine horror mingled with revulsion. She had never looked at him that way, no one had. Not even the villagers in their unending hatred of him.

"I won't repeat it. One moment you were behind me, and then I heard you making some unearthly sound. I turned and you were staring at the sky, gargling some kind of awful mess. It wasn't any language that I could possibly think of. When you did finally say something I could understand, I thought I was going to have to—"

She looked at her sword. When she looked back up to Fang, her eyes were filled with hurt. Whatever he said while in his fugue had almost forced her hand. She was fully prepared to kill him.

He was proud of her.

He swallowed, his mouth still dry. "You should have done it."

She put the sword away and he shouldered past her. The glen felt different than the rest of the Blackwood. It felt... separated. It was cold here, too, and Fang knew in his gut that this was the source of the cold in the woods. The chill and the evil leaked from this place like a seeping wound. Here, it even became gangrenous. For all its sinister atmosphere and wicked hallucinations, the trees here still retained a portion of their vitality. The green color of life clung desperately to these plants. It was as though they were draining it from their surroundings, sucking the essence from the world around them. It was then Fang saw these trees for what they were.

"Aldyrs. My gods."

Grayce looked at him from the corner of her eyes. "I remember that, too, when I first came here. Father told me about them. He said they were important. Or revered. Something like that."

"Something like that." Fang replied. This certainly added a somber weight to the grove, though it wouldn't need much to make this place feel out of sorts.

Even the air felt odd here. Everything in this void of normalcy felt out of place. Fang would have said it was a little abandoned hole that time had let alone, but the cabin centered in the little glade had nearly rotted away to nothing and the ravages of time were more than apparent. Holes pocked the ceiling and limp vines grew over the logs and around the windows. The door was rotted off its hinges; and combined with the vines that hung over the door, it gave off the appearance of a forbidding cave.

The feeling that encompassed him the most, however, was paradoxically the immediate urge to flee and a disquieting sense of belonging. The sensations only intensified when they entered the house. Grayce insisted on leading the way; however, she stalled quite noticeably at the doorway. Her breath quivered, and Fang wondered for a moment if she was slipping into a similar fugue as he had.

"Grayce?" he asked quietly. He reached out slowly to touch her shoulder, see if she was still with him.

"I'm fine," she replied before his hand reached her. She never turned around. Her voice was shaken but not otherwise in any great distress. "You—you wouldn't think I'd be so affected by an old cabin."

"With a dead person in it," Fang added, seeing the desiccated skeletal remains as he looked over Grayce's slender shoulders. "You were here at dusk?"

"Yes. It wasn't pleasant."

"I imagine," he said flatly, "and you found the statue here?"

"Next to him. Or her. Hard to say any more."

Fang stepped past Grayce and approached the lifeless figure. It was lying on the floor, recently disturbed. Thick streaks lay in the heavy dust and dirt that had settled on the table. It drew his eyes to the table's previous contents now scattered on the ground.

"Was this you?" He asked.

Grayce grimaced at the memory and answered simply, "Yes."

Fang inspected the corpse. He looked at the pages that were now in broken pieces on the floor. He couldn't read, but he knew the desperate lines of a crazed individual. He saw dried blood on the table under decades of dust—a pool of it. He saw where it ran down the front and continued its morbid flow on the floor.

"The skeleton; was the obelisk in the skull?"

"Yes, when I found it. I had to pry it off."

"They killed themselves. Let me guess, the pages on the floor talk about screams and whispers."

Grayce's face grew shadowed. She knew where the conversation was leading.

"Fang, this is not going to be you. Or me," she quickly added.

He grunted in reply. He looked back to the dried blood pooled on the floor. With the size of the hole in the skull and the way Grayce described having to pry it loose from the statue, there should have been far more blood here. The table would only begin to hold it before it gathered on the floor. But as he kicked away fallen chunks of timber and debris and moved aside the accumulated filth of abandonment, he saw the dark stain of only a small, irregular puddle.

He removed his glove and felt near the floor. The dust and grime had created a disgusting carpet on the floor. Now that some had been cleared away, he could feel the slightest bit of air moving through the boards. Fang had a sick feeling and asked Grayce to help him clear more of the room. It wasn't long before they found the line where newer wood met older planks. The entirety of the cabin was long-decayed, but there was still a visible partition where the previous owner had, at some point, covered at least one-third of the room with repaired slats.

"Unless we want to fall through, we should move," Fang suggested. Grayce may have been able to walk through here unimpeded, but together they weighed far heavier on the unsound floor; especially now knowing that there may be little underneath them.

"Fang, what is it?"

"Back away, toward the door."

Grayce, hearing the concern and urgency in this voice, quickly responded. Fang waited for her to move to safety, and then followed suit.

"You still haven't said what it is. Now's not a good time to keep secrets—"

"There's something under the floor."

Grayce's voice caught and her eyes widened.

"Under the floor?"

Fang found where the color of the newer wood began and stomped down hard. It cracked and trembled, but didn't give way. A second time and the older wood splintered and the wood came loose from its rusted nails. He worked his way along the haphazard repairs, obviously done in haste. Nearly half the way around, the partition in its entirety gave way. It crashed into a hole that appeared to be part of a tunnel. The unnatural dimness of the grove made it difficult to see to the bottom, but the tops of some of the broken boards still peeked above the blackness.

"How did I not see this?" Grayce whispered, afraid to conjure up something from the darkness or make some hidden beast aware of their presence. She then remembered the resounding crash of the floor collapsing, and realized anything in the tunnel already knew they were there.

"This place is decaying; there still may be something we're not finding. We may bring the whole thing down on us if we keep trying."

"Then what are we going to do?"

"We're going to wait."

Her brow crinkled and she had the look that Fang had come to love about her.

"Wait for what?"

"Something is down there, and we're going to find out what. Probably kill it."

She looked into the musty, foul-smelling abyss that lay before them. Surely, something called it home, but, "How do you know something's down there? Maybe, this is some abandoned warren," she finished her thought out loud. His answer chilled her, sent the hairs on her arms standing.

"Because I can hear them."

THEY SPENT the better part of the afternoon looking around the cabin's immediate surroundings. Each time they breached the perimeter of the grove, Grayce noticed Fang's brief twitch in his shoulders, a catch in his breath, or a tight squint of his eyes. Eventually, he hesitated before even stepping back into the grove altogether. A few times, she noticed he went out of his way to avoid it.

"Still nothing," she called out. They were no longer concerned about discreetness. They, particularly Fang, wanted attention and were looking for company. He had the both of them looking around for any possible entrances to the tunnel under the cabin. Fang surmised it was likely a way for the wolgs to travel. They may possibly have a cave nearby, or, even more disturbing, have a massive network of such tunnels that allowed them to hide all this time when he thought they may be truly wiped out.

"Wait," she said to herself. Something caught her eye in the underbrush. It was partially buried, but certainly not natural.

"Fang!" she shouted, "You need to see this!"

Fang came running over. "What—"

He didn't finish his question. A smoothly molded bit of metal protruded from the ground. Fang dug it from its resting place and Grayce saw a look of awe in his eyes for the first time. He held it with both hands, turning it over and over as clumps of dirt fell from its crevices.

"What is it?" she asked, her curiosity spurred by his own.

"The Keeper told me of these; the smith, too, once. They used to wear this in the old times."

"Before The Rupture—"

"It was armor. Soldiers would wear it for protection; Sword-bearers like us."

Us.

A small, but meaningful slip of the tongue, no doubt. But it made her smile nonetheless.

"This is heavy," he continued. "But I imagine nothing could get through this. I wonder where the rest is."

Grayce kicked about some of the foliage and underbrush. She wasn't finding anything, until a haphazard kick caused her toe to slam painfully into something. She cried out, or cursed, rather, and expected to find a buried rock. To her great delight, it was another piece of tarnished metal. "There's more here, Fang!"

She pulled the armored glove from the ground, having to force it to release its long-buried hold. Even the glove was heavy. The men and women who wore these must have been powerful, indeed. Though tarnished, it still retained some of its silvery sheen in places. It was the most beautiful thing she'd ever seen.

Grayce handed it to Fang. His eyes pored over the relic. If

they could find all of the pieces, it would fetch a fortune with a traveling merchant, or the material itself could provide their smith with a mountain of helpful possibilities.

"It's a gauntlet," Fang said. "There should be two."

Grayce and Fang continued to look; their beleaguered minds finally finding some respite in the search for their treasure. It was a welcome reprieve, and they didn't mind straying from their mission for a moment to find something so greatly useful. It would prove a vast boon to their community, and to themselves.

A short distance from the gauntlet they found its mate. Fang scowled when he had a moment to look it over. Bright streaks in the metal, now rusted from exposure, crisscrossed the part of the gauntlet that would have protected the forearm.

"Well, I know what happened to whoever this once belonged to."

"Do I want to know?" Grayce asked. She found herself becoming infected by his cynicism.

"They were attacked by beasts. Probably wolgs, or worse," Fang added after a moment of recollection. "It would take terribly strong fangs to do this to such fine steel."

"And now we know why the pieces are so scattered." Grayce felt sick at her own conclusion. "They were eaten. Torn apart." She looked about the area they had been searching. "Their bones are probably all around here."

Fang shook the dirt and decayed leaves from the gauntlet. He slipped his hand in and flexed the fingers. It felt strange. Like having a second, third, even fourth layer of skin and metal flesh. The leather of the palms felt thicker than anything he'd worn before. It was decaying, frayed, and stiff in places, but Fang could imagine the strength and protection these once provided. How long had these lain here? Who wore them before, and why were they alone?

Grayce called to him. She found more. This time, there were several pieces together in one place. The greaves, boots, even parts from a belt with some remaining leather were clumped together near a tree. Fang had the ill impression that the soldier was rent in half by at least two animals, and they fed on him separately. The armored plates on the legs bore copious heavy markings of an attack. Fang traced his fingers over them, and images of the two black-eyed, braying fiends that escorted Her flashed in his mind like a waking nightmare. If anything could have left these marks—

He shook the thought from his head. They scoured the thicket until they found the remaining pieces. Neither of them could believe it: a full set of armor. Thick, heavy plates supported by equally thick leather. One must have felt like a walking turtle wearing it, and equally as quick. Fang could only imagine the number of blows you would sustain from being unable to maneuver properly; however, he could also see those blows bouncing off the tarnished steel like a stick to a rock. They laid the armor out like it should have been worn, creating an outline of a human body on the ground. Grayce picked up the helmet. It was her favorite piece. It looked like it may have had a plume on the top at one point, but this had long rotted away. She put it on. It was a little too big.

When Fang smiled, his face looked so foreign to her. "I don't think you're going to grow into it. The smith is going to have to melt it down and forge a smaller one."

She gave him a quizzical look. "You're not going to wear it?"

He shook his head sharply. "That's too much metal for me. I prefer to be able to move."

She took the helmet off and looked at it again. "I suppose you have a point." She still wanted to wear it. She would ask the smith to melt it down, after he was done begging her to keep it himself.

A howl pierced the stillness. It caused Grayce's breath to catch, and Fang's face to drain of color. It wasn't a wolg, although it shared hints of the beast's bloodcurdling wail. It came from within the woods, and a second one followed, closer this time.

"It's them," Fang said, barely louder than a breath. "They're coming."

Fang held one of the metal bracers in his hand, turned it over in his hands.

"Help me get these on," he said in a low voice.

"Why do you need help?" Grayce asked, her eyes scanning the trees for the beasts.

"This is heavy armor. It requires two people to put on properly. You won't be able to wear it. It's been forged for someone bigger than you," Fang added the clarification awkwardly when he saw Grayce glowering at him.

"And what am I supposed to do?" Grayce whispered, afraid the creatures could hear them as though they were standing just outside of her vision waiting to strike.

"They might go for me if I'm wearing this, see me as the bigger threat."

"I understand," Grayce nodded, her eyes still darting about.

She helped him get the armor on, buckling the straps and hoping that some of the more worn and rotting ones held. They drew their swords and waited. The demons could come to them. They heard a third howl, but it was muffled and strange. It was long minutes before they heard another. The howls were coming from the same distance. They were no longer moving.

"Where are they?" Grayce asked, just as much to herself as to Fang.

They listened. A fourth one. This one muffled, too.

"They're at the cabin," Fang said through clenched teeth.

"Oh, gods, I'm not going back there." Grayce was overcome with a mix of fear, and anger at that fear. They'd had such good fortune after they left that place, and now she felt as though they were being drawn inexorably back.

"I don't want to either," Fang replied, with no small amount of empathy. Another howl echoed behind his words. "But they're not coming any closer. They—they want us there."

"And we're going?" she returned incredulously.

She saw his jaw clench. She recognized that look in his eye. It was the same he would get when the villagers were worked up at him.

"We came here for answers, for an end to this. I'll take it in blood if I have to."

She breathed deeply and exhaled. She would never let him go this alone. "You're right. I wanted those things dead. Let's make it so."

They kept their blades ready and moved slowly back towards the cabin. They hadn't wandered far, and it shook them to realize just how close those things really were. They stopped when the grove came into sight. Logically, they were surveying the area for any shadows, or noises, or anything that may give away where the creatures were. One step at a time, they approached the border of the clearing and looked again. As they drew closer, a dozen possibilities ran through their minds. Were the creatures still here? Were they mistaken and it really was wolgs, and not the larger, braying demons? What if Fang went into another trance, and left Grayce to fend for herself. Was that their plan altogether? Worst of all, what if She was here?

Fang gripped his sword so tightly the leather of the grip could be heard squeaking in protest. He stalked forward. "Come on."

Grayce followed behind him, ready to strike at anything that so much as flinched in the bushes and underbrush—duskrat or demon. When they reached the clearing, Fang stopped just short of the grassy border. She saw his shoulders rise and fall with a deep breath. He stepped through, and continued walking undisturbed. It must have stoked his courage and removed his doubt, for he walked with more purpose than he had before. They went straight for the tunnel. Rustling, growling, and barking could be heard below. It was a vicious sound, and they deeply wanted not to go.

"How are we going to see?" Grayce asked.

Fang looked around for a proper branch. He used some of the rags, dry-rotted wood, and old pages from the cabin to create a set of torches. They'd each take one, in case they were separated by accident. They would stick together, with Fang in front as the tunnels were too narrow to walk side by side, and keep their swords ready.

They dropped into the tunnels and were quickly thrown into pitch blackness. The gray light of the opening kept shrinking behind them. Their footfalls echoed flatly in the close quarters, and the sound of their breathing could be clearly heard. The braying and screaming that brought them here could not.

"Did they leave?" she whispered harshly. It came out louder than she expected.

Fang didn't turn around. "I doubt it. They're hunting for us."

She nodded, but was so lost in the sound of her heartbeat in her ears that she forgot Fang couldn't see her. They both stopped at the sound of rustling up ahead. Fang crouched, his sword in front of him, when he stood back up abruptly.

"Just dirt settling," he breathed in relief.

So, he was frightened, too. Grayce wasn't sure if that was a relief or added to her own distress. He was facing the source of his own demons. She was preparing for the most dangerous confrontation either of them had ever faced. Even together, they were little more than children lost in the dark.

The thought of one of those things, *Her* children, coming at them suddenly from out of the dark, began to overtake her. Fear squeezed her and made the already narrow tunnel close in. She looked behind her with a sharp turn of her head, feeling at any moment claws would tear into her back and pull her into that bloody and painful darkness.

Grayce chastised herself. Stupid, childish girl!

*What if one of those demons did show? What would you do? Piss yourself? Hide behind Fang? Give in and let them devour you or, worse, present you as a prize to their mistress?*

Grayce tasted bile. She angrily spit into the dirt. It was enough to give Fang pause.

"Are you ok back there?" He still didn't turn around.

"I'm fine," she huffed. "Where do you think we are?"

"I think we've been travelling northeast for a bit now."

"Deeper into the woods," she completed his thoughts. "So, this bitch owns the woods. She probably cursed the forest."

Fang winced at the insult. "I'd be careful about insulting Her."

She grimaced. "Why?"

Grayce wondered if he was beginning to fall under her influence. Maybe she should have cut him down at the grove.

She shook those thoughts from her head. Working up her courage had begun to make her angry at things that didn't warrant such a response. Fang's answer came quietly.

"We're in Her domain," he whispered, "we know what She can do."

Grayce only need a moment to reflect on what Fang said. She understood his fear.

"I don't think we do know, Fang. We don't even know what She is. We don't even know if She is a 'she.' A god? A demon? Worse?"

"What could be worse that a god or a demon?" Fang asked, thinking aloud.

"I don't know. That's what scares me."

"Me too."

Grayce's nose twitched. She stopped and took a deep breath through her nose. It wasn't much, but it was better than the closed in, musky odor of the tunnel.

"Fresh air!"

Fang quivered at the thought of what waited for them when they left. He should have been thrilled to see the grey daylight again, but something in his gut did not sit well. He had years of instinct built up to tell him when something was not right in these woods. He had little choice but to press on, however.

"Grayce," his voiced carried back to her in a gravelly tone, "be ready for anything."

Any relief she felt at the thought of being out of the tunnels was drowned by the weight of his voice. She drew her sword and clenched her jaw. Fang may have been out of sorts, but he knew the woods. If he was nervous, she was nervous.

The dull light engulfed them as they left the tunnels. The still air was a godsend after the tunnel. The woods spread around them. The typical trees of the Blackwood were now dotted here and there by the occasional aldyr, though they looked no better than their bulky oaken cousins. Grayce was then hit with a strange sense of déjà vu. This area felt familiar. They didn't get turned around, did they? This was a different exit; it had to be. The spacing of the trees, her slow and measured pace; Why did a feeling of familiarity tug at her so? Anxiety then settled upon her and soaked into her bones like a dull, persistent rain. She imagined the bodies of dozens of villagers hanging from the trees. The ropes groaning like the tree branches would if there were wind. She looked to Fang and saw his face was ashen. His jaw was set and his eyes were fixed. She drew her sword. If he fell under Her sway again, she wouldn't hesitate this time.

Fang's pace slowed. She saw him tilt his head, as though he

were listening to something. She didn't hear anything, so she stopped. She let nothing distract her from trying to hear what it was he heard. She wanted to ask, but didn't want to distract either of them. Still, though, she heard not a sound and his body had tensed as though he was bracing for a strike.

Was he hearing Her? Was She speaking to him again? Grayce heard the leather of her sword's grip groan as she gripped it with white knuckles. Suddenly, she feared the worst. Fang stopped moving, only a few paces ahead of her, and it sounded like he also held his breath. He must have been controlling his breathing; his shoulders heaved up and down rhythmically.

Fang wheeled around on her. She flinched, to her irritation, and saw murder in his eyes. His jaw was clenched and the corded muscles of his neck tightened like stretch ropes as his nostrils flared. She dug her feet in; prepared for the explosion of his blind fury.

The explosion came, but not from Fang. A sound like a hundred dying men burst from her right. The brush and briars disintegrated as a red-jawed and skull-eyed canine face barreled toward them, propelled by unnatural strength and unwholesome thirst. Fang's blade flashed and Grayce raised her own on instinct driven by fear and tinged with anger.

Her feelings of betrayal caught in her throat, fell to her stomach like lead, and were replaced by a new kind of panic. Fang pivoted to her right and Grayce saw but a breath of steel before a black wall slammed into him. Her nose was licked by a musty odor followed by that of stale viscera. Her own blade was readied as she turned and saw her mentor on the ground, wrestling with the slavering demon-wolf. The creature was snapping and biting in a wicked frenzy and seemed not to notice the outpouring of crimson gushing from its abdomen. It was wholly an unnatural abomination. It twisted and curled on the blade that must have been driven nearly to its spine. The wound grew worse in a matter of moments. Before her mind had a moment to consider how to react and drive a second blade home, the thing should have long been dead. Rather, it only grew more vicious.

"Gods," she muttered.

Her senses returning to her, Grayce brought her sword-edge down in a sweeping arc, landing a blow behind the beast's ears. She expected to see the gruesome, multi-eyed head rolling across the gray-green grass, but her sword clanged against the spine and only managed a shallow gash. Still, it should have been fatal, but the beast fought on. It was becoming difficult to tell the creature's slavering and Fang's grunting apart. It was all she could do to avoid being eviscerated by the vicious claws that kicked and swiped about. She could only imagine what Fang was dealing with, still struggling half-buried beneath the incandescent beast.

Grayce recoiled as bloody froth plopped from its slavering, red-stained teeth around Fang's face. He roared as he once more attempted to shove the beast off of him. The vile thing barked, an unnatural, otherworldly sound, and quickly placed Fang back on the ground. It swiped at him, but the gore-stained daggers it bore as claws careened off the new-found armor. Despite the age and tarnish of the steel, it was still strong enough to protect its wearer from a brutal evisceration; though, not without consequence. Sparks flew where contact was made and three deep gouges would forever be a reminder that even steel would not hold off this nightmare for long.

Fang had a look of grim determination. Or was it acceptance? Whichever the case, Grayce did not care for it. The profane creature had haunted her people, her village for as long as she'd known. Now, it threatened her mentor and the closest person she'd had to a friend. Her anger heated the lead in her stomach and it spread to her arms, her hands, her feet. A molten rage seared the fear from her muscles, blackened her heart against its cold, dagger-shaped claws.

The maw of the beast opened. Leather-dry lips retreated over blood-red gums where seated within were yellowed teeth of innumerable number and various lengths, though all were sharp as needles. Fang looked into beady, black, soulless eyes set deep within bone-like sockets. From this too-personal proximity, the creature could be mistaken for one left rotting in the woods; half-consumed by maggots and carrion-seekers. But the worm-tongue lolling about within the long, narrow muzzle that licked up the last of his resolve, as though it tasted his very soul, testi-fied to it being a very living and hungry thing.

He could drive his sword no deeper. It clung to life as though it hated the idea of being and existed only to do so out of spite. Blood fell from where Grayce's sword had struck, yet it barely distracted the thing. Fang's sword arm was trapped. His free one held out feebly against the barghest's throat, but it inched ever closer. Fang waited. He was ready. End it—and let him sleep a dreamless sleep.

A fierce roar sounded out. Fang awaited the sudden, unspeakable pain of his head being thrashed between a thou-sand teeth and felt a hot liquid splash his face.

Blood.

It poured down his face and into his mouth. It tasted foul and wrong. He knew then that it wasn't his own. The roar changed to a repeated staccato of grunts, each followed by another spray of blood. Fang was able to look past the beast's head to see Grayce hacking fiercely over and over again at the creature's neck, each blow landing in the same spot between sections of the stone-tough spine into the flesh and muscle between.

*Brilliant, girl.*

The fur-and-chitin-covered demon, child of that night-marish Bitch whose form was forever carved in stone and would haunt Fang's waking eyes forever, howled in bloody anguish and frothing rage. It tried to howl, to call for its twin, but choked on the blood from Grayce's enraged assault. Fang gripped the unwholesome fur around the jawline, felt it cutting into his hands, and pulled. He heard tendons snap and muscle creak as planted his feet and *pulled*. Now, the creature tried to get away. It was too late. He used the force of the creature trying to pull away to aid his own purpose—tearing off its damned head with his bare hands.

*Just. Fucking. Die.* Fang screamed in his head. Aloud, he could do no more than grunt and shout as his efforts bore ghastly fruit. With a stomach-turning crunching and squelching, the beast's head tore free. A final swipe from Grayce and it was fully severed. Blood poured over the tarnished steel breastplate, and Fang pushed the spasming, kicking body away as it fell to the side with a wet *thud*. He tossed the beast's head away, still snap-ping reflexively like a decapitated snake.

There was a howl in the distance of the human-like kind. The sound of a mother mourning her child. It could be heard in the soul. In the back of the mind where childhood superstitions and primordial fears dwelt. The part that She called home. She knew what they had done.

Fang and Grayce looked wearily at one another. She managed a weak smile, her chest rising and falling sharply with exertion. Fang, still attempting to stand amid the gore-soaked ground, gave her an affirming nod. When he reached a kneeling position, he stopped and looked around.

"What is it?" Grayce asked between breaths.

With a lip curled, he said, "There were two on the statue."

Her eyes widened in realization. She heard the sound of brush being trampled. It was faint, then quickly became thundering in seconds. Fang stood, scarcely managing to expose an inch of blade from its sheathe before the second barghest tore like a hellish thunderhead from the trees.

"Grayce!" He shouted.

Grayce spun on her heels before Fang even parted his lips. She couldn't take in a breath before the world was spinning about her, death and damnation pressed its weight on her, its claws pounding around her. A flash of teeth and gray sunlight, then all went black.

Fang made it to his feet, his sword drawn and ready for blood. His feet reacted before his thoughts could and he bolted for the beast. He roared, hoping to bring its attention away from Grayce. It looked up at him. She was on the ground, motionless. He saw a small pool of red below her head. He didn't stop running. He swore he saw the creature smile.

The jaws snapped, twice in quick succession. It leapt at Fang. He dropped to his knees, his maneuverability lost in part with the heavier armor. His first instinct was to raise his blade, but he wouldn't make the same mistake twice. He let the creature land behind him. Fang spun on his knee, slashing as far behind him as he could, hoping to beat the creature's reflexes. His blade caught resistance. A sharp sound similar to a man's last gasp coupled with a raven's cry told Fang that his ploy worked. He stood, turning on his heel, and saw the creature limping. It could barely utilize one of its hind legs. Infernally resilient and steel-boned they may be, but severed tendons will not function. Demon, wolf, or otherwise. It was crippled and, for once, Fang felt he was the one feeding off another's fear.

They circled one another, both limping from injury and with murder in their eyes. In the soulless black sockets of the beast, he could see a great, malevolent intelligence. The only advantage Fang had against this hellish creature was the lack of control it seemed to have over its bloodlust. If he drew it in too close, one wrong move and its claws would open his throat ear to ear. The creature was smart enough to not go for the armor now. It would find the softer parts of him. He couldn't run, not until he could see if Grayce still lived. And he doubted he could outrun the creature, anyway. Fang snarled and readied himself.

The creature balked at him; it feigned a charge then darted left. It stopped, yelping when it landed on the wounded leg. It was testing him. It would make no sense for the creature to have left its wretched companion to fight alone and not overwhelm him and Grayce. Although, he also did not put it past the barghests to have no small amount of hubris. That had cost them; this one would not allow the fate of its partner to be its own. Or, more horrifyingly, it was simply smarter.

Fang held the blade in a two-handed grip, pointing its sharpened tip at the beast. If it was brazen enough to charge him, the barghest would meet with a pierced brain or an open throat. Fang knew, however, that if he was to be flanked, he was not in a position or stance to defend against it. He hoped against hope that the statue was an accurate depiction and this was the last of the two. His body involuntarily shuddered at the thought of the loathsome artifact. From his nightmares and the visions that had assailed him, it was certainly accurate in its depictions so far.

Did the beast just... purr? The barb-like clumps of fur around the shoulders and hackles trembled and the cadaverous head lowered and tilted, just slightly, as though welcoming a caressing hand. Could they sense even the thought of Her, their Matron, their Mother?

"You can feel Her, can't you?"

It hissed at him. The wicked intelligence in its eyes was unsettling. Fang fought back the urge to shrink away and find a deep, dark cave to curl up in; to hide and wait for a quiet death.

"Is She the bitch that bore you?"

A low, guttural growl escaped its throat. It paced back and forth, measuring him up. Maybe this was how Fang could beat it. It felt, it hated, it loved. It loved Her.

"Your friend is dead. Or was it your mate?" he said, his disdain embellished for effect. "Did you both come with Her?"

Another growl-purr.

"Are you Her pets? Her children? I don't care. I'll send you both back to whatever hell-stained plane of existence shat you out."

The barghest pawed the dirt violently, sending dirt and moss scattering into air behind it. It snorted and barked. It appeared the beast knew what Fang was trying to do. Regardless, its hatred and bloodlust were too much temptation for it to hold off for long.

"I'm going to gut you; throat to groin. Then I'm going to find her. She's looking for me. She wants me."

A staccato hail of barks and prolonged braying flew from the beast's crimson jaws. Fang twitched and expected the creature to charge. It hopped forward, kicking dirt with its hind paws in a desperate attempt to avoid a fatal charge. But, it had shown its weakness. Fang lowered his head, his eyes squinting and brow furrowed.

"You can't stand that, can you?" he whispered, glaring the beast in its wet, black eyes.

"You're Her pets but She wants others to play with. She needs fresh flesh, fresh minds for Her nightmares." Fang smiled, "You're jealous. You sad little pup. You're just a jealous, cuckolded fucking *dog*."

The barghest brayed and frothed. It wanted his blood more than it could bear. Fang had no idea what drove these creatures or where they came from; human souls damned to a prison of bone and sinew, tied to The Mother of Screams for eternity? Wanting Her, forever at Her side, but denied their desire? Or were they truly just the most loyal of demoniac companions who will suffer no slight of their Mother?

It didn't matter either way. This one was too smart. It had eternity to bait him and wait. Fang only had so long before exhaustion claimed him. He breathed a heavy breath. He flexed his hands, cracking old and tired knuckles. With eyes on the beast, he gripped the straps on the shoulders of the breastplate, worked the dry and cracked leather until the tarnished steel fell around his ankles. Seeing his torso exposed, the beast ran a wet tongue up and over the skeletal orbs of its nose.

It launched itself on its powerful hind legs, springing towards Fang. It took but a pair of leaps before the creature closed the gap with him. It wasn't falling for the same trick that killed the other one. Fang tried to feint – slip low and then cut to the side – but the barghest did something unexpected. It pivoted, turned and bared its flank to Fang, and slammed into him. His blade barely connected with the surface of its piebald flesh as the muscle, corded like steel, crashed into his exposed body and sent him hurling back to the ground.

He felt pain shoot through his leg as the great teeth punched through tendon and scraped the bones of his ankle. The creature threw him bodily by the leg and Fang felt his knee pop from the force of the throw. Crashing to the ground, he rolled over and over again until his body came to stop by colliding with the gray trunk of a tree.

Dry-heaving and breathing in croaking gasps, Fang sat up against the tree. He more felt than heard the thumping of heavy paws coming toward him. His vision blurry and his will spent, he realized his blade must have fallen from his hands during the tussle. By instinct alone, he reached for the blade he remembered giving to Grayce. The fog of memory cleared slightly as he remembered picking up the blade when he checked her body moments ago. His fingers grasped worn leather, comfortable both to his hands and his soul, with wrappings worn to fit his grip.

His vision was a blur: red flashes mingled with a white haze. He saw light and shadow dance in his eyes and knew not if it was the muted sunlight of The Blackwood dappling through the sick trees or the abhorrent claws of his nemesis bringing an end to his suffering. Fang felt the weight of denouement. The thud of fiendish paws on wilted grass and tainted ground pounded heavy and sudden in his ears. His adrenaline took him for a moment and Fang saw a skeletal maw stretch open before him. A wet, red tongue like a rat's tail flicked and curled back like a snake prepared to strike. The moaning lamentations of some distant hell rattled from the beast's throat. The stench of forsaken souls languishing in agony wafted from its maw and drove Fang to action.

Thrusting the blade before him and demanding his aching left arm to grasp the hilt with a second hand, he aimed the point of the blade at that infernal gullet closing upon him. His shoulder, aching with dull pain before, exploded in white-hot agony as the weight of the beast drove the blade brain-deep, through the back of its own skull, and fell with its full weight upon him.

There was a moment of thrashing, the death throes of a demon faced with oblivion, and then the final twitches of a corpse that doesn't yet know it's dead. The beast weighed more than a half-dozen men. Fang had no hope to move it in his condition; however, it didn't matter. He knew he was mortal and a fragile one at that. His breathing came steady but ragged. It was still hard to see. His vision felt narrower. The weak and dappled light grew dim. It was time to sleep. For the first time in a lifetime, he would sleep a dreamless sleep. He felt arms wrap around him. One last, long, exhausted breath and he let go. As darkness took him, he heard a filthy, familiar voice caress his ear like a spider walking along his lobe:

*Welcome home, sweetness... Fang.* Mine.

A hand ran gently along his face. Fingernails touched his cheek and cut like razors.

His soul shuddered and wept.

~

HER HANDS CLENCHED, gripping piles of something both limp and crisp. Grayce swore she heard a voice, a man's voice, calling out. Her eyes opened and she groped about for her blade.

"Fang?" she called out, rolling to her side.

"Fang?" she tried again. Then, her eyes adjusted and her head stopped spinning. She remembered a wall of matted fur, piebald skin, a skeletal face and corpse-like eyes slamming into her. Though she felt no pain at the moment, her muscles promised her days of discomfort and soreness. Sitting there, working her way out of a daze, she noticed a mound of disgusting animal nearby, huddling close to a tree. She felt around for her sword again, keeping her eyes fixed on the pile of needle-like hair. Finding no trace of her weapon, she stood on unsteady legs and took in her surroundings. One headless barghest lay where she had decapitated it. The trees blew almost noiselessly in a limp breeze. The air smelled of copper – or was that her? She dabbed her nose and her hand came away tinged in red.

*Damn.*

She recalled her and Fang's discussion – that there two of the beasts. Both now lay dead, but could there be more? There were only two on the statue, so she had to rest her hopes on that. Now, where was Fang?

The thought had barely finished when she noticed an arm protruding out from the side of the second dead beast.

"Fang!"

She ran to him, using all the strength she had left to move the four-legged demon as much as possible. It was just enough to see Fang slumped against the trunk of the tree. The barghest's head lolled to the side and Grayce saw the point of a blade sticking out from its skull. She reached around pulled the blade free. Black blood poured from the now-open wound. She looked at Fang, her heart aching. His eyes were empty. His jaw slack. These were not entirely unexpected, but then she saw the tears. They ran down his cheek, leaving trails in the dirt on his face like scratches. She had never once seen Fang cry, or even show the effects of crying. Never in all their years in the shitty little village.

"What made you cry, Fang?" she asked aloud. It would always haunt her. She felt he was ready for death at any moment. She hoped he slept well.

It only seemed right to try and bury him. But, she had no way to dig a grave and nothing to fuel a fire. She stood there, looking about for anything that would mean she wouldn't have to leave him. The small house was back in the forest and she didn't recall seeing anything there that would help. She looked at him again and closed his eyes. Then, she looked up and realized the tree he had died against. It was an aldyr: dead and without any leaves to speak of. It was the only one the area. The rest of the trees were typical of those found in the Blackwood. She crossed his arms across his lap.

"As good a gravestone as any, friend." she said.

She wiped the fetid blood from the blade and sheathed it. Grayce also took the other blade they had found as well as the breast plate with the great tree emblazoned on the front. She doubted anyone would believe her story, but believed that none would care. The gifts she brought back would hopefully build some goodwill.

When she returned to the village after her eventless trek

home, she was greeted in a manner unlike any she seen before. The stares of the people followed her. They went about their tasks and cast only furtive or distrustful glances her way. An occasional eye wandered to the armor and extra sword she bore, but only resulted in increased suspicion. It was reaffirmed to her why Fang had become the emotionless stone of a man she knew.

She visited the blacksmith first. Grayce would never let them have either blade, but knew that to keep all the treasures would not be allowed and she would have a riot on her hands. So, the breastplate went to the smith. He grunted his thanks and she left wondering what he would possibly do with the steel. It didn't seem fit for farming tools, that was for certain.

Her next stop was her own home. She took two nails from the smith as part of her compensation for the breastplate – the rest to be discussed at a later time – and used them to hang Fang's old sheathed blade above her door. The village would remember the old Sword-bearer whether they liked it or not. They would also accept the new one.

This led Grayce to her final stop for the day. In the time that she had been gone, the new Keeper appeared to be as busy as the old one. He was reading the dusty pages of some old book when she entered and recounted the last few days events. She was surprised at how little emotion she showed outwardly when describing her return to consciousness and discovering Fang. She was also surprised at how much it ached, inwardly. The Keeper took out the Book of Lines and opened to Fang's page. He wrote "Deceased - Day Nine" in elegant letters.

"Day nine?" Grayce asked.

"I'm starting to date our time here," he replied with a measure of cheerfulness in his voice. "The previous Keeper didn't think it mattered, but I think we should try to improve our way of life. And for that, we need stability and measure of records beyond the colored system of lineage and skill."

Grayce looked out at the filthy congregation listlessly going about their usual chores. The Keeper was right about one thing: there was only improvement to be had. It couldn't get worse. However, seeing as how she had been so readily made a pariah as the new Sword-bearer, she felt it was already a lost battle. These people were so mired in their misery they knew nothing else.

She looked down to see that the Keeper had turned the Book of Lines to her own page. There were so few marks there. She thought she was trying to find herself, her place, but was helping in any way she could until then. To see the story of her life tallied with a handful of colored marks that counted fewer than the farmer next door sparked a twinge of shame in her. However, the Keeper took the smallest pot from the shelf. The one she knew held the red ink. He dipped in his quill and made several red marks under her name. She had a purpose, now. It was inglorious and spited, but it was hers. It was taught to her by one of the best men she knew.

When she lay in bed that night, the fire crackling weakly to fight the chill, she thought of those tears on Fang's face. He had been alone. Held so much at bay for so long. Perhaps, in his final moment, he realized he was free? Could they possibly have been tears of joy? She hoped so. She closed her eyes and tried to clear her head. It made it easier to fall asleep when she pushed her thoughts away – bottled up like her father's inks.

Sleep slowly edged its way upon her. Rolling like lazy waves. Then she felt the deep beneath its slumbering surface. A howling like dying men echoed from the black. Teeth prowling about her. And in the distance spaces of her unconscious mind, a scream.

## THE CHILDREN OF THE VALLEY

DERO AND MALDIN TOOK A SAFER ROUTE DOWN THE SIDE OF THE trail. Still, this path was steep with treacherously loose stones and patches of soft dirt ready to give way. A broken ankle or head wound from a fall would be life-ending out here. The last village was a few days' walk back east, and the plains from here to there were not generous in the manner of water or food.

The route through the western mountain range that Dero and Maldin chose looked to be a once-popular road, judging by the remnants of cobblestone and the occasional shattered sign-post, from before the world fell. Heltik, their third man, was a dangerously stupid braggart who wanted to prove his manhood by walking a tougher stretch of the road about a hundred feet away from them. The man-child maneuvered over a patchwork of broken terraces. Jagged, knife-sharp rocks protruded from the small step-like cliffs and Heltik was in danger of stepping onto an entire patch of mountainside that could disconnect and plummet into the valley below. The quake that accompanied the end of the world shook this part of the upper continent loose, leaving nearly the whole mountain a thick swath of detritus. The paved portion soon gave way to the shattered remains of the

Belgalant Mountains. Their footing would be unsure from here onward.

"You'll wish you followed me when I get to the bottom first!" Heltik shouted.

"You'll wish you'd stayed with us when your head is crushed under a chunk of the mountainside, you dumb rotter," Maldin hollered back.

Heltik gave a too-loud laugh in his croaky, broken voice. He was too thin by half to sound the way he did; it never sat right with Dero. Every time Heltik opened his mouth it sounded like a drunken demon cackling in his gut. Red, patchwork facial hair speckled his face and his blue eyes held no intelligence in them. In fact, they made him look like a fish from the nose up. Dero found the man untrustworthy, even for a brigand. The last village should have sustained them for another week, at least, if Heltik hadn't insisted on having his way with the people the way he did.

Not that Dero minded Heltik's activities. He engaged in his fair share of debauchery while there, but this was about survival. Who knew when they'd find the next stop with ample food and water for them to take? Or, gods forbid, some ale or wine.

A shout from Heltik's direction drew their attention. They listened for a moment, and Maldin opened his mouth to call out for their companion. He was cut off by guttural laughter. "Almost bit it, right there."

"Stupid git," Maldin returned. Their voices echoed among the barren stones and dead shrubs.

"Until we get to the bottom, shut it!" Dero shouted. "We don't know who or what's around the corner in that valley."

"Probably more rocks," Maldin mumbled. "I'd kill for a loaf of fresh bread."

"We probably will when we find one, brother," Dero replied, absently invoking the term of endearment.

They'd taken several lives over food before. But that hardly made anyone a criminal these days. Dero had seen decent folk stoop to levels he'd never have imagined. As the eldest of the three, he could still remember as a young boy the frightful tales of highwaymen and the morals taught him by his mom and pop. They were vague recollections, and faded more every year. He felt like each memory of the old world lost created a new wrinkle. The other two liked to goad him into a fight over his age. One day he gave in, and the scar on Maldin's forehead would forever serve as a reminder for him to not try that again. True, he had enough wrinkles to look like their father, maybe even grandfather, but he'd survived long before they came along. And each gray hair in his beard he'd guarantee counted as another year he'd outlive these two.

The remainder of their trip along the abandoned road was uneventful save for a few more loose stones and questionable footholds. No further racket occurred from Heltik's general direction, not even the sound of shifting or falling stones. Maldin wouldn't have minded hearing evidence of an avalanche nearby, but he kept such ideas to himself.

When they reached the base of the mountains they were exhausted. They built a small fire in an alcove, away from the treacherous ruins of the Split Road, as it was labeled on a map in the last village. Heltik insisted the alcove would be safe, but Maldin cursed him for a fool and could only imagine what creature may call it home. Dero had to step between them again. Dero drew one of his blades and tossed a large stone into the empty space. Only the echoing return of the stone followed.

Satisfied that it was safe, they set their packs upon the dry ground. The alcove was covered in a fine layer of powdered rock. They had to take care when setting up camp for fear of rousing a cloud of choking dust. Maldin removed the last of the rations from among his share of the supplies.

"A dry hunk of bread, some sprigs of bay leaves, and a few pinches of salted pork. I hope that valley of yours has something in it worthwhile, Dero, or we're dead. Starved or worse," Maldin cursed. He glared at Dero through the stringy black hair that constantly fell over his face. Where Heltik was a brash, guttural mouthpiece, Maldin was a pale, brooding ghost. He preferred wine over women and quick kills over torture. The opposite in every way to Heltik.

Dero dropped a few dented canteens on his blanket. "We've got water enough for a few days yet. We can scavenge for food in the valley."

Heltik spit. "How do we know there'll be food in the bloody valley?"

"The elder of the last village. He said there were creatures in the valley and forbade his people to go there."

"So why are we fucking going there?" Maldin cut in.

Dero took a swig of the water. "We have swords. Heltik has his axes. You see anyone else recently with a decent weapon? People are spent. Their soldiers are dead because this world is shit. Their scouts and horses are dead because this world is shit. They don't have anything b—"

"Because this world is shit," Heltik said, taking one of the canteens. He began to drink deeply, draining it.

"Slow down," Dero warned sharply. "It's all we have."

Heltik shot him a scathing look but lowered the canteen. "You said it yourself; there's a valley around this corner, with living creatures in it. Living creatures need water. We'll get more."

Heltik finished off the canteen and then tossed it back on the blanket. "You know what that valley won't have? Women. I need a woman. Right now."

"Didn't you just have your fill? It was your doing that tipped them all off in the first place," Maldin sneered. It appeared even Heltik's last friend was losing patience for him.

"I had some, but not my fill," Heltik smiled with his full set of filthy, brown teeth.

Dero stared until the reprehensible scab felt his glare. Heltik caught his eyes and the smile began to fade.

"You're a rotten, sick, little shit, Heltik."

He genuinely looked hurt. "What? And you're better? How many men have I seen you kill in cold blood, aye? Fifty? A hundred? How many before we even met?"

"I've killed plenty. More than any soldier. But I never hurt any women or children,"

Dero growled.

"Nag, nag, nag. I gave 'em all a better death than most would have. I don't have no qualms about who I am; but I ain't never betrayed none of my friends, either," Heltik added venom to his last words.

Dero's hand gripped the sword at his side tighter. If Maldin hadn't brought him along, insisting that they needed the extra blades, Dero would've struck him down months ago. He had a thought, though, and it made him smile inwardly. The last of their rations would be gone by tomorrow morning. The water wouldn't last much longer, especially with Heltik in tow. The valley wouldn't be guaranteed to have drinkable water, so they may have to ration further. That wouldn't sit well with the brown-toothed gutter rat. Maldin wouldn't be too sad to see him go at this juncture. Cutting him down would ease the consumption of the water and provide a bit of good meat as well. Many a problem could be solved tomorrow.

"Get some sleep," Dero ordered, knowing he'd be awake until he heard the other two snoring.

Maldin and Heltik laid out their roughspun blankets by the fire. They squirmed and attempted to get comfortable on the scratchy material. Hopefully, the next town they crossed would have better linens to take.

Dero sat up for some time. That valley would be their biggest hope. In the deep recesses of his mind, he knew what the three of them were refusing to tell themselves. They weren't even sure if there *was* a valley in the first place. Before they killed him, Dero had befriended the village elder and learned about the surrounding area. The same had been done time and time again whenever they found a small enough hamlet. The bigger towns were more difficult, but men with weapons could find pay easy enough when they couldn't just take what they wanted. He hoped their weapons would be enough for whatever they may find in that stretch between the two close, hugging mountain ranges. The map was drafted before The Rupture. It had marks and crude lines attempting to adjust it to the changed world.

The Belgalant Mountains must have looked magnificent once, but they had been laid low. Rough etchings showed the boundaries of the mountains were larger due to their peaks collapsing. The name of the range was crossed out and someone had written in "The Shattered Peaks." There must have been tunnels, which meant dwarves, under the mountains as chunks of the range sunk into the ground. This left pockmarks dotting the now flatter, wider landmark. One of the scars ran through the mountain and provided a route to pass without going over the smaller but unstable peaks. This scar also ran into a newly formed valley, their current destination.

The elder forbade his people from going there due to the danger. He knew of traders and caravans that had travelled west from time to time, but he'd never seen any of the same merchants return. Could be they found a better life or a decent place to call home. Maybe they avoided the valley altogether, or, most likely, they died. Tomorrow, one way or the other, the three of them would find out as well.

THE SUN ROSE in a clear blue sky for once, instead of behind grey clouds or in a blood-red haze. Dero took that as a good sign. They gathered up their supplies and, after Dero nearly removed Heltik's hand for gulping down the water again, began their last trip around the bend to this mythical valley.

The day was cool and a strong breeze pushed through the mountain path to the west. The wind seemed to grow stronger until they could feel dirt careening off their mail. They didn't tend to wear it openly, but nearing the valley they felt it better to be prepared. Their cloaks began to whip around their feet as the walls of the mountain grew narrower and the wind stiffer.

Maldin took the opportunity to speak to Dero while the wind covered their voices. He stepped closer to him and began to speak while looking forward.

"I know Heltik isn't long for this trip," he began. It took a few more moments before he continued. "I've known him a long time, when our men ran the northern stretches of the Old Roads."

"You told me all this before, brother."

"Yes, but what I haven't told you since is that he is not the same man I remember. He was a killer, a good one. He could make people talk when we needed them to, but he never did anything like I've seen since we've been on our own."

"Nothing that you ever witnessed."

"There's honor among brigands, Dero. You didn't run with us, but he and I were taking jobs every day together. He saved me a time or two from guards, rivals—hell, even wolves once."

"He's good with those axes."

"He is. He won't go easy when the time comes."

"It won't matter," Dero said decisively. They traveled in silence from then on.

Eventually, they came upon a nice wide path that opened out of the side of the mountains. The wind weakened but remained persistent at their backs. The path ended and led into a sweeping, gently sloping hillside. The way was as barren as the mountains themselves, but it was what waited at the bottom that drew their attention.

The green foliage drew a stark line against the otherwise brown wastes. It appeared a great scythe had come through and wiped clean the land at the edge of the mountains, leaving the valley untouched. Ferns and large-leafed plants were clustered together so close you couldn't see the ground below them.

Heltik laughed with his guttural croak. "Well, look at this."

A hand clapped Dero firmly on the back. "Well done, brother. We may make it a little longer."

Even Dero dared a quick smile. Then his face quickly dropped. He looked from one end of the valley to the other. He scanned slowly, trying to see around and through the vibrant green foliage carpeting it.

"Shit."

Maldin began to look about as well. "What? What do you see?"

"It's what I don't see," Dero said, fuming. "Water. No river, no lake, not even a fucking cow pond."

Dero could hear Maldin's audible sigh. "The plants are big, and they cover everything. Maybe there's water underneath we can't see. It may not be much, but we could make use of whatever we find. There's too much green here to not have any water."

"Maybe."

It was possible, and it gave Dero some hope. He glanced over to see Heltik wearing a concerned expression. He normally had some shit-eating smirk on his face. Now, he looked worried— even afraid.

"What is it?" Dero asked.

"Something's out there." Heltik drew his axes, both sharp and well-honed. He was, for all his faults, a monster with his axes. "I saw it."

At first, Dero wasn't concerned. It may have been game, which would be a relief. Game meant food and there wouldn't be animals without water of some sort.

"Probably an animal. Let's hunt," Maldin said impatiently. "We've seen all we can see from here."

Dero and Heltik agreed. Maldin led the way. When they neared the valley floor, a multitude of roots, half-buried and as thick as a man's arm, preceded the greenery. This was a lush and fertile area. There must be water somewhere. Dero decided they wouldn't leave until it was found. They'd uproot every fucking plant here if the need arose.

They pushed aside broad leaves and moved around fat-trunked ferns. All manner of lush plant life was to be found here. The footing was as shaky and uneven as the mountain trail as a result of the carpet of leafy vines and roots curling about the base of the squat boles. Maldin caught his foot in a tangle of roots and nearly fell face-first into a mass of branches. He cursed and drew his sword, hacking away at the tangle that caused his embarrassment.

Heltik began cutting away at the vegetation with both axes. He hacked and chopped anything he could reach, at times looking like he was in a blind rage. He stopped to catch his breath and saw Dero and Maldin staring at him in a combination of annoyance and confusion.

"You said you wanted to find water, didn't you?" He spat at them. "Help me cut."

Dero and Maldin drew their weapons and began swinging in heavy, lazy arcs to clear away the dense plant life. Below the leaves and fronds lay roots, brambles, and curling vines in flat patches like a dead man's veins. Where was the damn water?

In a short time, Dero reached a peak point of frustration. He cursed, roared, and began chopping at the vine-matted valley floor. He stumbled over a shrub, which enraged him further. He cursed the plants as though they were people who'd wronged him. He cut away at them and remembered the faces of all the guards, merchants, and travelers from his days as a brigand. The slashes became their screams. The impact of his blade on bark melded with the memory of his blade cutting through protective leather.

When he regained control and the red haze no longer clouded his vision, he tried to slow his breathing. Nothing remained of that world any longer. The paved roads were broken and overgrown. The cities were in ruins; haunted and too dangerous to ever dare approach, even for three hardened killers. Their old gang was dead, as were any friends they once had. Every day was a slow trek through misery and every hell imaginable. So, they took what they needed and what they wanted. They mourned not at all for those they left behind them, caring not if they left them alive or dead. Alda surely didn't care.

As he stood there seething over fate and other pointless things, he noticed something. It was in the dirt, which he could finally see after cutting the vine-covered floor into countless uneven curls of dead worms. It was a relief one moment, and a cutting realization the next. He got a bitter taste in his mouth.

Maldin came over, wisely waiting until the moment of rage had passed and saw Dero staring at the ground. He looked and saw nothing but dirt. It was dark—and wet. In a panic, Maldin dropped to his knees and began pulling handfuls of moist earth from the ground and throwing them aside in heavy clumps.

"No. No no no no," He repeated, over and over with each handful that came out. A foot into the ground and he began pulling out handfuls of mud. He kept digging until finally, Dero pulled him to his feet.

"It's no fucking use. The water's in the ground. The plants are getting what we can't."

Maldin was breathing heavily from exertion and frustration. "Maybe the water is feeding from the other side of the valley. Maybe there a creek in a cave or underground—"

"Underground?" Dero asked derisively.

They both looked back at the hole made by Maldin's maddened digging. It wasn't just wet mud now. A small amount of brown water had emerged and was sitting at the bottom, taunting and disparaging them.

"There's your underground," Dero said, with gruff resignation.

Dero contemplated what they could do next. They could keep searching. What else did they have to do but survive? Past this valley there was supposed to be a forest and a lake, but with no hydration between here and there, none of them would make it that far. Then he saw it. Something stood out among the vast greenery. A pale, white spot several hundred feet away. He squinted, trying to get a better look, then it moved.

He lifted his sword, and Maldin's shoulders tensed. "What? What is it?"

Maldin trusted Dero's instincts almost more than his own. If he raised his sword, it wasn't without cause. He was quick to anger and quicker to kill, but Dero could smell danger like a bloodhound.

"I don't know yet." It was a growled whisper that told Maldin to shut up and prepare his weapon. He was familiar with this tone from Dero. It never ended well.

Maldin followed Dero as they walked as cautiously as they could over the tangled ground. Gripping his weapon with both hands, he was prepared to strike hard at whatever came. He walked a few steps behind and to the side of Dero. He looked ahead and finally saw what the old bandit was focused on. A small, pale dome peeking from the green. He stopped a moment, taken aback by the discovery. His periphery caught sight of something else. He heard a rustling sound and looked over to see another of the strange shapes to their left.

"Another one," Maldin said in a low voice. "What is it?"

"Whatever it is, another one just showed up by that one." Dero pointed to the first bald spot in front of them. Indeed, a second one was now nearby.

"They're surrounding us," Dero said.

"What the hell are they? Maybe it's just another plant."

"That just started popping up among the others? More likely some dangerous animal or worse. They're hunting us, and we're going to have to kill a whole herd of them." Dero was looking forward to this in a small way. At least they could drink the blood for now and save the water.

Dero heard Maldin suck in a fearful breath and turned to see him staring at an empty green expanse. He jerked his head back to where two other small bald patches should have been sitting menacingly, finding nothing there.

"They're gone," Maldin observed. To Dero's disbelief, whatever it was had genuinely vanished beneath the leaves.

A choked and gargled cry drew Dero's attention back to his companion. It took only a few seconds for him to realize what occurred before his own eyes. A hand axe was buried almost to the hilt in Maldin's skull, cutting him down to the nose. Maldin's mouth hung open in the unvoiced scream of one already dead.

His convulsing form collapsed to the ground as Heltik pulled the axe from his head with a sickening crunch.

"Had to be one of you first," Heltik croaked. "Would've preferred you, but Maldin was closer. Shame. I think I could've made him see reason after I chopped you down like one of these fat little plants."

Dero was livid. He felt the blood run through his neck and the heat around his collar. He forgot, albeit momentarily, of the hidden things that lurked around them. He didn't recall those pale, still forms in time to prevent him from lunging at the dead man who murdered his brother.

Two axes swung up and intercepted the blade meant for Heltik's neck. The sound of the weapons connecting echoed through the valley. It was difficult enough to navigate the grasping and shifting tangle of the floor's vegetation when they weren't fighting; now, it was all Dero could do to outmaneuver the faster Heltik. It felt for a moment, Dero swore, that the floor had moved on its own. He parried and shoved Heltik back hard enough to cause him to stumble. It put some distance between them and Dero remembered that something was waiting in the underbrush.

Perhaps it was the look of concern on Dero's face, the desperation with which he shoved wiry Heltik away, or both, but Heltik hesitated. He smiled in the manner that made Dero's blood churn.

"Struck a nerve, have I?" he croaked. "What? You thought you were some murderer with a code and that made you better than scum like me, and now you figure out that we have more in common than you'd like."

"Shut up," Dero whispered harshly.

Heltik continued to grin at him with those rheumy eyes. "Oh, come on, now. Don't—"

"Shut your shit-rank mouth. Something's out here."

Dero thought he heard Heltik laughing again; that guttural, staccato clicking that scratched his nerves raw. When Dero looked at him, however, Heltik's pocked face was marred with a frown. The noise was coming from behind him. Dero swung his blade in a quick, but sloppy arc. The desperate move should still have cut down whatever was behind him or, at least, drove it back.

A grisly surprise was waiting for him. Blood, dark as wine and thick as jelly, was splattered among the broad leaves. He had to look for a moment to find what it belonged to. A pale, gaunt figure lay among the brambles of the valley floor. At least, a body lay there. The head was missing. Dero must have been graced with a lucky swing and decapitated the creature.

As he looked closer, it appeared quite human, albeit small and sickly. The skin was a pasty gray, and stretched too tight over small, thin bones. Was this a child? He grimaced at the thought. Then he took in the horror that was its hands. There were only four fingers, too long by inches, and possessing an extra knuckle. The fingernails, if this were appropriate to call them, were short and pointed. The creature lay on its side and Dero felt a sickening temptation to turn it onto its back so he could get a better look at the thing. A sudden sound of disturbed foliage reminded him of the murderer whom he had turned his back on.

Cursing himself for a fool, he stood and wheeled on Heltik. Dero prepared his sword for a fight, but to his surprise saw only Heltik's back. The murderer was charging clumsily through the brush. Dero was cursing Heltik for a coward, when he saw what drove the man into his mad flight. A dozen of the pale domes were sitting silent around Dero. They were as still as the plants. Every few seconds, one would bob just slightly, barely perceivable.

Dero backed away slowly. He looked to his left and his right, trying to spot any more of the elusive creatures. It disturbed him to realize he had yet to see one alive and whole. He found another patch of blood soaking yet more leaves, and wondered if Heltik took one of the creatures down before he turned and ran. Dero then realized it was brighter, more human. It was where Maldin had fallen. He edged his way over to his brother. The gray-white shapes had not moved.

When he reached the spot where his brother lay, his jaw clenched in conjoined anger and repulsion. Maldin's skin was as white as those long dead. His skin was pulled tight, leaving his teeth bared in a pained rictus. His eyes bulged from strained sockets. Strangest of all, his body was marred with numerous holes. They ranged in size from small pinpricks to as large as a stab wound. A chittering sound came from the distance, behind the dome shapes. One of the creatures lurched slowly along the waist-high greenery, dark red rivulets pouring from along the bottom length of its torso. Dero's stomach lurched at the thought of these creatures as hideous tenders of this infernal garden, literally feeding it with the blood of those who trespass. That one was using Maldin's blood. His disgust began to heat and reforge into anger. Dero looked at the unmoving domes again, then to Heltik.

The brown-toothed and black-souled villain had made little progress. Whether it was the result of the difficult terrain or the sinister little occupants he could not tell. He was panicked, however, and now both axes appeared to be covered in blood.

Dero sneered and began to chase after him. First, his brother's killer would die. Then, he would leave this cursed valley and never look back. He began to chase after his mark and discovered why Heltik was having such difficulty. The roots and brambles seemed to shift as he ran. It was as though the plants themselves were slowing them for those horrid little creatures.

A scream pierced the silence of the valley. Dero looked up

from watching his steps to see Heltik flailing uselessly with one arm. The other arm, along with the entirety of that half of his back, was engulfed in a wing of pale-grey skin. Thin bones ran under the wing like the frame of a tent. The head and upper jaw of one of the child-like creatures rested on its maw on Heltik's shoulder. Then, Heltik turned and Dero beheld a true horror. An ovular wing of the same pale skin had attached itself around Heltik's chest and stomach. As Dero stared, rapt with terror, he realized these weren't wings, but the body of the creature folding around Heltik. Teeth lined the flaps of skin and dug into Heltik, through mail and leather, and the upper mandible gnawed into his shoulder and upper arm. Heltik howled in agony, and Dero, for a moment, considered ending it. Heltik fell to one knee, his free hand dropped the axe, and he toppled backward into the brush. His screams faded, and Dero smiled.

He began to make his way quickly, but more carefully, for the edge of the valley floor. The guttural clicking began again. It surrounded him and echoed off the mountains. It reminded him of the cicadas in the woods from before. His pace slowed but never stopped. He had to continue forward. Dero thought he heard a hiss: sharp and quick. It jolted him, made him lose his balance. His foot caught a root looping from the dirt and he fell forward. It was a hard, jarring fall. It took a moment for Dero to regain his breath and look around. Being under the broad leaves felt like he had fallen into a different world. Much of the sun was blotted out. The ground was a tapestry of roots and vines that snaked among each other like guilty lovers in a tryst. Small insects crept in and out of holes in the trunks of the waist-high boles. It smelled of wet dirt and mildew. Wet dirt... he was so thirsty. It was beginning to occur to him how much he really needed water.

He dug into the earth with his hands, so desperate for a drink that even the soil-saturated water beneath the ground would suffice. He felt his hands sink into wet earth and began digging faster. Pulling up chunks of mud, he stopped, noticing the stains on his hands. A small amount of fluid had built up in the bottom of the hole. He looked at his hands, his heart growing cold, and saw they were stained with blood. He dipped his hand in the liquid that built up and pulled it away, up to his face. It looked like he had run his fingers knuckle-deep into a fresh wound. These plants were not feeding on water. These creatures were their ghastly keepers. The grounds of this valley were soaked in blood. This was an unnatural, unholy place. He stifled a frustrated, fearful scream. Something moved in front of him.

He sucked in a breath and held it. Two red orbs caught the glint of filtered sunlight. They flashed, veins exposed within the bulging white eyes, and an eager clicking followed. Dero stood and ran as fast as his legs would carry him. He nearly stumbled half a dozen times in a matter of seconds. He hit a patch of brambles and it tore through his trousers to the flesh below. He felt a red heat and knew he was bleeding; he ignored the sudden panicked thought of potential poisoning. Who knew what unnatural horrors this valley had yet to reveal.

The edge of the greenery, opposite from where they had entered, was within sight. He felt a sudden elation, then came to an abrupt stop. A cold hand squeezed his insides. One of the domes, the head of one of those vicious, child-like abominations, was directly in his path. He waited, hesitated, and began to slowly side-step around it. He saw no others, and when there was ample space between himself and the evil thing he would run again.

Then the pale object did something new. It moved toward him. He tasted bile, parched and painful. He froze for a moment, watching the unbroken, loping stride of the unknown atrocity. It moved with a haunting grace. Dero steeled himself, cursed himself for a coward, and forced his feet to move again.

The creature followed Dero like it was attached somehow. It flowed effortlessly in his direction no matter where or how suddenly he shifted, and it was getting closer.

"What are you?" he shouted, the valley and its inhabitants be damned. "What are you?"

The fleshy dome moved to within a few feet. Dero gripped his sword and was prepared to fight for every inch of his journey to the valley's end. He wasn't dying here today, especially not to these things.

A fringed spine attached to the domed head showed itself above the waste-high foliage, shuddering and bobbing like driftwood on a disturbed lake, and then began to rise. It looked nearly identical to the body that lay beheaded further behind him. Perhaps a little bigger. Dero would have called it hunchbacked, but he soon realized it was not something so simple.

The spine bent at too many angles, as a curled, gouty finger would do. The top half of a head, vaguely human while also barely worth being described as such, cocked sideways as it looked at him. Sharp teeth as thin as fish bones sat unevenly lined behind all-but-absent lips. The bottom of the skull seemed to disappear into fleshy folds attached to the thing's chest. The nose was little more than a small, triangular orifice that puckered as the thing breathed, like the mouth of a fish.

The eyes—sweet gods, the eyes—were swollen, milky spheres lined with bloodshot red veins that stared at nothing. The creature didn't even appear to be looking at Dero, but behind him. He jerked his neck around to see nothing lurking behind him. When he turned back to the creature, it had moved closer. The cloudy eyes slid downward, revealing themselves to be a thin membrane covering a set of blood-red spheres that shimmered with malice. The creature made the sound he heard in the world below the brush: a blood-chilling clicking.

He saw no mouth, only a vertical scar running from below the nose to the infected-looking folds where the chest and jaw met. Dero thought, with sickening dread, that no worse a fate could befall a creature. His words tempted fate, and fate replied in kind. The creature unfolded, its spine uncurling and cracking like old knuckles. The scar ran the full length of the creature's vaguely human body. It ran from the nose to the sexless groin. The folds beneath the half-skull quivered, and the scar ripped open. It continued to tear down the center of the creature until the chest and belly of the being opened and unfolded. He recognized the fan of flesh that gripped Heltik and felt his bowels loosen.

Wet, red flesh lined with hundreds of teeth in dozens of sizes trembled and shuddered. They clicked together in a strange unison, then in a chaotic disharmony. A guttural croak emanated from somewhere on the creature, and its many-knuckled fingers flexed and tensed. Dero made a move for his blade, but the creature moved with surprising swiftness. He felt a warm, wet embrace around his stomach and chest. It was quickly followed by thousands of knives pressing into him at once. He screamed, feeling a nauseating pressure upon his whole body. The creature was consuming him.

With a strength borne of terror and survival instinct, he grabbed the creatures head in his hands. He pressed his thumbs into the red, menacing eyes and squeezed with everything he had. He heard an audible pop and felt something warm splash against his face. A soul-shattering howl nearly ripped the hearing from his ears. The pressure was gone, and the creature had fallen back and disappeared under the leaves.

He stumbled, weakly, toward the mountains on the other side of the valley. Each step was agony; he forced one foot in front of the other. He felt cold and began to shiver. His shaking hands could barely feel the rivulets of blood that ran down to his fingertips. When he felt he could no further, when his will began to give in to fatigue, he saw the most lovely shades of brown and gray. The dead wastes of the world he was familiar with were stretched before him.

Dero smiled weakly. Then he heard the water. A constant dripping that made him unbearably thirsty. He knew he would find it, now he just had to follow the sound. It was nearby, so close. But where?

*Drip. Drip. Drip.*

He looked around, out towards the mountains, up to the sky, and out among the cursed green. Finally, he looked down. He saw the drops of blood falling from his soaked clothing and his stained hands.

*Drip. Drip. Drip.*

He sighed, dropping to his knees. It was the last he had in him. Several pairs of red eyes were watching him. The eyes of the dead. The murdered. The robbed. The innocent.

"I'm sorry," he said weakly. "It was you or me."

The eyes closed in. He felt pressure on his arm, but only barely. He turned and stared directly into a pair of crimson, hateful circles. Its body engulfed his arm similar to the way one had taken Heltik's. He felt a warm hug against his back. The pain was only brief. Too much blood had been lost to feel much else. He felt himself fading and laid down on the roots and vines. He smelled the wet earth and was chilled in the dappled shadows.

In moments, all was still again. The blessed green waited. The valley was silent and peaceful once more.

## ASHES OF ALDYR

Annica watched the caravel sail into the shabby, worn harbor of her riverside village with great interest. Being next to the wide, shallow waters of the River Leen, she had seen several ships come and go. There weren't many these days and fewer arrived every year. None of them looked like this ship, though.

Clean planks shone in the sun that filtered through the midday clouds. The ropes hanging from the mast and riggings weren't frayed or broken, flailing limply in the breeze. No smell of stale salt water and dead fish followed the caravel into port. The crew looked strong and healthy as they bustled about with their tasks on the deck. And the sails; they were something truly magnificent. Large and white like a gull's wings, they weren't marred by any holes or half-hearted patch-jobs. They fluttered proudly in the riverside gusts. The symbol embroidered on the sails was a large green tree with wavy, serpentine branches.

When the ship sailed to a stop, a uniformed woman with eyes like glaciers walked down the gangplank to greet Benli, the stooped, grizzled harbormaster. Benli wasn't tall by any means and his posture made him look even shorter next to the blonde-haired captain. Benli had several days' worth of patchy stubble and dirty clothes. The captain had impeccable short-cropped hair and buttons made of what must have been silver on her vest. Annica smirked at the sight. They couldn't have looked any more different next to one another.

"Are you the harbormaster?" the captain asked.

"Aye. Not much of a harbor for not much of a village, but it's a place to rest your backs. Even ships like yours," Benli grunted.

The captain smiled at the harbormaster. She had a swagger about her even when standing still. She looked over to where Annica stood. A crowd was gathering ever since the ship was sighted on the river. Everyone wanted to see the glorious vessel pull into port.

"We bring a trade offer to your village," the captain began as she continued looking at Benli, but spoke loud enough for all to hear. "We won't need to use your tavern or inn. My crew will be happy to stay on board our ship. We would like to offer some supplies as payment for our docking fees. Food, a few barrels of wine, and medicine for your apothecaries."

The captain gestured behind her to the boxes and barrels her crew were stacking on the dock. Benli ran his hand over his mouth and scratchy face, his eyes wide. Food was always welcome, especially if it provided some variety in the villagers' diets. Wine was rare enough, but to also receive medical supplies for the healers? The supplies' value was at least five times what the fee would be, but the harbormaster wasn't turning it down.

The captain stood straighter and looked back to Annica and the other villagers. She spoke loudly and confidently.

"We'll stay ported until morning. At that point, we will leave. Anyone who wants to come with us, back to our island, is welcome. We have room for fifty passengers. There will be no questions asked. We won't be coming back along the Leen again —ever. All we ask is that you bring a single bag to last you a two-week journey. I'll be back in this very spot tomorrow morning to receive any who wish to join us."

The captain nodded politely to the harbormaster and returned to her ship. They gangplank was retrieved, showing that no one would be boarding until the morning. The captain wanted to give the people time to consider her offer.

Annica could hear discussions and arguments coming from several homes for the rest of the day. She had only herself to be accountable to. Her parents had both passed in the last few years, sickness claiming them both throughout her teenage years. She lived in the house her family had grown up in for generations but was little more than a hovel as time and disrepair constantly sought to claim it. Her bag was packed within a few hours.

The next morning, Annica woke and took her time preparing for her journey. She looked out the windows to the fields that she helped the farmers work for meager returns, both in her pay and their crops. She lay in her pitiful bed and stared at the ceiling, seeing light poke through the many holes in the thatching. She rose and walked over to the fireplace and casually pulled a loose stone from the masonry, letting it fall to the ground. The only thing causing her to doubt the decision to leave was her fear of the unknown, of leaving behind what she knew—unenviable though it may be.

As Annica stared at the stone she let fall, she wondered how much of the unknown was worth fearing. Especially compared to her existence here. She grabbed her bag and left, not even bothering to close the door.

The captain was waiting right where she said she would be. The harbormaster was nowhere to be seen but was likely helping himself to some of the wine somewhere. Annica approached the captain who smiled at Annica as she sat her bag on the ground.

"What have we here? Another one?" the captain said, her voice husky and sultry.

Annica looked past the captain and saw an elderly couple boarding the ship. Several other villagers could be seen on the deck. Some smiling and talking, others looked hesitant or even afraid.

"Where are we going?" Annica said, looking the captain in the eyes.

Stepping aside and pointing an open palm to the ship, the captain replied, "Come aboard and I'll answer all—well, most— of your questions."

Annica looked past her again at the villagers. The sailors all but ignored them. No one guarded the gangplank. Annica even saw one person walk back down the gangplank and into the village, their bag over their shoulders. The captain's eyes flicked over to see the villager walking away and grimaced. When she looked back, she likely saw the hesitation on Annica's face.

"We're taking a risk on you all, too, you know. We don't know what type of people we're picking up, only that we take all comers. You need to give us some credit, too."

Annica sighed and picked up her bag. The captain chuckled and placed her hand on Annica's shoulder. The tall woman smelled like leather, whiskey, and citrus.

"You're making the right choice. Just wait until you see the open ocean. That alone will be worth it."

Annica smiled at the captain and left to board the ship. She had never seen the ocean. Now was as good a time as any. As she approached the ship, she saw the figurehead was a large rose, with vines underneath curled and spread along the length of the first quarter of the ship. It looked like it was painted gold. It couldn't have been real gold, could it? Annica stared at the golden rose figurehead until she reached the gangplank. Most ships had people, mermaids, dragons, or other such creatures at the head of their ships. This ship was unique in this way, as well. She turned and looked back. She only felt the slightest pull to stay behind, but ignored it. She was leaving the wilted memories of this life behind.

~

WHEN ALL THE PASSENGERS BOARDED, the gangplank was retrieved and the caravel set sail. Nearly a dozen villagers had decided to join the captain on her voyage. True to her word, the captain gave a short speech welcoming the other villagers along with Annica.

Introducing herself as Captain Sisironi, she welcomed them aboard the *Dawn Rose*. The figurehead made more sense to Annica, now. Their next stops were a few more villages along the Leen. There, they would make the same offer to the villagers. If their allotted passenger space was filled before reaching the final village, they would depart immediately for their new home at Nel Aldyri.

Annica went to raise her hand to get Captain Sisironi's attention. She wanted to ask what the name meant. Her village was called Ashwater, for its port and the ash trees that commonly grew around it. Nearby villages and towns, even the abandoned ones and those forbidden by the town elders to travel to had monikers tailored to their surroundings: Longroad, Cobble-crone, Feveroak, and the like. There was nothing as lyrical as 'Nel Aldyri'.

She felt someone lean in next to her ear. A young man's voice whispered, "It's elvish. It means 'City of the Aldyr.'"

She turned and recognized the face. She didn't know his name but had seen him helping out the smith, carpenters, and other physically laborious professions with their more taxing labor. She smiled, thanked him, and turned her attention back to the captain.

Annica heard the same speech three times, once for each village in which they stopped. Captain Sisironi accrued less than half of the passengers she had room for but didn't appear disappointed. After those final few boarded, Annica joined the villagers on the deck to hear the speech one last time. However, Captain Sisironi had more to add as they sailed away from their most recent port.

The captain explained that the next few days would be spent sailing the open ocean to the island where their new home awaited. It would be three days aboard the *Dawn Rose* and the passengers were expected to behave themselves. Captain Sisironi's face grew stern when she said that they would not be turning around, so anyone causing trouble only had one place to go. Her head turned to the side of the ship, where all eyes followed. The shores of the mainland had passed, so there was nothing but gentle waves out to the horizon.

Captain Sisironi also said they had plenty of time to make their decision about boarding the *Dawn Rose*, so anyone wanting to return to their villages would be welcome to swim back. She smiled as she said this and Annica assumed she was trying to ease the newcomers' anxiety while also making it quite clear the ship wouldn't be returning to the mainland. For anyone or anything.

"So, make yourselves comfortable," Sisironi bellowed, "We'll all be home shortly. The next few days will be spent on the waves of the Wailing Ocean. If you've heard the rumors, I assure you, I've made this journey many times. The superstitions and sailors' tales have been grossly exaggerated. The dead are nothing compared to the numerous vortices that could suck this ship down like a sober deckhand's first shot on shore leave."

Annica heard worried whispers spread among the gathered

villagers. Being from port villages, they had all likely heard the haunting tales that flowed in with crews from the ghostly waters the *Dawn Rose* now tread. She also noted Sisironi shrug as the captain's joke failed to impress.

Sisironi tried to assuage what she assumed would be superstitious fishwives' tales. When the sky opened during The Rupture, the world broke with it. Not just its soul, as could be seen with the dying of the aldyrs, but entire chunks of the world had shifted, deformed, and caved in. A large portion of Alda collapsed into itself. Some wondered if a sleeping god had awakened, or a lost subterranean society had existed that no scholar had ever discovered and the quakes shook the world above it loose. Regardless of origin, the waters of the seas that belonged to the old world rushed in. Whole kingdoms disappeared in moments. Untold millions perished as cities and temples, forests and deserts sank beneath the sinister waters.

That many deaths, so sudden and so terrible. The villagers feared what had sunk into the bones of every person born on the Leen and all other rives that led to those waters: the wrath of the drowned dead. Listen closely, legends said, and you could hear the moans in the tossing waves; feel your blood chill as a gull's cry echoed with countless screams; smell the rot of death on the salt air; see their chill hands reaching beneath the surface; taste the tangible horror of all those left to haunt the ocean floor. The sinking of whole cities and regions caused permanent whirlpools—powerful, permanent vortices—to appear like a portal to these realms of the drowned dead.

"The Wailing Ocean," a voice said, causing Annica to startle. It was the young man from her village. "Supposedly, it continues to expand as the tears of the damned cause the waters to rise every year."

He leaned on the side of the ship, looking over the ocean with her.

"That's quite grim," Annica said, smirking but raising her brows at him.

"I wonder, if you get pulled over the side by ghosts, do you get to choose where you haunt? I'd just want to be as far away from the Leen as possible," he continued, his rising pitch making it clear he was joking.

Annica chuckled. He was certainly charming. Knowing someone with a sense of humor might make the trip more bearable. Three days on the ocean, especially this ocean, didn't sound entirely thrilling.

"I'm Annica," she said.

"Edrik," he replied. "If the stories about this place didn't exist, you'd never think it was supposed to be haunted," he continued, looking out over the calm waters that rolled with the steady winds. Lines of whitecaps caught the sun as the waves crested. It was warm and peaceful—almost too good to be true.

But the hours passed and no disasters struck. No endless hordes of the ancient dead came for them in the moonlight. No unspeakable beasts crawled from the waves to drag the *Dawn Rose* down into the depths. Nothing evil or hungry or even regrettable assailed them. Annica enjoyed her time with Edrik, seeing the ocean and taking in the clouds that rose like castles and the breathtaking sunsets.

Annica watched as dolphins followed them in the ship's wake. She talked with Edrik, learned about his life growing up in the same village, and how he'd seen her around just as she'd seen him. They were both raveled so in their daily drudgery that neither ever thought to reach out to the other. Yet here they were on a striking ship, sailing to a new home they'd never seen.

It made Annica want to speak with the captain. Ask her more questions. Captain Sisironi always seemed to be roaming the decks most mornings and evenings. She didn't treat the passengers with any manner of disdain. Annica found the captain's constant smiling almost off-putting, in a way.

"Captain?" Annica asked as she approached on their third and last day of the voyage.

The tall woman in her uniform was standing at the head of the ship, watching the ocean pass by. The sun reflected off the rose figurehead. The third day on board the ship and Annica still felt she was going to wake up in her ratty bed, the glint of gold coming from the sun poking through the holes in her ceiling rather than the intricately carved sculpture.

"Yes?" she replied with a slight smirk.

"The city you're taking us to, Nel Aldyri, is it like the other villages we stopped at along the way? Like mine? I've never seen a ship like this and I just can't imagine there would be a place for us there without—"

The captain, chortling, cut her off. "You still think we're going to make slaves out of you all?"

It wasn't Annica's only thought, but she couldn't deny it. The captain read Annica's hesitation in her mannerisms; the way Annica grimaced and looked down, embarrassed.

"You have nothing to worry about, girl. If we wanted slaves, we wouldn't have sailed into your village with an offer and trade. Just wait until you see our soldiers. Best-equipped in the world, I'd wager, especially since The Rupture."

Annica looked back up at her and managed a small smile. "It's Annica," she said.

"Well, Annica, you'll earn your keep, certainly. And you'll work as hard as the rest of us to do so."

Annica nodded and looked back to the ship's deck. Several of the passengers were staring out to sea, watching the waves pass by as the captain had been doing.

"I counted after each village. You only met half your goal, at most. Will your elders be disappointed?"

"You're a smart one, aren't you?" Sisironi said, her smile growing wide. "They most certainly won't be. We've never met our quota. In fact, this is one of the largest groups we've ever brought back."

The captain's smile waned. "It's getting bad out there. Every year it's worse. We had no incidents this year, but most years we run into empty villages, hostile ones, or worse. We were lucky. This was a good year. I imagine within the next few voyages we'll be forced to take soldiers with us. They already make their own excursions with other ship captains into more dangerous territory. Not all of them come back."

"I'm sorry," Annica offered politely. Life had been a cold gamble since she'd been born. Nel Aldyri must be quite the place, indeed, if the mainland seemed uniquely horrible for its citizens. "Well, if this turns out to be a dream come true, I can't thank you enough."

"And if it doesn't?" the captain teased with a gleam in her eye.

Annica looked out over the water. It's surface beautiful and glistening, where below lay ruin and bones. She shrugged. "No real surprise, I suppose."

"You're far too macabre, Annica. Enjoy the trip. We're almost there."

The captain spoke truly. A warm afternoon with Edrik on deck was interrupted by a long, sharp blow of a whistle. Passengers gathered at the head of the ship to see an island off the horizon.

The ship came alive as the hours passed and the island grew larger where the ocean met the still-blue sky. Sisironi began barking orders to the sailors, preparing to dock the ship at Nel Aldyri. The captain ordered all villagers to the passenger quarters to keep them out of the way. As Edrik and Annica turned to follow the crowd, she heard him mutter, "Was that a tree?"

Annica looked back, tipping on her toes just in time to see the hazy outline of the island: long, low, and flat. Sprouting off its western side was the largest tree Annica had ever seen. She didn't get to see much else as they were all ushered below decks.

THE NEXT TIME they came above decks they were met with a bustle of activity and the noise of a busy harbor. Gulls called, sailors shouted, and there was an energy here that Annica had never before experienced. Buildings were painted, stone houses were properly mortared, and smells both enticing and distasteful mingled in the air. This was a city untouched by The Rupture.

The captain set her sailors about their tasks then called the villagers together. Everyone gathered, but many heads continued to turn and many necks craned to look out at the hopeful, unfamiliar surroundings.

"Welcome to Nel Aldyri," the captain shouted. "First, you will follow me to the Hall of Receiving where you'll be allocated a role within our society. Some of you may even find your way back here, working for me," she chuckled.

"Come," Sisironi barked as she gestured for all the villagers to follow her.

Every villager did so obediently without complaint or question. If they felt the same way Annica did, it was because they were still dumbstruck at the sights before them and could only follow out of instinct. A few sailors helped guide the villagers to the gangplank and followed behind to ensure none were lost.

The Hall of Receiving was a single-story building made of stone with a large, doorless arch for the main entrance. The captain stopped by the door and motioned for them all to enter.

As Annica passed, Sisironi looked at her and said in a quiet, friendly voice, "Welcome home."

Inside, there were few decorations but the building still had plenty of large windows that let a soft breeze flow through the room. One large table with a few simple chairs sat in one corner. Paintings of aldyr trees hung on the walls. It was simple but not wholly utilitarian.

Annica saw the captain standing by the entrance for a few minutes before she nodded, spoke to someone out of earshot, then nodded again and left. An elderly gentleman entered, followed by a number of other official-looking individuals of all ages. They were all dressed in white and green robes and carried themselves formally, nearly floating as they walked. They looked almost bored, judging by their expressions—except for the gentleman. He had a seemingly permanent, practiced smile on his face.

Annica and Edrik watched as the robed officials whispered among themselves for a moment. Then the smiling gentleman separated from the flock and approached the villagers. The haggard newcomers from the struggling villages looked awkward in this pristine place that seemed stolen from time. His eyes scanned the gathered strangers and he opened his arms, as though preparing to embrace the lot of them. He then clasped his hands together with a gentle clap.

"Welcome, all of you. Welcome, welcome," he repeated softly. His grey eyes flicked to Annica for a moment then back to a stare that seemed to encompass all of them and none of them.

"You are in the Hall of Reception, where many have preceded you," he continued. His voice was soft and aged, grandfatherly in its warmth. "I am Nostrado. The people behind me are my fellow Receptors. Our society here, our island, our city, is built on hard work and community. Just like the days of our ancestors. To maintain this wonderful balance, everyone must have a role to fill. To begin, we'll ask a series of questions. We ask that you be honest, as everyone has a place here. No one will be tossed aside or left despondent. You'll soon see we have no beggars in our streets."

Nostrado continued, asking the villagers to first line up along a wall. There was some apprehension, but his gentle nature eased most of it among the villagers. He walked slowly in front of them. After he finished he stepped aside and summoned over two of his fellows. A younger woman, light-haired and dark-complexioned, and a middle-aged gentleman with a square jaw that appeared to still be quite muscular under his robes stepped over to Nostrado. They were carrying parchment on a wooden board that was fixed with an inkwell. Both held quills in their free hand.

They conversed among themselves before the two summoned officials took their own walk along the line of newcomers: one in front, one behind, and then switching places. The staccato scratching of quills rising and falling as they went from villager to villager. Whoever was in front took names, each time, so that both officials had the name of every villager.

When they'd finished inspecting the villagers, leaving Annica feeling like one of many fish strung up on a dock for sale, they met with Nostrado and began conversing quietly again. In a short time, the elderly gentleman addressed them again.

Nostrado pointed out the old among them, asking them to step to one side of the large room. Annica recognized the elderly couple from her village she'd seen walking up the gangplank only a few days ago among them. The old wife was clutching a pendant to her chest. It was cheap metal, tarnished and unappealing, but she held it close like it was her most precious possession. The pendant was a six-pointed star with a rose in the center; the symbol of an old-world goddess of hope and good fortune, if Annica remembered correctly. The young woman that had been inspecting the villagers went to the gathered elderly and escorted them from the room. Annica's eyes lingered on the old woman and her pendant.

"Our elders have a special place among us, having survived so many years," Nostrado said. Annica thought it strange he spoke of them that way, likely being near the same age. "Now, for our next selection, I'd like the following to step forward: Nikus, Lot, Dayna, and Edrik."

Four villagers stepped forward, Edrik included. They stood with confused looks on their faces, glancing back and forth at each other trying to piece together the purpose for which they'd been chosen.

Nostrado nodded firmly at them. "Yes, strong, able-bodied. Young and, I hope, eager to learn. You're prime recruits for our military. It's second to none and a proud position here. Congratulations."

Upon hearing their appointment, none of the new recruits complained. One seemed quite pleased. Edrik looked to Annica and simply shrugged. The squared-jawed official led them from the room and Nostrado continued his filtering of skills and talents. Carpenters, smiths, and masons were separated, then apothecaries, midwives, and others with highly valuable skills. They were all led from the room by a different green- or white-robed official. Finally, only Annica and a handful of others remained.

The last separation was simple: literate and illiterate. Annica, a young woman, and a gruff-looking man stood where placed in the literate grouping. The rest were asked to simply stay put. Nostrado called over one of the last officials remaining then instructed those who couldn't read or write to be sent to the docks. New sailors and dockhands were always welcome.

Almost immediately, one long-haired, scrawny man began

shouting. He refused to work the docks, stating he was more useful elsewhere. He bellowed that he didn't leave a dying fishing village to come work at the docks of another. Annica felt that these docks were probably quite different from those he'd known, but the man continued to cause a scene.

It must have been only a minute or so before guards came into the room. They brandished dangerous-looking swords and wore fine steel breastplates engraved with the same strange tree symbol as the *Dawn Rose*'s sails. They were intimidating and efficient, subduing the man and dragging him away with what seemed like minimal effort. She could imagine Edrik bearing such armor soon and a smile came to her face.

"What will happen to him?" one of the remaining villagers asked.

"You'll soon see when you leave this hall that we have no gallows, either. Don't worry, I'm sure Holdyn will come around," Nostrado answered in his warm, inviting voice. He must have known the man's name from the notes taken so far by the many officials, Annica surmised.

"Now," the gentleman piped up, clasping his hands together, "what will we do with you three, hmm?" His calmness was somehow reassuring and unsettling at the same time. He approached the last three villagers remaining: a young man, a little girl not yet in her teenage years, and Annica.

Annica watched him go first to the young man—thin-framed and with a large forehead that glistened like a wet egg from sweating. Nostrado took the man's chin between his fingers, looked in his eyes for a moment, and sent him with an official to be an archivist at their library. The young girl next to Annica was taken by the last official to be a disciple at something called the Temple of the First Son, the only place of worship in the city according to Nostrado.

"All that's left is you, dear," Nostrado said, patting Annica on the shoulder. "I'll have to escort you myself. First, let's see where you're going, yes?"

With his hand open, flat, and palm up, Nostrado placed the tip of his fingers on Annica's chin and lifted her eyes so she could see into his. It wasn't much, as she was nearly as tall as the old gentleman, but the formality of his posture made him seem much taller than he was.

He looked into her eyes, the only sound his breathing going in and out in a steady rhythm. Annica felt the wind on her skin. She could hear the leaves rustle in the trees and bushes outside. The salt in the air was sharper, her heart louder. She saw his gray eyes widen slightly, his pupils dilate.

"You... are coming with me to the temple," he said, but his hesitation made a rock appear in her stomach. His demeanor broke momentarily. The near-dreamlike sensations from a moment ago faded as a feeling of alarm crawled up to replace them.

"I can catch up with the other two—" Annica began, but Nostrado raised a hand that quieted her.

"No, I'll take you myself. Please, follow me."

They left the Hall of Reception and Annica saw the streets of the city for the first time. They were paved, all of them, and the stone buildings still had all the stones in the right place. Wooden shops looked inviting and market stalls didn't sag or appear ready to crumble into kindling. A man sat on a street corner playing the lute, its melody echoing off the walls of buildings and reaching Annica and Nostrado even as they turned a corner. It was there the music stopped.

The placement of the structures became less tightly packed. The buildings punctuated grassy lawns and unclaimed space still covered in bushes and trees. The street led up a steep incline until they came to the crest of a hill. A building lay at the end of the street that looked like it sprang from a storybook. It was flat-topped, built of some kind of white stone, and had ornately carved pillars at the top of stairs that encircled the entire front of the structure and along roughly one-third of the sides. Hanging between the pillars were long white banners with the same symbol from the ships at the harbor: a green tree with waving, serpent-like branches.

Annica felt a tickle in the back of her head. She ruffled the back of her hair, fearing something landed in it. Her hand grasped nothing but locks of hair. The brief panic left her and her eyes were drawn from the majesty of the temple to the sprawling fields opposite of it. From this vantage point, they could see the last of the city's buildings spreading like spilled rocks until they came to a sudden stop. Beyond lay the tree that Annica had seen just before their arrival. It was the largest aldyr Annica had ever seen. Indeed, it was the largest tree Annica had ever laid eyes on at all. And it was in full bloom.

Her eyes lingered there, stuck on the tree like she was searching for something among its massive boughs. She couldn't pull them away. It was as though the tree had a soul of its own, like the elves always believed, and it spoke to her. Unlike the symbol of Nel Aldyri with the wavy, tentacle-like extensions, the branches of the actual tree looked completely normal, albeit massive. The blossoms must have been beyond count and the ground around it was stained with patches of red, no doubt from the untold number of aldyrfruit that fell unclaimed to the ground.

Annica felt a hand on her shoulder and she turned to see Nostrado nodding in the direction of the temple. Groups of people stood around the temple grounds in robes of sheer white or solid green, looking like flocks of birds until Annica and her escort came closer. She saw a fountain in the center of the grounds that trickled water into a basin where actual birds drank and bathed.

"It's like something out of a dream," she muttered.

"Indeed, child. Indeed," Nostrado replied.

Inside the temple, the tall ceiling and large floor spaces felt open and provided a sense of grandeur. Annica noticed there were fewer green-robed individuals than white-robed ones. No matter the color of their robes, everyone stood straight and formal. Their faces were masks of academic detachment.

Nostrado led Annica near the back of the grand foyer. He bid her wait for him as he approached a regal-looking woman whose hair Annica couldn't decide was black streaked with gray or vice versa. The disinterest on her face mixed with another, more domineering expression: authority.

The white-robed Nostrado approached her and bowed his head slightly as she looked over to him. The woman's eyebrows raised and her smile caused wrinkles to appear next to her eyes, marring her otherwise smooth skin. She was a handsome, older woman who radiated an aura of power and control.

The two quietly discussed something between themselves. Annica noticed the woman's brows lift before looking over at her. Annica averted her eyes and began looking around at the other people; some wearing green or white robes and others obviously citizens from the city.

From the corner of her eye, Annica saw the two approach her. They were of equal height and Annica noticed that the woman was wearing a robe that was both green and white. She was the only one Annica had seen wearing both colors.

"Annica, this is Helyn," Nostrado said, moving aside and giving room for Helyn to have Annica's full attention.

"Lovely to meet you, Annica."

Helyn's voice was strong and unaffected by age. She sounded much younger than her appearance would suggest. Annica smiled and returned the courteous greeting. Helyn seemed to regard her strangely for a moment before turning to Nostrado.

"Thank you, Nostrado. You may return to your duties," Helyn said plainly. Nostrado bowed his head and left, fading into the crowd that grew denser near the entrance of the temple.

"Walk with me, Annica."

Helyn led her to the top of the dais at the back of the main vestibule where it sat in a large alcove. The large, open-arched entrances to two other rooms were located on either side, directly across from the dais; however, the alcove was of ample enough size for room to walk behind the dais. This revealed yet another entrance. Unlike the other two, this one had a set of wooden, heavy-looking double doors that were closed. The tree symbol of Nel Aldyri was ornately carved into the front and split in half by the separation of the doors. A statue of the same large tree with spindly, leafless branches was in the center of the dais' apex and it was here where Helyn led Annica. Upon closer inspection, the cream-colored statue was not carved of stone, but rather it appeared to be polished wood.

"Is this—"

"A tree?" Helyn finished her sentence with a proud smile. "It is *the* tree, my dear."

Annica's confused look gave way to understanding, then her mouth drooped open. Helyn continued, "You saw the great aldyr. His roots run throughout the island. You'll find them growing into and as a part of many structures. This particular root, so large and strong, it became the site of our temple. Our most talented Third Sect practitioners shaped it into what you see: the symbol of our city, His city, and polished it as smooth as stone without so much as harming a splinter with stone or metal. But you'll learn all about that. You're very lucky, you know. To be among other such fortunate people."

The older woman looked out over the crowd in the temple. Their clustered murmurings rumbling like a soft wind in the large, open space. The various groups consisted of combinations of white-robed, green-robed, and casually-dressed individuals. None seemed to act with any superiority or subservience to the other.

"You see them, yes? The worshippers. The workers. The merchants," Helyn said flatly, Her eyes panning over those she spoke of.

"Um, yes?" Annica answered, confused.

"Those in white robes are disciples," Helen said, nodding to a group near a wall who all wore the immaculate ivory-colored clothing, "They carry the word of The First Son to the world outside. It's dangerous work, as I'm sure you're aware. The mainland isn't so welcoming. Especially to those who seek to bring change. The green robes are magi." Helyn pointed to a cluster of them near the temple's entrance.

Annica's ears pricked at the word. Stories of magi were little more than drunken whispers where she was from—and most other places, from what she'd gathered from passersby in her village. Many folk blamed them, and magic altogether, for causing The Rupture. Annica, however, had always been fascinated by them. She listened attentively as Helyn provided insight on the people Annica only knew from legends and fishmonger's tales.

"Where disciples are purveyors of The First Son's will, the magi are the conduit for His power. Although only a mere morsel of it. The power of The First Son is truly beyond comprehension, as you'll soon learn."

Annica looked at Helyn and squinted at her. The older woman's eyes flicked over, met Annica's, and her wizened face broke into a wide grin. Annica's mouth opened and it took several seconds before she spoke.

"You mean—"

"You're going to be a mage, dear."

Annica felt a smile pull at her still-open mouth. She couldn't help it. She was scared and excited at the same time. This must have been why Nostrado was so eager to bring her here, himself. No other magi trainees, or apprentices, or whatever they were called had been called out among the newcomers in the Hall of Reception. She was the only one.

"I'm going to be an apprentice? Or something like it?" Annica said in breathless tones.

Helyn, still grinning, looked back to the gathered people in the temple. "We don't have such a hierarchy here as they did in the old world. Yes, I'm a 'leader' of sorts; a position handed down since our little haven's founding. Officially, I'm the arch-priestess. A name chosen by the founders since the temple houses both magi and disciples. I run the temple, arguably the most important structure on the island, and the mayor runs the city. He remains in his manor draining the city's wine supplies, more oft than not."

Helyn leaned over and whispered loudly, making it clear she was joking when she said, "It just takes a few of us to keep the rabble in line."

The archpriestess returned to her more composed posture. "We all learn from one another in this temple, Annica. Those who are proficient in one discipline may be quite inferior to others in a separate discipline. We all serve one purpose, in the end: working together to take the will and word of the First Son into the world. Besides, if a certain skill or level of uniqueness earned one the right the rule, you'd be queen of this island."

Annica's eyes opened wide. What could Helyn have possibly meant by that? What made her use Annica's name and the word 'queen' in the same sentence? Why had Nostrado looked so concerned during his evaluation?

"Helyn, archpriestess, I don't—"

"I'm sure you don't understand," Helyn interrupted, finishing Annica's sentence. "Come with me and I'll let you find some answers, yourself. Tomorrow, I'll answer what I'm sure will be many more questions."

They both walked down from the dais and to the hall on the left of the main foyer. It led to a room lined with long tables, fewer open windows and no arched doors, and several large sconces on the wall. Helyn explained that this was the dining hall, which connected to the dormitories for the magi. The hall opposite this one was where public worship was held and from there led to the dormitories for the disciples.

Both women crossed the empty dining room and into a large open arched entrance that led to a short hallway with multiple, additional hallways branching off from each side. Each of these hallways was lined with multiple doors on each side, which in turn were attached to very small rooms. Annica's room was in the third hallway to the right and the last door on the left.

Helyn escorted her into her room, opening the door which appeared to be left unlocked. Candles burned softly in a wall sconce in the windowless residence. The room was quite small; so small the trio of flickering candles created ample light that flickered off a single bed in one corner, a shelf with two green robes and nightclothes in another.

"You have everything you'll need here. You may take the clothes you have, which appear quite... used, place them in this basket," Helyn gestured to a small wicker basket by the door, "and set it outside to be sent to the laundry. They'll likely come apart in the wash, anyway, but as a mage, you'll only be wearing your robes from now on."

Helyn approached the small reading desk along the wall opposite the bed. She touched her fingers to the top of the bindings as though blessing them. "This is your focus tonight," she said, her eyes lingering on the leather bindings. "I recommend starting with *Timmerian's Primer on the Aspects of Magic*. It's quite prosaic but important for those who are unfamiliar with magic, as Nostrado claims you are."

Helyn regarded Annica in a manner suggesting the arch-priestess was looking for affirmation of her assumption. Annica self-consciously cleared her throat and nodded meekly. She doubted fearful rumors and gossip counted as even base magical knowledge.

Pulling a book from among the dozen or so volumes on the reading desk, Helyn tilted her head and smiled at Annica. The older woman held the book out with both hands. Annica took the book and looked into the gray-green eyes staring back at her. The archpriestess must have been striking in her younger years. Annica could imagine those eyes once looking like a fierce ocean storm, but now all she could see were somber and myste-rious depths.

"Read this, cover to cover if you can. The dinner bell will ring and if you choose to join us we will discuss what you've covered. If you decide to remain in your quarters, I'll make sure dinner is brought to you. If you do choose to dine in your room this evening, you must come to breakfast tomorrow. We must discuss some matters. Not the least of which is what you discover in these books."

After Helyn left and softly shut the door, Annica looked at the cover of the moderately sized book in her grip. Near her old village, another town, Lot's Fork, stood on the edge of an old forest where a library remained intact. The books were from all from the old world and barely held together. The cover on this treasure she held was soft and the binding firm but worn. Though it was in fine shape, it was also plain and undecorated. The title was inscribed in an unassuming script; the words drafted in dull prose with little flourish. Some of the books in the Lot's Fork library, when she managed to visit, had pages with intricate designs on some of the lettering. A few had illustrations. This book on the basics of magic held only plain, academic words.

And she was fascinated by it.

Magic, to the superstitious and uneducated like herself, was often feared or outright reviled. Whispers of witches in the dark parts of the forests were used in tales to keep children in line. Young men and women entertained their bored minds with stories of old men who made pacts with unspeakable things to gain power, only to become slaves to their new otherworldly masters. If someone went missing, the level-headed blamed wolves, bears, or brigands; the delusory insisted they were taken for some dark arcane purpose by those magi who yet remained in the world.

Annica had always felt there was more to magic than darkness and evil rituals. It had existed for thousands of years before The Rupture, so how, she thought, could it be solely responsible for the shitty state of the world, now? She'd wanted to learn more, but could never find books on the subject and any time she had asked was quickly hushed and dismissed.

Page after page turned softly as she devoured the trove of magical clarity given her. She smiled as she read about not just 'magic' in and of itself, but specifically, five separate disciplines of the art.

The first discipline, simply referred to as 'The First Sect', as each subsequent discipline was similarly named, was that of raw, arcane energy. It could be used to levitate objects, propel them across rooms, provide bursts of expansive force, or, conversely, crush the life from someone. According to the book, it was the easiest to learn but held limitless depths that only those with innate, instinctive connections to the First Sect could reach. Hand gestures, both simple and complex, coupled with appropriate incantations were required to channel this magic, but it could be learned by most all magi.

The Second Sect was the control and manipulation of the primal elements: fire, earth, water, and air. In the words of the author, Thaddeus Timmerian, the elements were combined into one discipline as more often than not those with a talent in this area shared a universal level of skill across all aspects of it. That was the most common occurrence, he wrote, but not a certainty. Those who tended to exceed in only one elemental aspect of the Second Sect, rare though they were, could control that one aspect with ferocious singularity. The gestures required to channel such magic were more simple, but the caveat of the Second Sect was that only those with innate talent could focus it into being. No amount of practice and study would allow one to summon the most basic of these spells. This limitation only intensified the dangerous power of the most potent of its practitioners.

The practice of imbuing physical paraphernalia with arcane properties was the bailiwick of the Third Sect. This sect required some physical component coupled with simple incantations to infuse the magic with the mundane; it was often called alchemy by the more scientific-minded.

The elves were without equal in this discipline, but specialized in using the Third Sect to grow their fabled tree-cities and turn their ancestral arboreal homes into something unlike any other forests in the world, imbued with magical enchantments.

Annica frowned, saddened at the fate of the elves and the unique trees. The aldyrs were tended lovingly by the long-lived people and their efforts were all for naught. Annica remembered sitting among the lone aldyr grove near her village and wondering what happened, why they all went extinct.

Except, now she knew there remained a living aldyr. As she thought about the massive silhouette from her first glance aboard the *Dawn Rose*, its boughs casting their shadow over the outer farmlands of Nel Aldyri as seen on her first approach to the temple, Annica felt the back of her head itch yet again. It was no longer a simple prickle of her skin. She felt it beneath her skull, in the back of her mind. This disturbing sensation segued into the next pages of her studies.

The Fourth Sect: the art of death and the undying. The tone of the academic prose shifted. The author seemed to write with more hesitation and punctuated his descriptions with more colorful commentary on the nature and processes used in this discipline. The author even hesitated to call it a discipline, as its practice had been outlawed by civil societies for decades at the time of the book's writing. The idea of necromantic practices, and worse, were then briefly described before the author quickly moved on, as though the mention of such hideous practices would mark his work. The existence of infamous practitioners of the Fourth Sect, the creatures they summoned, and the fiendish deities the dark artists claimed to worship were, at most, loosely referenced or inferred. The skills required to operate such magic were as vague as its results. It was difficult to tell if the author omitted such details out of fear or disgust, but Annica assumed it was copious amounts of both.

Annica placed a mental pin in such a topic to discuss with Helyn. The fear and loathing emanating from the text were reminiscent of the attitudes Annica was familiar with. Could one discipline in an entire field of study truly cause a universal hatred of magic? Her questions only grew more complicated with the final chapters on the Fifth Sect.

A soft knock caused her to start. She looked up from the book. A second knock, still soft and polite, echoed from the door. She put the open book aside, pages down, and stood from the bed.

"Come in," she said; as much a question as a statement.

A green-robed man with a shaved head, red stubble stark against his pale skin, entered with a wooden tray. A bowl of savory-smelling stew, steam curling up from within, sat next to a chunk of bread torn from a loaf. A ceramic cup completed the meal being delivered to her as Helyn promised. Annica didn't intend to skip dinner with her new host; she simply became lost in the studies that had so readily enraptured her. The smell of the food and wine in the cup mingled and met her nose, causing her stomach to growl audibly.

"Appears I'm quite on time," the man smirked, his voice husky despite his thin, even gaunt, appearance.

"Thank you," Annica replied, slightly embarrassed but eager to accept the best meal she'd had in days. The wine alone was a rare luxury she would relish.

The red-pated man left the tray on the reading desk, bowed his head slightly, and left. Annica felt sudden pangs of regret at not arriving at dinner, but this was quickly overcome by the vicious rumbling in her belly. She ate her meal quickly, realizing it wasn't the best meal she'd had in days or weeks, but months. She finished and drank the wine, taking one large swill at first, then slowly sipped, wishing it would last forever.

Setting the cup down, she turned and let her eyes linger on the book still lying with its utilitarian cover staring back at her. The last section she'd read had been unpleasant and unnerving, but there was one more section yet to read. What would those pages contain? Taking one more sip of the wine, Annica returned to her bed. Flipping the book over and leaning against the wall, she continued reading.

Turning the page to the descriptions of the final discipline, Annica felt this part of the book may have been written by a different author. Any and all previous methods could similarly be used for this sect, or so the author had witnessed in the few instances of its application. She had the impression of child-like wonder being poured into these final pages. The Fifth Sect was discussed with a barely contained astonishment that bordered on veneration. As it was explained, this honored discipline connected with the medicinal arts and rejuvenation of the physical and spiritual self. But it seemed many believed it was much more. It seemed that in the waning days of the old world, such cherished magic was fading. Scholars discussed and magi fretted over the increasing lack of pupils with talent in this discipline. The Fifth Sect, in Timmerian's time, was disappearing.

Annica turned the last page slowly, letting the paper run along the tips of her fingers. She was prepared to close the volume, think on the bounteous arcane information she had just devoured in a single evening. To her surprise, a tiny note was folded and tucked in the spine where the page met the back cover. She opened it carefully, the paper being thinner than the book's sturdier pages. Several lines of flowing text were written on the back of the last page. They were in a different hand than that of the author:

*THE MAGI HAVE GONE. We've run them out. I say 'we' in the sense of 'my fellow beings.' Dwarves have always been distrustful of magic, but even the elves have become suspicious. My friends in the academies have become distrustful even of me, as persecution against magi grows more violent by the day. Only Thaddeus continues to speak with me.*

*Practitioners of the Fifth Sect are all but non-existent, or so my magi friends tell me. Meanwhile, the dark practices grow darker. The vile practitioners of the Fourth Sect grow bolder. Only the fear of what they hide in the shadows of their isolated halls keeps the people from doling out justice upon them.*

*The common magi have fled to their more remote conservatories, creating sanctums for their fellows. Due to the repulsive practices of their counterparts, their final bastions are invariably, and incorrectly, tied to the reputations of their heinous brethren.*

One of the most interesting aspects of magic that Thaddeus related to me was what remained after spells had been cast. A mote of the magical essence remained behind, marking the area in which it was used. This doesn't mean that one can be walking along and feel the fire of the Second Sect that was cast ages ago. Magic is a common occurrence, yes, but it would take repetitious or exceptionally potent use to leave a noticeable trace behind, but it does occur. That's why there's a slight tingle in the air at the academies—daily use leaves a lingering sensation of the magic behind. When potent enough, even non-magi can sense it. Such a presence would also make using such magic easier, as the mage could draw on that lingering essence.

To me, this points to some truly disturbing conclusions. The Fifth Sect fading. Who remains to practice it? What if its essence is lost forever? For that matter, how active have the heathens of the Fourth Sect truly been at work lately, for such dark and unwholesome days to be upon us? What stains are they leaving in their wake?

If magic does leave its mark, I have no doubt the worst of human, dwarven, elfkind have utilized this to the pinnacle of horrific effect.

The Fifth Sect is gone. Would that someone brilliantly endowed in this discipline existed, that could leave instead a sanctuary of hallowed ground. A safe place for us to shelter from the cloying darkness of our time. Rather, we live only to see out the last of days as the darkness closes in. I've hesitated to admit it, but I do feel the magic in the air here—common man I may be. And, I dread to say, it is not a resonance of fire or water, of soil or fruit or prickling arcane energy. It is a hollow dread in my chest that leaves an aching spot wherein my heart lies. It is teeth and black sinew; grasping coils with piercing barbs beneath oily flesh; a thousand-thousand blinking eyes beneath the water's surface.

The Fifth Sect is gone. This is what remains.

~PATRYK PREEN, *Year 1282 of the Sixth Cycle*

.  .  .

ANNICA FOLDED the note and returned it to where it was tucked in previously. She closed the book, stood, and returned it to the shelf among the other volumes. There were many other texts available to her; various sizes and numbers of pages; leather of various faded shades of black, blue, brown, crimson. She would have a chance to read them all, but her eyes grew heavy and she had much to think about.

Removing her robe and donning the sleeping gown folded on her plain shelf, Annica returned to the bed. It wasn't luxurious, but it was much better than what she'd left behind. It was clean, soft enough, and it felt safe. She lay down in her bed, pulling the simple sheet over her and allowing the candles to stay lit as she knew not who would be back to light them again in the morning.

Annica didn't mind. The soft light flickered off the wall, appearing to grow weaker, the shadows thicker, as she felt her body slip into the waves of sleep. Her eyes began to shut, seemingly of their own accord. Just as her sense of relaxation peaked and her mind slipped away, the lights and shadows on the wall contorted and took the shape of serpentine tree limbs. Her heart shuddered for a moment before she gave in to sleep.

THE RINGING of a bell greeted Annica as she woke. It was soft at first, then grew louder until it sounded like it was coming from within her room. It echoed in the dark until finally, Annica's eyes opened.

The room was still dark. Soft light peeked in from below her door, providing the only way for Annica to see. She heard noises outside; the sounds of people gathering and the low hum of soft conversation. She got up from the bed and donned her green robe. She ran her hands over the cloth. Simple, but comfortable. She smiled. She was one of the magi.

She opened the ever-unlocked door, something that still unnerved her, into the narrow hallway. A few other magi were leaving their rooms and greeting their peers. All the green-robed magi, Annica in their midst, made their way from the dormitories to the dining hall. Several white-robed disciples were already present. The tables were beginning to quickly fill with the groups of the temple-dwellers and had the appearance of snow-speckled grass.

Salt-and-pepper strands stood out among the crowd and Annica approached the table quickly. Helyn was breakfasting with yet more people that Annica didn't know. Nostrado was nowhere to be found, nor was the man with the shorn red hair. The table was also quite full. Helyn was conversing with a young blonde woman with bony cheeks and sad eyes. The archpriestess' eyes found Annica's.

"So glad you found us," Helyn greeted the new magi warmly. Seeing no place for Annica, Helyn looked to the dreary-eyed woman next to her. "Mya, please go get Annica some breakfast. She's new here."

Annica opened her mouth to protest, but Mya stood immediately, gave Annica a strange, lingering look, and left quietly.

"Sit," Helyn directed; and Annica obliged.

"How was your first evening?" Helyn asked as she dined on eggs and tomatoes.

"I did as you instructed," Annica answered. "I finished *Timmerian's Primer*. I am so sorry I missed dinner, I was caught up in my reading and didn't even hear the bell."

Helyn chuckled. "I think you made a good choice. That was important information we need to discuss today. And dinner was... middling."

Annica jerked her hand back as a plate was suddenly slid in front of her. Eggs and fruit stared back at her from the plate. Mya's glossy, strange eyes lingered on Annica. Her long, tangled blonde hair framed a face that at first gave the impression of one gaunt and sleep-deprived. Looking at her more closely, Annica could see beautiful features worn away by a rough existence.

"Thank you," Annica said. Mya hesitantly nodded and walked away.

The awkwardness of the gaunt woman's departure hung in the air. Helyn popped a small, bright tomato in her mouth and swallowed it almost instantly, then said, "Don't fret about her. She had a rough start with us. Life off the island was hard on her; as it was with many. She once was one of our emissaries but returned from one voyage and was never the same."

"An emissary?" Annica asked, poking at her food with a fork. The encounter with Mya left her less hungry than when she had arrived.

"Brave souls we send forth from our island. Ship captains venture out to find new blood for our city, disciples go to spread word of the First Son, and our militia guards them both. Sometimes the soldiers are sent off on their own to scout the lands and return with and news of the state of the mainland. It's never good. If I'm being honest about it, they don't always come back."

Annica's eyes looked up from her plate to Helyn, then broke from the archpriestess' emotionless gaze and flicked back to her food. Annica grimaced.

"Don't worry," Helyn chuckled dryly. "Magi are only ever sent with soldiers in the event they find a sanctum. And then only when said magi have proven their expertise. I have a feeling you won't be going anywhere anytime soon, if ever. You're too important."

Annica furrowed her brows. Now seemed a good a time as any to begin her questions. "That reminds me—"

"Why do I keep saying you're special?" Helyn interrupted. Annica raised her eyebrows and Helyn nodded. "Why don't we go for a walk? Into the city this time. I assume you're done eating?"

Seeing a smile curl on up on the edges of the aged woman's lips, Annica self-consciously set her fork down and cleared her throat. "I'd love to."

"Very good. Leave your plate. I'll have someone gather them up for us. We have important things to discuss."

Annica rose, feeling guilty about leaving dishes behind for others to clean, but the archpriestess waited for no one. Helyn stood and immediately began departing for the main foyer. Annica followed until they reached the outer plaza where the fountain still trickled and birds sang; the massive aldyr still towering over the outskirts in the distance.

They left the plaza and went to a quiet area that appeared to be used for meditation and study. It sat off to one side of the temple in a concave area of light-colored, polished stone arranged in a circular pattern. Vines and grasses from the surrounding area grew over and down along some of the seats, giving the sunken concourse a natural, peaceful ambiance. "Tell me what you learned, Annica."

She looked up at Helyn, seeing the archpriestess looking in the direction of the aldyr. Her expression was blank and her hands tucked into her sleeves. Annica tucked her hands into her robe. She wasn't sure if there was a proper way to stand like a mage, so she simply mimicked the archpriestess. Then, Annica told Helyn about all she remembered from her first, and late, night of study.

"The Principle Triad," Helyn said after Annica had finished speaking. "The first three magics are the most common and are critical disciplines. Some fundamentalists believe they are the only disciplines that matter at all."

"The Fourth Sect—death magic or black magic, I can't recall its other name—it seems the world would be better off without it. Especially if it caused The Rupture," Annica added.

Helyn shrugged. "Death magic. The Black Rites. Void Summoning. It has many names, just like the other disciplines. Which is why our ancestors always found simplicity in a numerical system. It has a purpose, as well. We try to be open-minded in Nel Aldyri, especially at the Temple of the First Son." Helyn looked at Annica and had a sparkle in her eyes, a glint of sunlight on the surface of the gray-green waters. "Like the Fifth."

"The Fifth Sect? Life Magic?"

"Tell me what you learned about it."

The archpriestess seemed quite eager to hear Annica's response. It was Annica's turn to shrug.

"The book said it was quickly going extinct by the author's time. It was tied to healing, life, light; positive things of that nature."

Helyn put her hands on Annica's shoulders. The older woman suddenly seemed much taller. She looked at Annica and her eyes had changed, the gleam gone from the water's surface and waves began to form.

"Not just life and rejuvenation, but empathy. Creating. Existence, itself. There is a mote of the Fifth Sect in the birth of every child who comes into the world to further create; in the death of every man and woman and beast that leaves room for others to coalesce into the world and *be*. The Fifth Sect is so many things. And you are the only one on this island who can connect with it."

Annica looked back at Helyn, fighting the allure to drown in her powerful gaze and simply agree. "What are you saying?"

Helyn removed her hands from Annica, tucking them into her sleeves once more. "Remember when I said if skill or uniqueness led to power, you would rule this island?"

"Yes," Annica replied, still unclear on what Helyn was referring to. It appeared the archpriestess caught on to her new pupil's confusion. She took a breath and continued in the patient manner of an instructor.

"We once thought Nostrado could use the Fifth Sect. At least, in some small way. We came to discover that the First Sect could provide those most talented in that discipline with empathic abilities. Nostrado does indeed have significant prowess in the raw arcane, but no other signs connecting him to the Fifth Sect. You see, it's theorized that empathic sensitivity is a basic skill to one connected to that most elusive of talents."

"And you think I have it? I can use the Fifth Sect?" Annica said, a glimmer of joy blossoming in her chest, then sinking to her stomach where it came to sour. What could all this mean for her?

"We're going to find out soon," Helyn said in a fairly chipper tone. "You and I are going to start today. We'll begin with the basics, as do all magi, but I truly don't wish to linger on such trivialities. You and I have so much more to move on to."

Annica nodded, nervous but anxious, but then something occurred to her. "Archpriestess—"

"Helyn."

"Helyn," Annica corrected, "You are the archpriestess. Don't you have duties of your own to see to? Didn't you say all magi are partnered with others? To learn and grow?"

"Indeed. But who here is going to be able to teach you in a discipline that only you can possess? You are the sole practitioner of the Fifth Sect we have *ever* had, Annica. There are no other records of someone with your potential ever existing on Nel Aldyri."

"So, how am I going to learn?"

"You are going to work with me. Personally. I will take you under my tutelage directly."

The sour spot in Annica's stomach rose to her chest again. "That sounds amazing, actually."

"Yes, it will be. We are going to learn much, you and I." Helyn appeared as enthusiastic about Annica's learning process as the new mage was.

"This is lovely," Annica remarked, taking in the quiet. She noticed the massive aldyr was also easily visible from here. The Temple of the First Son was built in plain view of the tree from nearly all angles.

"I'm glad you like it. You and I will be spending a lot of time here," Helyn said with a smile.

And, indeed, they spent a lot of time there. Aside from her meals and nightly time to read and study, Annica was with Helyn from morning to dusk. Over the next week, Annica not only spent her time learning in detail the Principle Triad, but she also began practicing actual spells. As it turned out, Annica wasn't too adept at much of the three core principles. Although, she did excel with aspects of fire magic. Helyn reined in Annica's progression slightly when the new mage nearly lit half the concourse on fire.

"Remind me never to make you angry," Helyn said, wide-eyed with shock and exertion from putting out Annica's flames that afternoon.

With her skill, or lack thereof, in the first three magics established, Annica remembered what would come with the fourth. She informed Helyn of her apprehension. The archpriestess shrugged off her concerns, informing Annica that they could discuss the practice, but not dive into actual applications if she was uncomfortable. Annica expressed her gratitude at Helyn's understanding.

Annica quickly learned that even discussion of the Fourth Sect was enough to cause her stomach to turn. The initial information from *Timmerian's Primer* spoke mostly of the practice of necromancy and cavorting with capricious devils from the bowels of the world. The practices Helyn spoke went further beyond and made such pursuits sound like tamer evils. Demons wanted slaves and to sate their own bloody desires. There were other creatures that existed beyond the anchors of reality that human, elf, and dwarf-kind knew. True practitioners of the Fourth Sect knew this and their obsessions ran deep. The knowledge of these extraplanar beings crawled like black-barbed roots into the minds of warlocks and cults of worshippers that sought out these beings.

There was little to nothing known about these beings, other than some of their names. To those who practiced this aspect of magic, there was no proof or precedent that any power or reward awaited at the end of years or even decades of study. Rarely were new spells or powers to be found by either luck or misfortune; and those that were discovered often extracted a terrible cost in either the blood in one's veins or the stability of one's mind. Regardless, the men and women who studied the deeper truths of the Fourth Sect found that the more they gazed into that abyss, the less they knew, and the more acute their obsession became.

Annica realized her head was aching from scrunching her forehead and grimacing at Helyn's lesson. She asked if they could move on, repeating her complete lack of interest in the heinous and reprehensible aspect of the Fourth Sect. The morning had been bright and soft clouds floated in the sky, but now the day felt colder after such talk.

"Of course," Helyn chirped, pivoting immediately. She was apparently quite used to discussing such horrible rites and pursuits. An archpriestess must be knowledgeable on all such things, Annica supposed. "There's only one aspect of magic left to discuss, isn't there?"

Helyn's eyes sparkled. Realization dawned on Annica, and

she grew both nervous and excited at the same time. Annica began to think that all the training from the week had been leading up to what Helyn really meant to study: Annica's connection to the Fifth Sect.

"Where should we even begin?" Annica asked, shrugging. "You admit yourself that there's no one who's ever used such magic on the island before."

Helyn nodded, conceding her point. "All I have are books and conjecture. That's why we're going to do a little experiment, you and I."

Annica looked at the archpriestess like a teenager who'd just been dared to spend the night in a haunted mill. "What do you mean 'experiment'?"

"Don't worry," Helyn replied cheerily, "We always start with the basics, yes? There's only one real place I can think of to start."

"Based on conjecture," Annica pointed out.

"Yes," Helyn said matter-of-factly.

Helyn stood and beckoned Annica to follow. As the new mage did so, she noticed Mya sitting alone in the concourse. The girl pretended not to notice them, staring instead toward the great aldyr, but Annica noticed her pale green eyes, the color of a deep and sickly bruise, flick towards her for a moment. After their eyes met, Annica saw Mya's bony fingers begin to pick and pull at one another as if they had a mind of their own. The sickly girl never looked at Annica again but was obviously trying very hard not to do so. Annica was forced to put the issue out of her mind, as Helyn was quickly outpacing her; the archpriestess herself being overcome by excitement.

～

THEIR WALK from the temple to the city proper carried them down a winding path from the crest of the hill. Near the temple, mosses and grass traced between the cobblestones like green rivulets; the nearer they came to the city the flatter and more worn the stones became, the verdant coloring disappearing from constant use by heavy merchant carts. Annica voiced her concerns about any danger her initial tests with the Fifth Sect could pose to the city folk. Helyn assured her that today's test would be completely harmless, but Annica remained hesitant.

They reached the city square when Helyn stopped and asked Annica to close her eyes. There was no context provided. No explanations. Just a simple instruction. Annica did as Helyn asked.

"I don't want you to focus," Helyn said softly. "I want you to feel."

So, Annica tried to feel. She felt the breeze from the harbor, smelled the salt from the sea carried among the stones. She felt the subtle vibrations in the ground from the people traversing the roads to and from the markets. It felt calming, relaxing, but normal for a place such as Nel Aldyri.

She took a slow, deep breath and tried to relax even more. Annica began to wonder why she was out here with no training. What did Helyn expect from someone who did not know what they were doing?

"You're distracted." the archpriestess said straightforwardly.

Annica's eyes opened and she turned her head to see Helyn watching her. "How do you know?" she asked, not intending to sound flippant.

"I can see it on your face: scrunched up like you ate a sour apple. Stop letting your mind wander. Stop trying and let it happen naturally."

Annica took another deep breath and closed her eyes again.

She felt the same cool air and gentle indications of a busy afternoon, but also something else.

Agitation.

She didn't feel any such emotion toward Helyn or herself. She realized it wasn't even her that was feeling it. She felt a strong agitation towards a man.

Then, Annica became acutely aware of the conversations surrounding her. They were a loud hum, indiscernible as she expected the mingling discussions in a city square to be. But words began to lift themselves above the clamor.

They weren't insulting, but they weren't friendly either. An irritation burned in Annica's chest. She wondered why this man was trying to cheat her. This wasn't the normal price. Annica began to smell something unpleasant. Or, perhaps, just unfamiliar. Then, Annica recognized the smell of raw meat. Not putrid, but uncooked.

"You're a scoundrel!" Annica said aloud. Her eyes opened and she realized she was still with Helyn in the city square. The archpriestess looked pleased.

Helyn asked what happened and Annica explained. Nodding her head, Helyn told Annica to try again; to see if she could go even further.

Annica closed her eyes once again, eager to see what she would feel this time. She shut down her mind. Let all thoughts of excitement and consternation flow from her head to her heart and then out to her fingertips. She let the noises of the conversations lull her into a trance. That's when the sensations came to her again, stronger this time.

She felt hot. Her body burned—no, not her body—her muscles. They ached and burned like she'd been working the fields in her old village all day. Annica began to sweat. She could smell it; the pungent odor of exertion. She heard the sounds of metal on metal. She heard muffled shouts. Then her mind shrieked at her. She heard muffled shouts again.

"Annica," she heard, but only scarcely.

Again, "Annica." The voice shouted but sounded as though it came through a thick fog.

"Annica!"

Hearing her name finally cut through her fugue and pummel into her ears, Annica opened her eyes and felt her legs nearly give out beneath her. She sucked in a breath. Her eyes adjusted to the light and she didn't recognize where she was.

Her feet were perilously close to the edge of a steep hill. It overlooked what must be some sort of arena or training ground. As she continued to stare at the circular patch of dirt encircled by a low fence, Annica saw the sun glint off moving steel. It was indeed a training ground and the city's soldiers were currently training.

"Annica," Helyn said through winded breaths. The arch-priestess was running toward her up a road that sloped up the side of a narrow hill; similar to the one by the temple. Coming to a slow stop, chest heaving, and robes swaying, Helyn looked at Annica with eyes wide.

"My gods, I haven't seen anyone move like that," Helyn panted.

"What happened?" Annica asked, her eyes still lingering on the sparring grounds. "How did I get here?"

Helyn chuckled. "You ran, girl. And you kept running. It was like you were possessed. You weren't sprinting, but you were jogging at a steady pace. You didn't slow down for anyone. Not even me."

"I felt like I was here... there... down there with the soldiers," Annica said, confused.

"Empathic magic. More potent than any practitioner of the

First Sect in our temple, that is most certain." Helyn said cheerily, still catching her breath.

"Edrik is down there, isn't he?" Annica asked casually.

"Is he?" Helyn echoed humorously.

"I know he is. I can feel him."

The archpriestess had been leaning with her hands on knees, but now she rose and stretched her back. Finally, in control of her breathing, she looked across from the hill they now stood on. Parallel to them, on the crest of another hill that was hazy with low clouds, sat the Temple of the First Son. Annica had indeed led the two of them for quite a run.

Following Helyn's gaze, Annica thought the temple looked quite beautiful from here. She wondered why both hills had steep, sloping sides towards the city and sharp cliffs on the opposite side. Then, she realized why. The cliffs were naturally formed, but they seemed to provide an almost purposefully staged view of the great aldyr.

The tree cast its broad shadow over the flat lands before it. The farms and sown fields soon dissipated into fallow meadows and untamed patches of forest. There, the unthinkably massive roots of the aldyr began to surface, raising the ground like low hills. Annica's eyes followed the hills as they gave way to the base of the tree. The limbs spread out with its countless blossoms. A cold shadow spread over her, chilling Annica to her bones.

Turning around, she saw the shadow fall over the training grounds. She looked up, expecting to see grey clouds carrying rain, but the skies were clear. Feeling left her body, with naught but a dull tingle remaining in her fingers. It felt similar to when she channeled the Fifth Sect, but stronger, more intense, and cold. The more it took hold of her, the more vastly different it felt.

Something had changed. Her mind flinched and the tree

was suddenly before her. Her feet were planted, unmoving, at the base of an aldyr so large it swallowed her field of vision. The shadows had grown deeper until it seemed night had fallen in all its dark splendor. The wind howled and pulled at her robes and hair. An odd sensation tickled her feet. Looking down, she saw the ground was wet. Cold drops began to prick at her skin. The power of the rain grew quickly to a crescendo as the moist earth grew saturated and the water rose around her ankles.

Some deep, inherent terror rose within Annica's chest. It radiated from somewhere deeper than her heart, beyond the roots of her soul, and spread to her conscious mind. She wanted desperately to scream, but the sound died in her throat, locked behind gritted teeth.

The frigid water had risen to her waist. It smelled stale, old; as though it flowed from a hidden reservoir from deep within the world after eons of stagnation. What terrified her more, however, was that the water was not empty. Somewhere below its ink-black surface, there were things that crawled; slipping around her ankles, pulling at her robes as the wind had done previously. The water had exposed the tree roots, or at least that's what she tried to convince herself it was.

The water rose and rose, reaching her chest and stealing her breath with its chill. When it touched her chin, Annica threw her head back to breathe. The branches of the tree were now barren. Their twisting appendages more resembling the serpent-like branches of the city's sigil. Beyond, pale violet light radiated from unknown moons. This was not the ashen face of night that Annica knew; rather, a gaunt and pallid pretender surrounded by dead and dying stars. This sickly illumination was just enough for Annica to see those profane branches subtly writhing in its wake.

The water reached her mouth. Whatever lay below the

churning waves followed, slipping into her mouth as she choked on the water that filled her lungs and threatened to drown her.

Her arms seized, flexing at her sides like wooden planks. Her legs followed suit, stiffening so that she was forced onto the tips of her toes. Her eyes rolled back into her head exposing the pure whites of her eyes, and all fell to darkness.

Soft yellow light greeted her waking eyes. Annica could see the gentle shadows dancing off the ceiling. It took a few moments, but she came to recognize her room at the temple. A tingling sensation coursed through her extremities as though she had just woken from a terrible nightmare; however, she only remembered seeing the great aldyr by the training grounds and then... nothing.

Annica sat up, leaning against the wall. She was still in her deep green robes. Her mouth was dry and her head ached from front to back with a sharp pain. Rubbing her eyes with her hands, she became aware of another presence in the room.

"Gods!" Annica shouted.

Mya flinched at the reflexive outburst. She sat on a stool next to Annica's reading desk, which had a cup sitting on top of it. Thin wisps of steam curled from within. Reaching into a small satchel, Mya pulled out a small platter and unwrapped something covered in a cloth. It was a hunk of bread. When Annica relaxed after seeing her, Mya approached the bed, cup in one hand and a platter with bread in the other.

"I'm sorry, Mya, you scared me is all."

"It's ok," the pallid girl replied. She retreated back to the stool and sat there, eyeing the wall nervously.

"Mya, what's wrong?" Annica asked. The cup was warm, the contents smelled sweet, savory and inviting. She sipped gingerly, the tea inside still hot but palatable. She stared into the cup at the lingering flecks of what she assumed to be leaves and cloves. They truly lived well here in Nel Aldyri.

In just moments, Annica had completely forgotten about the horrible fugue. However, Mya's purposefully avoiding looking at her continue to prickle Annica. Mya's eyes looked everywhere around Annica except at her; the fidgeting girl refused to even looked in Annica's general location.

"Mya?" Annica repeated, scratching at an itch on her shoulder.

Mya's lips churned and stretched, like words wanted to escape but she chewed on her lips to keep them imprisoned. Her eyes fell on Annica's fingers, gently scratching at what felt like a scar. Was that there before?

A quick, choked sound escape from Mya's chapped lips. Her eyebrows scrunched, her breathing halted and, for a moment, the girl was actually still. Mya lowered her head and let her wheat-colored hair cover her face.

Annica felt uncomfortable. Not just at Mya's behavior, but at something else; at something seeping into the air. It crawled on her skin, radiating from this newfound scar, and it almost seemed as if Mya felt it, too.

Mya shot up from her stool, grabbing the platter, and stiffly approached the bed. Her eyes darted to Annica and just as swiftly. Back and forth, meeting Annica's gaze for a moment than flicking back to some other spot to avoid letting their eyes meet for too long.

"I just—" the nervous disciple stuttered, "I want— are you done with your tea? I really want to go."

Annica sat up straighter. She went to put her hand on Mya's, her heart breaking at the sight of the nervous wreck of a girl, quivering and fidgeting. Mya pulled her hand away before she could provide any comfort. Annica noticed Mya's eyes had become jaundiced since they last met. The sickly eyes kept glancing back to the satchel.

"Mya, please tell me what's wrong," Annica pleaded with sincerity.

She refused to speak to Annica. Huffing, Mya took the tea from Annica, grabbed the plate, and walked, still stiff-legged but more swiftly, back to the desk where the satchel waited. Mya rolled the bread up carelessly and shoved both it and the plate into the satchel. Carrying the cup in one hand, tea slipping over the edge and onto the floor, Mya stormed out of the room.

Annica climbed out of bed and went to her door. The sickly, once-beautiful girl was walking in short, rapid steps as though too long of strides were somehow painful. Annica thought to call out to her, but decided against it. Her mind went back to Mya shoveling everything back into the satchel. Her efforts were haphazard, but she was sticking everything on top of something. A book. Yes. Annica had seen the pages of a book in the satchel.

Normally, that wouldn't seem out of place in a temple and dormitory of study. Something nagged at Annica, though; it pulled her back to the desk. None of her books appeared missing. There were no empty spaces. Annica then saw something out of order. One of the books was put back upside down. It was *Timmerian's Primer*.

Annica pulled the book from among its fellows and opened the cover. The copy seemed to be in the same well-cared for shape as it had always been. She flipped through the pages. No loose bindings, no pages torn out. She grabbed the spine and shook the book, letting the pages and covers flop loosely in her hands.

Nothing fell out. The note was gone. Why did Mya take the note from the back of her book? It did strike Annica as odd and would explain Mya's more feverish anxiety. She'd only met the girl once before, but Mya was much more nervous this time.

Annica would have to confront her, gently, about the issue tomorrow and get an explanation. Or try, at least.

A yawn escaped her and Annica wondered how she could be so tired after being unconscious for so long. She returned the book to the shelf and removed her robes. She let the cool air of the stone room linger on her skin a moment while she retrieved her nightgown. The itching had stopped, but where did this scar come from? She would not be surprised if she had a few cuts and bruises to be found after losing consciousness, but nothing could possibly have scarred so quickly. Her struggling mind wore on her and she yawned again.

Annica crawled into bed, sighed, and watched the candle-light dance on the walls. It was becoming a habit. She closed her eyes and tried to sleep. Her mind slipped into the soft velvety blackness of slumber. She was just conscious, however, of things twisting and coiling at the edges of the darkness.

THE RINGING of the breakfast call woke Annica and her mind instantly cleared of any dreams she may have been experiencing. It always maddened her that thoughts once so vivid slipped away with such abruptness. She sat breathing through her nose, as she felt the images that played across her mind's eye during last night's sleep were important.

She put this out of her mind as she dressed and joined the gathering crowd of green and white in the dining hall. She could see over the heads of the amassing, hungry crowd to the main foyer beyond the door opposite her dormitory. The carved statue of the aldyr caught her eye; after a moment she caught herself absent-mindedly rubbing the unevenly-shaped scar on her shoulder.

Pulling her hand away, she stared at her fingers as though

she'd find answers there. Another mage accidentally bumped her, apologized, and went on his way. It was enough to break her distracted thoughts and she began looking for Helyn.

Instead, she noticed Nostrado by the single closed door behind the great aldyr statue. Recognition sparkled in his eyes as he smiled, though it was not as warm as when they first met. Having no one else familiar to speak with, Annica went to him. He always had the smell of clean linens about him, as though his clothes were washed more thoroughly than any other or he changed many times throughout the day.

"Annica, my dear, how are you enjoying your time here?"

"You remember my name?"

"Of course," he chuckled. "You were quite a special find."

*Like pearls or a rare bird?* Annica thought sardonically. She had been feeling a bit like a trained animal, the more she thought about it.

"Where does this door go?" She asked, looking at the large, ornate door that was always closed and, she assumed, the only one in the temple that was locked given the keyhole in the front.

"A special branch of our temple. It contains a library restricted to certain individuals." Nostrado regarded the door with either adulation or apprehension, Annica couldn't decide which.

"I thought all things were equal here?" she asked flatly.

Nostrado smiled half-heartedly, his head lowering, seemingly taking her tone as incredulous. It wasn't her intent. She was, at most, passively curious. He placed his hand on her elbow and squeezed gently.

"We have to allow for some measure of hierarchy, don't we? Some magic is simply too dangerous for the inexperienced."

There was much left for her to learn as it was, so Annica merely nodded and, inwardly, shrugged off the door. She had plenty of mystery and magic to understand as it stood without worrying about secret libraries.

"Have you seen Helyn?" she asked as her mind dwelt on the subject of learning and mysteries.

"Of course," Nostrado replied and led her around the dais. His outstretched hand led Annica to see Helyn near the middle of the room again. "Her usual spot," he added.

The archpriestess sat at a table near the center of the feasting throng. This time, however, Mya was not with her. The seat normally reserved for the restless girl was empty and Annica helped herself to it after getting her meal.

Helyn was uncharacteristically quiet; somewhere between thoughtful and brooding. Breakfast was relatively quiet, with Helyn only asking if Annica was feeling better and voicing genuine concern over the new mage's health. Annica assured her that all was well. Helyn also diplomatically avoided any comment on Mya's whereabouts.

One thing was clear: there would be no further lessons today. Helyn wanted Annica to rest, take some time to herself. The temple, the city, and the harbor were Annica's to explore and enjoy. She was asked to remain within the city's limits, however, and to not explore the hinterlands beyond for now. Helyn wanted to be able to reach Annica if need be.

Annica was given a small brown sack, fastened with a green cord, and filled with what appeared to be some manner of coin. She'd only read about currency and its uses in the societies of the old world, and even the *Dawn Rose*'s captain had bartered with her village harbormaster rather than pay him. This was yet another practice that Nel Aldyri sought to return to the world, as Helyn explained. The currency was little more than a thumb-nail-sized chunk of gold stamped with a rudimentary tree. The archpriestess said the smiths were still perfecting the practice.

Helyn practically shooed Annica from the table. She left the foyer and began exploring the city, free to do as she pleased. She bought fresh bread for the first time, and wine made from aldyr-fruit. The taste wasn't entirely pleasant to Annica and she thought perhaps aldyrfruit just wasn't for her. She told the wine merchant it was magnificent, regardless.

Down the street a raucous noise came from a busy pub. Rife with the smells of alcohol and the sounds of drunken instrument playing, Annica never imagined a place of gathered drunks that weren't there simply to drown away the drudgery of life. Despite the comings and goings of many people in various states of inebriation, a head of short-cropped blonde hair stood out.

"Captain Sisironi!" Annica shouted.

The head turned and two sharp blue eyes found Annica immediately. The tall captain made her way deftly through the crowd, like her own ship cutting through the waves.

"Annica, it's good to see you, girl," Sisironi said, a warm smile on her face. The mug in her hand and the glow on her cheeks spoke to her enjoying her time in the establishment. "How are you enjoying the city?"

"It's like nothing I've ever seen, that's for certain. Seems almost perfect."

The captain barked a half-drunken chuckle. "Not many places like this left. Trust me, I know. But, it's not perfect. These blundering assholes aside, we have our share of crime and the like. You keep those spells handy, you hear?"

For the first time, Annica felt as though she could see sadness mar the captain's face; crack the ice of her eyes.

"You'll have to forgive this lot," Sisironi said, waving her mug at the crowd. "A lot of the folk like to celebrate the return of the ships. Though, I imagine any excuse to drink is celebration enough for them. If you ever want to talk in a quieter place, we'll have to meet at my humble home. Next to the harbor. It has a walrus out front; can you believe that? What fool thought a ship captain would want a damn walrus in front of their house?"

Annica chuckled, half-heartedly, and kindly took her leave from the captain. Although a good drink did sound enticing, the captain was obviously making progress on enjoying many of them. Annica would like to take her up on her offer of a visit, if she remembered making it after today.

A few streets over, several armored guards patrolled the streets, but one, in particular, stood out. Near the gardens, Annica spotted a dark-haired man she instantly recognized; another friend in the new city.

"Edrik!" she shouted.

Her friend, whom she hadn't seen since the Hall of Reception, turned and looked as if he'd heard a ghost calling his name. His eyes darted everywhere but in her direction. Her mouth mimicked the words, "here, here", and her hand waved in hopes of him noticing.

Edrik's eyes fell on her and he smiled. It had barely been a week since their arrival on the island, but it was still a relief to see him. A breath of relief escaped her and their steps quickened together.

She felt his arms grab her in a strong but friendly embrace. The pungent scent of worn leather and a sharp tang of polished steel filled Annica's nose. She had desperately needed to see a familiar face. Edrik's timing could not have been more perfect.

"I've been worried about you," he said in a voice full of mirth. "Where have you been?"

A smirk curled from her lips, but her brows furrowed at him all the same. "I could ask the same of you. Are you some kind of dangerous warrior now?" Her eyes took in the sight of him in full armor. It was simultaneously intimidating and impressive.

Rattling his sword in its sheathe, he was beaming as he replied. "You could say that. I've been training day and night. All the new recruits have, actually. My inauguration into the Darm Aldyri is tomorrow morning."

"The what?"

"'Army of the Aldyr," he clarified, smiling. "If it wasn't for the elvish terms, their naming conventions would be very boring."

Annica grimaced. "Even still, it seems a little single-minded. Fanatical, even."

Although she couldn't see the great aldyr from here, she turned to look in its direction. Thankfully, there was nothing but unassuming buildings surrounding them, laced by a web of cobblestone streets. The last thing Annica wanted to do today was allow unpleasant thoughts to linger. An idea came to her.

"When are you free from your duties?"

"This afternoon, after a change of the guard at the western gardens. The captain of the guard gave me the afternoon free as a reward for my performance leading up to the inauguration."

In her excitement, she squeezed one of his hands in both of her own.

"Perfect," she exclaimed, "I'll wait for you there."

He returned to his patrol and faded into the afternoon crowd with his comrade. Hunger began to gnaw at Annica's stomach. Had it been that long since breakfast? The coins suddenly felt heavier in their pouch and remembering she had money made the smells of bread nearby grow stronger.

The stalls were busy and the merchants, though harried, were friendly and accommodating. It was difficult to tell if their friendly demeanor was due to her green robes. She couldn't remember from her readings if magi were held in high esteem before The Rupture when they subsequently became the maligned target of society's hate and distrust. Regardless, the shopkeeps in Nel Aldyri held much friendlier demeanors than those back in her old village.

It was strange to think about that place from before. After a week in Nel Aldyri, Ashwater felt like another life. There was no nostalgia or regret when she thought of those who remained behind, only pity. Eking out a living on wilted crops from malnourished soil, sleeping in moth-eaten beds, under leaking, rotting roofs was not a life. Surrounded by people who lived, a city that thrived, where music played, bread baked, and children played—that was life.

Who would've thought currency would return to the world? Her fingers traced the smooth, uneven edges of the coins. As her fingers traced the tree symbol on the surface, her scar began to itch again. It tingled, ran up her spine and into the base of her brain. She knew which direction the tree lay in and her mind was pulled there, to the west where the great aldyr grew.

Squeaks and laughter brought Annica's attention back to the street she so precariously stood in. City folk meandered around her like a gentle stream around a rock dropped in its flow. The people paid her no mind, not even the children who had bumped into her that were now frolicking away.

Annica smiled. This was living.

The western gardens had fewer visitors than she would've thought. The paved stone terraces with their wood-and-wrought-iron tables were mostly empty. The stones were shaded by trees of various sizes and species. Lush, large-leafed trees grew next to delicate willows. Ivy and other vines crawled from planters and along the iron fence that separated the upper terraces from the steep hill on the edge of the gardens. Like other places built along the western edge of the city, the gardens ended in a sharply declining hill overlooking the aldyr.

Keeping her back to the large tree, Annica poured the contents of her satchel onto one of the tables. Her route through the market passed one of the magnificently-scented bakeries. Bread, cheese, and fruit filled a satchel she purchased to carry it all here to meet with Edrik. A small jug of wine completed her purchases. Helyn gave her plenty of the Nel Aldyri coins to enjoy herself with. Annica was happy to indulge, not knowing if it would ever happen again.

A few nibbles were all she would partake in for now. Edrik would likely be quite hungry after his patrols and she wanted to have plenty for them to eat while discussing their experiences. The prospects of conversation with her friend owned her thoughts and attention until a soft orange glow shone from behind her.

It was still midday, from her knowledge, so this couldn't possibly be a sunset. She would have gladly turned to see what the source of such radiance was, if her body wasn't frozen in place. The breaths came and went sharply through her nose. Her hands trembled as she silently screamed in her mind for them to move. Whatever had held her there in the chair had released her.

The jug of wine was knocked over, splashing on the ground as Annica whirled around. The horizon was a wall of fire, something she would have once thought beautiful. But, against the great aldyr that loomed black against the flaming sunset-like vista like a burnt offering, Annica felt a familiar horror grip her. A low, reverberating drone radiated against her. It was like nothing she'd ever heard, and she could not be sure she actually heard anything at all. It was somehow both deafening and non-existent. It became hard to breathe.

A part of her consciousness, somewhere deep beneath the layers of her waking, subconscious, and dream-state mind, woke up; an instinctive part, the part that connected with her ancestral kin, that lay buried under a blanket of civility and stone houses, that had forgotten the raw fear of being one creature amid a vast web of predators that could take you in the dark and sink in their teeth. That part had awoken, and it trembled at what it saw.

A hand grabbed her shoulder and a voice called her name. It was distant, like when Helyn called for her during her trial of the Fifth Sect. The name echoed beyond a cloth veil again. When Helyn called to her, she was lost in an empathic connection with the world around her. This time, it felt like she was held prisoner by something else; her mind was not her own.

Struggling against the powerful influence was useless, but there was also a powerful feeling of anger and confusion born of ineffectiveness. Whatever the power was, it wanted more than just to hold her there. It prodded her thoughts like ravenous birds pecking at an armored shell.

"Annica?"

The voice tore through the veil like a dull knife, pushing until it gouged through the stubborn material. Her nerves were frayed, the torn edges of what remained of her mental fabric. But she was free from the aldyr's influence. The hand whirled her around, another joining it as they both gripped her arms. Brown eyes stared back at her. It took several moments for her to recognize Edrik.

"Annica, what's wrong?"

Her breaths came in ragged gasps as she tried to keep her mouth from gawking open. Her tongue was swollen and she tasted blood. She must have bitten it during the ordeal.

"You were like a stone statue, I swear," Edrik said, his brows furrowed in concern. "Did I scare you?"

A hoarse, "No," managed to squeak out of her throat. Her hands trembled and her heart thumped in her chest, the sound reverberating in her ears.

"I don't feel well," she mumbled, her drooping eyes staring weakly at the emblazoned tree on Edrik's armor. The tree was everywhere. There was no escaping it, especially in the open-aired streets and plazas of Nel Aldyri.

The world grew hazy and began to list from side to side.

Annica plopped onto a bench. The breeze felt cold against the sweat that prickled on her arms and forehead. Her slow, heavy breaths forced themselves through dry lips.

Wrapping his hand gently around her wrist, Edrik was shocked to feel the cold dampness of her skin. Annica appeared like she was going to faint any moment.

He swallowed hard, feeling the fear radiating from her like cold, packed snow. "Annica, what is going on? Do you need to lie down?"

"It's happening again,"

Her words were weak, her eyes unfocused. Even after taking her face in his hands, putting his eyes right before hers, she still was not looking at him. Strands of dark hair stuck her face like cobwebs. He gently pulled them aside, tucked the strays behind her ear.

"What is happening again? Annica?"

Finally, her eyes found his. Her muscles tensed and she sat up. Now she was gripping one of his wrists. What *did* she mean by that? What was happening again? Her memories flickered like weak candles, scorning reality.

"I'd like to go back to my room," she said, eyes wide.

Edrik nodded stiffly. "I'll walk with you."

Her strength returned as they made their way to the temple and the aldyr faded from view within the city. Edrik pressed the issue of what Annica meant when she said it was "happening again." She explained the events of the day prior. How she connected with the energy and life of the city, unknowingly led the archpriestess on a chase through Nel Aldyri, and, finally, her nightmarish vision with the aldyr. After showing her scar from her fall into unconsciousness, Edrik's pace slowed noticeably.

"That was you?" he asked in a low voice, realization blossoming in his eyes before they became doused in shadow.

"What was?"

"There was a commotion by the sparring fields the other day. A mage had to be carried from the hill overlooking the hinterlands. I heard later she had passed out. It seemed like nothing at first. A small quake shook the island not long after; it may have even been the next day, perhaps. It was more of a shudder, nothing I was overly concerned about. I'd almost thought a strong wind had blown in like back in Ashwater. But, my captain was on edge for several days after. The temple requested additional patrols and I was on a few of them. I'd hoped to see you but never did. Things were tense there."

As he continued speaking, Annica wondered if she heard him correctly. Her question lingered just behind her lips, fearing to open the door to a truth she was afraid to know.

"Edrik, did you say 'several days'?"

Pursing his lips, Edrik hesitated for several long moments before answering. "Yes. If that was you, Annica, that passed out on the hill... it was several days ago."

Annica's heart lurched. No one told her she had been unconscious for so long. She assumed at most a single evening. Had she struck her head that hard?

"I thought it was only one evening," she mumbled in disbelief.

"It was longer, much longer," Edrik said, his voice rising with concern. "If you were that hurt they would have sent apothecaries."

"I only woke up to Mya in the room."

"Mya?"

"Just a girl," Annica clarified dismissively. "Something isn't right. I woke up with this scar, too, but I thought it may have just been from my fall."

Edrik's finger traced the jagged outlines of the pale, raised surface of Annica's skin. He'd never seen anything shaped like this, but a random fall could produce such a strange-looking wound. Although, if Annica believed she had only been unconscious for a single night such scarring would be impossible. She was certainly the temple mage that was carried away and she was certainly unconscious for longer than she thought, but this didn't explain the strange reaction of the temple afterward.

The sky turned into a dull flame as the sun began to set. The Temple of the First Son rose into view and Annica made every attempt to avert her eyes from the ever-present tree that loomed dark and silhouetted against the horizon's fire that was quickly turning to sickly, bruised purple.

The temple grounds were quiet. The trickle of the fountains echoed weakly as Edrik and Annica passed between them. When they reached the entrance, Annica surprised herself when she took Edrik by the hand.

"Will you come in with me?" she whispered, as though her voice would carry to every person behind the closed doors within. "Something doesn't feel right. I... don't feel right."

Squeezing her hand, Edrik attempted to provide some passing comfort. Night was moving in quickly, draping itself like a heavy blanket over the island. The only other living beings in the temple were scattered disciples snuffing out every other candle, leaving only dull light and dense shadows to lead the way back to Annica's quarters.

Annica stopped so suddenly it caused Edrik to jerk her abruptly forward as he continued walking. The doors were always unlocked, but she never left hers ajar. A beacon of yellow light several inches wide greeted them as light poured from the open space of Annica's doorframe.

She told herself it could have been the disciples tending to her room's candles. But candles in individual rooms were often left in the purview of the occupant. And doors were always shut securely, providing at least a little privacy and respect.

All of these things she attempted to disregard, hoping that

they were a result of her frayed mind. Inside the confines of her simple room, all appeared in place. Her bed was still made from this morning. Her shelves appeared untouched. The candles glowed softly and all was quiet.

Her bed beckoned to her. After removing her boots, she sat on the edge of the soft mattress and ran her feet over the cool wood on the floor. Just once, it seemed the anxiety that chewed at her stomach may have been just that; a bad feeling and nothing more. Her hand patted the soft blanket, signaling Edrik to join her. He came in, casually pulling the door behind him but leaving it open a few inches.

The bed shifted as he sat down, creaking from the weight of his armor. The small metal pauldron was cool against her head as she lay it against him. It wasn't the most comfortable, but his presence made up for what his shoulder lacked. At this moment, friendly company was what she most desired.

Her mouth opened in a deep yawn that forced her eyes closed. When they opened again, she found herself looking at the books on her desk. Something was off. The feeling was a soft twitch in her consciousness at first, then peaked when realization dawned on her. One of the books was turned upside down. Although not overly stringent regarding neatness, her books were indeed something she valued. Putting a book back upside down was simply something she would not do.

When her head rose sharply from Edrik's shoulder, the way he stiffened gave away that he felt her own tension.

"What is it?" he asked, his voice low but harsh.

"I don't know," she replied, but so distracted was Annica by the inverted binding she wasn't sure if she actually said the words or not.

The green lettering on the book's spine was easy enough to read, even upside down: *The History and Peoples of Alda*. Her hand hovered perilously near the tan-covered book as though it would jump out at her. Cautiously removing it from between its fellows, Annica looked at the front and back covers. Finding nothing unusual, she opened the book in the same manner as the other volume that contained the old letter.

Edrik turned toward her slightly as Annica sat back on the bed. His eyes moved between her and the dreaded book with the mundane title in her hands. The front cover felt as though it was made of iron as she opened it slowly. The breeze off the pages glided under her sleeve as she flipped briskly through the pages. Once again, a lone piece of paper waited between the final page and the back cover.

This parchment, however, was quite fresh. It lacked the brittleness and fading ink of time. The small piece of paper, no larger than her hand, contained a lone image: a rough, broken diamond shape, lines thick and uneven, with curled, jagged barbs where each side met in a corner. In the center sat a plain, unassuming, and rough-edged dot that, as she gazed upon it, felt deeper than the nothingness. As deep and empty as the end of time itself.

There was writing scratched on the paper. The language wasn't one she recognized, at least not at first. The longer she stared, the more the words seemed to coalesce and make sense. Whispers licked her ears, crawled into her brain.

BAC'THULE. *The Void and Vessel. The Inheritor King. The First Herald of the Obscured Throne—the unmaker and bringer of Oblivion Bliss.*

VIA MORTIS INFINITUM.

.   .   .

THE HORRIBLE WORDS repeated themselves until they split, over-lapping, and became indecipherable yet intimately knowable. The lines became a chant that layered upon itself until it was as indistinct as a rushing wind and tossing waves. A horrid sense of recollection washed over Annica. A cold familiarity covered her in goose-flesh, but full comprehension was yet out of reach, like she was underwater grasping at the surface, seeing the light break against the prospect of life-giving breath and understand-ing; it lay just beyond her fingertips.

"Hey," Edrik barked. The paper fell from Annica's hands. Edrik practically jumped from the bed, he was nearly out of the room before Annica could react. "Stop!" he shouted as he barged out the partially open door, throwing it open the rest of the way.

Perhaps it was a combination of her catching Edrik by the forearm and her shocked concern at his sudden actions, but, regardless, the Fifth Sect ignited within in her. Edrik's heart was beating like a terrified animal. The thundering within his chest resonated in her head.

"What is it, Edrik?"

The disciplined reaction to protect and the innate trembling of fear mingled in Annica's gut. These were Edrik's emotions; flowing from his being into hers. It became difficult to tell where his fright ended and hers began. Edrik's, though, did have a sharpness to it that Annica's lacked. This fed her own fear, creating a resonating echo that built into near-panic.

"Edrik," she managed to force with her tongue dry, "what is going on?"

"Gods," he replied, his chest still heaving, "he was right there."

"Who?"

"Fuck... right there," he continued to ramble. "He was looking right at us. How did I not see him?"

"*Who?*" Annica repeated, her voice rising in panic.

"Someone at the door. I looked over and there was someone there. They took off as soon as I noticed them."

"What did they look like? Was it another mage or disciple? What color were their robes?" Her breathing calmed somewhat at the prospect, but Edrik's fear was still raw and continued scratching at her own emotions.

"They were black. Who wears black robes?"

Fear no longer scratched at her barely-controlled demeanor. It ripped into it, leaving reason and comfortable assumptions in tattered pieces.

"No one wears black robes... not that I've heard of," she said, her voice quiet.

"They're gone now. No chance we can catch them."

"We can't lock our doors," she thought aloud. "What if they come back?"

Edrik was quiet a moment. His heart still beat rapidly with distress, but now something more resolute was there, a levee holding the chopping waters of his will in place.

"I'll stand watch tonight. At the front of the hall. If they come back..." he let the words trail off and punctuated his thought with a hand on his sword. "I'll inform my captain about what happened. I'm sure he'll understand. The importance of the magi and disciples are stressed to us."

Her arms wrapped around him in an embrace, surprising both of them. She let her head rest against the steel of his breastplate, although the engraved tree stood out against her temple almost painfully. Wishing to alleviate the discomfort but not wanting to let him go, she raised her head slightly to look into his eyes.

"Thank you."

He smiled, nodded, and squeezed her a little more tightly.

Edrik closed the door and reassured her that he would be only a few doors away at the end of the hall. Even knowing that an armed soldier waited dutifully for the dawn brought little comfort to her troubled and racing mind.

Annica slept only in short fitful bursts until Edrik knocked softly and opened her door. The sound was weak, tired like her. The only reasonable explanation is that morning had come. Somehow, it took forever to arrive, and yet she also dreaded having to face the day already.

Edrik's upper half leaned into her room. His eyes were bloodshot and he walked as though his back ached horribly. Annica could only imagine how she looked.

His gruff, exhausted voice cut through the chill in the room. "It's morning. No more black robes showed themselves. Not even a shadow out of place."

Sitting up in bed, a weak "Thank you," was all she managed before a deep yawn took control. Edrik nodded.

"I need to report in. I'm going to have some explaining to do about my post, but I think they'll understand. I hope they will, at any rate."

"If not," her smile strengthened, "the archpriestess' personal student will set them straight. We'll see how seriously they take the magi."

A frail chuckle was all he could manage. Her eyes looked as tired as his, red and sunken, and her hair was a mess. What other mysteries surrounded this girl? Despite the night's harsh toll, she still had an alluring beauty—like a pale moon on a cold night. And, with some measure of grim relevance, something was haunting this girl.

"I hope to see you again soon, under better circumstances."

After Edrik took his leave, she felt the room grow colder. The idea that it was the absence of his presence was the most comforting excuse, so Annica clung to that. Pulling the blankets back over her aching body provided little additional warmth, at most a mockery of the comfort they should provide. A warm cup of tea was likely the best solution, so Annica rose, groaning, from her bed.

Standing with her feet on the cold floor, her clothes felt abnormally heavy. She realized she was still in her mage's robes, now wrinkled from tossing restlessly throughout the night. Annica slowly and clumsily put on her spare robes. The crumpled clothes were tossed haphazardly into the laundry. It was too early for the morning meal, so Annica would have to go to the kitchens to find tea for herself.

To her surprise, Helyn was in the dining hall, in her usual place and by herself, leafing through a large tome. The archpriestess looked up with barely contained disinterest until her eyes fell on Annica.

"Annica? Gods, you look terrible. Are you alright?"

The struggle to tell the truth about the previous day and night tossed about in Annica's head before tumbling to her stomach. Nervous thoughts about what her mentor would think of her recent episodes, for lack of a better word, or the black-robed stalker that Edrik swore he saw. Fear prevailed over reason.

"It was a very long night, archpriestess."

The archpriestess wore a veneer of incredulity over her ill humor. She didn't believe Annica. That much was certain. When she spoke, her words dripped with sarcasm.

"I have many different interpretations of what a long night with a soldier standing guard to your room could entail."

Despite her insides turning to ice, Annica's face flushed.

"It was my hallway. That he was guarding."

"Regardless," Helyn replied shortly before taking a sip from a cup of steaming tea sitting next to the large book, an action that Annica felt was the archpriestess punctuating the end of the topic, "we'll continue with your studies today."

Helyn's eyes looked up from her current page once more,

lingering on Annica. She gently pushed the ornate brass kettle toward Annica's side of the table. "There's extra cups just there, in the kitchen. You look like you need a cup or three. We'll deal with some light study today."

Annica shuffled away from the table meekly. She imagined the gaze of the archpriestess pressing into her back as she passed through the door to the kitchen. Having thankfully broken line of sight to Helyn, Annica sighed deeply. Fetching a cup from the stores, she braced herself to return to the table where her mentor sat.

The room suddenly felt cavernous. The weak, chill light of early morning barely held at bay by the pungent tea Helyn enjoyed. The archpriestess let the revelation of her knowledge of Annica's guest hang in the air for several long moments, a few turned pages. If she knew that much, then Annica could only assume Helyn knew nothing was amiss between her and Edrik. Perhaps the archpriestess merely wanted to make the point that the temple was in her charge, as was Annica, and such things wouldn't go unnoticed.

Regardless, Helyn eventually began to inquire more into Annica's troubles. No satisfying answers were provided. Helyn suggested it may have to do with pushing Annica into tapping into her Fifth Sect potential too early. As a result, they would avoid such training for the time being, allow her mind and body to recover, and focus on the other sects.

The rest of the day was spent in, as Helyn promised, light study. Helyn wanted to avoid other incidents involving tapping Annica's potential so carelessly. That she was magically proficient was without question, so the need for her to learn control was paramount. There was much reading and manipulation practice, all the while Helyn was directing her with cold disinterest.

The archpriestess lacked the spark and enthusiasm that was

present when she and Annica first began her training. Helyn was detached, almost uninterested in Annica's progress any more. The events of the previous night were a stark contrast to the mundanity of this routine.

Finally, Annica had enough. As the last sparks of a failed spell fizzled out, she approached Helyn. She'd left the issue alone, but it had been gnawing at her all day. Helyn's dismissive attitude only exacerbated the problem.

Taking a deep breath, Annica asked, "Who is Bac'thule?"

It was subtle, but Helyn twitched. Her composure cracked briefly, but sharply. The archpriestess looked around casually. Her eyes scanning those other magi practicing around them. "Where did you hear that name?"

"I found another letter in one of my books. It had a strange diamond-shaped insignia on it with very strange, actually, disturbing, content written on it. Albeit, very brief."

"I see," Helyn replied, trying to be nonchalant.

Helyn dismissed Annica after that, letting her know they would talk soon and to put the contents of the letter out of her mind. Helyn would have Annica's personal library audited for any other strange material and any books replaced that were tampered with. Helyn encouraged Annica to take some time herself and enjoy the rest of her day. It was a sudden and awkward end to their conversation.

Things felt vastly different in the temple. Annica could sense it—a different energy resonating from every person and stone. She tamped down those feelings, fearing that connecting to the ebb and flow of the Fifth would open her to whatever baleful presence always seemed to find her when she used that magic. The magic of healing and creation seemed to bring her only nightmares and darkness.

Thankfully, that night passed without incident. She dreamed of nothing, and there were no nightmares left unremembered;

no hollow spaces in her mind to greet her as she woke, tinged with foreboding. Breakfast was typical, and Helyn was still taciturn.

Annica's training sessions that day were held in one of the several recessed training areas for magi. The training focusing mostly on Annica's skill she previously exhibited with fire magic. Though, the lessons were trite and rote. Helyn's instruction felt as though it was being directed straight from a textbook. Summon the flame, make it form a circle. Make it grow. Dissipate. Light the sconce at the far end of the arena. Light three at once. Five at once. All of the tests she passed and each one was followed with the same, tedious response: "Very good." Had Annica so failed the archpriestess?

Helyn dismissed Annica for a few hours, providing only the vague excuse of 'temple business'. The archpriestess encouraged Annica to experience more of the island, stressing that Annica had only spent her time in the city proper.

"Nel Aldyri is more than just these stones and shops," Helyn said, with the first smile Annica had seen from her in two days.

Despite her hesitance, Annica took Helyn's advice and took a quiet walk to the edge of the city. Tight alleys and stone streets gave way to open lots of overgrowth and buildings that reminded her more of her old village; that is if the buildings were in any sort of respectable shape.

The dirt road crunched beneath her feet as the occasional cart and driver or traveling farmhand passed. The overgrown lots became vast swaths of plowed and growing fields. Patches of trees or small herds of animals mottled the countryside. It should have been serene, quaint even. Instead, there was an innate sense of wrongness. A sour feeling crept up her arms and back, like venom dripping upon her and burning her soul.

The sensation held a familiarity to it. It reminded her of magic, but not like any she had practiced. The letter from the back of the primer mentioned that magic left its mark. This must be such an echo or, given the aspect of magic that she feared lingered here, a stain. Such an awful, gnawing miasma of the arcane must be the wretched taint of the Fourth Sect. Annica shuddered.

Suspicious eyes had fallen upon her. It wasn't an unfamiliar sensation. Feeling like you were being watched was a common thing in Ashwater. The dark nights, the distant sounds of beasts on the prowl during the twilight hours, even the cold wandering eyes of judgmental and cantankerous neighbors left one looking over their shoulder fairly frequently. Annica had felt that familiar weight of being watched for some time on her trek this afternoon.

Sometimes, the feeling came from the houses. Gathered in clutches of twos and threes, with the occasional single home with relevant outbuildings, the denizens of the hinterlands worked in their surroundings like sluggish ants. They toiled slowly and persistently. They would stop and turn their heads as the mage from the city passed by. The sounds of chopping wood, the smell of manure, the cries of the occasional child melding into a discomforting harmony that was channeled at her through their lingering, following eyes.

This, however, was preferred to the alternative—she was also being watched by something else. Something *other*. She knew from where it came and cursed herself for being stupid enough to take Helyn up on her offer to visit this quiet and unsettling place. The tranquility felt fake. The incessant buzz of the insects mocked her. And she was closer than ever to that great, bestial aldyr. The tree was calling to her, beckoning her forward—no, commanding. There was brutishness behind the feeling, some seething anger.

She pushed back against it. Forced the caustic presence from her mind. It didn't go quietly. Annica's breaths came faster. Each time the call wrapped around her mind like perverse, grasping fingers, she pushed back harder. Whatever was keeping that appalling, pleading, furious presence at bay Annica held on to. She concentrated, using her newly honed skills to focus on the power that wrapped around her like a shimmering membrane. It felt warm and familiar, like the first touches of the Fifth Sect. Cold, coiling appendages groped at her soul, hungry and violent, but slipped away like slimy tendrils off wet rocks.

A cold sweat beaded on her forehead, chest, and back. Annica realized she was running, her hair trailing behind her like a dark pennant heralding her return to sanity. The stone walls of city buildings growing closer as her feet pounded on cobblestone streets. Once again, she had run an incredible distance without stopping, coming to as she entered the boundaries of the city proper.

Stopping next to a lamp post, Annica placed her hand against the cold iron and leaned against it. The physical exertion was catching up to her. To her left was the road that would take her back to the Temple of the First Son, her room, and more questions. Ahead lay the path to the harbor where it all began. To her right lay unfamiliar parts of the city. And behind her the aldyr and its accursed countryside. None of these promised safety or rest.

Tears welled in her eyes. Where could she go and find any respite? Where in this strange city could she be safe, both body and mind?

Edrik. She felt safe with Edrik. But there was no possibility of her being with him at the barracks. She didn't even know if he was on patrol at this very moment, walking this city with steel useless against the horrors that assailed her practically since she arrived at this menacing island.

The walk back to the temple was slow and begrudging. Helyn would likely be of little help. Dismissive, even snide, remarks were certainly unwelcome at this juncture. Her room—what awaited there? More cryptic letters and intrusions?

As the temple came into view, the faint sounds of shouting interrupted her pitiful thoughts. Soldiers and civilians both were pleading with someone. The group circled the edge of one of the training arenas. Running to see what the commotion entailed, Annica saw someone standing on the opposite side of the fence that separated the grassy rim of a recessed arena with the steep side facing the rest of the island. This particular portion of the hillside was akin to a cliff. The person being pleaded with was considering leaping from it.

Annica tried pushing her way through the crowd. They parted more willingly when they noticed her green robes. Annica began shouting to the poor individual. It appeared to be an older woman, judging by the longer blonde hair that tossed in the breeze, and the telling white robes indicated they were a temple disciple. Annica's voice must have reached them, for they turned to look directly at her.

The pale blue eyes of Mya stared back at her. The girl was nearly unrecognizable. Her eyes had grown so pale Annica wondered if she'd gone blind, except for the terrifying look of recognition that was there. Her hair was as thin and wispy as the smoke of dying incense and her skin nearly translucent. Her dry, cracked lips curled up like she would begin weeping at any moment.

"Mya?" Annica called out.

"Annica," Mya wheezed. "You're still here?"

Annica forced a smile, anything to keep the poor girl holding on just a moment longer. A tear rolled down the girl's fragile, pale face.

"No," Mya whispered, "No. The notes were supposed to scare you away! Make you leave and not get me in trouble! No, no..."

The groan that escaped the parched mouth was like an

ancient door closing for the final time. Paper-dry skin surrounding bruise-colored sockets suddenly scrunched around her eyes as her bottom lip quivered pitifully. Annica was able to approach Mya, nearly to within arm's length, but the girl simply hung her head and turned her gaze away. Mya then did the unexpected and, with startling speed and agility for one that appeared so broken, leaped back over the fence and clutched onto Annica like a drowning woman.

"You have to get away," Mya croaked. "You have to! They'll use you, break you, they won't let you die."

Annica had no time to ask Mya what this meant, as two soldiers plucked the frail creature off of Annica. Knobby fingers clutched at her like dead branches. Mya's belligerent ranting was lost as Annica recognized one of the soldier's dragging her away —Edrik. He quickly gave Annica a sad, fleeting look before hauling away the rambling, maddened girl. The crowd closed in around them and she lost sight of both her friend and the crazed Mya.

The walk back to her room was quiet and a weight pressed on Annica's heart. She felt terrible for Mya, frightened for them both, and desperately wanted to see Edrik so they could talk at length about recent events. Ignoring the concerned whispers and stares from the clusters of magi and disciples that she passed, she reached her room and slammed the door shut. The wood felt cool against her splayed hands as she pressed against it.

After a moment to collect her thoughts, Annica went to her bed and sat there where her mind promptly ran amok again. Amid Mya's pendulous fits of whimpering and rambling, the basic conclusion that Annica could draw from the bits of words and phrases she put together as that she had to get away from this place—a thought that she already entertained—and that they didn't like her. Who was 'they?' The temple? The city? The island?

After weeks of churning over fears, rationalizations, and endless questions, Annica stopped and let her mind simply wander. At first, the books held her gaze; particularly the one that had once been used to slip her a cryptic letter. This caused little but more fear and agitation, so she let her eyes close.

Breaths came slow and measured. It contrasted sharply against the roiling, silent chaos of her mind. But, within that chaos, a tranquility began to grow around it—cupping it like gentle hands around a wounded, frightened bird. The Fifth Sect slipped into her, or she into it; this wasn't clear, but Annica did not entirely care. Calmness and warmth were present and welcome, for once.

The stillness of the natural world around her. The old stones of the hinterlands, the oaks and pines of the forest, the stillness that gave way to the bustle of Nel Aldyri. The city was slowing, people returning home to their families, but it was still so much more lively than the tranquil wilds. A smile crept across her face for perhaps the first time in days or longer.

Then, amid the calmness and warmth of the natural order of the fields and forests and the souls and lanterns of the city, there was something else that began to creep into her consciousness. Like cold fibers, something was among the people and stones and trees. Something hungry. Something cold and leeching from the warmth.

Like a great maw in the dark waters beneath the sea, where the sun reflects on the waves, rows of teeth waited with ravenous impatience. It couldn't surface. Or it wouldn't. The intent of this vile thing was difficult to judge. All that was clear is that it didn't belong on this island, in this world, in this existence. But the icy, fibrous voids were everywhere. They filtered into homes. They ran beneath the streets.

Most of all, they were in the temple.

A sharp pain shot through Annica as she saw the fibers wrap like the thick ropes used on the *Dawn Rose*'s moorings. They coiled up in the tree-shaped roots that rose from the dais in the temple proper. Her breathing quickened and she both felt and saw the fibers leave the city and grow into trembling tendrils in the hinterlands beneath the rocks and trees and farms. The tendrils spread through the island like a hungry web, assimilating, wrapping, and binding together at the great Aldyr where *they* became *it*. A thing of unknowable intent, but boundless in its maliciousness.

Annica struggled to define what it was. The nearest she ascertained was that the thing beheld the same principles as a doorway: defined by its emptiness and purpose, recognizable as a shape, yet not actually, physically there. Or was it? The concept eluded her as to whether this was a viscous mass of sinister portent, or simply nothing at all. Her mind began to burn, as though her consciousness fought for air, drowning just below the surface where it could breach into understanding. So much noise as she sought to grasp the reality before her. So much flailing of sanity trying not to drown in the incomprehensible.

She shut herself off from the magic. Withdrew into the safe and comforting physical confines of her dormitory. Stone walls that could be felt. Flickering candles that could be seen. Paper and wood that could be smelled. And silence. Her heart thudded. Her hands and teeth clenched—and her resolve strengthened. There was no doubting her course of action now.

Against her better common sense, Annica knew she had to reach Edrik. He was likely at the barracks and she may have to pull some sort of rank as a mage. She still hoped she had such pull. The prospect of having to flee this island on her own caused a tight knot in her gut. The idea of leaving Edrik behind caused it to grow tighter still; however, she would have to be willing to follow through if it came to that.

There was nothing to gather, no food or clothing in her room that she could take with her. Looting the temple larder could get her caught before she even began her flight from the island, so that was yet another option she didn't chance. Annica left her room hoping that the one other person she had to meet could help her in this regard. Otherwise, escape into the Wailing Ocean with no supplies would be a slow, lonely death. Though, she doubted it was much worse than what awaited in Nel Aldyri.

The hour had grown late while Annica was lost in the flow of the Fifth Sect, or perhaps it was the influence of whatever darkness dwelt in the great aldyr. Every time she felt its malice, time became irrelevant. Regardless, darkness now draped over the city, casting shadows that almost looked alive. This, to her, was the true face of the city. Weak, scattered lights from a few windows called out like lost souls, while thick clouds trimmed with pale, unfeeling moonlight sat motionless overhead.

The town was silent as she passed one closed door after another. Annica neither saw nor heard any guards, even as she drew closer to the barracks. She thought she was either very lucky, or the town had disappeared overnight.

It occurred to her that she might make it to the barracks without incident, when an armored figure grabbed her arm and pulled Annica in like a caught thief.

"What are you doing?" a voice asked harshly. Despite the tone, she knew who had seized her.

"Edrik? How did you find me?"

"Your feet don't bear you as quietly as they should."

"Why—why are you alone?"

The firmness of his grip softened; his fingers parted slightly. With a hurt tone, he replied, "I've been practically ostracized of late. After that night in your dormitory, it's as if I broke some unwritten rule."

"It makes no matter. I'm leaving. I want you to come with me."

Her firm voice and resolute glare did little to assuage Edrik's immediate misgiving. There was no simple way to leave Nel Aldyri. They were on an island days from any nearby coast; he knew as he had watched on their journey, seen the maps as part of his training for potential quests to the mainland.

"That will never work, Annica—" he began, before she wrenched her arm free, nostrils flaring.

"I am not staying here a moment longer, Edrik," she flung the words at him in a harsh whisper. "This island is evil. Not necessarily the people, but the island itself. There's a shadow here that covers everything; it infests everything. It's trying to—I think it's trying to infest me. I—I don't know a better way to explain."

Annica waited for Edrik to scoff, roll his eyes, or smile in some condescending way. To tell her that she was having nightmares or that her studies were getting the better of her. When he replied, she didn't know if the words were comforting or further fueled her sense of ill foreboding.

"I believe you."

She stared at him, disbelieving, until he continued to speak after a few moments.

"I do, I believe you, but what can we do? Where in the low hells are we going to go? We're on an island days away from any coast, let alone other towns."

"We'll take some supplies with us, take a ship, we'll sail straight until we hit solid land and keep going."

"Who's going to sail this ship? I don't know how, do you?"

Annica took a deep breath. Perhaps her plan needed more refinement, but the weight of providence was growing heavier.

The night was dark, and the darkness was growing thicker. They would have no more time to plan. Unfortunately, Edrik was right. She didn't know how to captain a ship.

"Come with me," Annica said, the words whipping about with her as she turned sharply to walk away.

Edrik huffed. "I told you, I would love—"

"Not to the harbor. Not right now. I want to see someone else."

"Annica,"

"Just another hour of your time, Edrik, please. Are you on patrol?"

"No."

"Then why can't you—"

"Because I have to escort you back to the temple."

The words fell like an iron ball between them. Annica stepped back, reflexively. Edrik breathed heavily out through his nostrils.

"Why do you have to do that?"

He could hear the betrayal in her words. The hurt that caused her to reel back from him and the fear that momentarily flashed in her eyes, which quickly turned to anger.

"Why?" she asked again.

The silence was painful. Not even the sounds of insects could be heard. That strange fact struck him now at the most awkward of times.

Edrik cast a quick glance back toward the barracks, the glow of numerous large torches causing an orange glow around the adjacent buildings. The northern and southern guard towers loomed against the night sky like fire pokers; fresh orange embers at their tips.

"They saw you coming, Annica," Edrik explained, indicating the windows and their respective guards at the top of the towers.

"I was sent to escort you as they thought it would cause less of a stir. Are they wrong?"

Annica looked deep into his eyes. She couldn't tell if that was disappointment in his voice. Despite the pressing darkness, his squinted eyes had sorrow hiding in the lines beneath them. He was under orders to take her back. That left them with quite the conflict.

"I'm not going back, Edrik."

The firmness in her words left no room for argument. If he was taking her back, there would be a struggle. It was a good thing he was prepared, the moment he was ordered to return her immediately, to disobey those orders.

"Will you just follow me for a while? Give a passing attempt that you're cooperating?"

The look of betrayal changed to one of confusion; a softer but still cold expression. Edrik took her gently by the forearm and felt Annica resist at first. Her muscles tensed, then just as quickly relaxed. A moment of renewed trust passed between them.

Annica followed where Edrik led. The glow of the barrack torches faded as they walked. Still, no insects sang. The world began to feel fake, as though a candle had been blown out and took all substance of being with it. She looked around, focused on trying to hear and hesitating to use the Fifth Sect for fear of what waited in the darkness for such a tempting beacon to be lit.

"I hear it, too." Edrik's voice was low, a brusque whisper. "The silence. Nothing living stirs this night."

"Then you know why I can't go back. I see we still walk the path to the Temple of the First—"

"Don't say that. Please," Edrik interrupted. His voice croaked, almost breaking. "That name, please don't."

"Edrik,"

"We're not going to the temple. I only needed to get out of

sight. Get away from the barracks. Who was it you needed to see?"

Annica hesitated. Not out of distrust of him, but from the fear in his voice. "Captain Sisironi," she said flatly.

"Do you know where she lives? I haven't seen her since the day we arrived." He sounded incredulous. Annica assumed he was following her out of blind desperation at this juncture. For the first time in days, Annica smiled.

"I think I do, in fact. She invited me to visit her in the housing district next to the harbor."

Edrik replied with only a nod. Once they passed a few more streets, he released his hold on her arm. His hand gripped the sword tucked in its scabbard. His eyes scanned the streets and houses for any signs of life. People were alive within those walls, but at the moment everything appeared much like the towns and villages back home—dark and empty. Something stirred that drove human, animal, and insect alike into hiding like mice in the shadow of a great flying predator.

The sound of lapping water greeted them as they reached the harbor-adjacent dwellings. Two-story townhomes of gray stone sat back to back, one side facing the harbor and the other facing a deep canal that separated this district from the other homes on the opposite side. They were well-maintained, with thick ivy growing along the walls and winding through the steps that led up to the front entrances. Back on the mainland, these would be considered small, individual palaces.

Neither Edrik nor Annica knew who lived in these domiciles; however, Annica only needed to find one particular individual. The townhouses, for the most part, were almost identical. It took a few moments for Annica to notice that all of them had separate marine-oriented creatures carved into the stone newel posts at the base of each landing. Her eyes spotted a pair of otters, then dolphins, followed by perched seagulls, and, finally, a duo of plump walruses.

"There," Annica said, pointing and directing Edrik's attention to the penultimate house on the street.

Edrik allowed Annica to lead. She knocked on the door, softly at first, then gave a few quick, sharper raps. The heavy door opened, revealing a heavy-eyed Sisironi in evening attire. Her short-cropped hair was pulled back into a short ponytail. Annica saw that, despite her comfortable shirt and pants, the captain still wore a dagger sheathed in a loosely-fitting belt.

Staring at the weapon, Annica asked apprehensively, "Expecting company?"

"Ship captain. Dangerous journeys. Surely, you remember some of what we've discussed? It leaves me overly cautious," she answered drowsily. Edrik's eyes flicked to the dagger and back to the captain. Their eyes met momentarily and, Edrik admitted, uncomfortably.

"What are the two of you doing out here?" Sisironi asked pointedly.

Annica glanced over her shoulder to the main street. Seeing no one, feeling ill at ease regardless, she asked, "May we come in please, captain?"

The tall woman stood aside and her tired but stern eyes softened. "No need to be so formal, Annica. Come in."

The interior of the home was quite different from the cold stone that formed the exterior walls. Warm wood panels and soft furniture adorned the modest-sized rooms. From the small receiving room, Annica heard a crackling fire coming from another room, spreading its warmth all the way to the front door. In this home, Annica almost felt safe.

Sisironi started to lead them into the main room, where the comforting fire awaited. Annica was tempted to oblige and follow, but she couldn't. She wanted to be here, with Edrik and the captain, and forget for a moment everything that awaited outside—the temple, Mya, Helyn, their coming days of fleeing on the ocean, and whatever ghastly darkness dwelt within the great aldyr and spread its corruption to the city. It was these things, however, that drove Annica to speak up, causing the captain to stop mid-stride.

"Sisironi, I have some things to discuss with you. Some things to ask of you."

The captain turned and regarded her quizzically. "I'm not sure I like the sound of your tone, Annica. What has you worried so, girl?"

Edrik and Annica exchanged glances. The courage and gall that so drove her earlier fizzled in her gut. What if Sisironi refused to help? What if the captain reported them? She was likely as good or better a fighter than Edrik. The doubts were closing in, threatening to stamp out her plans and hopes before they took root. She had to ask now and press her case.

"I'm leaving the island." The words came quickly and confidently.

"*We're* leaving the island," Edrik added, his eyes fixed on the captain.

A smile crept across Sisironi's thin lips. Her eyes flicked back and forth between the two of them. She giggled in her husky, sultry way. Pausing to look at them both again, she then chuckled louder.

"I'm all for a good tease, but it's very late."

"I'm serious, Sisironi," Annica repeated, firmer than before. "We're leaving. Tonight. I was hoping you may be able to help us, but I'd rather risk death on the ocean than stay on this island for a moment longer."

The smile faded. Sisironi's thin, toned arms crossed and she settled her weight onto one leg. Whenever she stood in such a way on her ship, Annica remembered it was to give a sailor or rowdy villager a verbal thrashing that sent them away with their tail between their legs.

"You're coming to one of the captains of Nel Aldyri to confess your plans to steal a ship? Have you bribed any crew? How many are willing to turn traitor? How many provisions have you stocked up?"

Annica placed a hand on the increasingly irate captain's arm. It felt like she was trying to calm a large cat that was ready to spring at her. The captain looked at her with piercing eyes and Annica knew there would be no diplomacy that would work. Only the raw truth of their situation; at least, the truth as Annica knew it.

"I don't know what loyalties you have to whatever superiors you answer to, Sisironi. But there's something dark on this island. Not just evil, something wrong. I've felt it, more than once. I won't stay here and be subject to its influence any longer."

The look in the captain's eyes shifted. Edrik knew that look. As brief as the pit in one's gut when they look over a cliff face to see the fate that awaited them with one purposeful step. As flickering as the shadows of a dozen sparrows fleeing the sight of a hawk. It was the look of fear slipping out from behind the mask, only to be quickly covered again by something more comfortable. Orders, delusion, or self-soothing lies.

"You've heard, too, haven't you?" Edrik asked matter-of-factly.

Annica's head swiveled to face him. Her brows furrowed.

"Heard what, boy?" Sisironi countered. Her muscles tensed under Annica's grip.

"The whispers. The things captains, lieutenants, and other old-hands are talking about. They won't risk any details, but they've been frightened. For weeks now, they've been saying a lot of unusual things."

"Those that have been here for a while have their superstitions. What of it?"

Edrik took a step toward Sisironi. A slow, purposeful step that may have just been that proverbial step off that gut-softening cliff. Sisironi didn't move, only meeting his step with a harsh stare.

"Superstitions. I saw them from one of the barrack towers. Lined up by the temple, just a few days ago."

Sisironi's eyes narrowed in thought. "The Temple of the First Son?"

Edrik's skin grew cold. His face paled. Annica's frustration with him obviously withholding something from her faded when she saw how he reacted to mere mention of the name of the place she had been sleeping and studying.

"Ever since I figured out what happened with Annica," he began, but his voice choked. He cleared his throat, licked his lips, and continued. "Annica had been acting strange after we met for the first time after arriving here. When she said she was the one who fainted on the hill that day, things started piecing themselves together. Remember the tremor?"

Sisironi nodded, her jaw muscles tensing.

"That was not long after Annica was taken away. Just before I met her, patrols were doubled by the hinterlands. People were going missing. Then, after I was ordered to stay away from Annica," he looked over to her at this juncture, his face begging forgiveness, "that's when I saw one of them. Talking to my captain. I'll never forget."

Turning from the captain, Annica took Edrik's shaking hand in hers. "One of the black-robed men?"

"Yes," he answered in barely a whisper. "I learned quickly upon our arrival that my captain was a strong man. No nonsense, no frailty, not an ounce of weakness in him. But, after speaking to the man in the black robes. I've never seen the captain shake before."

"I've never seen any black-robed men," Sisironi thought aloud.

"I don't think I was meant to. They must have heard me approaching. The man turned. He looked human, but his face was, I don't know—cold and gray. His eyes, though—gods be good—his eyes held nothing but the worst kind of emptiness. When I heard him utter that name, the temple, something shook within me. I felt like a rabbit in a snare."

Edrik paused, needing a moment before he continued. "When they noticed me the black-robed man said something to my captain and left quickly. The captain spoke to me immediately, told me the other man was very important and powerful, and to let the matter drop."

"What did you do?" Annica asked breathlessly. The look in Sisironi's eyes spoke the same question.

Edrik answered simply, "I let the matter drop. I was also told not to speak to you again, on penalty of dereliction of duty."

"A very serious offense," the captain added in a grave tone. "I've never seen anyone come back from such a sentence."

"Come back?" Annica pressed.

"Taken away, I assume to our dungeons. Or executed perhaps, but they never inform the public of such things."

"And that never struck you as odd?" Annica questioned, her tone openly accusatory.

Sisironi took a noticeable offense.

"That the powers-that-be don't hang people in town square? No, I didn't think to question such morbidity, Annica."

"Not the executions, the disappearing of people. Wouldn't the mayor and archpriestess want the criminals' offenses and punishments at least known? To prevent further crimes?"

"I'm neither the mayor nor the archpriestess." Sisironi shrugged.

"What about the tree, that damned giant aldyr?"

Annica's voice was beginning to rise. Sisironi's expression grew dark.

"That aldyr is the lifeblood of our city, girl. The magi and disciples have made that quite clear."

"I'm sure they have."

"What do you mean by that?"

"I've read about the aldyrs, Sisironi, even before I came to Nel Aldyri. Nothing about them says they grow even remotely that large. The farms out by them; the people act strange, *look* strange."

"And the aldyr is at fault for that? It's a tree; a slightly magical one, according to the elves here in the city, and our elders, but it helps our crops grow, sustains wildlife, leaves us prosperous—just like those damned trees supposedly did for ages before they all died. Except for this one, except for ours!"

To Edrik's surprise, Annica wasn't growing frustrated. Rather, she looked at Sisironi with sympathy.

"How many trips did you say you've made to the mainland?" Annica asked in a measured, patient voice.

"Many." Sisironi replied, in a tone neither measured nor patient.

"And how many villages or towns or cities have you seen that could even begin to compare to Nel Aldyri?"

The captain's lips parted as though she were about to speak, but they quickly closed. They pursed, becoming a pale line on her square-jawed face.

"And how many living aldyrs did you come across? I'm guessing not many, but you probably found a few of their number on your journeys. All dead. And nothing here seems to be too good to be true? Too convenient?"

Sisironi's expression softened, just enough for Edrik to see the exchange between the two women grow measurably more defeated and saddened.

Sisironi's shoulders dropped as she spoke. "You loved this place when we last spoke. I know it isn't perfect, but are you truly talking about fleeing out onto the ocean because of some questionable practices by the nobility? That seems extreme."

"It's not the only reason," Annica replied. "I have others. I need to leave this island, with or without your help. You warned me, even drunk, you *warned* me about this island. Don't you remember?"

"I said we had our fair share of crime and weren't perfect, Annica—"

The look in her eyes told Sisironi that her mind was made up. This girl, once under the personal tutelage of the archpriestess, wanted to abandon everything.

"I'll help you. If you tell me why you truly want to go."

Silence hung awkwardly in the air as Annica mulled over her words. Realizing that any explanation she offered would likely make her seem insane, she struggled to simply say *something haunts the island and it lives in the aldyr.*

"Annica?" Sisironi pressed. "That's my condition."

"I've been having visions. And nightmares, during the day, at night—they strike at any time, it seems."

"Visions?" the captain replied dubiously.

"I'm connected to the Fifth Sect," Annica said flatly. "Apparently it connects me to things. People, nature, and other such things. I can feel something coursing through this island, Sisironi. And it all focuses back on that damn tree. The aldyrs may have been something good, or represented prosperity or some such in that past, but that's not the case here. This aldyr is bloated, stretched to the seams with something evil and *angry.*"

"It certainly casts a new light on the behavior of the city

elders and officials," Edrik added with another long look at the captain.

Sisironi was quiet for some time. Her head downturned, eyes flicking back and forth, she contemplated the situation. She tossed her head back, closed her eyes, and sighed.

"I can't go with you."

Annica's eyes lit with hope. Her mouth opened to speak, but stopped when Sisironi lifted a subtle finger. The captain's other hand went to the handle of the dagger at her waist. Edrik saw this, and he barely managed to grip his own sword when Annica gasped.

Sisironi's eyes opened wide, her mouth open and throat calling for air. A narrow, red-covered blade protruded from her chest. A black-robed individual was standing behind her where moments before no one was there. The figure appeared seemingly out of nowhere, as silent as snowfall.

"Don't move, girl."

The voice coming from behind Annica wasn't Edrik's, and Sisironi had already fallen to a heap on the floor, blood pooling beneath her. The figure before her had yet to make a sound. The baggy robes made them an indistinct, dark shape. Their cowl hung low and the shadows of the room were thick, hiding their face. Whether they were male or female, human or elf or other-wise could not be discerned. The figure before her was merely a specter of wicked portent.

"Turn around," the gravelly, male voice instructed. "My companion won't harm you."

Doing as the voice instructed, Annica turned to see Edrik at the mercy of another black-robed individual that looked iden-tical to the other one. This figure wrapped an arm around Edrik, a pale hand gripping a long, slender dagger that was pressed tightly against Edrik's windpipe but had yet to draw blood.

The voice spoke again, coming from within another thick

cowl. "Him, however, I would very much like to hurt. Obey, or watch him bleed out like the other. I'll leave just enough of his throat intact to call out your name."

Annica felt the fire of the Second Sect burn in her. She knew that Edrik would be dead before she could get the spell invoked, so she tempered her rage. For now, they were at the mercy of this dark, cowled figure.

Keeping his blade at Edrik's throat, the gravelly-voiced figure unsheathed Edrik's sword and tossed it at Sisironi's corpse. It landed with a sharp clang in her friend's blood.

The second figure stepped over the weapon and the body and pointed their dagger at Annica, motioning for her to turn around. Annica turned slowly, letting her glare linger on the faceless hole where she wished a face was staring back.

Following the robed figure's command, they left the house— the captain's body left unceremoniously where it fell. Glancing back, the last few minutes replayed in Annica's mind. She wondered if anything could have been done. Guilt began stinging her in the chest. The captain died because of her. Edrik was being walked through the shadowed streets of this evil city with a knife to his throat because of her. Wallowing in pity began to feel quite tempting.

Not a word was spoken by the black-robed pair during their march. The second figure—still silent so far—maintained a firm grip on Annica's shoulder. She kept imagining the sharp blade pointing somewhere behind her. Edrik and his tomb-voiced captor walked ahead. It wasn't long before Annica realized they were making their way toward the Temple of the First Son.

The firm hand jerked and Annica stopped. The temple grounds lay before them, empty and dark. The two figures stood quietly, almost reverently, for several moments before ushering Annica and Edrik forward again.

Their captors led them to within the temple foyer where

they stopped again. In view of the aldyr statue standing at the end of the room, the two figures began muttering something in a strange, guttural language. The hand on Annica's shoulder was quivering and tightening painfully.

"You're hurting me," Annica whispered harshly.

A sharp pain rang in her lower back. The tip of the dagger. Annica clenched her teeth against the sting and moved forward. The pair finished their throaty prayers—at least, she assumed that's what the illegible stream of gibberish coming from their mouths were—and continued leading them both to the back of the grand room. There were fewer lit candles than usual this night, and it made the aldyr roots look even more menacing, if that was possible. Larger, spindlier; seeming almost as though they were moving. Annica tamped down the churning fear in her mind and told herself that it was only the candles. The roots were not moving. The black, tentacled voids were not squirming beneath their physical prison.

She repeated this over and over as they came to a stop at the large, ornate double door. The only locked door in the building, that she could recall. The robed man took a single key from within his robes and pushed it into the lock. Turning, it made an obnoxious scraping sound as the lock gave way.

The man pushed the door open and the yawning hall beyond breathed as though it were alive. A smell of dampness and damnation rolled from that black throat. A shudder stole through Annica, leaving gooseskin on her flesh.

Prodding them like cattle, the two figures acted eager to move through the door into the foul-smelling darkness beyond. One step inside the door and Annica knew immediately why it appeared so dark. This wasn't a hallway or darkened room, rather a stairway that began moving downward under the temple.

After the initial fear and hesitation wore off, Annica realized

that the stairs were quite gradual in their descent. The corridor
was very different from the temple and the city. It was old; the
worn, damp stones of the walls barely discernable from natural
soil. Sconces held torches that provided weak light, and each of
them spaced too far apart. The darkness between was terrifying
and complete. For minutes at a time, Annica felt as though she
was walking through a never-ending pit to be consumed by
darkness forever. Then, the fiendish light of one of the sconces
would greet her like a scorned lover—reluctant and half-
hearted.

The stairs sloped gradually downward and continued for an
amount of time both sluggish and immeasurable. There was
nothing to mark the passage of the minutes or hours. Each time
Annika and Edrik attempted to speak to either their captors or
each other, a jab from a sharp knife silenced them once more.

The darkness grew thicker as they walked. It didn't make
sense, as nothing about the ancient, cloying hallway physically
changed; however, the pitch black gloom felt as though it
grabbed at them between torches, now. The pulsing blackness
was no longer due to the flicker of the torches, but by the dark
itself—breathing and quivering for living warmth. Annica's
thoughts turned to the struggle of tiny prey caught in the throat
of some cold, ophidian monstrosity. Would her tiny heart beat
until it finally gave out and the shapeless hunger surrounding
them, when finished feeding, return once again to craving what
it could never be?

No matter the destination, Annica was ready to confront
anything that didn't involve this wretched, unending corridor.
Her thoughts had gone numb and she didn't know exactly
when. Walking became a rote exercise in muscle memory. At
times the path grew steeper, taking them downward much more
noticeably. Though, it never grew any brighter. Any less nauseating. Any less despicable.

Whispers reached Annica's ears. They slid through the darkness and slithered unintelligible within her frayed mind. A hand clutched her heart with shaking fingers. The hall *was* alive. Their fate was, indeed, to be a sacrifice to some hungry, monstrous thing in the dark.

After a few moments, sanity graced Annica just long enough to recognize the sound as coming from the robed pair. They began their guttural prayers once again. After a moment more, she saw why. The corridor broadened, opening like a funnel's top into a large cave-like alcove. Sharp, dripping rock formations on the floor and ceiling encircled an open archway. The alcove's tooth-filled, maw-like appearance did not assuage Annica's fearful imaginings of a voracious creature awaiting them.

Edrik and Annica led the way through the archway at the prodding of their escort. The room beyond was more copiously lit. Solid stone floors and walls with a wooden table and chairs greeted them. There were hints of life here, not just dilapidation and throbbing darkness. Annica welcomed the change, though only for the most fleeting and superficial of moments.

The silent specter escorting Annica led her to a chair. The hand painfully wrenched her down into the cold, hard seat. Edrik cast a shadowed glance back at her as he was led out of the room through a closed door to their right. Alone with whatever creature had haunted her every step since Sisironi's home, Annica felt cold, both physical and otherwise, seep into her bones. No fires other than the sconces burned down here; and down deep they must truly have travelled.

The figure sat opposite Annica, the black void under its thick cowl threatening to draw her in and leave nothing but an empty shell in her place. Two pale hands emerged from the long sleeves and pulled back the hood. Staring back at her was a young woman with hair as red as blood and skin as pale as a grave worm. Their gaze met and Annica could only describe the feeling of looking in this other woman's green eyes as what it must feel like to have broken glass dropped onto one's face. Annica focused her breathing through the discomfort, attempting to identify her. Unfortunately, the young woman remained a mystery. Annica didn't recognize her from the temple, the city, or the outskirts.

"Not many can do that," the woman said in a thick, husky voice.

"Do what?" Annica asked flatly, as pinpricks continued to poke around her eyes.

"Look us in the eyes. Stare at us for long. It becomes quite discomforting, I've been told."

Annica refused to reply.

"It must be fairly painful for you, right now."

The feeling was more uncomfortable than painful, but Annica wasn't giving this sanguine-haired woman the slightest bit of gratification.

"Now you speak? Have you grown tired of poking me with your knife?" Annica replied, her words dripping with contempt.

"I was told not to speak to you, but the one giving those orders is no longer here. Besides, that walk is ungodly boring."

She spoke with measured arrogance. The tone reminded Annica of the nobles she'd overheard in the city. The woman must like the sound of her own voice, because she continued talking as though Annica were a caged bird there only to listen.

"Besides, it's not often I get to meet with others. Look them in the eyes," she cooed, with a gesture to her face. "Our gifts are so underutilized in this spoiled city."

Annica's eyes narrowed.

*What gifts?* she wondered.

The woman smirked, just slightly. Did her eyes see more than just Annica's disdain? Could those acid pools cut through her thoughts and see Annica's question?

"I haven't learned how to quite control it yet. They told me I had years to go before I learned to control it enough to not cause trouble. I don't see the issue. I doubt our Great Bac'thule would mind. Instead, we continue to wear these ungainly hoods."

Bac'thule. Annica recognized that name. Her mind flickered and her body flinched as the sound of that name passing her ears and flowing into the deep crevices of her hidden thoughts.

"You know that name, don't you?" the woman asked, sitting forward, her voice rising at the idea. A smug smile crossed her face. She bit her lip, as though she were considering something, then sat back in her chair. "I hear you're touched by the Fifth Sect. Is it true?"

Annica's eyes lingered on the woman for a few moments. She could say it was true, or she could lie. If the archpriestess had been so interested in her because of that magic, what would these people do?

The archpriestess—did she know of these black-robed fiends under the surface of their city? Edrik said he'd seen them lined up by the temple, but that didn't mean the disciples and magi were aware. Annica realized she could reach out with the Fifth Sect and see who else was in this subterranean hold, but that dreaded name reminded her of what happened previously when she tapped too deep into her talent. But, maybe, Annica could reach out and connect with this room; or just a part of it.

Rolling her eyes in annoyance, the woman scoffed and looked away from Annica; unaware that the mage was tapping into just enough of the Fifth Sect to get a sense of the area immediately surrounding the table. The moment Annica felt the tingle of foreign emotions, she stopped and would go no further. Feeling the vile emanations of this woman was enough. Her emotions were cold and sharp; there was no real hate in her, only unfeeling, sociopathic arrogance; and her soul was as black as the slithering tributaries that Annica once observed coursing under this island and converging on the aldyr.

For as terrible as this woman felt within the empathic folds of the Fifth Sect, the person that entered the room and came to stand next to her was exponentially so. What Annica felt and saw there cause her breath to catch. A subtle choke escaped and she was grateful to see neither had noticed.

"Enjoying yourself?" the man asked sarcastically to the woman. With his cowl pulled back, Annica could see the pasty skin and wrinkled face of a bald, elderly man. He looked no more threatening than a cobbler, but Annica knew better. She was now also able to put a face to the gravestone voice that threatened her and Edrik at Sisironi's.

"You killed my friend," Annica said coldly as memories of the tough but jovial captain returned, pushing her fear aside.

The man's head turned slowly and purposefully. He grunted an acknowledgment to Annica's question, or perhaps to her existence. Looking back at the woman, he awaited an answer to what Annica would have assumed was a rhetorical question.

"She doesn't react like the others. And I looked into her eyes for some time."

"Interesting," he replied in a low voice, looking back to Annica. Their eyes met and the sensation was much worse. Annica sucked in a breath as the uncomfortable, glass-like feeling from before exploded into a thousand glistening shards in the back of her eyes that felt as if they were literally cutting her flesh to countless ribbons.

"Bac'thule is the Herald. The Void and the Vessel. He is our path to The Obscured Throne, the Un-Maker," the black-robed man spoke with a stilted, haunted measure. He slowly rounded the table to come near Annica, his voice like the dead singing from within their sarcophagi. "We invite Bac'thule in. He is the gift He bears. He makes us vessels for Himself as He is a vessel. We become heralds to the great nothing of existence."

He stopped in front of Annica, staring down at her with his arms at his sides.

"That doesn't make any sense," Annica said, wincing in his presence.

"Existence is nothing. Bac'thule is the avatar of nothing, The Void, an infinite vessel yearning to be filled," he proselytized, clasping his hands in front of him. "*Via Mortis Infinitum.*"

"The infinite is the way of death," the woman repeated softly.

"Get up," he ordered.

Annica looked up at him defiantly, forcing her pain and fear down with all she could summon. His hand reached out slowly and gripped her arm, but to Annica it may as well have been a striking snake. She recoiled, but his grip was firm. Pain shot through her arm unlike any she'd experienced and she cried out.

"Get. Up." he repeated harshly.

Though her legs shook, Annica stood and braced herself with her free arm on the table. The man released her arm. It throbbed; her heartbeat sent fresh waves of pain from where he touched her.

"Who are you people?" she asked through gritted teeth.

"Walk," he replied.

As they passed the woman, she stood and followed them.

Annica heard the woman speak from behind her: "The Black Gnarl."

The man sneered, and the look in his eyes—that Annica in all her power tried to only catch from her peripheral vision—was one that made Annica suddenly pity the poor being behind her.

"Don't look at me that way," the woman said indignantly. "What does it matter what we tell her now?"

"Shut your mouth," the man whispered with seething malice.

"She should be honored. The last seals will be—"

With a swiftness Annica didn't think possible in a man of his age, he grabbed the woman by the throat. Annica turned her head slightly, looking over her shoulder at the display. The woman's mouth moved, but no sound came from her quivering lips. Her young, pale hands grasped and tore at the liver-spotted claw that held her with unnatural vigor.

"I said 'shut your mouth,' lest you be made to offer yourself to Him."

The fear in the woman's eyes changed from that of simple, unbridled panic to one of soul-shrinking fear. Her hands no longer grabbed at his. She simply proceeded to try and unsuc-cessfully inhale life-giving air. After allowing another moment to ponder his words, the man's hand opened. The woman gulped in air with a look of chastised obedience. Without another word, the Hooded Man—as Annica had come to name him—turned around and they left the unadorned room through the door where he had entered.

The round alcove was even smaller than the previous room. The dome-shaped space, lined with rough-hewn stones placed in swirling and diamond-shaped patterns, made Annica uneasy on her feet and physically nauseous. Roots had grown between the stones over the ages, tracing the mortared spaces between them. The shoots that lined the diamond-shaped patterns of the stones brought to mind the strange, barbed diamond symbol Annica had seen in her room. The blood-haired woman said their name—the Black Gnarl. This was their temple, as the temple above belonged to the First Son.

A closed door lay to the right; made of heavy wood, it wasn't yet heavy enough to conceal the muffled sounds of conversation coming from within. Ahead, yet another open, shadowed mouth of an archway gaped at Annica. The temple and its disturbing underbelly seemed composed of nothing but waiting mouths, whispers, and pain.

The longer she stared at the archway, the more she felt such things weigh on her. The room beyond the archway could not be seen. There was light in there, somewhere, as the palest flickering of illumination danced beyond the lips of the stone archway. An innate dread bloomed inside her, and her instincts begged her to flee though it would mean her death.

"Take her. I will be in shortly," he growled.

The woman placed another heavy hand on Annica's shoulder, pushing her through to that dreaded room beyond. A single torch was ensconced on her left, providing the only light. Once past the threshold, the hand jerked her to a stop. The momentary dancing of light told Annica that the woman had retrieved the torch to guide them.

Sheer darkness surrounded them. The torchlight fought a losing battle against the seemingly living blackness of the room. The woman pushed Annica onward for a dozen steps at most, but it might as well have been a hundred. There was no measure of space. This room could have been a hundred square feet or thousands, but for Annica, the torchlight provided a pocket of existence where all else outside simply ceased to be.

The light showed only bare, dirt flooring with scattered rocks. No other walls were visible within the light. No sounds came from the shadows, not rats or voices or falling soil. This place was an utter nothingness.

"You were friends with Mya, yes?" the woman asked, her voice low and eerie.

Annica was silent, her defiance overcoming her need to

know what happened to the strange, pitiful girl. But it didn't hold out for long.

"I didn't know her well. She seemed troubled."

"Turn," the woman said mechanically. A few more paces later her stiff grip pulled Annica to a stop again.

The woman stepped in front of Annica for the first time. The light hit the woman's eyes and, instead of flickering against them, was absorbed, creating orbs of terrifying blackness against the white sclera.

Worse, there were now things hovering on the edge of the torchlight. A dilapidated table drew Annica's immediate attention. Only a small part of the table was visible—just enough to see a desiccated hand lying palm up on the corner of the tabletop. Annica's stomach grew empty and cold, bile rising into her mouth.

Backing up to Annica in her sight, the woman held the torch directly over the table, where the corpse of Mya lay in an open-mouthed, wide-eyed, and silent scream. Thin, vine-like roots had grown around her wrists, throat, and body. Or, as Annica continued to try and reason through her terror-numbed state, were these vines used to constrain her? These thoughts and more ran through her mind as the woman continued to stare at her, a bemused expression on her face.

"If she wasn't your friend, perhaps that's all for the better. I only assumed as it was your name that was last on her lips."

"Mya," Annica whispered, "What did they do to you?" Sorrow lined her voice as a tear rolled down her face. The girl's panic-riddled, belligerent state of mind was more understandable now.

As Annica closed Mya's lifeless eyes and stroked the last remaining strands of the girl's hair, the wicked woman turned and looked at them both.

"She was my test," the woman explained conversationally. "I was tasked with discovering more about the Fifth Sect with her."

Careful to avoid her gaze, Annica looked toward the woman at the mention of the Fifth Sect.

"Yes, she had it, too. Not even a mote of your talent, but it was there. It mostly served her in that she was quite physically resilient. We tested many things on her. Spoiled food, virulent tonics, cutting; anything to test what healing powers the Fifth Sect granted her. She couldn't cast magic to save her life, obviously," she chuckled at her own grotesque joke, "but had something inherent in her. Since I continue to have trouble with, well, these eyes of mine—His gift of gazing into the void, as it were—I was given her to work with my control. They hoped to find more about the last seals with Mya's continued torment. Tragic for us, that she gave out as pitiably as she did. Selfish bitch. Her contribution was meager at best, leaving us with some scraps to offer up to Him."

The woman spoke scientifically, with calculation and educational pomp. Behind this though, was a sadistic glee. Annica felt it. Her sorrow and anger made her hands shake and she felt control slipping away. Tears fell more freely.

Avoiding this woman's eyes left Annica staring behind her. Half hidden in darkness, the torchlight bounced off a column of rock. Covering the rock was a black, soot-like substance.

Reacting instinctively, fueled by her emotions, Annica lunged at the woman whose arm was still outstretched with the torch. Her callous gloating left her vulnerable. In her frenzied state, Annica was only somewhat aware that her hand had grasped the woman's face, partially covering those vile eyes. Throwing herself bodily into her waist, Annica pinned the woman against the column and smashed her head into the rocks. A throaty grunt coupled with a wet crunch preceded the woman slouching to a heap on the ground.

The light in the room dimmed significantly as the torch landed on the ground. The thought of being stuck in the pitch dark with corpses left to feel her away around until she starved to death, struck Annica sharply. She grabbed up the torch before it could go out and breathed, relief filling her when its light cast itself against the darkness again.

She spent a few moments trying to remember the number of steps they had walked and in which direction, in order to get back to the door. Keeping one hand on the table, she stretched the torch out and walked around. Her breath caught when she saw that no matter where she shined the torchlight, more tables waited at the edge of the blackness.

With aching slowness, Annica approached one of the tables. Another body, as shriveled as Mya's, lay atop it. This one was a withered husk that must have been here for some time. She recognized something atop what remained of the chest. Covered in ash and teetering over a collapsing chest cavity was a pendant. A rose emblem sat in the middle of a six-pointed star. Annica's memory returned to her first day in Nel Aldyri and the elderly couple that was taken away from the Hall of Reception. She whimpered, a cry breaking in her throat at the thought of how many helpless people had been shuffled down through that awful tunnel to a fate they could never imagine. She left the table and went to one more after another, each with bodies in various stages of decay. Some were little more than ash, with even the bones down to brittle splinters.

She heard a soft sound and turned to see yet another table holding another sacrifice. The body consigned there to its doom had yet to reach a severe state of deterioration. Holding her breath, she shined the torch over the poor soul. The same supple roots that wrapped up the others tightly bound this man to his place.

Annica noticed something else here, something she'd

missed on the others. The ends of the roots had petal-like growths on them. They stuck to the exposed skin of the man, making a sickly, squelching sound when Annica tried to remove one from his neck, noticing the growths were more like appendages, and the petal shape more akin to a flat tongue.

Beneath the leafy, tongue-like growths, the skin had turned black and was melting away. A thin, dark fluid ran in rivulets down his throat. When she, recoiling in disgust, released the growth it reattached itself to its victim. The man moaned painfully.

Annica couldn't scream. Her disgust and horror choked her. A pit boiled in her gut until she fell over, retching. She fell back on her knees. A shuddering sigh came from the table. The horrifying thought that Edrik was in here somewhere nearly made her vomit again. Picking up the torch, she began turning in all directions, her thoughts racing. She could search for him but still had yet to find a wall to guide herself out of here. There was no knowing how many unfortunate people were trapped here in this disgusting place.

Remembering Edrik was taken into a room apart from here, Annica's resolve strengthened. The torch tight in her grip, Annica ran. She could only move so fast, her small pocket of light limiting her flight. Sights better left ignored passed through the torchlight as she frantically tried to not trip and fall. Her eyes watched the ground carefully, trying not to pay any mind to the horrors in the shadows. She would find a way out of here, find Edrik, and leave this place forever.

Before she could react, a hand reached out of the darkness and caught Annica by her robes, slamming into her chest. Breathing became a fight as the wind was knocked out of her. The Hooded Man emerged, holding a torch Annica had not seen for watching her step and ignoring what she knew to lay in the dark. She cursed herself for her foolishness.

The Hooded Man's strong hand pushed her back, leaving her gasping for air. He continued to stare at her, a scowl turning his old face into a mass of wrinkles. His strength was inhuman; his demeanor even more so.

As breathing came easier, Annica felt her courage harden. The woman, now dead and unmourned, had talked of the Fifth Sect and its power like Helyn and Nostrado before her. Annica hesitated to fully embrace it, to sink herself into its flows once more, but perhaps a more concentrated use of the Fifth Sect could help her—shield her.

The Fifth Sect could still be felt, even here, and she began washing herself in it. The sensation was akin to filling her hands in a hot spring and pouring the contents over her. She gathered the magic around herself, pulling it to her like a vortex, rather than floating and being carried away. Her breathing slowed, became more regular. The painful, inexplicable sensation caused by locking eyes with the Hooded Man was significantly lessened. From his annoyed expression, he must have sensed something was amiss.

"Hmph," he grumbled.

Annica gripped her torch, preparing to club him with it. She stepped forward to strike him as hard as she could when the Hooded Man's free hand rose, stopping her in her tracks. The image of the barbed diamond was carved into the Hooded Man's palm, scarred and pale. The strange dot in the center was darker, a pinhole in time opening wider and wider, threatening to draw her in and claim her forever. The world stood still and vibrated all at once. The screams of billions filled her ears until the sound became empty and pointless as existence itself. All the memories that had been locked away, that her fugue states of late kept from her in black pits of memories and that her nightmares gave her but momentary glimpses of, flooded her. The sheer, unflinching terror threatened to break her, but her mind held. The thinnest fibers of the Fifth Sect wrapped her sanity in its fragile web, barely leaving her a sentient wreck rather than a drooling husk. Her jaw slack and eyes drooping, Annica felt herself slipping into a waking coma—aware but unable to move.

The Hooded Man grabbed her, spun her around, and pushed her against a wall. She grunted in pain as she slammed against it. With the terrible symbol, a ritual written in pain and blood and other horrible things on his hand, gone from her sight, Annica felt her faculties returning to her. Though, it was just in time to see roots curl from their resting place and grip her tightly. The wall and its grotesque draperies embracing her and holding her there, standing. She fought against them, but could barely move her legs or arms against their unholy grasp.

"Your magic; it's something else," the man said, looking at his palm. "Every other poor soul I've cast that spell on withered before me or fell into a state of catatonia from which they never recovered. Yet, here you are, merely stunned into blissful silence."

"Kill me. Don't give me to these things," Annica said in a harsh whisper. Tears threatened to fall down her cheeks, but she forced them away.

"Things?" he replied, an insulted curl on his lip. "These are not *things*, girl. It is He—or at least his influence—made tangible."

The Hooded Man turned, the light and warmth of the torch momentarily fading, and when he came back around he was pulling a wobbly chair with him. Sitting down, he regarded Annica quizzically.

"Where is the woman who brought you in here?"

Annica stared back at him, a hint of a smirk behind her eyes. "Dead."

If a person could shrug with their lips, that is certainly what he did. "She did something foolish," he said matter-of-factly, with no question in his voice. He turned his head and spoke to the darkness, "Lavyna, you idiot."

"Why am I here? Why won't you kill me?" Annica said in exasperation and hopelessness.

"Because you have a higher purpose here."

"The Fifth Sect."

The torchlight flickered on his face, the black orbs of his eyes dilating momentarily.

"Yes, in a sense."

"Then do what you must; I'm already tired of talking to you." Her voice was growing hoarse and physical exhaustion was quickly settling in. The Hooded Man remained silent. "Just cut my wrists, my throat, let them feed quicker."

"He can't touch you." Annoyance and anger drenched his words.

Seeing the confusion on Annica's face, the Hooded Man sighed and continued speaking with a voice as empty and emotionless as his eyes.

"I'm not talking with you because I need conversation. I'm simply at a loss; which I'm not fond of."

A moment of clarity came to Annica. It was something that the woman, Lavyna, had said. Seeing a man this powerful contemplating a mystery helped her put the pieces together.

"Seals, this is something about seals. You need the Fifth Sect and don't know how to use it." Mya had uttered something along these lines to Annica before being taken away.

"Clever," he replied, then leaned forward. "But don't think this gives you power over me. I've murdered more users of the Fifth Sect than I can count, all in the name of study. I will do it again."

He sat back, looking at her again. Annica's head hung low, her eyes looking up at him, though she focused on anywhere but that horrible, uncomfortable gaze. She tried wrapping the

Fifth Sect around her again, seeing if it would tear these monstrous things off her.

"Don't try it," the man said flatly, "I can sense it. Your precious talent will do you no good right now. You think the Fourth Sect is just, what, death magic? Summon some bones and ghosts with virgin blood to fight your bullies? How many primers have you read that tell you that, hm? Parlor tricks for amateur conjurers. I am a practitioner of the true Fourth Sect. A master of its darkest secrets, girl. They don't talk about my magic in those books. They only dare breathe the words 'death magic' because they can't bear the thought of what it truly is— the magic of the cosmos, of what lies beyond. Of the *other*. The magic of what waits on the other side of reality. The closest connection we have with the Inheritors. You've heard of the theory of the saturation of magic? Feel this place, girl. Haven't you felt it since the door in the temple first opened? The embrace of the Fourth Sect is strong here; resonating in every speck of dirt and inundating every breath. I am drenched in it," he spat, his mouth nearly frothing. His free hand held the arm of the chair in a white-knuckled grip. "You cannot fathom what things I can wreak in His name. They will find who is worthy. I am worthy. Perhaps you may be, as well."

"Bac'thule," Annica thought aloud, recalling the name that gripped her heart and mind with a numb terror. The Hooded Man flinched at the mentioning of the name.

"Yes, Bac'thule," he repeated, looking around the room. He appeared to regain control of himself, becoming as cold as he was before.

"There are others, but He—He is who we seek to bring forth. That part of Him that dwells on this island is little more than His shadow. Others have existed here in some small way for millennia. Whoever stole this world away from Them hid it well, but a piece of the Inheritors was always here. They are always searching and He is always waiting. He is why you are still alive, until such a time as we discover how we can use you."

"You don't know how to summon Him."

"No," he said after a moment. "Forty-four seals. After centuries of work my order broke forty-four seals. Eleven for each sect of magic. Some more difficult than others. Each one unique. But the eleven seals of the Fifth Sect, those we could not discover. As it were, they are needed to complete the rituals of the Dread Praises, to bring the Inheritors to us and begin their reign in full, but we could at least receive Them in part."

He paused, watching Annica. She was confused at first, not knowing what he expected, but then her eyes widened as the things just beyond the shadows of her mind began to stir again.

"The Rupture..." she began before trailing off, her words dying on her lips. Then, something about his explanation occurred to her. "If you were there, that would make you—"

"Old. Over a century. I told you, worm, the Fourth Sect can do things you can't imagine." He sighed. His lips drew back in a sneer revealing a rotten mouth of decaying teeth and diseased gum tissue.

"The Rupture," he scoffed. "A cowardly name for returning a jewel to its rightful owners." he lamented. "It is a *reclaiming*. Our world is Theirs, as all things belong to the Inheritors, the creations of The Obscured Throne. His machinations are unknown to us but these worlds belong to His Inheritors, make no doubt about it. Bac'thule is not only counted among Them but the greatest of Their kind. You'll learn this soon enough. I've seen a king's anger when his namesake is threatened—stolen— but it is nothing compared to a god's. By some ancient rites completed so long ago they're beyond recollection, our world was sealed off. Bound and protected by its unique connection to the magic that became the Fifth Sect. What is missing is the connection between breaking the Fifth Sect and allowing the

Inheritors, the timeless children of the great and demoniac demiurge, to take back what is theirs."

"And torturing me is going to do that?" she asked matter-of-factly.

"Perhaps," he answered. His tone was quite academic. "You're the strongest natural talent in the Fifth Sect I've ever seen. If there's a way to begin breaking the eleven seals of that sect, it's with you. The other forty-four were just a start. Mere cracks, like I said, that finally weakened the veil of reality just enough to allow the reclaiming to begin. Many of the greater species long-dormant or waiting for the streams of our existence and their unexistence to merge crawled forth through pits in stone or tears in reality. Ygiddra, a lesser brother of Bac'thule, was one of the first, you know. I was there for his arrival. Not what I was intending, mind you, but the first creeping spores of his great garden showed me that we were successful. The Rupture that so many bemoan over happened mere hours later. I continued my search for Bac'thule as Ygiddra's pestilent veins began creeping through all corners of this world ." The Hooded Man reached over and lifted one of the vines on the nearby table, bringing it in front of him to observe. It twisted slowly in his grasp, the tongue-shaped leaf-appendages shuddering as it sensed a fresh sacrifice. "The similarity of Bac'thule's current prison is not lost on me." He tossed the spindly, supple root aside. It curled around the leg of the table then sat still. The Hooded Man continued lecturing Annica, while Bac'thule's influence continued tugging at her magical protections.

"Our founders discovered the first scrolls that spoke of the Confluence. Scrolls so old that we could barely touch them without their crumbling to dust. It took powerful magics to read and handle them. Once reconstituted, we discovered what their unknown author titled them: The Dread Praises. Four sects had been successfully translated, then some fool with all the preparatory forethought and dexterity of a fucking mountain ape caused the destruction of the final scroll detailing the seals tied to the fifth and final sect. And now, I'm cursed with conversing with you, trying to discover the nature of these final seals."

He looked out into the darkness again, turning his head to see all around him as though the answers would come crawling out of the darkness; dark and bloody and bearing the damnable testimony that would give him the answers to how Annica could break one of the last eleven seals. His gaze returned to Annica and he continued speaking, his voice resonating in the cavernous room.

"But Bac'thule. He is the First Herald. The Void and Vessel, the avatar of nothingness itself, whereupon the Obscured Throne rests; always being filled and forever empty, such is the gift he provides us."

Annica understood the sharp pain that came from the gaze of Bac'thule's followers. The Void and Vessel has hollowed them out, left the windows to their souls as empty as the realm of the Obscured Throne.

"The aldyr that these city wretches revere so highly is merely a conduit for Him. Or, more appropriately, a prison. A crude vessel, but one that was once connected so intimately with this world. Ironic, really, but a means to an end. The Obscured Throne will come. Its calling will liquefy the minds of the unworthy. Though it is a greater honor than they deserve. Much more of an honor than is meted out to these offerings here. To say they are consumed is only due to our limitations in describing in our pathetic tongue what the Inheritors are and what They do. It is more accurate to say they are extinguished. Their lights snuffed out. As Bac'thule is nothing, so are they who are given to Him. We who follow, those who facilitated the Confluence, will scream the Dread Praises until our throats are raw. If we are lucky, we shall catch a glimpse of the Unmaker ourselves before we wink out of existence."

"Do you think you have some sort of claim to this throne?" Annica sneered.

Some horrible, crackling sound escaped his lips. It may have been a laugh, but if so it was the worst kind of sound that could be associated with such an expression. "The Obscured Throne is not an object, little mayfly; more a sentience. Greater than all of reality and unreality. The great demiurge responsible for everything. And we await Him."

Annica struggled against the grotesque bindings holding her against the wall. Her protective weave of the Fifth Sect still lingered and she felt Bac'thule's influence in the Hooded Man lash out and prod her for weakness. The man was cruel and insane and had been ruling his followers within the underbelly of Nel Aldyri like a shadowy priest-king. The horrific rites they were performing, the unspeakable things they were doing. Annica recalled the still-living victim and the black, oozing wounds he suffered from. She remembered the ones that were decomposing beyond recognition—not decomposing, but disintegrating, their bodies reduced to the faintest amount of ash as nearly every mote of their being was consumed.

Consumed by Him. Bac'thule. This vicious and angry hunger was familiar. The wave of nightmares that returned, courtesy of the Hooded Man's dark spell, was filled with thoughts of Him. Her shoulders tingling where the strange scars were. Irregular and distinctly shaped, like the appendages that fed on the helpless victim somewhere in this room along with many others. What fate awaited her here?

The Hooded Man and his followers attempted to offer her up to their god—one of these Inheritors. But something happened. She still lived. She was released to walk among the city again. Why?

Perhaps, the Fifth Sect was more than just a conundrum for the Black Gnarl, more than a mystery. It was a foil. It was the opposite of everything they were, everything their gods were. Whoever, or whatever, had sealed this world off from the Inheritors had woven a new magic into the world itself: the Fifth Sect. It was more than medicines and rejuvenation. It was a magic unique to this world and its people. It didn't come from the Obscured Throne or the Inheritors—and they had no hold over it. Bac'thule didn't consume her because she was a bearer of this magic, the bane of the Inheritors and all their dark purpose. Annica could reach out and connect with the deepest parts of this world, where the Hooded Man and his great lord, Bac'thule, could merely hollow it out and string along their soulless puppets.

The Hooded Man was correct in that the human language lacked the ability to truly describe Bac'thule and His ilk. It was not hunger that drove Him, but the need to fill the void that Bac'thule himself embodies. Bac'thule is a hungry vessel, one that consumes everything placed within it; one that will forever suffer to only be, ironically, temporarily filled. That is, until the Obscured Throne comes and makes all nothing, even His Inheritors, and creates what must be the Oblivion Bliss that Annica read in the note left for her once upon a time before the true nightmare of her reality became apparent.

"Where are you, Gideon? Where is she?" a woman's voice, breathy and muted, called from the darkness.

"Damnable woman," the Hooded Man, Gideon, muttered viciously under his breath and stood from the chair. Lifting the torch, he walked toward what Annica assumed to be the direction in which the entrance lay. It was not the way she expected; in the dark, she had become completely turned around. Had the man not found her, she may have become lost down here forever.

The light of the torch quickly grew dim against the oppressive, unnatural darkness. A second light moved to greet it, like fireflies at night. Hushed voices reached Annica, though the conversation was indiscernible.

Lowering her head, Annica felt hopelessness crawl over her. It writhed and flexed on her skin with the snake-like roots that bound her. The feeling pressed in with the heavy darkness that felt as though it had a physical weight of its own.

In the quiet of the wretched chamber, soft voices came to Annica. Echoing off the walls, the harsh whispers were just perceptible if she stayed still and quieted her trembling thoughts.

"Why is she here? What purpose does this serve? You tried your way and you failed," a woman's voice scolded.

"Speak to me that way again—" Gideon began, his voice filled with venom, before being cut off.

"Or you'll what? Your branch of our devotion is rotting this city. You rule under here for a reason, you miserable shit!"

The voice that replied trembled with rage. "While you've been worshipping and putting on pretty faces, I've been studying, Helyn. Reading the Dread Praises day and night, studying everything down to the most basic of magic in all sects looking for clues to the last seals. This girl is the only key we have and she belongs down here where she can be studied."

"You mean tortured?"

"Don't be so dramatic. I saw your face when the girl was offered up. You need a more iron gut if we're to finish our work."

Annica's eyes widened as the revelations reached her ears. Had it been shame or even compassion that drove Helyn to distance herself from Annica after she'd first collapsed those several weeks ago? Annica strained her ears to listen, focused on the voices as though they were right beside her.

"I'm close," he continued, "So close. It has to do with the

Fifth Sect's connection to this world, blocking or counteracting the Fourth's. The Fourth connected us with the Others and the Fifth is shielding this world from Them. Somehow this girl will be our key."

The voices grew quieter for a moment, too quiet to hear. The two small orbs of light moved and flickered like their bearers were maneuvering around each other, then the light of one torch grew as it approached her. The second light began to follow.

A pair of flaming eyes, surrounded by weak halos, approached Annica. Like a demon swathed in shadow, the two mismatched eyes slowly grew larger until it seemed the beast would lunge at her. Instead of some bowel-loosening fiend from the pit, a familiar face looked back at her. The light was weak and the shadows it cast sinister, but the old eyes of Helyn stared back at Annica with something in them that Annica hadn't yet seen in the archpriestess' face: pity.

"Annica," Helyn breathed, sympathy softening her usual terseness, "I never hoped to see you down here."

Annica looked back at Helyn, anger marring her expression.

"Please, don't look at me that way. I've come to help."

"Help? I heard you, you know. Just now. You let them take me, Helyn. You let them take Mya and all these others. How long have you been feeding victims to the Black Gnarl? Are they the true rulers of Nel Aldyri?"

Helyn looked more hurt than angry. It didn't temper Annica's fury whatsoever. Helyn had been training Annica, personally, and to what end? If Annica was merely meant to be offered up to Bac'thule, why bother with the training? Annica asked as much, spitting out the words.

"Annica, don't let these macabre zealots sway you. Their methods are reprehensible, but there is a dark and light side to all things. Animals kill one another to feed their young.

Surgeons cut their patients, removing limbs and worse, to cure them. The First Son is the same."

Helyn spoke to Annica in a way that sounded both reverent and pleading. She wanted Annica to understand. That was never going to happen.

"Bac'thule is the First Son," Annica said, glaring at the woman once her mentor.

"Yes, the First Son of the Obscured Throne; the one who will unmake this world and create something wholly new!"

"The Un-Maker. You want to destroy the world and you're trying to justify this to me? An apprentice? A prisoner?"

"I want to explain our reasons to someone who could be such a great part of our work."

"You tried to *feed* me to your fucking god!" Annica screamed, the pain and fear and confusion of the last weeks of her life pouring out of her all at once. The sound echoed off unseen walls and left her throat aching. The Hooded Man appeared behind Helyn, holding his torch at chest-level, the flames doing little against the darkness that seemed to live and thrive around him.

Helyn's expression drooped, becoming the taciturn look Annica recognized from after her first fugue. Before Annica had any knowledge of the horrors of Nel Aldyri.

"I was overruled in that regard. When you were returned to us in the temple, I was forbidden to work with your talent in the Fifth Sect pending further research."

"And Mya? She was by your side quite a lot. She was tortured as the Black Gnarl's plaything. Why didn't you help her?" Annica asked, with fresh tears building in her eyes. "Or were you overruled in that regard, as well?" she added with blatant scorn.

Helyn didn't answer, but the look on her face spoke volumes.

"You have no power here, do you?" Annica's eyes flicked to

the Hooded Man behind Helyn. His face obscured except for his wrinkled, cracked lips. "They have the real power, don't they? They control the city from down here, in this festering hole with their victims."

"And our knowledge. And our power." The Hooded Man croaked. "Until we can fully open the way for Bac'thule. Then, we will control all, sitting on our black thrones in the world unmade and remade."

Annica sneered. "The Un-Maker will remake the world?"

"The Dread Praises are clear," he replied, those parts of his face that were visible giving no sign of the derision in his voice. "the Obscured Throne will bring his blissful oblivion to us all."

"This isn't an uncommon belief, Annica," Helyn added, her soft tone a sharp contrast to Gideon. "The dwarves have similar principles with their forge gods. We in the temple just happen to believe in less ghastly practices than our brethren in the Black Gnarl."

Helyn, for all her stoic tenacity and authority in the temple, appeared to lose her nerve in the presence of the shadowed man behind her. Her words seemed forced and self-justifying.

"Void, vessel, herald, and also son. Bac'thule is all these things. The First Son is the essence of nothing. Again, a void and a vessel," Helyn continued, "and a vessel can be filled with wine as much as it can be filled with blood. We just fully believe it can be wine."

A feeling of dumbfoundedness struck Annica. Gideon was callous and malicious in his insanity, but Helyn was dangerously, stupidly naïve in hers.

"You're wrong," Annica said pointedly. For a moment, it appeared like the hint of a smile danced on the man's cracked lips. Helyn's shoulders shifted in frustration at her former apprentice's defiance.

"And so are you," Annica said, looking at the man, whose

face returned to its unreadable, impassive state. "I've felt the First Son's intent—Bac'thule—I don't know if it was Him or my own mind trying to keep it from me, but coming to this wretched hole woke the memories in me that my mind tried to lock away. Call it His presence, if you want. I don't care. He is a vessel for the Obscured Throne or whatever waits beyond, and if it gets here it will obliterate everything. We will be less than a memory. Nothing you do or say is going to grant you some sort of clemency. Whatever fate awaits the rest of the world awaits you."

She emphasized these last words, watching as the man's swollen tongue licked his lips. They squirmed on his face like grave worms as irritation fomented and stretched them thin, revealing his yellowed teeth sitting in his blackened gums.

"It doesn't have to be that way, Annica," Helyn said, almost pleading. "Look at our city. Look at how we prosper where the rest of the world consumes itself!"

"Have you ever considered that is what 'The First Son' wants?" Annica replied, openly sarcastic with the honorific. "Bac'thule needs the seals broken. The vessel needs to be filled with the blood and souls of this world, it seems to me, and He has plenty of underlings at his beck and call here; working to break the seals so He can finally break this world and all of you with it."

Annica's eyes never left Gideon. From what little she saw of his face, her words must have held more than a little truth in them. Her words hung in the air, mingling with the rank presence of the Fourth Sect that saturated the area.

Helyn looked defeated. Maybe she cared for Annica somewhat, but her part in the vulgarity of Nel Aldyri's true side was without redemption. Annica would never cooperate with them or help them find the eleven seals of the Fifth Sect. Annica reached out, just momentarily, to see within Helyn. Though she wasn't fully hollowed by Bac'thule like Gideon or Lavyna, there was no doubt that the roiling, lashing tendrils of nothingness had taken root within her.

Sensing Helyn's defeat and seeing Annica's defiance, Gideon stepped forward. His padded boots shuffled near inaudibly. His face came so close to Annica's that she could smell the sourness of his breath. The magic of unlife radiated from him like a sharp, cold aura. Her breath caught and she struggled not to whimper reflexively against such close proximity to utter nothingness—a true disciple of annihilation.

"You'll stay here then. Listen to this silent song, bathe in this pool of obliteration, until your mind utterly breaks and insanity takes you. Then, I'll come back. I'm all you have now. Look at me, see that I am nothingness, like Him, and I am all you have."

His words crawled down her spine, raising the hairs on her neck. She fought against the fear, but Gideon had become a true servant of the infinite Vessel. The Hooded Man suited him much better than any other moniker. His name was lost along with what remained of his humanity long ago. It was the only explanation Annica had for the unnatural, unwholesome aura he radiated that froze her logical processes and made her want to crawl into the wall and hide in the safety of darkness until the Inheritors came to take them all.

She focused on her breathing. That had always been a strategy that prevailed for her. It connected her to the Fifth Sect, it calmed her nerves, it focused her. She breathed in and out. Slow, long breaths through her nose. Strangely, she realized despite the number of bodies that must lay in the darkness, there was very little smell. They truly were being wholly consumed down to their most basic elements until nothing but a soft ash remained.

A notion sparked within her mind. Ironic, given the idea that came to her. Her skills in magic had been limited to the Fifth

Sect, for the most part. This is what was most valuable to her captors. But, she had been given other training when Helyn was told to back away from the Fifth Sect studies. Her talents in other sects were limited, but there was one that she seemed to take to.

Bac'thule was consuming the victims of this sacrificial chamber until they were little more than ash, their remains smearing the walls. His shadow fed to sustain his weakened form holding onto their reality through the aldyr. If this was a glimpse at what He and the Inheritors wanted for her world, she would pay unto him in kind. She closed her eyes, removing the image of Gideon's wretched face, cowled and unnatural, from her mind.

Annica pressed her arms against the wall, her palms facing outward. The roots tightened, pulling her arms against the wall, unaware they were helping seal their own fate. She focused on what little warmth could be found in the chamber. The heat of the earth below them, the torches carried by her tormentors. Curling her fingers inward, one at a time, then uncurling and curling them again, she stoked the magical flame building around her. Flushing, she saw the heat of her magic coalescing in uneven points around the chamber, like a viper seeing the heat of its prey. She couldn't control where it was going; she still lacked that level of skill, but she could build a lot of the magic energy very quickly and release it to do its work. It didn't need to be accurate.

Annica felt the room growing warmer. She opened her eyes and, when he saw another type of fire there, Gideon's face curled into a grimace. He stepped back, casting the torch around to see small fires catching around the chamber. She didn't excel at many aspects of magic, but she was quite good with fire.

"What are you doing?" he asked in a harsh whisper that showed, for the first time, a hint of fear.

Helyn began looking around with signs of panic, as well. "Annica, what are you doing?" she repeated.

The small fires grew, feeding on roots large and small. Old, dry tables lit up like copious pyres. The victims on them, doomed as they already were, fed the fires even more—but they would no longer feed the horrifying vessel. They would not suffer obliteration.

The fires grew and Annica finally saw the chamber in its entirety. Dozens of tables, lined up somewhat neatly in rows, held atop themselves the bodies of so many men and women. Nearly every table was occupied. The rocky column that Annica had slain Lavyna upon was but one of many. They were also shown to be, in truth, massive roots that contained large stones embedded in their fibers. These were the largest roots of countless others. The smallest were those that bore the appendages used to drain the sacrifices of their life essence. Roots of countless other sizes ran along the ceilings and walls; as individuals and corded like ropes. A disturbing shape formed as Annica took in all the horrors of this chamber: it was shaped like a diamond, with the large hole in the ceiling near the center, where the largest of the roots congregated. The entire fiery scene appeared pulled out of hell itself.

Annica realized why the trek through the darkened tunnel took so long. They had traveled to beneath the great aldyr itself.

The roots holding her remained taut. The fires hadn't affected the aldyr or the vile god inhabiting it. The magic of the Second Sect still burned within her; she continued to feed it. The fire would burn this chamber to the ground, but what would it do to a timeless being like Bac'thule?

Her mind raced, not knowing if her efforts would be in vain. Only moments had passed and the fire was already spreading, but she still remained bound to the wall. Her studies in magic and its many sects were still amateurish, but she wasn't without tenacity and imagination. One more risk, one more chance to defy the Black Gnarl and their heinous god.

The fire of the Second Sect still burning in her veins, Annica closed her eyes and reached out to the Fifth Sect. The chamber was momentarily alight behind the darkness of her eyelids with the flames spreading across the roots and tables, heating stones and flesh. As she continued wading into the sensations of the Fifth Sect, she felt herself drop off a precipice. The light of the fires and the dim lights of dying people in the room grew into tendons and tendrils of darkness, a black spider's web. The figures of Helyn and Gideon mimicked this darkness, with the exception of a cold light tracing the fibrous void within them—traces of their corrupted souls given over to their empty god.

Annica felt the call of that vessel once again, threatening to overcome her, reaching in to claim her soul and hollow her out. She stared with shut eyes at the congealed nothing above them, the insides of the great aldyr hollowed out. The black tendrils billowed like submerged weeds at a lake's edge. The call to succumb to Him was stronger than ever before.

Annica saw the source of Bac'thule within the aldyr. She saw the fiendish rope uncoil and spread its dread fibers into the city, into homes and markets. She saw Him infiltrating everything, claiming it for His own before the Black Gnarl even brought their sacrifices to this withered chamber.

She felt Him. A brush of the Void and Vessel on her mind, a hint of the nothing He promised. It was enough to send a flood of warm tears down her face as she kissed the damnation of oblivion. He couldn't touch her, but she reached out and inadvertently touched Him.

All this in a span of moments. But, in that moment she connected with Bac'thule, she took advantage. The fire of her magic spread along the dark threads, up the roots and into the

boughs; along the threads that spread out among the island.
The fire spread a thousandfold.

Helyn witnessed a moment of defiance become a flame that
threatened to consume them all. Annica opened her eyes, tears
streaming down her dirty cheeks, and Helyn recoiled in fear.
She bumped into Gideon, who gripped her arm tightly. Annica's
eyes were alight with liquid fire. Darkness and flame fought in
her gaze and then flickered, died, and Annica screamed.

Gideon grabbed Helyn as she fell back into him. The woman
was reeling from her former apprentice, but he was much more
concerned about the fire breaking out in the chamber. His
glorious palace was under assault. He moved to grab Annica by
the throat, choke the life from her and stamp out her pitiful fire
magic. After putting one foot forward, however, he felt his strength
give. He stumbled, his ankle jerking and threatening to drop him
to the floor. The feebleness of age flooded his bones. He tasted
blood and bile. His connection with Bac'thule was unprecedented,
unique, and gave him power previously unheard of—but it was
waning. The feeling of the sweet nothingness pulled away from
him. As it did, the cold of the Void gave way to a blistering heat.

The Fifth Sect laced the room like gossamer threads,
mingled with the fire magic. It pulled the connection to
Bac'thule from him like a net pulling fish from water; a net of
burning hot diamonds. The magic of the Fifth Sect was tracing
Bac'thule's essence, carrying Annica's fire with it. Bac'thule was
protected by the void, the great nothing of His birthright.
Gideon was not. He opened his mouth to scream, but his lungs
were already smoking. His organs already on fire. His skin split,
his blood boiled, and his veins sizzled. The last thing he saw was
his robes catching fire.

Helyn screamed as Gideon fell to the floor, his mouth open
in a silent scream. The leader of the centuries-old cult of the

Black Gnarl died a quivering, flaming mass on the floor of his sacred chamber, beneath the very throne of his god in this world. The smell of burnt flesh was overpowering. She backed away, looking at Annica in abject terror and disbelief, then fled through the door that led to the alcove beyond.

An unbearable vibration resonated through Annica's skull. Crying out, she shut her eyes and could only fight against the pain. The sensation dulled and an instant wave of relief rushed over her. Then, it came back, pummeling the inside of her mind. She gritted her teeth as her muscles tightened like taut ropes against the pain. When the wave of agony subsided once more, Annica recognized the sensation as being akin to the resonance of a scream without the shrieking sound.

The repulsive cords loosened and fell like dead worms stuck against the wall. Annica fell to her knees, caught off guard by the sudden release. Another psychic scream pierced through her, contracting her muscles and causing tears to fall from her tightly shut eyes. Once it had passed, she gasped for air and wasted no time standing up. The smell of burnt flesh and smoke filled the room. The fires were growing quickly.

The exit door was to her left and easy to be seen by the firelight. She ran, the fires catching above and around her, spreading along the root system quickly. Annica choked on the quickly thickening smoke.

Cool air crashed against her as she breached the doorway to the alcove. Falling once more to her knees, she coughed and choked, then began breathing in air free of smoke and ash, but now musty and thick from moist soil and stone.

Annica stood to her feet, grateful to be free from that unspeakable chamber. Looking back over her shoulder, she saw the smoke pouring out across the ceiling from the doorway. Escape was the only thing on her mind, but in taking in the alcove, she noticed the other door. The one that Edrik had been taken through.

She cursed herself for being so thoughtless and immediately rushed to the door. Annica tried the handle, finding it locked on the other side. She shook the door violently. The damp air left the locks and hinges rattling in place. With desperation setting in, Annica threw her shoulder against the door. It thundered in its frame as dull pain shot through her shoulders.

The second attempt was equally as painful. And the third. And the fourth. Each effort punctuated by a cry of anguish. On her fifth try, her body aching from the effort, the door shattered inward. Her frantic efforts won out and she pushed the ruined hunk of wood inward. It was a small room, big enough for only a few people. A desk with books and scrolls sat against the wall. Annica's eyes were then drawn to a heap on the floor.

There, Edrik lay motionless. Some of the smoldering appendages swung limply where Annica could only assume he was strapped against the wall. Worst of all, his armor had been removed, leaving him in his shirt and pants, and on his exposed skin were irregular-shaped bruises. Edrik had been strung up for some horrible purpose in this small room, perhaps interrogation or experimentation, but Annica would likely never know.

Throwing herself to the ground, Annica shouted his name. She shook him, called to him. Edrik's eyes fluttered open and he took a sharp, ragged breath.

"Annica," he whispered, wheezing and with bloodshot eyes, "where are we?"

His body shook. His skin was pale and clammy. She touched his arm, grazing one of the bruises which caused him to wince. "We're under the aldyr, Edrik. We have to get out of here, now."

Edrik's eyes swam, disoriented. He shook his head and allowed her to help him stand. She put his arm around her shoulder and they began making their way to the door.

"Wait," he said abruptly. She felt his weight shift, pulling her in another direction. She gave in, letting him lead her. They walked to the corner by the desk where Annica saw his armor, weapons, and other belongings sitting on the floor. He reached down and clumsily pulled his sword from the sheath. "Now we can go."

As they reached the door, Annica saw from the corner of her eyes the flaccid vine-like extensions catch fire. Soon, the whole of the ground around them would be ignited by the expansive root system. The thought of racing against time through the insidious tunnel back out made her heart pound in her chest.

They made their way through the last room before the tunnel. If there were any other cultists here, they had all managed to flee—including Helyn. The original room was empty and only the long, dark tunnel remained.

The route back was uphill, which made the situation more difficult, but Annica was somewhat grateful it was only a gradual incline. The fire from her magic that clung and crawled along the aldyr's roots ran along the walls of the tunnel like red and yellow stars. Fires caught here and there and Annica couldn't shake the image of the tunnel collapsing around them, or the fires exploding and burning them alive down in this wretched place.

Thankfully, Edrik began to regain his strength. Soon he walked on his own, then broke into a near jog. Annica had trouble keeping up, but he grabbed her arm and prodded her on. With no way to tell how long the tunnel actually was, they could do nothing but make their way up and up, hoping to find the end of this demonic throat before it swallowed them whole.

With their lungs burning from both exhaustion and the smell of burning wood, their legs shaking from exertion, and their morale all but spent, the sight of the large double-door leading to the temple caused an unexpected shout to escape their lips. Although Annica was sure she only imagined her excitement, as she was too fatigued to actually feel anything.

They landed heavily against the door, which felt like it was made of stone. It creaked open, heavily and slowly. The expected rush of cool air never came. Instead, the two were greeted by a roaring inferno. The carved statue of the aldyr in front of the doors was wholly ablaze.

Edging their way past the display, screaming and shouting followed them through the temple. Through the open arches and windows, fires could be seen blossoming around the city. They ran through the foyer and out to the temple grounds. Citizens, guards, disciples, and magi were all out of their houses. The fires were so numerous that the night sky was ablaze with false daylight. Water brigades were at work trying to put out fires, but there were too few people and too many buildings ablaze.

"We have to get to a ship," Edrik said, shouting above the clamor. He grabbed her arm and they began running again.

Wails and shouts and cries assailed them as they ran past people trying to put out fires, find those who had gone missing, or simply trying to find safety. A pang of guilt struck Annica sharply. This was her fault. What sort of price was she, and the city of Nel Aldyri, paying for her fighting back against the Black Gnarl?

"Annica," a voice shouted for her. It was faint, but each repeated attempt grew louder. "Annica!"

Annica turned to see Helyn stalking toward her. The once authoritative and coldly confident woman was now dirty and disheveled. Her eyes wild storm clouds glossed over with unspent tears.

"Annica, what have you done?" she accused, her voice harsh and strained.

Annica took in the scene again. Buildings burned, the city

was collapsing, but so was the evil temple and its abhorrent chambers in the belly of this awful place.

"Fire magic, Helyn. You had me study that quite a bit."

Helyn's forehead creased in disbelief. "No fire magic can do this. None!"

Helyn lurched towards Annica, but the firelight flashed off of a familiar surface: steel. Edrik pulled Annica back and brought the tip of his sword up to greet her old mentor. The blade positioned perilously close to her throat.

"Leave us alone, archpriestess. Your time with Annica is over. Leave now with your life, and don't even try to cast anything. I'll put this blade through your throat before you can even twitch."

Helyn looked surprisingly defeated. The stormclouds dissipated, leaving her eyes filled with a sullen gloom. She backed away, leaving her hands at her sides. She looked at Annica forlornly, then turned her head to stare blankly at the city as it burned down around her.

The two of them continued fleeing up the main street of Nel Aldyri. Their feet sloshed through puddles of water from the vain attempts to douse the fires. Annica knew it to be a useless endeavor. Her strands of Fifth Sect magic could not harm Bac'thule, as Bac'thule could not stand the touch of her, but she could use the gripping void of Bac'thule to hold the essence of her magic in place. She weaved the diamond-pure lace of her spell around Him, around every dark fiber of his evil presence that stretched into every home and business and storehouse on the island. Then, she lit the diamonds on fire. While wading deep in the Fifth Sect and casting out her glistening strands, she also conjured her wild, untamed flames of the Second Sect. It took all her focus, everything she had, to not let the fires burst out of control in the chamber, but she did it. Combining the two sects, the fires raced along every inch of Bac'thule's presence, and began to burn.

There was no stopping these flames. They would consume everything that Bac'thule touched. There may have been innocents caught in Annica's fiery wrath. She would never know for sure how deep the reach of the Black Gnarl ran, but if any of the blameless died because of her she would carry that burden with her forever. It was likely a far better fate than awaited them here.

The tall masts of the docked ships greeted them as Edrik and Annica reached the docks. To their dismay, many of the ships were already on fire. The flames consuming the buildings had jumped to the ships' sails and began to ignite their wooden hulls. Time was quickly running out.

They stopped at the edge of the stone-wrought harbor where the long wooden docks led out to the ships. One yet remained attached to its moorings, drifting lazily on the water despite the death, chaos, and insanity surrounding it. The flower-and-stem figurehead of the *Dawn Rose*, Captain Sisironi's ship, glistened like a beacon. The light-colored wood with its polished finish shined so brilliantly in the firelight that Annica worried for a moment that their last hope had caught fire, itself.

Annica smiled and turned to look at Edrik. His chest pumped with each heavy breath, an open-mouthed smile on his face; however, his smile faded and he looked back over his shoulder then left to right, as though searching for something. His breathing slowed. It seemed his optimism was fading, each breath releasing more of his hopes.

"We'll never be able to sail that, just the two of us."

He glanced around again. What was he hoping to find? Others desperate to leave the island? They were all fighting to stop the fires consuming their homes. The anarchy continued to rage behind them, the fires here in the harbor peaceful by comparison. They could board the ship, hide there and hope for the best. This was certainly a better place to die than beneath that vile tree with those wicked people.

"Wait," Edrik said, his eyes squinting and shoulders stooping as he looked out and past the larger ship. "There's a smaller ship, just there; a schooner or something. We might be able—"

His voice cut off, replaced by a gasping choke. Annica heard the *thump* of his knees as Edrik fell to the ground. She turned to see a black-robed figure pulling a narrow dagger, dripping red, from Edrik's side.

"*Via Mortis Infinitum*," a deep voice rumbled from within the cowl.

"*Via Mortis Infinitum*," another voice followed, completing the horrible phrase Annica had already memorized.

She followed the voice behind her where another of the Black Gnarl stood with their hands raised to their chest. Both palms were splayed open like they were holding an invisible ball. Their palms began slowly closing, and as the invisible ball shrunk, a black orb swathed in blue, crackling light appeared. Annica recognized the spell. Lightning was simple, effective, and lethal. She didn't know why it held such a different color but assumed it had to do with some foul tampering by the cultist preparing it. She didn't care to find out what variation of spell they were casting.

Annica reached out, felt the heat of the flame burning within her palm as she gripped its magical essence. Like a lash, she pulled a roiling band of fire from the inferno consuming the structure behind the cultist. Annica smiled to herself. Her control of fire magic was getting better with each spell. The force of the blow was enough to stagger the person, but not enough to catch their robes ablaze.

Edrik grunted and shouted beside her. She turned and saw him stand to his feet, face curled in pain. Edrik's attacker must have expected him to stay down, for he stumbled back in shock, hesitating. Edrik swung a quick backhanded stroke that caught the man across the throat and chest, opening a gushing wound.

The member of the Black Gnarl fell to the ground gargling their own blood, their head leaning too far sideways.

Edrik turned his attention to the second member of the cult, who was preparing the same spell they attempted to use on Annica. They worked quicker this time. Edrik made two quick steps toward the cultist, his sword-arm preparing a strike, when blue and black streaks of lightning leapt toward him. Edrik screamed as his sword arm was enveloped. Annica's eyes widened in horror as the flesh of Edrik's arm shriveled, tightening against the bones like dried paper. The skin of his fingers pulled back until his fingernails fell and the bony tips were visible beneath ruined flesh.

Edrik fell back to his knees. His face dripping sweat and his mouth open in a silent cry of pain. Annica's fury built once again.

She pulled all the flame she could possibly muster into one more assault against the wretched member of the Black Gnarl. She screamed—a hoarse, angry scream—and pulled down gouts of flame with each hand as though she were ripping the burning stones of a mountains down. For a moment, the robed figure disappeared in the blaze. When the flames dispersed, the figure was fully engulfed from cowl to boots. Their arms waved wildly, screams of agony coming from under the sounds of burning cloth and crackling skin. They threw themselves into the harbor, the flames disappearing under the water's surface. They never came up.

Annica, too, fell to her knees. Falling back, she felt the exhaustion of her reflexive spellcasting take hold. It was like jumping a large gap carrying a barrel full of stones. She was utterly spent.

Edrik moaned beside her. The fear for his safety rejuvenated her and she went to his side. He cradled his ruined arm, pieces of it flaking away and carried off on the ocean breeze. She felt a wet substance through her clothes and looked down to see his shirt sticky with blood; her robes were saturated where they touched.

"Edrik," she whimpered, not knowing what to do.

She hadn't practiced with the Fifth Sect enough to know how to heal anyone. She tried to wade in its eddies again, but found them further away. She had exhausted herself killing the second member of the Black Gnarl.

She persisted, feeling wisps of the life magic caress her. She then felt the essence draining from Edrik. Mostly from his stab wound. His arm was ruined, but it wasn't spilling his lifeblood onto the docks. Still, she wouldn't be able to heal him. She was too inexperienced and too weak. They would have to reach the boat and she could tend to his wounds there.

"Come, Edrik. We need to reach the boat," she said in a whisper, but with urgency.

He shook his head.

"Don't argue with me," she pressed gently, "let's go."

"No," he grunted, his voice shaking. "There's more coming."

Edrik's eyes stared back into the city. Annica followed his gaze and saw several more of the Black Gnarl making their way from streets and alleys. They approached slowly, likely preparing spells or hesitant to approach in too much haste after Annica's recent display of uncontrolled magic.

"We need to hurry," Annica repeated.

Edrik attempted to stand. He stumbled, for a moment, then regained his footing and composure. He held his shriveled arm against his body and took his sword up in his left hand. When he looked at her, his eyes told her everything.

"Go. To the smaller ship. You'll have to figure out how to get away. I'll hold them off as long as I can."

The words screamed inside her head. Reverberated through her skull and drowned out the pain and fear of the last several weeks. When she finally spoke, a barely audible whisper was all she could make.

"No."

"You have to. I'm dying, and I can tell you're too weak to heal me. No bandages will help this," he said, referring to the wound still seeping crimson at his side. "And my arm is gone. I doubt even the Fifth Sect could return it. I can give you some time, though. Go. Get away from this place, Annica. Get away and try to never think of it again."

"I—" she wanted to say something, but the words left her. Leaving her mouth open and empty.

"It's ok," he replied gruffly. "Please, go."

Annica left him, jogging, wanting to run and not make his sacrifice meaningless, but also wanting to walk and be as near him for as long as she could manage. When the boat came into sight, she moved faster. She hopped over the side of the hull and removed the rope moorings. She began fumbling her way around the boat until she found something, anything she could use to push herself away from shore just enough. It was slower than she liked, but she began moving. She worked with the one small sail until finally getting it raised.

The boat continued moving away from the shore of Nel Aldyri. The fires burned out of control over the city. The burning ships shared their fate with the *Dawn Rose* as the last of the ships, and the one to carry Annica and Edrik to this vile place, caught fire.

In the light of the blaze, Annica saw Edrik. His left arm moved more clumsily than his right, but there were two more dead Black Gnarl members on the docks than there were before. A few more were preparing spells and another was attacking Edrik with one of their long, slender daggers. She was prepared to watch him until he fell for the final time, but something else drew her eyes.

The great aldyr itself was fully ablaze. The burning city was nothing compared to the terrifying majesty of the gigantic tree burning in all its hellish glory. Worse still, behind the blaze, were shadows moving against the night sky. Flailing tendrils of darkness deeper than the night itself whipped and squirmed as the tree burned. His avatar consumed, the infinite Vessel, the Herald of the Obscured Throne, no longer had His own vessel to bind Him to the world. He was both freed from his prison and expelled from her reality.

A sudden, momentary flash of light so brief Annica felt it may have been her imagination blinded her. In a blink, she could see the fire still burning, but the ophidian-like branches were gone. Perhaps Annica had grown too accustomed to it after weeks in Nel Aldyri, with the First Son constantly pulling at her consciousness; constantly seeking to weaken and devour her. But Annica felt a release in the back of her mind. The tingling, itching sense of unease was significantly lessened.

She wanted to take comfort in this. To know that Bac'thule was gone—like Gideon and Helyn. Like Edrik. But she knew that a simple fire, even an inferno driven by the Fifth Sect, would not destroy Bac'thule. He was beyond such simple matters. She simply cut the rope holding Him here.

Annica laid down on the deck of the boat, big enough for her to stretch her legs. Her focus now was to survive. Rather, to continue to survive. Something tickled her nose, then the top of her hand. Running her hand along her forearm, she opened her palm to see crushed bits of gray powder. Annica listened to the sounds of water lapping against the sides of the hull. She watched as the sky turned a subtle shade of deep blue as dawn began approaching, where she caught a better glimpse of the ash that fell like infernal snow.

# EPILOGUE: 10 SEALS

*MY DEAREST VICTOR,*

*As you read this, you no doubt have also placed my body upon the pyre I once requested. I regret this also means that you are left bereft of any friendly contact in our lonesome sanctuary. We were the last, dear apprentice, and I feel I left you in this world with so many unanswered questions.*

*I'm writing this in the last hours I have left; you'll find this letter in lifeless fingers come morning. I wish we had more time, but this world was cruel long before The Rupture. My ailment has little to do with the events of that day long ago and is of a far more mundane origin. Were Willis the apothecary still among us, he would likely be able to treat me. But these are the circumstances we find ourselves in.*

*I wanted time to pen these final words for you, so you have something to remember me by. I've always been an insular individual and I thank you for giving me time to reconcile with my fate. I've been waxing nostalgic all evening, and I appreciate that you left me to my own devices for these last hours.*

*When you first arrived at our sanctum, your latent talents were*

*apparent to us. We had been the Trifold Sanctum for so long, prac-*
*ticing only those three sects common to our trade, that when a being*
*touched by the Fifth Sect arrived, it caused the greatest stir among the*
*bored and inert studies that we'd experienced in decades. You were*
*quite the minor celebrity.*

*We were many magi stronger then, only a few years ago. We had*
*members to spare, to train you, to search the world for signs of hope,*
*and to protect us from the evils that plagued the world in brute force*
*and shadow and within the ethereal places. We, the great-grandchil-*
*dren of those who experienced The Rupture first-hand, pored over*
*every text we could find to explain why the world hated us so.*

*According to historical text, many blamed us for The Rupture.*
*And by 'us' I of course mean magi in general. Remember this, if you*
*are to ever leave these empty walls. We have only ever known the*
*comfort of fellow magi and the occasional traveler. The fear and perse-*
*cution of magi may still exist in what remains of civilization for all we*
*know. The stories of what drove our founders out of their homes to*
*establish these academic sanctums around the time of The Rupture*
*still stokes my ire. I admit, I feel the horrors visited on the world are*
*sometimes deserved if we would treat our kin in such a manner, but I*
*would never say this openly. Especially, knowing what such horrors*
*lay claim to our world.*

*Perhaps it was a poor decision on our part to continue sending*
*scouts and ambassadors out into the world. Even when they stopped*
*coming back, we insisted. We continued out of desperation, for what?*
*Hope that things were returning to normal? That the world was*
*showing signs of recovery after being on its death bed for multiple*
*generations?*

*I don't desire to spend the last few hours I have left pondering the*
*same questions that haunted me every day. I would rather leave you*
*with something useful. I wish that something could be nothing but*
*kind words, but you are alone now. I am torn between encouraging*
*you to stay here within the safety of the walls of the Trifold, but what*

a languid and lonesome existence that would be. The only other option is to set out on your own. If you were to choose that, I would want you as prepared as possible.

I know we've discussed at length the reports our fellows have brought with them from the far reaches of Alda. We've not discussed them all, however. There are some things I want you to know if you decide to leave the safety of our sanctum.

There is a tower not three days ride from here, in a region called Thayn. It's tall, slender, with a sturdy keep at its base and surrounded by abandoned farms and hamlets. It may have been beautiful once, but now pushes up from its cursed grounds like a rotting, skeletal finger. The power of the Fourth Sect radiates from it like corpse-stink, blighting its surroundings. I've no doubt that's what drove off the populace over the years. There were rumors arising not long before The Rupture of the tower being haunted. I've no doubt the Black Gnarl were involved. Even the monstrosities that arrived in the wake of The Rupture avoid the area. I would caution you against travelling here and find an alternate route around.

The same can be said for the Withered Groves. It was once called the Blackwood, long ago, but has since become the playground of some vile entity. We decided to rename it, in the event we ever made contact with some sort of civilization and could begin rebuilding. It seemed appropriate, given the pitiful and unusable state of the entire forest. Given the rumors we've heard of the place, it may even be some sort of dark goddess we've never heard of. Regardless, she seems content with her forest. The Blackwood was isolated before The Rupture, save for a few scattered villages, but they quickly abandoned the area. There is nothing but ruins left, now, though one village, in particular, has shown definite signs of being haunted. When Grashar returned from his sojourns to the northeast, he spoke of that village next to a lake that the old maps call Stillwater. He swears the ghosts there noticed, looked at him, but left him alone. They carried on in their duties like they were still alive.

There is no reason I can possibly think of to visit those forsaken woods, Victor, and you would do well to avoid them, same with the valley further east. In fact, if you are ever in the east at all and catch a foul odor in the air within the valleys, turn and run.

This leads me to my gravest warnings, apprentice: Ligothi and Carnelia are to be avoided at all costs. Records show that Carnelia was struck particularly hard by The Rupture. We have little to go off, as only the first few days provided enough survivor accounts to build some sort of history on. They speak of something akin to eyes or mouths opening, followed by faceless creatures made of living darkness who stole people away. The black eyes would open again, throwing the desiccated remains of the bodies out. Anyone we've sent there in the last twenty years has never come back. The last member who returned with any word said, "The city is dead and the cold eyes still watch over it."

Ligothi is just as dire. Some sort of sinister plant growth has claimed the city. Old Ligothi appears to be the worst, but the strange growth and the pale, gaunt, and hunchbacked creatures that dwell therein reach as far as the outer borders of the inland parts of the city. Temira was sent after Norlan after he didn't return for several months. She reported that she found him near the border, trying to warn people away. According to Temira, Norlan shouted that he'd been 'infected' and could feel his mind and even his soul being 'integrated' and 'absorbed'. I shudder even as I write about these horrid memories. Temira said that Norlan used what he claimed to be the last of his own willpower to immolate himself. She returned to us not wholly the same woman who'd left. That is the whole truth of why we forbade travel to Ligothi.

Temira returned with a name on her lips, one that sent our scholars into a frenzy: Ygiddra. She mumbled it in her sleep and when asked about it, even years later, would shake and turn pale. We researched the name as much as we could. We knew it was connected with those charlatans, the Black Gnarl; those truly responsible for the hatred all magi now bear. We looked up every text and scroll we could find on them. We discovered something quite frightening in our examinations.

Ygiddra was but one of several great beings worshipped by the Black Gnarl. Some of that fiendish cult were drawn to this god of the Timeless Garden, others to one called Bac'thule. These were the two largest branches of their cult, but several smaller ones sought out other beings, as well. We assume the goddess who dwells over the Withered Groves is one, also, though we'd never actually discovered a Black Gnarl presence there. Of all the separate divisions of the cult, they all seek one of these ancient beings above all others: something called the Obscured Throne.

We have very little knowledge on whatever this thing may be. From all accounts, even the Black Gnarl themselves don't truly know. In our own library is contained a few excerpts from their greatest tome—the Dread Praises. We don't have a complete copy and, even though if we did our understanding of these beings would much further along, I'm grateful we do not. I can deduce from what I've read of the excerpts that full knowledge of the book brings a terrible price. Some of our pages are mysteriously blank; in all my arcane studies I can only surmise that these pages were meant for certain eyes. I dare not dwell on what those pages contain, or what unenviable consequences await those who read them.

We learned only bits of information about this Obscured Throne. Nothing was clear on if it was a creature, a god, an actual throne, the embodiment of sentient malevolence—or, rather, complete lack of comprehensible emotion as we can discern it—or even a combination of these. One thing is for certain: it seeks this world with fervor, feeling Alda to be stolen from it.

It was also I, Victor, that made a connection I feel few others have ascertained. One night after several heads of the council and I had pondered over this vile tome, I had an inkling to look over some other texts. I pulled a number of volumes on ancient history, dead elf-kind religions, and even folklore.

I was amazed to find that the Dread Praises filled space between all those stories. Not gaps to be filled, necessarily, but details in between the lines. A repulsive mortar filling in cracks in the foundation.

My findings left me trembling. I put them out of my mind, wishing not to dwell on them too much at the time. As days passed I let myself try to forget it all together, but in the dark hours of night, when the clouds crossed over the moon or hid the stars from my eyes and all I could see was the black of the great beyond I remembered the conclusions I drew. I never dared have another living being validate my findings, but I am certain of my discoveries.

There have never been conclusive answers on the origin of our world. Different peoples of different religions have their own creation theories, but most align with the belief that our world was saved from a great, living darkness. What exactly saved us changes according to various dogmatic beliefs. Most stories consist of multitudinous beings, often god-like, fighting this ancient evil in some sort of climactic battle. I say most, not all. The Dread Praises add a new angle to our world's origins. The great darkness is that of the Obscured Throne—of course, such a heinous tome would be open about this matter—but there was no battle at the beginning of time. The world of Alda existed long before any such confrontation; however, it was a wretched place. A living hell and bleak existence. Over time, the humanoid creatures that lived here began to learn how to harness the energies of the world.

Magic. The original magic.

Eventually, the most powerful among them discovered some way, some rare and nigh-unreachable hope, that they managed to get a finger-hold upon. The world was locked away from the Obscured Throne and its terrible children: Bac'thule, Ygiddra, the goddess of the Withered Groves, and their ilk. The tome speaks of these ancient gods as the Inheritors. The beings branded the world with forty-four seals; eleven seals for each of the four kinds of magic. Apparently, it was completed with great difficulty, as eleven of the seals required the use of the magic connected directly to the Obscured Throne—the Fourth Sect, as we know it. But, they overcame this obstacle and saved the world from its abhorrent existence.

Over millennia the stain of the Inheritors and their Obscured Throne weakened. Life flourished. Those beings were our farthest reaching ancestors; over hundreds of generations becoming human, dwarves, and elf-kind. The aldyr trees were discovered growing some decades after the sealing of the world. The Dread Praises speak in harsh tones of the world gaining its own soul, a separate entity from the Obscured Throne that flourished outside of Its influence. The aldyrs were the physical embodiment of this. This is why my people cherished them so. With this new energy radiating from the world came a new kind of magic. The Fifth Sect was unique. It still is. It's tied to the life of this world; not the animals and humanoids and flowers and fish, but the life of Alda itself. The fact that such magic is all but extinct speaks to the worst of hidden and horrible fears. Why? Because when our ancestors discovered this magic they fashioned eleven more seals. This caused no end of frustration to those who still worshipped the Old Ones. This is why there is even more to be found in the Dread Praises of the aldyrs and the Fifth Sect than there is in any mainstream historical texts. They, the first of the Black Gnarl, wanted to know everything of the aldyrs and the Fifth Sect so they could destroy it.

This brings me to my most crucial parting words for you, Victor. I believe one of the last eleven seals has been broken. Being one of the last of my kind, as far as we have uncovered, I could still feel the last remaining echoes of the aldyrs that survived The Rupture. The return of the Inheritors corrupted the soul of the world and the sacred connections of my people to Alda began dying. In all of the world, at least one must have been clinging to life. One night, perhaps a decade or so ago, I experienced a nightmare such that it remains fresh in my memory today.

An aldyr, larger than any of the dried husks I've seen, was alone on a rock in the sea. Night came and went, but when the sun rose the night clung to the aldyr like tar. Time passed in flashes of light and dark but the tar stuck to the aldyr, pulling its branches and forcing it to grow far beyond its natural size; bloated and sick. Then, a bolt of lightning struck, setting the aldyr ablaze. The tar slipped away into the ocean, leaving the aldyr to burn, scorching the stone upon which it long rested.

When I woke, I knew the last of the aldyrs were gone. To be honest, my connection with the near-extinct species was already weak to begin with and so the pain of loss was fairly fleeting. However, it was the nature in which the loss occurred that dug its thorns into my heart, scarring it. The seals were vaguely mentioned in most histories. After reading our excerpts of the Dread Praises, I realized that some of the ancient poetry was, in fact, referencing these seals. The black tome was more direct.

I've left the pages of the tome on my desk. If you leave, I suggest you take them with you. You may find the reference to the seals useful. They are still cryptic, such as the one that states; "When a sick man made whole forever tends his garden". The ones that strike me cold with fear are those that refer to the last eleven, including the one you can read that speaks of the "last of the soul's fibers fraying and dead." There has been more than enough in our conversation to know what the soul's fibers refer to. And I know they are all dead. At least one of these last seals is broken, Victor. The rest are only a matter of time.

You are one of the last of those touched by the Fifth Sect. This magic came to be after the world was taken from Them. It will protect you, at least for a time. I cannot say which fate would best suit you, apprentice. Stay or leave, either will offer little comfort in one way or the other. I only hope to leave you some lasting guidance in these final words. I would hope you could find some way to seal this world away *again. Thus far we have only dealt with the minor inconvenience of the unspeakable terror that is the Inheritors. The Obscured Throne is still a complete and horrifying mystery to us all.*

*If you go, seek out knowledge of the seals. Make it your last—our last—torch in the looming darkness that threatens to blot out the very stars of our existence.*

*Perhaps you will be the next in a line of lost stories that society will bicker over when the world is safe again and all the peril of annihilation has come to pass. That is the thought I choose to part with, Victor. Please, take care of yourself. And never forget me.*

*~NETHARA THEL Minos*
   *Archmage of the Trifold Sanctum*
   *and Headmistress of the Academy at the Trifold*

VICTOR LOOKED at Nethara for several moments after finishing the letter, letting his thoughts dwell on her last words. She died in the same manner in which she chose to live: graceful and dignified. She looked no older than his thirty years despite being over a century in age.

He had some theories of his own in that regard. The death of the aldyrs took more than just an emotional toll on her people. They lost their arcane affinities, their long lives, perhaps even a part of their souls.

A deep ache cut into his heart as he pulled the sheets over her pale face and hollow eyes. After reading her letter, her illness took on a new, sinister aspect. If he remembered correctly, she became ill near the same time as she stated she suffered that horrible nightmare. This led him to the terrible assumption that other elf-kind perhaps experienced the same thing. It was a high possibility that they were now as extinct as the aldyrs themselves.

This was something else he would have to discover in his travels. Storing himself away like unused clothes and waiting for death was not how he imagined the rest of his life. He wouldn't presume to say long life, as that was actually quite unlikely once he set off outside the walls of the empty sanctum.

He added the pages of the Dread Praises to his belongings, attached Nethara's letter, and left her room. Casting one final, heartbroken look back, he closed the door. He truly hoped this would be her peaceful resting place for all eternity. The impact of her death would likely strike him hardest on some cold night by a low fire, but for now, he had to remove himself from the Trifold grounds.

Stepping out of the archmage's residence, the wind echoed along the many other white-marbled walls; their interiors devoid of any living presence. All other members of the academy had either passed and were long-since burned on a pyre, had left of their own accord to strike out on their own, or never returned from their academic sojourns.

This place was nothing more than bittersweet memories and fresh heartache. The leaves of the trees rustled in the breeze as loose slat windows creaked and complained. He stood there for several moments. Minutes, hours... he couldn't say. Finally, with a long-suffering sigh, Victor walked to and through the threshold of the Trifold Sanctum's wooden, twin-doored gate.

The magi had long since been exiled to such places. Now, there were few who cared if Victor practiced magic or not. Most of what he learned was through the texts his fellows had gathered over the centuries since the infamous Rupture. He had only gone on a few short-ranged sojourns and never saw much of the horror that others returned ranting about.

He didn't want to seek such things out directly, though he

wasn't fool enough to think he wouldn't come across them. He hoped he had the courage to face whatever things waited in the woods, the valleys, and the abandoned remains of civilization. It couldn't be worse than rotting away within those lonely walls.

Besides, if Nethara said one of the seals of the Fifth Sect had been broken, he believed her wholeheartedly. If he'd stayed at the Trifold, it would not just be himself that he'd resigned to death, but the world and perhaps even creation itself.

Victor carried with him the combined knowledge of his entire sanctum. There may be other sanctums, other holdouts of civilization, that know more. Or, perhaps, they know nothing at all. This meant bringing this knowledge to them was even more important.

The road ahead of him was worn and strewn with wind-blown leaves and refuse. Long had it been since people walked its path for any reason. He imagined he'd find most roads in such a state. He imagined he'd find most places in the same state as the Trifold. But, he walked on, into an unknown world, carrying a flickering light into a world sinking further into a dark misery and madness.

# MEET THE AUTHOR

Fantasy and horror have always been Russell's preferred genres. Some of his favorite stories often combine them–and the grittier the better. His eclectic tastes in this genre originated when he discovered Lovecraft's stories of beings so vast and incomprehensible that just thinking about them would melt your brain. Later, he would discover the more sinister but equally unfathomable creations of Laird Barron and, combined, these two influences would create Russell's desire to fashion his own story of cosmic horrors with a fantasy flair. Fantasy often holds many horrific aspects of its own, but Russell enjoys finding ways to take those and kick them up a notch.